ALSO BY L.J. SHEN

All Saints
Pretty Reckless
Broken Knight
Angry God

BROKEN KNIGHT

L.J. SHEN

Bloom books

*To Betty and Vanessa V, two talented women I
adore, and to all the Lunas of the world*

Published by Bloom Books, an imprint of Sourcebooks
P.O. Box 4410, Naperville, Illinois 60567-4410
(630) 961-3900
sourcebooks.com

Originally self-published in 2019 by L.J. Shen.

Cataloging-in-Publication Data is on file with the Library of Congress.

Printed and bound in the United States of America.
WOZ 10 9 8 7 6 5 4 3 2 1

*"Never to suffer
would never to have been blessed."*
—*Edgar Allan Poe*

THEME SONG

"Dream On"—Aerosmith

PLAYLIST

"Enjoy the Silence"—Depeche Mode
"Just My Type"—The Vamps
"Who Do You Love"—The Chainsmokers featuring
5 Seconds of Summer
"I Wanna Be Adored"—The Stone Roses
"Beautiful"—Bazzi featuring Camila Cabello
"Fix You"—Coldplay
"I Will Follow You Into the Dark"—Death Cab for Cutie
"The Drugs Don't Work"—The Verve
"I Predict a Riot"—Kaiser Chiefs

CHAPTER ONE
KNIGHT/LUNA

KNIGHT, AGE NINE

I drove a fist into the oak tree, feeling the familiar sting of a fresh wound as my knuckles split open.

Bleeding helped me breathe better. I didn't know what it meant, but it made Mom cry in her bathroom when she thought no one could hear. Whenever she glanced at my permanently busted knuckles, the waterworks started. It had also earned me a trip to talk to this guy in a suit every week, who asked about my feelings.

My earbuds blocked out the sounds of birds, crickets, and crispy leaves under my feet. The world sucked. I was done listening to it. "Break Stuff" by Limp Bizkit was my designated ruin-shit anthem. Fred Durst might look like a ball sack in a cap, but he had a point.

Thump.

Thump.

Thump.

Most kids liked fighting each other. Not me. I only wanted to hurt myself. When my body ached, my heart didn't. Simple math and a pretty good deal.

A pine cone dropped on my head. I squinted up. My stupid neighbor Luna sat perched outside our tree house, bouncing another pine cone in her hand and dangling her toothpick legs from a thick branch.

"What was that for?" I tore the earbuds from my ears.

She motioned to me with her head to climb up. I made no move. She waved me up.

"Nah." I tried to gather phlegm, spitting sideways.

She arched an eyebrow, her way of asking what my problem was. Luna was nosy but just with me. It sucked.

"Vaughn stole my bike," I announced.

I'd have beaten the crap out of my so-called best friend, Vaughn, if I wasn't so sure I'd kill him by accident. He'd said he wanted me to lose my shit. *"Get it out of your system."* Whatever that meant. What's a system? What did he know about mine? About anger? His life was perfect. His parents were healthy. He didn't even have an annoying baby brother, like Lev.

Luna threw the second pine cone. This time I caught it, swung my arm like a baseball player, and threw it back at her, missing on purpose.

"I said *no*."

She produced a third pine cone (She kept a stash in the tree house in case intruders came upon us, which was honestly never.) and made a show of throwing it at me.

I finally snapped. "You're so dumb!"

She blinked at me.

"Stop looking at me that way!"

Another blink.

"Goddarn it, Luna!"

I didn't care what Vaughn said. I was never going to *want* to kiss this girl. God help me if she ever asked me to.

I climbed on the tire swing and up to our tiny tree house. Vaughn thought he was too cool for tree houses. Good. It was one more thing that was Luna's and mine that he wasn't a part of.

Luna jumped from the branch. She rolled on the ground,

straightening up like a ninja and patting herself clean with a satis-fied smile. Then she started running toward our neighborhood. Fast.

"Where are you going?" I yelled as if she was going to answer.

I watched her back disappear into a dot. I was always sad to see her go.

This was all so stupid anyway. I didn't know anyone who could talk Vaughn into doing anything. Luna couldn't even talk, period. Plus, I didn't need her help. I'd walked away from him because, if not, I knew he'd get what he wanted from me—a dirty fight. I wasn't like him. Pissing off my parents wasn't a lifetime goal.

Sometime later, Luna came back riding my bike. I stood up, shielding my eyes from the sinking sun. It always burned brighter when the ocean was about to swallow it.

She waved at me to come down.

I threw a pine cone at her shoulder in response. "Rexroth."

What? her quirked eyebrow said. She could tell me a thousand things with her eyebrows alone, this girl. Sometimes I wanted to shave them off just to spite her.

"I always get even. Remember that, cool?"

Cool, her eye roll huffed.

"Now, come up."

She motioned toward my bike, stomping her foot.

"Leave the stupid bike."

We huddled inside the tree house. Instead of thanking her, which I knew I should, I pulled out the pages I had printed earlier and arranged them on the wooden floor between us. Our foreheads stuck together with warm sweat as we both looked down. I was teaching her profanity in sign language—the stuff her father and therapist never would.

"Says here *dick* is a 'd' hand shape tapping the nose." I mimicked the picture on one of the pages, then flipped it on its back. "Oh, look. If you want to say *fuck you*, you can just give the person your middle finger and pout. Convenient."

I didn't look at her, but I felt her forehead resting against mine. Luna was a girl, but she was still really cool. Only downside was sometimes she asked too many questions with her eyes. Mom said it was because Luna cared about me. Not that I was going to admit it, but I cared about her too.

She tapped my shoulder. I flicked another page.

"Waving an open hand on the side of the chin, forward and back, means *slut*. Dude, your dad will kill me if he ever finds out I taught you this."

She tapped my shoulder harder, digging her fingernail into my skin.

I looked up, midread. "'Sup?"

"Are you okay?" she signed.

She didn't use sign language often. Luna didn't want to talk. Not in sign and not at all. She *could* talk. Technically, I mean. Not that I'd ever heard her say anything. But that's what our parents said—that it wasn't about her voice. It was about the world.

I got it. I hated the world too.

We just hated it differently.

I shrugged. "Sure."

"Friends don't let friends get upset over small stuff," she signed.

Whoa. An entire sentence. That was new.

I didn't understand the point of speaking sign language if she was planning not to speak *at all*, but I didn't want to make her feel bad and stuff.

"I don't care about the bike." I put the page down and scooted toward our branch, leaving. She followed, sitting beside me. I didn't even like riding my bike. It was cruel on my nuts and boring to the rest of my body. I only rode it so I could hang out with Luna. Same reason I colored. I *loathed* coloring.

She cocked her head to the side. A question.

"Mom's in the hospital again." I picked out a pine cone and threw it at the sinking sun, over the edge of the mountain our tree was rooted upon. I wondered if the pine cone made it to the ocean, if it was wet and cold now. If it hated me.

Luna put her hand over mine, staring down at our palms. Our hands were the same size, hers brown, mine white as fresh-fallen snow.

"I'm fine." I sniffed, choosing another pine cone. "It's fine."

"*I hate that word.* Fine," Luna signed. *"It's not good. It's not bad. It's nothing."*

She dropped her head down and took my hand, gave it a squeeze. Her touch was warm and sticky. Kind of gross. A few weeks ago, Vaughn told me he wanted to kiss Cara Hunting. I couldn't even imagine touching a girl like that.

Luna put my hand on her heart.

I rolled my eyes, embarrassed. "I know. You're here for me."

She shook her head and squeezed my hand harder. The intensity of her gaze freaked me out. "*Always. Whenever. Forever,*" she signed.

I breathed in her words. I wanted to smash my stupid bike on Vaughn's stupid face, then run away. Then die. I wanted to die in desolate sands, evaporate into dust, let the wind carry me nowhere and everywhere.

I wanted to die instead of Mom. I was pretty useless. But so many people were dependent on Ma.

Dad.

Lev.

Me.

Me.

Luna pointed at the sun in front of us.

"Sunset?" I sighed.

She frowned.

"Beach?"

She shook her head, rolling her eyes.

"*The sun will rise again tomorrow,*" she signed.

She leaned forward. For a moment, I thought she was going to jump. She took a safety pin from her checkered Vans and pierced the tip of her index finger. Wordlessly, she took my hand and pricked my finger too. She joined them together, and I stared as the blood meshed.

Her lips broke into a smile. Her teeth were uneven. A little pointy. A lot imperfect.

With our blood, she wrote the words *Ride or Die* on the back of my hand, ignoring the state of my knuckles.

I thought about the bike she'd retrieved for me and smirked.

She drew me into a hug. I sank into her arms.

I didn't want to kiss her.

I wanted to zip open my skin and tuck her into me.

Hide her from the world and keep her mine.

LUNA, AGE THIRTEEN

I was named after the moon.

Dad said I'd been a plump, perfect thing. A light born into darkness. A child my mother didn't want and he hadn't known what to do with. He'd said that despite—or maybe *because* of—that, I was the most beautiful and enticing creature he'd ever laid eyes on.

"My heart broke, not because I was sad, but because it swelled so much at the sight of you, I needed more space in it," he once told me.

He said a lot of things to make me feel loved. He had good reasons, of course.

My mother left us before I turned two.

Over the years, she'd come knocking on the doors of my mind whenever I least expected her, barging through the gates with an army of memories and hidden photos I was never supposed to find. Her laugh—that laugh I could never unhear, no matter how hard I tried—rolled down my skin like tongues of fire.

What made everything worse was the fact that I knew she was alive. She was living somewhere under the same sky, breathing the same air. Perhaps in Brazil, her home country. It really didn't matter, since wherever she was, she wasn't with me. And the one time she'd come back for me, she'd really wanted money.

I was five when it happened—around the time Dad had met Edie, my stepmom. Val, my mom, had asked for joint custody and enough child support to fund a small country. When she'd realized I wasn't going to make her rich, she'd bailed again.

At that point, I had made it a habit to tiptoe to the kitchen at night, where Dad and Edie had all their big talks. They never noticed me. I'd perfected the art of being invisible from the moment Val stopped seeing me.

"I don't want her anywhere near my kid," Dad had gritted out.

"Neither do I," Edie had replied.

My heart had melted into warm goo.

"But if she comes back, we need to consider it."

"What if she hurts her?"

"What if she *mends* her?"

Experience had taught me that time was good at two things: healing and killing. I waited for the healing part to come every single day. I sank my knees to the lacy pillows below my windowsill and cracked it open, praying the wind would swish away the memories of her.

I couldn't hate Valenciana Vasquez, the woman who'd packed up her things in front of my crib, while I'd cried, pleaded, *screamed* for her not to go, and left anyway.

I remembered the scene chillingly well. They say your earliest recollection can't be before the age of two, but I have a photographic memory, a 155 IQ, and a brain that's been put through enough tests to know that, for better or worse, I remember everything.

Everything bad.

Everything good.

And the in-between.

So the memory was still crisp in my head. The determination zinging in her tawny, slanted eyes. The cold sweat gathering under my pudgy arms. I'd racked my brain looking for the words, and when I finally found them, I screamed as loud as I possibly could.

"Mommy! Please! No!"

She'd paused at the door, her knuckles white from holding the doorframe tightly, not taking any chances in case something inspired her to turn around and hold me. I remembered how I didn't dare blink, too scared she'd disappear if I closed my eyes.

Then, for a split second, her motherly instincts won, and she did swivel to face me.

Her face had twisted, her mouth parting, her tongue sweeping over her scarlet lipstick. She'd been about to say something, but in the end, she just shook her head and left. The radio had played a melancholic tune. Val had often listened to the radio to drown out the sound of my crying. My parents hadn't lived together, but they'd shared custody. After Val had failed to answer Dad's many phone calls, he'd found me some hours later in my cot, my diaper so soiled it outweighed my tiny body.

I hadn't been crying. Not anymore.

Not when he'd picked me up.

Not when he'd taken me to the emergency room for a thorough checkup.

Not when he'd cooed and kissed and fawned over me.

Not when hot tears had silently run down his cheeks and he'd begged me to produce a sound.

Not at all.

Since that day, I'd become what they call a selective mute. Meaning I could speak, but I *chose* not to. Which, of course, was real stupid, since I didn't *want* to be different. I simply *was*. My not speaking wasn't a choice as much as it was a phobia. I'd been diagnosed with severe social anxiety and attended therapy twice a week since babyhood. Usually, selective mutism means a person can speak in certain situations where they feel comfortable. Not me.

The nameless tune on the radio that day had been burned into my brain like an angry scar. Now, it popped up on the radio, assaulting me again.

I was sitting in the car with Edie, my stepmom. Rain slapped the windows of her white Porsche Cayenne. The radio host announced that it was "Enjoy the Silence" by Depeche Mode. My mouth went dry at the irony—the same mouth that refused to utter words for no apparent reason other than the fact that when I'd spoken words aloud, they hadn't been enough for my mother. *I* wasn't enough.

As the music played, I wanted to crawl out of my skin and evaporate into thin air. Hurl myself out of the car. Run away from California. Leave Edie and Dad and Racer, my baby brother, behind—just take off and go somewhere else. *Anywhere* else. Somewhere people wouldn't poke and pity me. Where I wouldn't be the circus freak.

"Geez, it's been a decade. Can't she just, like, get over it?"

"Maybe it's not about the mom. Have you seen the dad? Parading his young mistress…"

"She's always been weird, the girl. Pretty but weird."

I wanted to bathe in my own loneliness, swim in the knowledge that my mother had looked me in the eye and decided I wasn't enough. Drown in my sorrow. Be left alone.

As I reached to turn the radio off, Edie pouted. "But it's my favorite song!"

Of course it was. Of course.

Slapping my window with my open palm, I let out a wrecked whimper. I shuddered violently at the unfamiliar sound of my own voice. Edie, behind the wheel, sliced her gaze to me, her mouth still curled with the faint smile that always hovered over her lips, like open arms offering a hug.

"Your dad grew up on Depeche Mode. It's one of his favorite

bands," she explained, trying to distract me from whatever meltdown I was going through now.

I struck the passenger window harder, kicking my backpack at my feet. The song was digging into my body, slithering into my veins. I wanted out. I *needed* to get out of there. We rounded the corner toward our Mediterranean mansion, but it wasn't fast enough. I couldn't unhear the song. Unsee Valenciana leaving. Unfeel that huge hole in my heart that my biological mother stretched with her fist every time her memory struck me.

Edie turned off the radio at the same time I threw the door open, stumbling out of the slowing vehicle. I skidded over a puddle, then sped toward the house.

The garage door rolled up while thunder sliced the sky, cracking it open, inviting more furious rain. I heard Edie's cries through her open window, but they were swallowed by the rare SoCal storm. Rain soaked my socks, making my legs heavy, and my feet burned from running as I grabbed my bike from the garage, flung one leg over it, and launched toward the street. Edie parked, tripping out of the vehicle. She chased after me, calling my name.

I pedaled fast, cycling away from the cul-de-sac…zipping past the Followhill house…the Spencers' mansion darkening my path ahead with its formidable size. The Coles' house, my favorite, was sandwiched between my house and the Followhills'.

"Luna!" Knight Cole's voice boomed behind my back.

I wasn't even surprised.

Our bedroom windows faced each other, and we always kept the curtains open. When I wasn't in my room, Knight usually looked for me. And vice versa.

It was more difficult to ignore Knight than my stepmother, and not because I didn't love Edie. I did. I loved her with the ferocity only a nonbiological child could feel—hungry, visceral love, only better because it was dipped in gratitude and awe.

Knight wasn't exactly like a brother, but he didn't feel like less than family either. He put Band-Aids on my scraped knees and shooed the bullies away when they taunted me, even if they were twice his size. He'd given me pep talks before I'd known what they were and that I needed them.

The only bad thing about Knight was it felt like he held a piece of my heart hostage. So I always wondered where he was. His well-being was tangled with mine. As I rolled down the hill on my bike, toward the black, wrought-iron gate enclosing our lush neighborhood, I wondered if he felt that invisible thread attaching us too, if he chased me because I tugged at it. Because it hurt when one of us got too far away.

"Hey! Hey! Hey!" Knight screamed behind my back.

Edie had caught up with him. It sounded like they were arguing.

"I'll calm her down."

"But, Knight—"

"I know what she needs."

"You don't, honey. You're just a kid."

"You're just an adult. Now *go!*"

Knight wasn't afraid to get confrontational with adults. Me, I followed rules. As long as I wasn't expected to utter actual words, I did everything by the book—from being a straight-A student to helping strangers. I picked up trash on the street even when it wasn't mine and donated a selection of my gifts every Christmas to those who really needed them.

But my motives weren't pure. I always felt less-than, so I tried to be more. Daria Followhill, another neighbor my age, called me Saint Luna.

She wasn't wrong. I played the role of a saint because Val had made me feel like a sinner.

I pedaled faster. The rain slushed in sheets, turning to hail, pelting my skin with its icy fury. I squinted, passing through the gates of the neighborhood.

Everything happened fast: Yellow lights flashing in my face.

Hot metal grazing my leg as the vehicle tried to swerve in the other direction. A deafening honk.

I felt something hurling me back by the collar of my tweed jacket with a force that almost choked me, and before I knew what was going on, I'd collapsed into a puddle on the side of the road.

Just then, the sound of my bike exploding rang in my ears. The assaulting car shattered it to pieces. The seat flew inches from my head, and the frame glided in the other direction. My face hit the concrete. Dust, wet dirt, and blood coated my mouth. I coughed, rolling around and fighting what felt like the weight of the entire world to find Knight straddling my waist. The car careened to the end of the road, taking a sharp U-turn and zinging back past the gates of the neighborhood. The hail was so bad I couldn't even see the shape of the vehicle, let alone its license plate.

"Butthole!" Knight screamed at the car with ferocity that made my lungs burn on his behalf. "Rot in hell!"

I blinked, trying to decipher Knight's expression. I'd never seen him like this before—a storm within a storm. Although Knight was a year younger, he looked older. Especially now. His forehead was wrinkled, his pink, pillowy lips parted, and his soot-black lashes were clustered like a heavy curtain, damp from the rain. A drop ran its way down his lower lip, disappearing inside the dimple in his chin, and that simple image sent fire tearing through my heart.

It was the first time I'd realized my best friend was…well, beautiful.

Stupid, I knew, especially considering the circumstances. He'd saved me from certain death, pounced on top of me so I wouldn't get hit by a speeding car, and all I could think of was not Val, or Edie, or Depeche Mode, or how fragile life was, but the fact that the boy I'd grown up with was about to burst and bloom into a teenager. A handsome teenager. A handsome teenager who would have better things to do with his time than saving his awkward childhood friend or teaching her how to say *douchebag* in sign language.

I'd thought the memories of Valenciana nicked my heart, but that was nothing compared to the violent rip of it when I looked at Knight, realizing for the first time that he was going to break that piece of my heart he held hostage. Not maliciously, no, and definitely not intentionally. But it didn't matter. Hit-and-run or struck by lightning, a death was a death.

A heartbreak was a heartbreak.

Pain was pain.

"What the fudge?" he screamed in my face.

He was so close, I could smell his breath. Sugar and cocoa and boy. *Boy.* I still had a few years before it all started. Transfixed, I couldn't even bring myself to wince at his anger. How had I never noticed the graceful angles of his nose? The color of his eyes—so vividly green with flecks of dark blue, a shade of viridian I'd never seen before? The regal slopes of his cheekbones, so sharp as they outlined his mischievous face like pop art inside a thousand-dollar gold frame?

"Answer me, goddammit." He punched the concrete near my face.

His knuckles were as swollen as golf balls by now. He'd recently started cursing for real. Not a lot, just enough to make me cringe. I stared at him, steadfast, knowing he'd never hurt me. He wrapped a hand around his injured fist and let out a frustrated howl, then dropped his forehead to mine, panting hard. We were both out of breath, our chests rising and falling in the same rhythm.

"Why?" His voice was a soft growl now. He knew he wasn't going to get an answer. Our hair matted together, his penny-brown mane mixing with my dark curls. "Why'd you do this?"

I tried to wiggle my arms from out of the confines of his thighs so I could answer in sign language, but he pressed his legs against my body, locking me in place.

"*No,*" he growled, his voice thick with threat. "Use your words. You can. I know you can. Mom and Dad told me. Tell me why you did this."

I opened my mouth, wanting so badly to answer his question. He was right, of course. I could speak. Physically, anyway. I knew because sometimes in the shower or when otherwise completely alone, I would repeat words I loved as practice. Just to prove I could, that I was capable of uttering them aloud, that I *chose* not to talk. I repeated the words, the sound of my voice sending small shudders of pleasure down my back.

Old books.

Fresh air (especially after the rain).

Watching the moon watching me back.

Seahorses.

Dad.

Edie.

Racer.

Knight.

Now, for the first time, Knight was demanding my words. I wanted to say them. More than that—I knew he deserved to hear them. But nothing came out. My mouth hung open, and the only thing flashing through my mind was, *You don't just seem to be stupid; you look it too.*

"Say it." Knight shook my shoulders.

The hail faded into light rain, and my visibility cleared. His eyes were red-rimmed and tired. So tired. Tired because of me. Because I always got into stupid trouble he had to pull me out of.

He thought I'd tried to hurt myself. I hadn't. I kept opening and closing my mouth like a fish, but the words wouldn't come out. I tried to rip them from my mouth, my heart escalating, beating everywhere behind my ribs.

"Ahh… I… Hmm…"

He stood up, pacing back and forth, threading his fingers in his thick, wet hair and tugging it in frustration.

"You're so…" He shook his head, letting the drops fly everywhere. "So…"

I got up and ran toward him. I didn't want to hear the rest of his sentence. I wasn't keen on finding out what he thought of me. Because if he believed I'd driven straight into the car, hoping for a collision, he clearly thought I was way more screwed up than I was.

I grabbed his shoulder and twisted him around. He scowled.

I shook my head, frantic. "*I didn't see the car. I swear*," I signed.

"You could have died," he screamed in my face, pounding his scarred knuckles over his heart. "You could have left me."

"*But I didn't.*" I used my hands, arms, fingers to reassure him.

My lips trembled. This was about so much more than us. This was about Rosie, his mother, too. Knight didn't like people disappearing. Not even for a few days, to get better in the hospital.

"*Thanks to you*," I signed. "*You saved me.*"

"Remember *always, whenever, forever*? What happened to that bullshit? Where's your side of the bargain?"

He repeated my promise to him all those years ago, his voice dripping disdain. I opened my arms for a hug, and he stepped into it, melting into my body. We molded, like two distinct colors mixed together into something unique and true—a shade only we could paint with.

Knight buried his face in my hair, and I squeezed my eyes shut, imagining him doing it with someone else. Despite the chill, my blood ran hotter.

Mine.

I wasn't only thinking it. My lips moved, shaping the word. I could almost hear the word. I tightened my hold on him.

"Ride or die," he whispered into the shell of my ear.

I knew he meant his promise.

I also knew how unfair it was because I didn't know if I could save him if I had to.

If someone like Knight would ever need saving. Knight was a normal kid. He talked. He was athletic, outgoing, and oozed confidence. Edie had said he was so handsome, modeling scouts stopped

Rosie at the mall and thrust their business cards in her hands, begging her to let them represent him. He was funny, charming, well-heeled, and rich beyond his wildest dreams. The world was his for the taking, and I knew one day, he would.

I started crying in his arms. I wasn't a crier. I could count on one hand the number of times I'd wept since Val left. But I couldn't stop myself. I knew, then, that ours would not be a happily ever after.

He deserved more than a girl who couldn't tell him how she felt.

He was perfect, and I was flawed.

"Promise me." His lips touched my temple, his warm breath sending shivers down my body.

Shivers that felt different—like they filled my lower belly with lava. *Promise him what?* I wondered. I nodded yes anyway, eager to please him, though he hadn't completed his sentence. My lips moved.

I promise. I promise. I promise.

Maybe that's why he didn't trust me.

Why he'd sneak into my bedroom that night—and *every* night, for the next six years—and wrap his arms around me, making sure I was really okay.

Sometimes he smelled of alcohol.

Sometimes of another girl. Fruity and sweet and different.

Oftentimes, he smelled of my heartbreak.

But he was always making sure I was safe.

And he always left before my dad knocked on my door to wake me up.

For the next six years, before jumping through my window, Knight would drop a kiss on my forehead in the exact same spot where, shortly thereafter, Dad would kiss me good morning, the heat of Knight's lips still on my skin, making my face radiate.

I'd see him in school, his cocky swagger and whip-smart witty comebacks making girls drop their guards and panties. Tossing his shiny, thick mane as he showed off his pearly whites and endless dimples.

There were two Knight Coles.

One was mine.

The other everyone else's.

And although he always spent recess with me, continuously protected me, forever treated me like a queen, I knew he was everyone's king, and I only reigned in a small part of his life.

One night, when the moon was full and peering in at us through my window, *my* Knight kissed the sensitive skin beneath my ear.

"*Moonshine*," he whispered. "You fill up the empty, dark space, like the moon owns the sky. It is quiet. It is bright. It doesn't need to be a ball of flame to be noticed. It simply exists. It forever glows."

He'd called me Moonshine every single day since.

I called him nothing because I didn't speak.

Maybe that's how he knew, all those years later, that I'd lied—by omission. He wasn't nothing. He was my everything.

CHAPTER TWO
KNIGHT/LUNA

KNIGHT, AGE EIGHTEEN

"She's not here. You can tuck your vagina back in, Cole." Hunter Fitzpatrick yawned, flicking a red Solo cup against some tool's head.

Said tool turned around from his conversation with a sophomore cheerleader ready to talk smack. As soon as he saw that it was Hunter, he bit the inside of his cheek, glowering.

"Ew. Why so constipated?" Hunter growled in the Joker's why-so-serious voice.

Downing the last of my fifth beer of the night, I pulled my gaze from the front door, tucking the empty bottle into the back pocket of some girl's jeans. She turned around and laughed when she saw it was me.

I cupped and lit my joint, sucking on it as I watched the amber flickering under my nose. I passed the joint to Vaughn, releasing a plume of smoke and sinking back into the plush couch until it swallowed most of my upper body.

"Suck a dick," I told Hunter, my voice hoarse from the smoke.

"Any tips from a pro?" he teased, mumbling "sláinte" and knocking back a shot of something electric blue.

"Let me call your mom and ask," I quipped.

"Friday is a busy night for her; better call Hunter's sister." Vaughn, who somehow *still* held the title of my best friend, had a profile like an eagle and a voice so low it felt like black smoke seeping into your ears. "Side note: Knight wasn't looking at the door."

I had been. But I was also high and drunk and a little off guard. Nothing a few harmless flirts couldn't fix.

"Sure, sure," Hunter said in his Boston accent.

I pulled him into a headlock, messing his perfectly moussed, wheat-blond hair.

There was just one crack in my unshakable, good-natured, billion-dollar smile and hot-motherfucker-jock-stereotype persona. A barely noticeable chip. You could see it from one angle. Only the one. And only when Luna Rexroth entered the room and our eyes met—for exactly the first half-second, before I rearranged my features back into my usual smug grin.

Other than that—as far as anyone else knew, at least—you couldn't rattle me if you tried. And seeing as I was an untouchable legend among the mortals inside the walls of All Saints High, many people did. Often.

Why I thought she'd be here was beyond my basic-ass logic. The shit I was smoking was obviously more powerful than a nice tall cocktail of bleach and antiperspirants. Moonshine didn't frequent parties. She had no friends other than Vaughn and me, and she only hung out with us when we were riding solo, sans our harem of fangirls and shit-for-brains entourage.

Maybe I thought she'd come because summer break was crawling to its inevitable end. My eighteenth birthday had come and gone, and Luna was still dragging her feet about college.

Her dad told my dad he was trying to convince her to go to Boon College in North Carolina. It was highly populated with gifted students who had mild disabilities. She fit the profile perfectly. But she'd been accepted to Columbia, Berkeley, and UCLA as well. Personally, I found it damn near offensive she'd think about moving out of Todos Santos at all. There were a few academic establishments in San Diego, a stone's throw away from us, that should do her just fine. Luckily, I knew Moonshine, and she'd never leave home, so it didn't really matter.

"I'm in the mood for some ass." Hunter slapped my thigh, probably sensing I was spending too much time in my head. He leaned toward the coffee table to grab his beer, elbowing Vaughn in the process. "You in?"

Vaughn stared at him blankly, as if the answer were obvious. With his icy, pale eyes and raven-black hair, he looked like a dropout from a *Twilight* movie—a vibe a surprising amount of girls dug. More than anything, Vaughn had perfected the art of making you feel like a dumbass for asking him a simple question, the way he'd done to Hunter just now.

Fitzpatrick swiveled to me. "Cole?" He wiggled his brows.

"Bouncing chicks is my side hustle."

That was my official statement anyway. Also that I wasn't hung up on Luna Rexroth, who'd friend-zoned me so fucking hard even my nocturnal emissions were platonic at this point.

Hunter, an Irish polo prince—too posh to play football like me and too remarkably untalented at anything to be an artist like Vaughn—put two fingers in his mouth and let out a whistle that pierced through the music. The guys around us clinked their beers, trying to bite down their excited grins. When we wanted a piece of ass, that meant they were in for a treat too.

"Ladies, line up toward the entertainment room. Make it neat. No cutting in line. Chop, chop. If you're lovely, daring, and willing, you're an applicant we want to see. Just be sure to remember—we won't call you tomorrow morning, won't follow you on social media, and won't acknowledge your existence in the hallways. But we will carry you with us forever, like hepatitis B."

A herd of junior and senior girls scurried up the stairs of Vaughn's mansion in pairs, whispering and giggling in each other's ears. Vaughn threw parties every other weekend while his parents were in their Virginia castle, probably fucking the memory of their devil spawn out of each other's minds. The girls lined up outside the entertainment room, spines rod-straight against the textured gray walls. The line started at the base of his spiral stairway, snaking all the up way to a heavy set of black doors.

Vaughn, Hunter, and I strolled past them silently, lit joints clutched between our teeth. I wore white, destroyed Balmain biker jeans and a shabby *I Fucked Your Girlfriend and Didn't Even Enjoy It* tee that had cost me a grand, paired with vintage Gucci sneakers and a beanie I was pretty sure was made out of real unicorn fur or some shit. Vaughn still wore his painting attire and looked just a little dirtier than a guy who had spent the night in a dumpster, and Hunter was wearing a full-blown suit, bless his Great Gatsby, weird-ass heart.

Our names, moaned and whispered like a prayer among the buzzing girls, drowned in the angry tune pulsating against the walls.

"A Song for the Dead" by Queens of the Stone Age vibrated in my stomach as we glided the length of Vaughn's hallway, which was complete with gothic, high ceilings and giant paintings of his family members. It was actually creepier than a Stephen King book: Vaughn's scowling face staring back at you, life-size.

Let's admit it, the fucker gave the Grim Reaper a run for his money in the menacing department. And he looked extra dead in those paintings.

Extra pale. Extra cruel. Extra *Vaughn*.

Since the girls couldn't explicitly proposition us without staining their precious reputations—I'd always hated the double standard of *guys are players, girls are sluts*—they pretended to talk to each other, sipping their drinks.

We stopped to examine the line. The rest of the football and polo squad were behind us, loyal and on guard, like the good puppies they were.

I was captain of the All Saints' football team, so I had that shiny quarterback title and shotgun rights. But Vaughn had the street cred of Dracula, and Hunter's family was the fourth richest in North America, so suffice it to say, all our dicks were fool's gold and had pussies in their cards tonight.

Hunter stroked his chin, making a whole show of it. Sometimes I truly hated him, but most of the time I was indifferent to his theatrics.

"You." He pointed at a girl named Alice, with pixie-cut blond hair and huge hazel eyes. He curled his index, indicating for her to come closer. She exchanged looks with her junior friends, breathless giggles bubbling from her ample chest.

One of the girls pushed her toward us, whisper-shouting, "Oh my God, Al. Just go!"

"Take pictures," a brunette coughed into her fist.

Hunter jerked his chin to Vaughn. The latter ran his arctic eyes along the line, carefully and methodically. He looked like he was searching for someone specific. Someone who obviously wasn't there.

"You're choosing a fuck buddy, not a mortgage. Hurry up." Hunter rolled his eyes, throwing an arm over Alice's shoulder. She bathed in the attention, smiling up at him with stars in her eyes.

Vaughn ignored Hunter, as he did ninety percent of the people who talked to him.

I examined the line, my eyes settling on a girl named Arabella. She had huge blue eyes and tan skin. A senior too. She reminded me a bit of Luna—when she wasn't talking. But that was the thing about high school girls, wasn't it? They always fucking talked…other than the one whose words I wanted desperately.

No. That one never spoke a word to me.

"Arabella, baby." I opened my arms in her direction.

She unglued herself from the wall to strut toward me in her high, hot-pink heels and black mini dress.

Vaughn finally picked a girl, though he was grunting like a caveman about it. I'd have made a mental note to ask him why, but Vaughn never talked about girls.

Or feelings.

Or, you know, life in general.

I wanted to tell him if he didn't feel like dipping his dick in someone tonight, no one was forcing him. But clearly, that would have been hypocritical. Not to mention false.

We confiscated the girls' phones before they walked into the room and dumped them into a fruit bowl outside the door, to be guarded by a designated freshman who wanted to fit in with the cool crowd.

What happened in Vaughn's entertainment room stayed there too. We weren't bad guys, despite what people might have thought. We never spoke about the ladies who entered here—not between ourselves and definitely not to other people. If the girls wanted to brag, that was their prerogative. But there were never any pictures, any vicious rumors, any drama. The rules were simple: you got in, you had your fun, and on Monday morning, you acted like nothing happened.

Because nothing really had happened as far as we were concerned.

In the entertainment room, Hunter was full-blown fucking Alice against a pool table from behind while having a civilized, flat-toned conversation with her about her summer. He'd tugged her mini dress up and gone at it, barely even bothering to slide her panties aside.

Turned out she'd lost her virginity a few weeks earlier to some tool at Christian camp and needed a redo.

"I just want to come," she whined.

"Then you're not getting out of here until you do."

Her fingers were buried in the holes of the pool table, her half-bare tits dragging along the green, fuzzy surface. Hunter smoked a cigarette, his eyes drifting to *Spaced*, a British comedy, on the huge, flat-screen TV in front of us, while fucking her.

And they say guys are not good at multitasking.

Vaughn, who was obsessed with *Spaced*, stood against the wall, letting some chick I didn't know suck his dick. Arabella stood next to me, waiting for some action, but I just propped my shoulder against the wall, angled in front of Vaughn, ignoring the girl on her knees between us.

"Hope she'll go out-of-state," Vaughn said, verbose, one hand holding the ashy hair of the girl beneath him, the other scrolling through his phone.

He didn't have any social media profiles and was soundly against trying to impress anyone on purpose, just like me. I'd once caught him checking some chick's Instagram, though he'd locked his phone as soon as I noticed. I never got her name, and it was pointless to ask.

Anyway, Vaughn was talking about Luna now, so that was my cue to check out. I hated talking to him about her.

"Haven't you wasted enough years on this shit?" he probed, tucking his phone into his back pocket.

This shit? Oh, screw you, Spencer.

"Haven't *you*?" I clipped through a locked jaw. "You hate girls so much you won't even fuck them. Blowies are as far as you can manage without being repulsed by human touch. At least I'm capable of feeling."

"I'm capable of feeling." He lifted a cocky eyebrow, yawning. "Hate. Jealousy. Disdain." He looked down at the girl bobbing her head up and down, the apathy in his icicle eyes confirming no one was home behind them. "Besides, unreciprocated love is like a nice Jag—one you have to carry on your fucking back instead of driving. Nice and shiny on the outside but such a drag to manage by yourself."

"Drop dead." I smiled cheerfully.

"Eventually, and at least I won't die a virgin," he said blandly, running his paint-smeared, rough hands through the girl's silky, clean hair just to taint it.

I was about to knock his lights out mid-blowjob when Arabella dug her fingernails into my neck.

"You look a little tense. Let me help," she purred. "I heard you were a kinky bastard, Knight Cole. Care to compromise me?"

I'd yet to pay her any attention, let alone touch her. I wasn't stupid—she wasn't here for *me*. They all came here for the story. For the *glory*. It didn't matter who got them in the door as long as they were chosen.

"Not in the mood. But…"

I grabbed her jaw and yanked her into my embrace. She moaned as I crashed our lips together, her grunt of pleasure swallowed in my mouth. Her tongue tried to pry my lips open, but I slammed them together, ignoring the wrongness of it all. I never ever, ever kissed girls like this, but I was too stoned to care, and besides, my resolve was thinning after years of getting slammed down by Luna.

I smeared her lipstick like it was war paint, burying my fingers in her hair and messing it so it looked like she'd gotten fucked into the next decade. Then I pulled away, smirking down at her. Lipstick had smeared all over her chin, nose, and cheeks. I could only guess I looked just as wild.

"Maybe some other time?" Hope flared in her eyes, her smile drunk with newfound power.

"In a heartbeat, baby."

Arabella got her story.

I faked mine.

———

Twenty minutes later, we ambled out of the entertainment room, heading down to wrap up the party. I made a stop in the kitchen to grab my sixth beer and found Arabella, Alice, and Vaughn's piece leaning against the kitchen island, giving their exaggerated versions of what had gone down to their doe-eyed friends.

I knew my secret was safe with Arabella. No girl would admit that an All Saints' legend hadn't touched her after taking her to the room. Truth was, I didn't want any of the other chicks to set the record straight either, and the only thing kinky about me was my fondness for watching breath-play porn (don't judge).

I swung the fridge open and looked around for the Bud Light. I was still reeling from Vaughn's comments about Luna needing to go somewhere else. Somewhere far. The notion that I could forget her just went to show he'd never been in love.

And then there was the other thing. The reason I'd drunk myself to near-death tonight. I searched the kitchen counter for vodka and took a generous swig before resuming my hunt for beer.

Dear life,

It's cool. You can stop throwing shit at me. I'm already neck deep.

Yours,

KJC

My mind had started doing weird shit shortly after Mom's parents, Grandma Charlene and Grandpa Paul, died in a car crash and left Mom an orphan. That was five years ago. I didn't care about my losing them; it was Mom's pain that killed me.

That's when I'd first started secretly drinking, and whaddaya know, I never really stopped.

"Supersize burrito huge, not even kidding," Arabella exclaimed behind me, perched against the island and looking thoroughly fucked as she fanned her face dramatically.

She obviously hadn't noticed me, or if she had, she knew I wouldn't contradict her story.

"Too huge. At first I was like—how am I going to take Knight Cole? Am I even ready for this? But he ate me out for, like, thirty minutes. When his tongue ring hit my clit, I swear I started speaking fluent Swedish."

Gasps, snickers, and intimate questions exploded in the room. I shut the fridge, turning around with a beer in my hand, and bumped into a small thing.

A small, tan-skinned thing.

With molten silver eyes and a constellation of freckles on her nose and cheeks—a map I knew by heart.

Luna Rexroth.

I could practically hear the chip in my mask cracking open before I cocked my head to the side, nudging the base of the cold bottle against her nose and watching a drop of beer sweat make its way from the tip, dropping to her luscious, full lips. I tugged at a stray curl that bounced over her eye in hello.

Luna Rexroth was beautiful. Sure. But so were a lot of other girls. Difference was, Luna carried her beauty like it was something borrowed. Carefully yet casually, not making a fuss about it. *She* wouldn't stand in line for anyone, anywhere. She'd stand out, glowing with quiet pride.

Luna wore a white T-shirt rolled up at the sleeves, boyfriend jeans, and a pair of dirty, checked Vans. No evidence of makeup on her smooth face. Tragically, it only enhanced how much *more* beautiful she was than the other made-up girls. By the look on her face, I realized she'd been privy to the conversation going on behind me in the kitchen. She always gave me that disappointed look. That you-can-do-better-than-this look.

But I didn't think I could. Because the best—*her*—was not available to me. She'd made it perfectly clear.

Three times, in fact.

Three kisses.

All ending in disaster.

Kiss Numero Uno was a bit of a stretch, even I'll admit.

I'd been twelve, and she'd been thirteen. We'd been in a water park, behind a giant blue slide. We were laughing and splashing each other, and I'd just gone for it, the spontaneous fucker that I was. Up until then, the idea of Luna and me was, well, more of a fact. Roses were red. The sun rose in the east. A seahorse could move its eyes in opposite directions (Moonshine told me that herself), and Luna Rexroth was going to be my girlfriend, then fiancée, then wife.

Alas, she'd turned away and let out a little gasp.

Because she couldn't—*wouldn't*—talk, she'd just shook her head. Then, probably seeing the sting on my face, she'd melted, pulling me into a hug. Our hot skin had met almost everywhere. It was the first time I'd realized *why* I had kissed her.

Boner. I'd had a boner. Which was…not great.

Kiss Numero Dos occurred when I was fourteen and had a pretty good grasp of the fact that my cock liked Luna just as much as the rest of me.

By then I'd learned a bunch of tricks to avoid attacking her with it, especially since we slept together every night.

I'd been a freshman, Luna a sophomore. I'd been gaining popularity at All Saints High thanks to my last name and ability to throw a fucking ball, which was something the rest of the football team wasn't so good at.

Girls had been all over me, and I'd hoped Luna might've noticed all the notes that poured out of my locker whenever I opened it. We'd still been best friends. Nothing had changed. Well, other than me. I'd started to fill out my skin with muscles, and a few growth spurts had resulted in my reaching five eleven seemingly overnight.

It had been nighttime when I'd climbed up to her window like I'd done every single night for years after our families went to sleep. When she'd opened it to let me in, I'd pressed my lips against hers, whispering, "Take two."

Biggest fucking mistake I'd ever made. She nearly slammed the window on my fingers. It had grazed my nails before I'd pulled away. By some miracle I'd managed to hold on to her chimney, and it had taken Luna a second to realize what she'd done. Once she did, she'd pulled me back in and saved me from certain death.

That night, while I'd been pretending to sleep in her bed, she'd been for real writing me a letter of apology, in which she'd explained that she loved me but only saw us as friends.

This time, I'd accepted it. Not long-term, obviously. But I knew this was a Luna problem, not a Knight problem. I saw the way she looked at me when girls were around, when notes were passed to me, when my phone lit up with unanswered text messages.

There was hunger there. Desperation—that hot, green liquid that slithered into your soul when you watched something that was yours be admired by others.

And so, I continued to slip into her room every night. I got it. She needed time. Time? I had plenty.

I'd decided to show her I wasn't some kind of obsessed stalker. That I was capable of moving on. To bring the point home, I'd stopped ignoring other girls' advances. I'd started dating, texting back, and flirting.

I stayed closest to her, keeping my alliance firmly with the girl next door. But I also had a chain of girlfriends who came and went—a revolving door of glossy-lipped beauties who wore the right brands and said the right things. I paraded them around school and brought them over for family BBQs, expecting Luna to ease back into our friendship now that I wasn't trying to suck her face every time she looked my way.

Ironically, that's what brought on kiss number three.

Kiss Numero Tres happened when she was seventeen and I was sixteen. I call it The Kiss of Death because the damage it inflicted on our relationship was huge. Even now, a year and a half later, I was still dealing with the echoes of its destruction. For instance, Luna before kiss number three would have told me she was coming to Vaughn's party. Luna *after* kiss number three barely communicated with me about what she was doing or where she was going. We were still hanging out most days, but it had turned into a bad habit more than anything else.

Back to that kiss. I was fooling around with a girl named Noei at the time. But I'd still cleared the day for Luna's seventeenth birthday. I'd bought us tickets to a museum, even though the carnival was in town, because Luna hated carnivals—and zoos, and SeaWorld, and anyplace where animals were captured for human entertainment. I'd had it all planned out. Luna was a vegetarian, and a vegan curry place had opened in downtown Todos Santos, right across from the museum. I'd bought her a bunch of weird-ass shit from Brandy Melville and had a seahorse tattoo inked on my spine, hoping she'd get the underlying message: that she was my backbone.

Luna loved seahorses with a passion. They were her favorite animals—something about the male seahorse being the one to give birth... Mom gave me so much shit before she signed the consent for the tattoo, but she'd known it was a part of a bigger plan, so she'd let it slide.

And if that wasn't enough, I'd made Luna seventeen different birthday cards, all the while trying to downplay my excitement that we were spending the entire day together.

The day had been pretty perfect, as far as birthdays go. So perfect, in fact, that when I dropped Luna back at her door, she'd taken my face between her palms and smiled up at me. I'd stared at her like an idiot, thinking, *Should I or shouldn't I?*

Darkness had washed over our street. Our families had been inside, probably eating dinner. No one could see us—not that anyone would have cared. It wasn't a secret I'd chop heads and bring down the sun for Luna Rexroth.

Still, I'd kept on staring at her, searching for the okay in her face. By that time, I was pretty damn good at recognizing the okay in girls' eyes when I looked at them. But not with Luna apparently. Every time her eyes said yes, the rest of her said no. I'd decided this time I needed more affirmation before I fucked everything up and earned an unfriendly visit to my house from Trent Rexroth, Luna's dad, with his even unfriendlier baseball bat.

She'd pressed my hand over her heart through her shirt. It was beating so fast, I'd thought she needed me to squeeze it back into her chest. My fingers had involuntarily twitched against the swell of her breast. The hint of a puckered nipple under my palm had almost made my knees buckle.

Luna had worn thin sports bras. You noticed those things about a girl when you hung out with her all the time. My brain had short-circuited, refusing to come up with words to describe what was happening inside my body. I mean…

My.

Hand.

Was.

On.

Her.

Breast.

Why'd it feel so fantastic? In my mind, we were already fucking three times a day at that point—my morning jerk-off in the shower before practice, the rub-in *after* I got back from practice in the afternoon, and of course, the whack before bedtime to take the edge off prior to slipping through her window. I'd imagined us doing filthy things I was pretty sure Luna would never even think about, let alone do.

Meanwhile, in real life, I'd just nearly come from touching her tit. I'd been worried for my man card. Also for my sanity when it came to this girl.

"*Do you feel it?*" she'd signed.

I'd squeezed my eyes shut and breathed slowly through my nose. Opened my eyes.

"I never unfeel it, Moonshine." The words had come out laced with pain.

"*Promise not to break it?*"

Even my dumb teenage brain understood the magnitude of the situation. Never breaking our gaze, I'd put her hand on my own heart, so she'd know, without a doubt, she wasn't the only one whose heart had a chunk missing.

"Promise."

Luna had tipped her chin up, giving me the okayest-okay in the history of the goddamn word, and I'd gone for it, still half expecting to wake up from the dream. And that was it. My lips were on hers. Finally. Consensually. This time, she didn't pull away.

A low, guttural moan tore from my throat when our mouths met and molded. She'd poured magic into that kiss, and it had depressed me to know, after kissing dozens of girls before her, that I'd been right all along. My mom had said there were a lot of lids for every pot. But there was only one lid for this pothead. *Luna.*

Her lips had been soft, sweet, giving—like her. She'd smelled like coconut and ocean salt and pencil shavings. Like heaven. Her wild curls had framed both our faces. I'd wrapped a lock around my finger, and it had gripped me like a live wire. I loved her hair the most because that's how I recognized her in the hallways. Everyone else either had flat-ironed, thin hair or a tired, in-between mane that wasn't straight or curly. Some wore theirs in doll-like, perfect ringlets held by hairspray that made them look like fancy divorcées. But Luna looked like nature. It was like kissing the entire fucking forest from our spot in the tree house.

"Knight. Jameson. Cole!" A loud whine had cut through the air, jerking Luna's body away from mine.

I'd twisted my head, still drunk from that kiss. Noei had been standing in front of my door, mouth agape, a hand on her hip, one foot tapping on the wide step to my door.

"I knew it! I just knew it! And with the school's freak no less! I should've listened to Emma and Jacquie when they said so. You're such a cheater."

No. No. No. Just...*no.*

Pretty sure I voiced that aloud, because Noei had shouted, "Oh, hell yes!" and "I can't believe you," and "I thought you were the one."

Which, honestly, would have been laughable if it hadn't been for the unfortunate situation.

I didn't even entertain the idea of explaining myself to Noei. We'd never been steady. I'd never called or texted her, though I had messed around with her in public every now and again. I'd explained to Noei that my situation was complicated. That I didn't do relationships. That I had an endgame and it didn't include her.

"Moonshine, wait…"

I'd chased my best friend through the snaking, cobbled pavement leading to her doorstep. She'd moved quickly between the green hedges, ducking her head so I wouldn't see her face. She'd asked me not to break her heart, and I'd gone and done it even before our kiss had ended. Frantic, I'd grabbed her wrist. She'd spun around, her waterfall-gray eyes shooting fire I knew would leave blisters on my memory. I'd let go of her immediately. She'd raised her finger between us, warning me not to get closer, before launching into the longest speech I'd ever seen her sign:

"I love you, Knight Cole. More than anything. Maybe even more than myself. But I don't trust you with my heart. And when you hurt me like this, I feel little and vindictive. So vindictive you shouldn't trust me with yours. Whatever it is, we need to kill it before it kills us, you understand? We can't be together."

"But…"

"Friends." She'd mouthed the word.

I almost heard it.

"Listen, Luna, it's not what you think." I'd tugged at my hair so hard, it occurred to me I might pull it out completely. This was bullshit. I wanted to rip something apart. Maybe my own skin.

"Knight, no. Promise me."

I'd turned around and stalked back home, and that had been that.

Then, I'd thought I couldn't handle less than everything.

Now, I knew that when you're left with no choice, you can handle it. It just hurts like a thousand bitches in heat.

"Moonshine. Can I get you a beer?" I blocked her way to the other girls in Vaughn's kitchen with my huge frame, rolling my pierced tongue along my lower lip. Long gone were my five eleven days. I was a little shy of six three now, with the width of an industrial washing machine, hard and muscled head to toe.

These girls, they hated her. She'd hung out with Vaughn and

me, the most popular guys in school, until she'd graduated. Spent summer vacations and trips to the Maldives with us and with Daria Followhill, the alumna queen bee of All Saints High. Luna was cool as shit by association, and fuck knows she tried hard not to be.

It didn't bother me that Luna and Vaughn were tight. I trusted both of them. There was still a dull pang of pain every time she as much as breathed in the direction of a guy who wasn't me, but I'd learned how to control it over the years.

Mostly.

Now, Luna flashed the girls behind me the middle finger. By their lack of reaction, they either didn't see it or knew they'd never get away with answering her without feeling my wrath.

"What brings you to the lion's den?" I brushed my scarred knuckle over her cheek slowly, watching in awe as goosebumps broke over her neck.

She took the beer from my hand, tilted it back to take a small swig, then pointed at me with the neck of the bottle. All eyes in the kitchen were on us, but I was used to the audience. Luna, not so much.

"Just make sure to bring him back in time for our round two!" Arabella barked, staking her claim on me tonight.

Her minidressed clones laughed like hyenas.

Luna gave her a hard stare, then pretended to shove her finger down her throat. I bit down a smile. Luna turned back to me.

"Spencers' bedroom. Five minutes."

The Spencers' bedroom was soundproof, which was something Hunter and I gave Vaughn a lot of shit about. Didn't make any difference that Baron was Vaughn's dad—it still must've sucked to know someone was fucking your mom so hard she needed special walls not to wake up the neighbors.

Even though I couldn't hear Luna's tone, I knew she was pissed. I could read it in her delicate frown. Not that she had a case. Way I saw it, she'd rejected me—not once, not twice, but *three* times. What did it matter if I wanted to fuck every mouth in this room? We weren't together.

"Wrapping shit and coming up." I took a sip of my drink, turning around and slapping Arabella's ass on my way to ask Vaughn for his parents' bedroom keys.

I was being a little spiteful, but I gave myself some slack because of the extreme circumstances.

Right now, my breath was goddamn near flammable. Substance abuse ran in my family, so usually, I tried to limit myself to one joint and a beer at every party.

But usually, I didn't find out Mom was officially no longer a candidate for a lung transplant, which meant her team of doctors had basically given up on her.

Today, I did.

My mother was sick. *Really* sick. Rosie had cystic fibrosis. She'd been lucky to reach forty, let alone pass it by a few years. Recently, her treatments had become more intense, more frequent. She stayed at the hospital for longer periods of time. Sometimes weeks. Her lungs weren't coping. The rest of her body wasn't doing so hot, either. From the outside, she looked fine. Gorgeous. Vital. But inside, her liver and kidneys were collapsing. So was our family.

Frankly, I was surprised Dad hadn't ripped out his own lungs and tried to shove them down her throat when he heard about it. It had sent me on a binge this evening, and I wasn't completely in control of what I was doing. All I knew was I needed to numb the pain of Mom not getting her lung transplant and seeing her earlier, hunched over Dad's office desk, crying.

Five minutes later, I pushed the bedroom door open, letting Luna in and locking it behind us. The Spencers had the wildest bedroom I'd ever seen. If *Pimp My Ride* and Buckingham Palace had a love child, it'd be this place. Royal navy drapes decorated floor-to-ceiling windows and a matching California King bed filled the room. Everything else was in gold or deep bloodred, and there were self-portraits of the Spencer couple on the walls in sexy poses I was pretty sure we had no business seeing—the reason they locked this bitch whenever they weren't home.

I watched Luna slump on their bed, looking up at the ceiling and making a snow angel on their sheets. She looked faraway. Spaced-out. Perching a shoulder against one of the posters of the bed, I watched her, already on the defense.

"Why do you give yourself to anyone who asks?" There was a snow globe of unshed tears coating her eyeballs when she asked this.

Interesting, coming from Luna, who'd gone to extreme lengths to ignore my antics with girls this past year as well as the fact that there was a dick attached to me in general. I cocked my head to the side, inspecting her. I wasn't an asshole—definitely not to her and maybe not at all—but she was seriously overstepping if she thought she had a say in what, or who, I was doing in my spare time.

"Because I enjoy it." I shrugged.

She gave me a you-don't-look-like-you're-enjoying-it glare.

"Jealous?" I smirked.

She rolled her eyes.

"There's enough to go around. If this is a booty call, I'll gladly pick up."

No fucking way I was risking another blow to my ego—a *fourth* one—weeks before she started her college courses and could ghost me, even from across the street. I no longer had leverage on her. The All Saints' hero everyone was afraid of but also admired had officially retired from protecting her at school. I needed to play my cards more carefully to keep her around.

"When did you become such a sexist jerk?" She narrowed her eyes.

"Right around the time I was born. It's called being a guy."

I was reducing myself to my reputation, something I knew she loathed. After all, she was the weirdo who wouldn't talk. She knew that between the stigma and the person laid an open abyss and in its depth, the truth.

"Don't give me credit I don't deserve. I work full-time for my dick and take orders directly from him," I joked, trying to lighten the mood.

She snorted out a sarcastic laugh, shook her head, and swung her legs to the side of the bed, darting up and making her way to the door. *"Good talk, Knight."*

Whoa. Back. The. Fuck. Up. *What?*

She didn't get to shut me down two thousand times and then get pissy when I tried to move on. Or pretended to, for that matter.

I clasped her wrist and turned her around so she faced me. "You came here to throw shit at me?"

There was some anger in my voice, and it made me furious with her. I tried so hard to accommodate whatever wish she had for us. When she wanted kisses, she got them. When she wanted friendship, she got that too. What about what I wanted from her? What I *needed?*

"Because I have nothing to apologize for. If you're here to pick a fight, wait till I'm done with the party. I'll climb up to your room, and we can talk shit out. Oh, wait, that's right. You don't talk."

"Shut up, dumbass. Shut up before you ruin eighteen years of friendship in one drunken night." Her eyes zinged with fury, and she shook my touch off of her arm. *"Why wait?"* she signed. *"So you can squeeze in another girl?"*

Her hands moved fast. Luna was still partial to not talking at all, even in sign language, so her Pissed-O-Meter was obviously dinging.

"Two." I winked at her, knowing I would regret every single word that left my mouth but somehow unable to stop myself. "I'm a hell of a multitasker, which is something you would know if you weren't such a fucking coward when it came to us."

That was the beer speaking, not me. But let's be real—the beer wasn't wrong. I was team beer until the bitter end. Beer had more balls than I did.

I heard the slap before I felt it. It was the first time a girl had ever slapped me. Up until now, I hadn't been a player but the fucking coach. I'd abided all the rules of the game. I never led anyone on. With the exception of Noei, who simply refused to come to peace with my terms, girls mostly understood, even if they hated the fine print.

Luna took a step back, cupping her mouth. My gaze was hard on the wall behind her. I didn't even rub my cheek. Whatever emotion it evoked in me, I didn't show it. As I said—my mask was made out of solid gold. Nothing seeped in. Nothing poured out.

I was drunk and scared shitless by Mom's situation. Ruining one more thing about my life wasn't going to make any difference. I sighed theatrically.

"Moonshine, baby, we've been through this. Next time, aim for the balls. Quarterbacks are good at taking hits. Barely even felt it," I said.

She raised her hand in apology, lowering her head and squeezing her eyes shut. Luna was the type of girl who never hurt a soul—the caregiver, the nurturer of the crew. Vaughn and Daria thought she was obnoxiously sweet, but I'd take her sweetness over their black hearts any day of the goddamn decade.

"Forget it." I took her hand and kissed her knuckles. I was a fool for Luna Rexroth—incapable of being mad at her, even when she deserved it.

The horror of what she'd done still played on her face as she took another step away from me, the back of her legs hitting the bed. She wasn't scared of me, I realized. She was scared she'd do it again.

"Why are you here, Luna?" I asked softly.

She swallowed, looking away out the window. The Spencers' house was a dark castle, a large, ancient-looking property that stood out in the manicured neighborhood like a sore thumb. I wondered if Luna wanted to jump out the window, like she'd jumped in front of that car all those years ago. I also wondered if it really had been by accident that she'd pedaled straight into the car. For all our years of friendship, I didn't know what she was thinking ninety percent of the time.

"I came to talk to you about college. I'm ready to make a decision."

I nodded, leaning against the wall with my arms crossed. There was no fucking way she was leaving, no matter what her dad wanted. She hadn't even left the neighborhood for a sleepover without her family. Was it sick that I liked her frightened? Sheltered? Closed-off? Because it meant having more of her and less competition.

Yes, fucker. It is wrong on every single level, a voice in me confirmed.

Still, it wasn't any less true. I thought Trent was insane for even suggesting an out-of-state college, not to mention pushing it down her throat about a week before she had to make a decision.

"So?" she asked. "What do you think?"

"UCLA online."

Were we actually talking colleges right now? Our shit was faker than a Hooters waitress's tits.

"They have a good creative writing program," I continued. "Plus, you won't have to leave, so you'll be here with Racer, Edie, and your dad."

And me.

She nodded, turning toward a window, placing her fingertips on the glass, staring out. She'd just slapped me after accusing me of being a man whore. But the truth was, I needed more than a crumb of jealousy to keep me going. I'd been shut down one too many times, and I needed her to throw me a bone with at least a bit of meat before I reassured her that, yes, I was the same pathetic bastard who had loved her from day one. That I wished I weren't but I was hers, whether I liked it or not. And fuck knows I didn't like it anymore. Not for a while now.

"You're drunk," she accused.

I may have had a whiskey brain, but my dick, for all intents and purposes, was sober as a priest and admiring my best friend's feisty nature.

"Okay, Saint Luna." I threw Daria's nickname for her in her face.

"Maybe you have an underdeveloped frontal lobe. That's why you take so many risks."

She was babbling. She hardly ever talked, let alone about fucking lobes or whatever it was.

"Thanks for the medical assessment, but I don't think there's one thing about me that's underdeveloped. Of course, you would rather slap me around than find out, wouldn't you? Anything but allowing yourself to fucking feel."

My good-natured smile was on full display as I advanced to the door. I didn't stop on the threshold like I'd wanted. The beer or the joint, or whatever the fuck it was, took charge and told me Luna could use a taste of her own medicine. I breezed right back down to the party, my cheek still stinging from her slap.

Come after me, my heart begged. *I need you. Mom feels like shit. I don't know how long she's got. I need you.*

I looked behind me. Luna wasn't there.

I grabbed Arabella's ass as soon as I reached the kitchen, dragging her toward me and slamming my groin against hers. I was rock hard, mainly because Luna had touched me, but as I smirked down at Arabella, I realized that for tonight, she'd do.

"Someone's ready for round two," she hummed.

I leaned down for a pucker, showing PDA for the first time since...ever. I didn't kiss girls in public. It was one of the many things I didn't do in public to be considerate of a girl who couldn't bring herself to tell me how the fuck she felt about me.

Vaughn and Hunter were right. I was possessed, and it didn't matter that I'd grown up with her. I needed to come to terms with the fact that it was possible Luna and I weren't going to happen.

I closed my eyes, and Arabella did the rest of the job. Our open-mouthed kiss was drowned out by the sounds of her squeaking friends, deafening music, and the squealing of Luna's sneakers as she pushed past people on her way to the door.

I recognized the sound of her running away from me like it was my first language.

And I vowed, that night, to stop doing the chasing.

LUNA, AGE NINETEEN

Stupid, stupid, stupid.

I slapped my forehead as I dashed out of Vaughn's house so embarrassed I wanted to throw up.

It wasn't supposed to go down this way.

I was supposed to muster up the courage to go there and tell him I wanted to stay in California. So I could be near. Near *him*. And Rosie. And everyone I cared about.

I'd been waiting for him to bring it up all summer, but every time we talked about my college plans, Knight yawned his way into another what-are-we-eating question. There was an air of dismissal about his behavior that rubbed me the wrong way. Almost as if I were asking him if he thought I should become a space cowboy or unicorn vet—like the option of my going elsewhere for higher education was so farfetched, giving it thought was ridiculous.

He'd never once said anything about us. Maybe *us* didn't exist anymore. Maybe he'd finally given up on the idea of us, and I had no one to blame but myself. I'd done this. I'd pushed him away.

What killed me the most was that deep down, I knew he'd been right. I hadn't done my own thing my entire duration on this planet. I was frightened, dependent, and completely out of sorts whenever he or my parents weren't around. I'd managed to sail through life with no friends—no human connections outside of him and our families—and minimum communication with the world. I was, for lack of better description, a glorified bubble girl. Knight was a friend, but he might as well have been my babysitter. So even though

I was angry at him—for the one-night stands, for taking me for granted, for being right about my insecurities—I also couldn't resent his dismissal.

I wanted to prove him wrong. To go to Boon just to make a point.

We were growing apart anyway, going in completely different directions.

He was growing upward, in full bloom, while I was developing deeper roots, chaining myself in place.

Besides, what was the point of staying? We were never going to be together.

He was always surrounded by girls. Girls who were nicer than me. Who spoke with real words. Some of them even had great voices. Girls who wore makeup and trendy clothes and curled and flat-ironed their shiny hair. Girls who had sex with boys and knew how to use their bodies to seduce him.

Girls like Arabella.

Those girls were always going to be there, swarming around him, competing for his attention. I couldn't imagine being with him without being eaten alive by the notion that my competition had more to offer. Problem was, *not* being with him hardly made any difference. Jealousy still wrapped its green claws around my neck and squeezed every time I had a front-row seat to just how enchanting he was to others.

Case in point, I'd slapped him after seeing him with Arabella. Shame and embarrassment flooded my cheeks with heat. I rushed through the Spencers' front yard, skipping over people making out on the lush lawn. Twisting my head back to see if Knight was chasing me, I bumped into a hard chest. I stumbled backward, then looked up, and *of course*, it was Vaughn, propping a fresh keg on his ripped shoulder, his dirty black shirt riding up to expose his lower abs and glorious V lines—peppered with red-lipsticked kisses.

Just your luck, Luna.

Vaughn shifted the keg to his other shoulder and gave me a light nudge back toward his door. His mouth, forever pressed in a disapproving scowl, twitched with a taunting smile.

"What's the hurry, Rexroth?" He waited expectantly for my response.

Vaughn knew sign language and could read my lips and hands easily. All my parents' friends' kids had learned so they could communicate with me. Seeing as he made it a point to stress how little he cared for people in general, I was surprised Vaughn had made the effort. Then again, it was hardly an effort to him. One day his mother gave him an ASL book. The following weekend, he was fluent.

He looked over my shoulder. I instinctively followed his gaze. Through the glass door to the kitchen, Knight stared at both of us, a beer in his hand, an arm draped over Arabella's shoulder. She kissed his neck, dragging her hand past his belt and into his… I snapped my gaze back to Vaughn, squeezing my eyes shut.

"Oh, that's the hurry," Vaughn finished in his signature arsenic voice.

I wanted to throw up. I took a step sideways, trying to get around him, but he clasped my shoulder on a dark *tsk*.

"Now that the knight is not here to save his princess, let's have a little talk."

He led me like a captured animal, his hand on the back of my neck—caught prey dragged through the savannah—until we were in his cobblestoned courtyard. He spat me out on a curved stone bench tucked into a darkened corner nestled between carefully clipped pink rosebushes.

The Spencers didn't have a pool at their manor. Instead, they nurtured elaborate gardens that made Versailles' landscape pale in comparison. But the absolute best thing about the Spencers' estate was the heavenly slice of lush green grass with a white gazebo surrounded by cherry trees their landscaper treated with hysterical delicacy.

Vaughn crouched before me, like a father figure would, not a friend. But he had never been either of those things to me. He was Knight's cousin and best friend. His fondness for me—or lack of blazing hatred, more like—stemmed from familiarity and solidarity with Knight. We weren't as close as people thought we were. I knew where his loyalties lay. He cared for me, but if I hurt Knight, he'd tear me limb from limb and dump the rest of me like roadkill.

"You haven't picked a college yet," he pointed out.

I stared at him, waiting for the punch line. I felt like a punished kid under his scrutiny. Usually we only hung out when Knight was with us, and then Vaughn took his Vaughn-ness down a notch or two. Now we were alone, leaving him free to unleash the demons lurking behind his aqua eyes.

"Are you waiting for a special invitation from the Queen of England?" he asked in his usual aristocratic, flat-lined manner.

Privately, and only to myself, I could admit that Vaughn scared me. He seemed incapable of so many basic feelings. I'd never seen him cry, even though I'd known him since he was born. I'd never seen him laugh—fully, wholly, with abandon. He'd never had a crush, and he never spoke about, or to, girls. He was, in a lot of ways, like Lot's wife—a statue, made of salt and stone, standing on a cliff, emotionless and proud after watching with glee as Sodom—or Todos Santos—was set aflame by its sinners.

I couldn't answer Vaughn's question without looking like a complete, pathetic lunatic.

I was waiting for Knight to tell me to stay.

I was waiting for him to realize I could do it.

I could move.

I could leave him.

I could, I could, I should.

Signing nothing, I fingered invisible lint from my crop top. Vaughn shifted his weight to his toes, leaning forward. He pinched my chin with his free hand, tilting my head so our eyes met. His pupils pierced through mine, rummaging inside the dark forest of my mind, turning every stone and tearing every tree in search of my secrets and truths. I wanted to blink but didn't want to cower in front of him like everyone else. So I set my jaw, staring at him, unblinking.

"What's your game, Luna Rexroth?" he whispered.

Swallowing, I arched an eyebrow.

"Is it the power? Control? What's your kick?" A cold, dead smile spread across his pink lips. "You're never going to be with him. You don't have the balls."

Something deep inside me screamed at Vaughn to shut up. But I couldn't deny the truth in his words. I had no plans to be with Knight. Not when he was with everyone else. Now Vaughn was clutching my jaw, no longer gentle but far from the realm of hurting me. He touched me clinically. Like a doctor would.

"Move to North Carolina and get far away from here. Go to Boon, Luna," he clipped. "End the fucking, never-ending shitshow of Luna Rexroth and Knight Cole. The cat is tired, and the mouse is diseased. It's a fairy-tale love story that took many fucked-up turns and ended as a parody. I know the general assumption is I don't have a heart. Perhaps it's true. My brain, however, is fully functional, and I can see exactly where this is going. Save whatever's left of Knight's high school experience. He's a senior now. Go to a place where you won't shit on his parade every time he shows signs of getting over you. Let him move on with his life. As for you? Find out who you are. Live. Unchain yourself from your parents and him. It's high time, Rexroth."

"But I—"

He took my hands, drawing my curled fists to his chest and wrapping his long, pale fingers over them. His chest was warm. It surprised me. He looked cold as a tombstone. I'd always thought of him as a cold-blooded creature. A brutal, callous crocodile.

"Stop," he hissed. "You're good, Luna. Anyone can see that from a mile away. You volunteer at shelters. You take care of your own.

You've always done right by people. I bet if your shitty mom showed up, you'd give her a free pass too."

I winced at the mention of Val.

"He *pities* you." He let the word roll across the ground. It exploded between us like a smoke bomb, and I found myself coughing. "By the same token, you should show him mercy."

I couldn't believe what Vaughn was asking me to do. Except I could. I was frightened that if I let my guard down and truly let Knight in, he'd use me and dump me, and there'd be no escaping him because he was everywhere. We'd grown up together, and our parents were best friends. Our families were tangled like a tight, never-ending french braid, with no beginning, middle, or end. And if I stayed, it would be more of the same: us circling around one another. Always in the same universe, never on the same planet.

Vaughn noticed the shift in my expression, a cunning smirk playing on his face. Boon College had a good creative writing program. He knew it was my passion and hit the final nail in that coffin.

"Artists are terminally dissatisfied. With life. With love. With their work. You like being tortured, don't you, little Luna? Sadness has a bittersweet aftertaste. Keeps us going." He lit up his joint. "Being an artist is a miserable job. You're pregnant with your work, only to give the baby away. An entire year of careful strokes of a brush just to have someone else buy the painting. You can be miserable anywhere, Luna. But Knight? Knight could be happy. Right. Fucking. Here."

On one hand, I was scared to death. What if I was like the Bubble Boy of Houston? He came out of his bubble to be touched by his mother for the first time only to die moments later. What if I couldn't survive outside my bubble?

On the other, I wanted freedom. To make my own choices. Even if just to show Knight I wasn't a permanent feature in his life, like a piece of furniture. And to shut up arrogant, awful Vaughn Spencer.

He was right, though. The only way to deserve Knight was to outgrow my need for him.

"Put yourself out of your misery." Vaughn straightened up. His clothes were holed almost as much as his heart. "Because he never will."

That night, Knight didn't show up to hold me.

To protect me.

To save me.

The moon shone, peeking back at me, asking why?

I turned around, giving it my back, ignoring its invasive question.

The sun will rise tomorrow, I reminded myself. *It has to.*

CHAPTER THREE
LUNA

SEPTEMBER, ONE MONTH LATER

"She doesn't even speak in sign language much. Dude, she doesn't speak *at all*. Trust me. I've tried. She's a freak. A genius freak, because hell, she hardly ever studies and apparently aces all her courses. She straight-up has a seahorse poster on her wall. I can't even tell you what insane *Rain Man* vibes I'm getting from her. Oops, I think there's someone at the door. Gotta go. Bye."

April, my high-pitched roommate, swung the door open. When she saw it was me fiddling with my key, her face fell.

Initially, I'd been a little worried about my multicolored-haired roommate. Dad and Edie had prepped the college prior to my arrival, so they'd roomed me with someone whose mother was deaf. April spoke sign language fluently, and was a tiny thing from Montana with eyebrows so blond you could barely see them. She liked Dierks Bentley and soul food and whistling loudly when attractive guys walked by, which I found horrifying and amusing in equal measure.

"I didn't think you'd come back so early." She didn't sidestep to let me in.

I checked the time on my phone and shrugged, shouldering past her. My daily meeting with my counselor, Malory, had been canceled. Apparently, she'd come down with a stomach bug. But who knew?

Maybe she, too, had gotten tired of trying to reach a breakthrough with me.

I flung myself on my bed, opening my message box with Knight. *Nothing.*

I didn't know which part shocked me the most: the fact that I'd actually taken the step and gone to Boon or the fact that Knight had disappeared from the face of the earth since I had.

I was dwelling. Obsessing. Fixating.

I swung my legs sideways and perched in front of my typewriter. Dad had gotten it for me last summer after I decided to go away to school in the hopes it'd inspire me to write. Typewriters are everything laptops are not: authentic, romantic, and unforgiving when you make a mistake. If you spell a word wrong, you must start over.

Dad knows I love a good challenge, but right now I was also wildly out of my element.

Write.

Write what you know.

What's bothering you.

What you love.

What you hate.

Just do it.

My fingers hovered over the keys. I needed an outlet. April, in my periphery, squinted as she examined me like I was a wild raccoon that had burst into her dorm room.

"Right. Heading out now, Raymond. Ping me if you need anything. Not that you would, you little vampire, you."

She had compared me to Dustin Hoffman's character and *Twilight* in one sentence. Awesome. I wondered if she knew just how offensive that was to both autistic people and myself.

"Yo. Earth to Raymond."

That's it. I flipped her the finger. Screw that.

"Whoa. There she is. Alive and kicking. Digging it."

I stared at my blank page, waving her out.

"Okay. Okay. I'm going."

I heard her on the phone as she blazed through the narrow corridor of our dorm, laughing and laughing and laughing, and I smiled to myself. April was so happy.

Clearly, she wasn't an artist.

OCTOBER

Anxiety laced my legs like ivy, climbing all the way up to my neck. Some days, it felt like I couldn't breathe. I still attended my daily meetings with my counselor, but whatever courses I was able to switch to online, I did. One of my promises to Malory was to study at Starbucks at least twice a week. Be out and about. Let the world stain my otherwise pristine, sheltered life.

Knight was still MIA. He wouldn't answer my messages, and I wondered if he'd truly moved on, if all he'd needed was a bit of space from me.

I sent an email to Edie every week, and every week I received one back, always saying the same thing:

Make mistakes.
Be free.
Be bold.
Treat teenage as a verb, Luna.

Love you,
E

It felt like life continued without me, and my bubble hadn't just burst...

It had exploded all over my face.

Malory insisted I ask April to have lunch with me.

She said otherwise she'd have to report to my parents that, despite my amazing grades, I was not making any real progress in the ways that mattered.

She dangled that negative, lackluster report about my progress, threatening to send it to Sonya, my longtime therapist back home too.

I took April to a taco joint and ordered two of everything on the menu. Then I flashed the fake ID Knight had hooked me up with as a joke on my eighteenth birthday and got us margaritas too. I made an effort to speak to her in sign language, because texting from across the table seemed extra weird. I even smiled. I was desperate not to go back home with my tail between my legs. So I decided to fake it till I made it.

It worked.

April smacked my back when we left the restaurant. "You're cool, Raymond. Who'd have thought? Not me, that's for sure."

I was mentally exhausted from talking. I needed to close my eyes and shut the world out for a month or two.

"Hey, so my friend is throwing a party next week…" she started, and I darted my eyes to her pleadingly.

I'd die if she asked me to join them. I shook my head slowly.

April burst into howls of laughter. "Um, no, my little grasshopper. Redirect that thought. I was wondering if I could give you money for some beer and other liquor."

I nodded. That I could do.

She grinned, her eyes twinkling with mischief. "You'll need to lighten up eventually. You know that, right?"

I didn't, but people were starting to make it impossible for me not to.

NOVEMBER

Then there was a boy.

An actual boy.

With limbs and everything. A real boy. That noticed. Me.

Josh: Party 2nite?

"Ask him if the party's in his pants and if you can bring a plus one." April peeked at my phone over my shoulder, reading my incoming text message. "I'd climb Josh like a tree hugger saving a rain forest given the slightest opportunity."

I tucked the phone back into the pocket of my jeans, chuckling.

"Come on." She flung herself over my bed—we had bunk beds, and of course, I'd agreed to take the lower bunk on day one—kicking her socked feet in the air. "We've been here for months, and you haven't gone to *one* party. That's legit the saddest thing I've ever seen."

"I'm happy you've never had to deal with truly sad things, then," I signed to her.

I'd been doing a lot of signing lately. More than I had in years in Todos Santos. I finally got why Dad had been so desperate for me to come here.

It forced me out of my shell.

It broke said shell like a glass ball.

Truth was, I couldn't *not* sign. I needed to buy groceries. Communicate with people around me. Talk to teachers. *Survive.*

"I have some homework to catch up on," I lied, ducking my head to my MacBook. The typewriter next to it was getting dusty.

April threw a pillow at me, laughing. "Liar, liar, thong on fire. You're acing all your courses and flying back home tomorrow morning. You don't have anything going on. Come. Party. Chill. And give Josh a decent chance."

Something in my gut twisted at the mention of Josh's name. Not because I didn't like him. The opposite, actually. He was mute—as a kid, he'd suffered trauma to his vocal cords in a car accident and could no longer produce any sound—and I felt oddly defensive about our tender friendship.

I'd seen Josh on campus for the first time three months ago, in the cafeteria. He had a smooth, young face, dark skin, and striking features. He'd been clad in white jockey silk pants and a hoodie. A flock of girls had cawed around him, so loud against his comfortable silence. His eyes had met mine across the room as if I'd called his name. I'd clutched my books tighter to my chest and slipped out of the cafeteria.

I'd tried to convince myself he hadn't really noticed me, that I was just so thirsty for the attention I was no longer getting from Knight, I'd started imagining things.

Then, overnight, I saw Josh everywhere—on the front lawn on campus, at the local Starbucks, at the library, in three different lectures, and at the stables where I volunteered as part of my ongoing therapy with animals. No matter where I went, he was there, until we had no choice but to smile hello at each other—not because we knew one another but because it was pointless to pretend we weren't familiar with each other's faces.

April and her friends were gaga over him, so I found out his name and that he was teaching special needs kids horseback riding three times a week. The first time I noticed he spoke in sign language, my heart slowed, almost coming to a full stop.

He hadn't noticed me, focused instead on his conversation with April. They'd stood across the hallway from me, oblivious to my presence. He had a laid-back, confident smile, like he didn't consider his muteness a disadvantage. He had a roommate, Ryan, who'd sometimes interpret for him the way April did for me. And sometimes he'd type things on his phone to communicate. But he always walked with the self-assurance of someone unstoppable, inspiring me to think maybe I could feel that way someday too.

I knew with fierce certainty that our paths were bound to collide. We were both freshmen, studying in a small college in North Carolina, and both of us were mute. My instinct proved true about four weeks after I initially saw him.

I'd hurried into Starbucks to escape the drizzle, tossed my scarf and peacoat onto a table by the window, got myself hot cocoa, and had the barista, Nicole, punch the time sheet Malory had given me—testimony that I was keeping up with my twice-a-week sessions. I'd always kept my Starbucks visits as brief as possible, staying the twenty minutes Malory requested from me and dashing back home.

But this time, when I'd turned around to take my seat, Josh was perched on a stool at my table, clad in his jockey outfit and a smile that could melt hearts. Nervous but open. I'd liked that he was confident but still not completely well-versed in his attractiveness, like Knight was.

"Am I that invisible?" He'd tilted his ball cap down and signed to me, knowing I would understand him.

There was something in my stomach. Not exactly butterflies but not the usual empty hum I got when guys—even handsome guys—spoke to me. I'd lifted my eyebrows.

I could do it. I could answer him. I could use *teenage* as a verb.

"You weren't here when I came in," I signed, poking out my lower lip.

"Prove it," he challenged, knotting his arms across his chest.

He was long-limbed and lean—good-looking but not intimidatingly so. I could imagine him accompanying his mother to the mall or playing Xbox. Things Knight did, technically speaking, too, but he still looked too untouchable and beautiful to be bothered.

"That's ridiculous," I motioned.

I reminded myself to breathe. I was doing it. I was having a conversation. With a stranger. A breakthrough.

"Says who?" he asked.

"Says me." I nearly snorted.

"Pretty sure you'll need to prove your case and not vice versa. I've been taking some prelaw courses."

"Where's your drink, then? If you were here before, you must've ordered something." I bit my lip.

His eyebrows shot up to his hairline, where his hair was buzzed close to the scalp. He sighed. "You got me. I just saw an opening to talk to you and went for it. Clearly, my plan was not bulletproof."

"Are you stalking me?" I asked, mostly joking, but I couldn't help but feel a dash of panic too, a familiar tug in my stomach. I was not in the best headspace.

I couldn't get Knight out of my mind, as if talking to Josh was cheating on him, though he had no claim. I'd tried Skyping Knight a dozen times since I'd been at college, but he never answered. He did text me sometimes, and I kept reading and rereading his messages, trying to decode some deeper meaning, especially after how we'd left things at Vaughn's party.

We'd never talked about the slap. I was too embarrassed to bring it up, and these days he seemed to tiptoe around me, dipping his toes in mindless pleasantries but avoiding an actual conversation.

Knight: Broke my middle finger. Switching to running plays. Killing my pass percentage. I'm getting hit more. Texting less. Stay safe. x

Knight: Sorry couldn't answer. Need to rest. How's school?

Knight: Missed your call again. Sorry. x

Luna: How'd you break your middle finger?

Knight: Fingering the wrong asshole.

Knight: JK. Practice.

Luna: I miss you.

Knight: xx.

Luna: How is Rosie?

Knight: Fine.
Luna: You know how I feel about that word...
Knight: Sorry. Good. Mom's good. x

I sometimes wondered what hurt more: losing someone all of a sudden, like in a plane crash, or losing them piece by piece, like I did Knight. It was like feeling a once-warm body growing cold next to you in bed. Chills ran through my back. I wanted to throw up half the time I thought about him.

"Stalking you!" Josh had thrown his arms up, feigning exasperation and commanding my attention. "For your information, yes, I did stalk you. But only a little. And only when we were both already out and about. I don't know where you live or anything creepy like that. But I was walking on Main Street on my way to get chicken noodle soup for my sick roommate when I saw you walk in and thought, there's my in."

I'd smiled at him. Really smiled, for the first time in a long time. He was charming and pleasant and *normal*. Yes. That was the part I liked most about him.

"Luna," I'd signed, offering him my hand.

He took it.

"Josh. Joshua. Whatever you want to call me, really. Just as long as you do."

Josh had then said he really needed to go get his roommate that soup before he got kicked out of his dorm room.

"You're here a lot," he'd observed, flipping his ball cap backward.

I couldn't deny it, because Malory was going to make sure I'd be here, whether I wanted to or not. I shrugged.

"Mind if I invite myself to tag along sometime?"

I'd shrugged again, fighting the urge to shut him down. Vaughn was right. It was high time I made my own friends and connections—and life.

After that, Josh had come every day, even when I wasn't there. I knew because the baristas told me.

At the stables, I sometimes watched Josh teaching other kids who spoke sign language as I swept with a wooden broom. Sometimes, he'd buy me hot cocoa and put it outside the door, knowing how embarrassed I was to be given things.

We were just friends. I'd quickly made it clear I was still hung up on a boy from home. I told Josh that Knight was my ex-boyfriend. It felt less pitiful than being desperately in love with your childhood friend, who was probably screwing his way to the top of a Guinness record for being the most obnoxious, desired teenager to ever live.

I'd tried to Skype Knight a few more times before completely giving up. We'd just see each other at Thanksgiving. Our parents always spent it together, so we couldn't delay talking to each other much past that, no matter how much he dreaded it.

When I returned from my lengthy trip through my thoughts, April had thrown her head back on my bed and was rolling around and moaning Josh's name to highlight how hot he was.

And he was. But he wasn't Knight. Though I reminded myself that Knight seemed to have moved on. He didn't have an active Instagram account, but sometimes, at night, I stalked the accounts of girls he went to school with and found pictures of him from parties and football games. He looked happy, and that made me unhappy. The fact that it made me unhappy made me even *more* unhappy.

"Don't tell me." April rolled to a sitting position and blew a purple lock from her face. "You don't want to go because then Josh might finally kiss you, and you will lose the precious notion that the idiot back home is going to get back with you."

April thought Knight was my ex-boyfriend too. The lie had grown larger, wings bursting from its back. The more it matured, the less I was comfortable considering myself her and Josh's true friend.

"Let it go, Luna. You're going to spend the next few years away from this dude. It's over."

I swiveled in my chair and pinned her with a look.

"That is not what it's about," I signed.

Or maybe it was. But either way, social gatherings made me physically sick. However, I knew with Josh and April there, I wouldn't be alone.

"Before you say no to Josh, I want you to consider something." April sprang up from my bunk and sashayed over to my laptop, hovering above me. "I didn't want to show you this, but I guess I have no choice."

My heart jumped to my throat. April leaned down and punched an Instagram handle into the search bar, opening an account I was familiar with. It was one of the popular senior girls Knight went to school with, Poppy Astalis. He'd never mentioned her throughout our friendship, but of course, my weekly searches included her. She was an English rose, sans the thorns—all sweet, delicate, and trimmed where appropriate. Her father was one of the most well-known sculptors in the world, and after her mother had passed away, he'd agreed to take on a consulting job, assisting in opening Todos Santos School of Art, uprooting Poppy and her younger sister, Lenora, from their London residence.

Poppy was pretty, but she wasn't made from the same velvet, tainted cloth as the rich Todos Santos girls. She'd always been nice to me during the two years we'd spent at All Saints High together, and she was a straight-A student. She played the accordion, skipped most parties but attended the important ones, and from what I'd heard, she was always the one to drive drunk girls home before they did something stupid.

"Maybe this will inspire you to give up on the dickhead." April clicked on the newest picture in Poppy's Instagram, and my throat closed in on my heart.

It was a perfect Pinterest picture: pint-sized Poppy standing on top of Knight's helmet in an empty field, her arms wrapped around his neck, both of them lost in a deep, passionate kiss. He was still wearing his football gear, dirty and sweaty and so alive he nearly burst out of the screen. Gorgeous. Victorious. Like a god who'd descended from the sky. Friday night lights shone on the beautiful couple, highlighting his glistening, disheveled brown hair. Against the backdrop of the black night and empty bleachers, they looked like nothing short of high school royalty.

The caption read:

WeWon!#StillLikeRealFootballBetter#NoItsNotCalledSoccer #KnightColeForPresident #MineMineMine

The pen I'd been chewing slipped between my fingers, and I bent down to pick it up, hitting my head on the edge of my desk. I lost my footing. I didn't even feel the fresh wound on my forehead. I patted it, confused, feeling warm, thick liquid between my curls.

"Jesus, Luna! You're bleeding! We need to go to the nurse."

The nurse glued my head, which, of course, was super fun. Then she gave me a painkiller and asked me to promise her to be less clumsy next time. I nodded—what else could I do?—thinking deep down it was ridiculous to ask me to be less clumsy. No one *chose* to be clumsy. It was hardly a trait one tried to excel at.

But sure, I would try to be less clumsy.

Less quiet.

Less of a screw up.

More normal.

Less dead on the inside. Because that's what it felt like, seeing Knight moving on with another girl.

I needed a drink. And I needed it bad.

Knight had a girlfriend. Of course he had one. *Of course*. Or he wouldn't publicly kiss her. Everyone knew the infamous Hotholes weren't about public displays of affection. Yeah, they were just like their dads had been—hot assholes. Hence the name.

Knight, Vaughn, and Hunter completely disregarded the fairer sex as a concept. Publicly, anyway. Knight didn't have just any girlfriend either. Poppy was love material. Beautiful, kind, and sweet. She was probably the reason he'd stopped texting me. God, what a fool I was, telling him I missed him, coaxing him to answer me.

As soon as April and I got back to our room from the nurse, I took out my phone and texted Josh.

Luna: I need a drink.

The message was seen before I could put my phone down.

Josh: Is that your way of accepting my party invitation?
Luna: Yup.
Josh: I have a better idea. Meet me at the stables.
Luna: ...
Josh: !!!
Luna: We're not supposed to be there after hours.
Josh: Didn't you tell me you want to use teenage as a verb?
Luna: Yes. My stepmom tells me to do that all the time.
Josh: Well, she's right. Trust me?

Funnily enough, I did. I did trust him. Was it insane that I put my faith in this stranger? Was I going to get burned?

Luna: I'll be a little bit, but I'll get there.

I dragged myself to the communal showers. My gut twisted and clenched as the hot stream hit my body, and the Instagram image of Knight kissing Poppy played in my head on a loop.

I threw up straight into the drain, the sound of the water drowning the retching.

The barn, surrounded by a low wooden fence, was located behind the main college buildings, on a rolling green hill overlooking a water tower. The stable looked almost like an ordinary house, red-roofed and swan white. It nearly glowed in the dark as I pedaled my way toward it. I left my bike propped against the fence and hopped over. A trickle of fear slithered in my empty stomach. Everything was dark, silent, and deserted.

I'd always been shy and reserved but never cautious. I was actually a tomboy. Edie had taught me how to swim and surf at a young age. Dad encouraged me to loosen up and take risks. He'd signed me up for a martial arts class so I could defend myself but told me not to be scared of boys, so I never was.

I knew Dad would cheer for me had he known I was meeting Josh.

Edie would be elated.

But Knight? He would be angry. Furious. Betrayed. Even though Josh was exactly what I needed. Maybe if I'd taken more risks, met more Joshes and Aprils in my life, Knight and I would be together today. But then I'd never have met Josh and April at all, would never have left home in the first place.

Knight wanted to keep me small and his, and the dumbass that I was, I'd let him have his way.

But not anymore.

I was drained from collecting small pieces of romantic moments like shattered glass, tired of brief encounters with my best friend: half-finished kisses, friendly hugs that lingered. His hot erection pressing against my leg one dawn shortly before I went to college, while we slept together. It wasn't the first time I'd felt his erection, but it was the first time he hadn't pulled away. We'd both opened our eyes at the same time and stared at each other for a beat, his penis twitching against the side of my thigh. He'd thrust once before he turned away from me with a lazy smile. Stretching. Yawning. Denying what had just happened.

But Josh wasn't like that. Josh didn't have enough baggage to keep an airport busy.

I jammed my hands into the pockets of my blue All Saints High hoodie (the only thing I'd found that was relatively clean) and jogged to the barn. I closed the door behind me, relishing the warmth of the animals, so big and hot in their stalls, radiating heat.

The minute I entered the barn, I heard something crunching and released a breath. I knew it was Josh's way of showing me he was here. He couldn't talk, but he still found ways to communicate with me. He stood on the other side of the stable, next to the stall of a beautiful, black Arabian horse named Onyx. He was the youngest horse in the barn and always requested extra petting time whenever I was there cleaning or feeding the horses.

I surprised myself by launching at Josh, suffocating him with a hug. Only when I was in his arms did I realize how much I needed that hug, how I craved to be put back together after being broken by a simple picture.

When I pulled away, I blinked.

Josh lifted his hand between us, holding a bottle of Everclear.

"Say hello to your date." He winked.

"That's it? Not even dinner? Straight to business?" I signed, grinning.

"What are you implying?" His eyes bulged.

"Nothing. What are you implying?" I chuckled.

This was fun. Easy.

He laughed and shook his head, producing a bottle of cranberry juice from behind him and two Solo cups. He poured a shot of alcohol into each, then filled them with cranberry juice. He unlocked his phone and put on a tune. The band was called Drum Kithead. The singer had a voice like liquid lava, and Josh bobbed his head with a small smile, not an ounce of bitterness in him, clinking his glass with mine.

"We're riding this evening."

I didn't want to refuse him—not when he was the only person I could stand to be with right now. I took a sip of my drink. It was horrible, but I ignored the burn scorching my throat.

"Bareback," he added, causing me to choke on my drink. "Because it's more natural and stuff," he explained.

"I don't know how to ride."

"I'll teach you. You'll be a natural."

"How do you know?"

He looked at me with eyes so full, I didn't doubt he really saw me through them.

"Because you're always on your bike. You already have the balance. The core."

We finished our drinks and led Onyx outside. I knew what we were doing was wrong, and that if the owners found out, they'd behead Josh and fire me from my volunteer work. But it was difficult to deny ourselves things when we already felt so robbed—robbed of our voices, our ability to speak our minds, robbed of being normal.

He helped me mount the horse, then climbed atop, settling behind me. Josh communicated with Onyx by pressing his boot to the horse's side or tapping its head. Adrenaline rushed through my veins. Onyx was huge, but gentle. Josh's chest bumped into my back as Onyx galloped forward, and I heard my friend hissing voicelessly behind me. Josh's groin bumped against my behind. Again and again and again. Until it stopped bumping and started...grinding. Not on purpose, I don't think. I swallowed, trying to decode what I was feeling.

Offended? No.

Annoyed? Not that either.

Scared? Not by a long shot.

Instead of being mortified of jumping from no base to third base, I was...enthralled.

It felt good. Him. Hot. Hard. Pressing against me. At first he tried to scoot back, give me my space. But when I wiggled my butt on purpose and looked over my shoulder with a smile, he deserted his inhibitions and ground into me with delicious intent. Heat burst in my chest, trickling down to my lower belly, exploding between my legs. I found myself leaning forward so my butt pushed against him, grunting as silently as I could. Josh and I had never discussed the circumstances of my muteness. He had no idea there was nothing wrong with my voice but with my head.

When we got off Onyx, we were both panting. I pulled the hem of my hoodie down to cover my lower body because I didn't know if my jeans now had a lust stain the size of my head. Josh led Onyx back to his stall and returned, looking down and shifting from foot to foot. I felt like I needed to somehow apologize to the horse for what had happened on top of him. Not that it was intentional… but still.

"Hug?" Josh asked, probably as a peace offering more than anything else.

"Please." I smiled.

Josh squeezed me again. Hugging like a parent—a hug that wasn't to take, only to give.

"What do you want to do now?" his heart whispered as his hands signed.

I could read Josh fluently because I understood his struggle. And he was a wonderful open book that I wanted to drown in.

I closed my eyes, hearing Vaughn's words again. Edie's. Dad's.

Move on.

Use teenage as a verb.

He's happy. Be happy too.

There was no menace in my next move, not an ounce of bad intention or vindictiveness. Still, I took Josh's hand and pressed it against my breast, holding my breath and bracing myself. The world tilted, turning upside down, and as my stomach flipped, even I had to admit—he felt almost as good as the real thing.

I popped one eye open, the dull pain in the back of my head seeping through my skull. Wincing, I remembered the Everclear. I wasn't even drunk, so I couldn't blame whatever had happened between us on that. I was relatively sober, and a lot heartbroken, and Josh was... *Josh*. Perfect and safe and beautiful.

God. What have you done?

Rubbing my face tiredly, I examined my surroundings. My walls, my desk, my navy blue–sheeted bed.

Wait...*blue*?

I bolted upright in an instant, stifling a groan when my body reacted by sending a ball of nausea to my throat. Again, this must've been my lack of experience with any type of booze in any quantity. I glanced to my right, and there lay Josh, bare-chested, snoring softly. His arm was flung over my thighs, and when I looked down, I realized I was naked too. I scanned the rest of the scene frantically as I pieced last night together into a full picture. I remembered watching in awe as my nipple disappeared inside Josh's mouth, imagining Knight doing it to Poppy. How, to shake off the infuriating visual, I'd pulled Josh closer, spreading my legs for him. His hands had stopped fumbling with my hoodie to ask me if I was sure. I'd nodded.

"I'm a virgin, but I want this."

"Luna..."

"I'm tired of feeling precious, Josh."

I hadn't wanted to be left alone with my thoughts, and Josh's mouth and hands were the perfect distraction. He'd sneaked me into his dorm room, and when we'd walked in, he'd taken off his shoes and stared at his socked feet, like he was trying to decide something, locked in an internal battle.

He'd shaken his head a little, chuckled to himself, and walked over to the door, taking one of his socks off and slipping it on the door handle.

We'd started kissing. Then he'd backed me to his bed, and we fell into it and started doing other things. He'd asked me if I was sure again, and I'd rolled my eyes, pushing down the light-headedness and queasiness I'd been feeling.

I'd wanted to wash Knight Cole off of my body after what I'd seen. Wanted to fill myself with Josh. Safe, sweet Josh. Josh, who I would come back to after Thanksgiving. We'd ride Onyx and study at Starbucks and be a couple. A normal couple. I would never have to wonder where I stood with him.

"I take this very seriously," he'd signed between us.

Suddenly, I'd taken it very seriously too. *Us.* Things were fresh and crisp and uncomplicated. I hadn't seen him kissing other girls, or flirting with them, or texting them. He wasn't the town's football hero, the knight every princess wanted to be saved by. He was simply...Josh.

The first time he'd entered me, I'd closed my eyes and squeezed the muscles of his shoulders. The second time, my mind glossed over and all I could think about was the moment we were sharing. The third time, I knew, without a shadow of a doubt, that I'd rewritten my fate by doing this with him. That Knight would know. That whatever we had shared would cease to exist.

And it felt morbid. Like I'd lost a part of myself—a huge part that anchored me to the ground. But I also felt...relieved, empowered by a decision I'd made all on my own. Without Knight holding my hand. Without seeking silent permission in his cool gaze.

Back in reality, in this strange room, with the strange boy-smell of socks and aftershave and physical sports, my eyes traveled to the trash can next to his door. I peeled off the blanket, tiptoeing my way to it and peering inside. I saw the knotted condom, with traces of blood, and white, thick liquid swimming inside it.

I'd done it. I'd had sex. Here I was being sexual, and daring, and *normal*. I'd never gone that far back at home. Not with Knight. Not at all.

Then the full realization of what I'd done hit me, and that it wasn't with Knight.

It should have been Knight.

I closed my eyes, mouthing the word *no* so loud I was pretty sure Josh would have heard me if he'd been awake.

No, Knight didn't get to intrude this moment too.

No, he didn't want me. He wanted Poppy. Beautiful, put-together Poppy.

No, I couldn't believe I did this.

No, no, no.

My phone pinged on Josh's nightstand. His dorm room was so much bigger than mine. He and Ryan had nightstands and even shared a little closet.

One missed Skype call from Knight Cole.

Three new text messages from Knight Cole.

> Knight: Finger feeling better. Heart's still feeling trash. We need 2 talk.
>
> Knight: No more fucking games. Time to face the music.
>
> Knight: I can't wait to hold you. x

What was he talking about, hold me? Why did he sound like he didn't have a girlfriend? Like the kiss with Poppy had never happened? Was it my imagination running wild? No. April had seen it too.

I opened Poppy's Instagram again, and sure enough, the photo was still there. Three hundred thousand Likes, no less. Way too much for a high school kid. She only had about ten thousand followers. Nothing about this whole situation made sense.

I scribbled Josh a note, telling him I needed to catch my flight home—which wasn't a lie—and I'd text as soon as I landed, which I promised myself wasn't going to be a lie either.

On my way to my dorm, I passed the cafeteria adjoining the

different housing sections of the college. I spotted Ryan napping on a table, probably because he'd given Josh the room for the night. I bought him a croissant and a huge cup of coffee and asked the barista to give it to him. Then I got myself the greasiest grilled cheese ever made in the history of bread and cheese and chugged two gallons of water to try to fight my hangover from hell. I sneaked into my dorm and locked myself in the showers, not coming up for air until I was sure my body didn't smell of anything other than soap.

But it did smell of something.

Something I had no business feeling.

A sour, tangy scent I couldn't shake off.

A mistake.

CHAPTER FOUR
KNIGHT

I'd been watering the plants for forty minutes.

The fuckers drowned some time ago. If I wasn't careful, we'd have a second pool in our front yard.

It had rained all of yesterday, and the field had been muddy as fuck during the game. But none of it mattered, because Luna was coming home tonight. I'd been watching the Rexroths' empty garage for nearly an hour, hoping to catch Trent's Tesla rolling in with his eldest child, to spot Moonshine getting out of the car so I could do the casual oh-fancy-seeing-you-here-it's-not-like-I-fucking-waited-for-you-for-the-entire-semester-or-anything.

I'd never gone longer than two weeks without seeing Luna—even that had been a one-off vacation—and by fucking God, it had been a form of torture we should apply to child molesters. But not seeing her for months on end? That shit sucked the life out of me.

Her choosing North Carolina came out of left field. I'd been so unprepared, I'd spent the first month too angry to even acknowledge her absence.

Amazingly enough, everyone else seemed to be on board with this bullshit.

Vaughn had shrugged her decision off, and my parents reported she was doing great.

Great.

She was fucking doing great.

Awesome for her.

Not.

Me, I wasn't doing so fresh. Luna was my center. My fuel. I was running on an empty tank. I'd have self-destructed if it wasn't for Mom. But I couldn't do it to her. So I ran on autopilot, acting like everything was fine, but as soon as the weekend rolled around, I was all about drinking myself to death and popping whatever pills were available at parties.

Look, I was mad.

Okay, fucking furious, more like.

Luna had left. She'd just left.

I bailed on her ass *one* miserable night to show her that, in fact, it wasn't cool to slap me because she was a Jelly Nelly, and she'd. Fucking. Left.

Like my biological mom.

Like Val.

Like the people we *hated*.

All right, Debbie Downer, time to shut down the pity party before the fun police throw you in the can.

"Just a sec," I growled, answering Mom when I saw her face peering from the kitchen window.

She was probably wondering what kept me in our front yard. Come to think of it, Mom never called out for me. My bad. But she was here now, leaning against our doorframe, wearing a brown polka dot dress and looking beautiful with her hair twisted in a loose chignon. Rosie Leblanc-Cole offered me a pumpkin cupcake from an orange tray. I shook my head, turning off the hose.

"You are so transparent." She dipped her finger into a half-baked cupcake, sucking the batter.

She loved half baking shit. Lived for the batter. I liked that she liked imperfections. It made believing she actually loved me easier.

"Oh yeah?" I tore my eyes from the Rexroths' open garage to her.

Normally, I wouldn't entertain that type of observation, but Mom had more leeway. I wish I could say it was because I was a good son. Truth was, it was because I was a guilty one. Not that I'd done anything overtly wrong, but with Mom's situation and everything, being a shitface felt excessive and wrong.

"She's going to be here any minute." Mom grinned, calling me on my bullshit.

I dug through the pockets of my gray Gucci sweatpants. "Shit, Mom, I think I ran out of fucks to give."

"Funny, you look like you're full of them. Why else would you be standing here for four hours straight?"

Forty minutes, four hours. Who was counting? Not this asswipe, that's for sure. Apologies to California were in order. I might have created a drought.

"Didn't you tell me to take care of the front yard? Practically *begged* me, in fact?"

She didn't need to beg. For better or worse, I was mother-whipped. I hated people who took their parents for granted. My thirteen-year-old brother, Lev, and I didn't have that luxury. Lev was Mom and Dad's biological child. I wasn't. I'd be lying if I said it didn't sting, that I didn't wonder if they loved him *just* a little more. That I'd become a quarterback for All Saints High *just* because I wanted to, and not because I'd wanted to continue my father's legacy. That the clothes, rowdy reputation, and destructive smile weren't calculated moves to look and feel like Dad.

That was the real kicker, by the way.

Fate had a twisted sense of humor because I even looked like my adopted parents. I had the same green eyes as Dean Cole, the same shade of light copper-brown hair as Rosie Leblanc-Cole. The loss of a parent was a concept I was familiar with, seeing as my birth mother had given up on me. So the idea of losing Mom was…yeah. Not a place I could ever let my mind go.

"What about Poppy?" Mom arched an eyebrow.

Man, Mom was on top of her shit.

"What about her?"

My parents showed up at all of my games. So did Lev, although he sat with Jaime and Melody Followhill because he had the hots for Bailey, their daughter. I didn't have the heart to tell my little bro that falling in love with your best friend is trash. Akin to sentencing yourself to life in prison. I'd be better off never knowing Luna Rexroth existed.

"That kiss seemed real," Mom pointed out.

I dropped the hose and headed toward her, to the door. "Hate to piss on your parade, but it wasn't. I barely know Poppy, and sure, it'd be nice to catch up with Luna, but I'm not waiting for her ass to make a royal entrance."

I tramped back into the house, peeling my clothes off on my way upstairs and throwing them on the floor. I didn't want to admit how weak I was for Luna. It was pathetic. And unstoppable. I'd tried getting over her plenty of times, especially the last few months. I wasn't such a saint that I'd enjoyed twiddling my thumbs and waiting for her to realize we were the real deal.

After taking a shower, I plopped on my bed and tried to ignore the fact that the light in her window was turned on. Instead of peeking into it (bad form), I checked my email on my phone. There were a bunch from a few colleges I was considering—all close by. Being near Mom was imperative. That meant waving goodbye to college football, but that was a small price to pay. I was good at football—great, even—but my parents were more than capable of paying my way through higher education, and I didn't want to take the space of someone who needed that opportunity. It wasn't that I didn't want to play ball. I did. I just didn't want it enough to rob someone else of a chance to get out of their shitty neighborhood.

I knew a thing or two about getting breaks when you needed them, as an adopted kid who'd hit the parents jackpot. Karma had a sick sense of humor.

"Hey, I know your birth mom sucks ass, but here's an amazing, one-in-a-lifetime mother. But here's the real kicker, boy—she's a temporary mom. She'll die in a bit. That'll show you to appreciate people!"

Yeah, screw you, Karma.

In the ass. Sans lube. Sans spit. Sans everything.

I swiped my screen and three text messages popped up, one after the other.

> Poppy Astalis: So, this is quite weird and oh so embarrassing, but...I've got a voucher for an ice cream place. Not that you need a voucher to afford ice cream. I don't even know if you bloody eat sugar, being into sports and everything. But I don't want it to go to waste, and Lenny is busy, and Papa is...well, you know, Papa. So I was thinking maybe...Oh, wow. I should NOT be sending you this message. LOL. Quite clear on that. This is silly. Sorry. But since you're not going to read it...well, I quite like you. And I quite enjoyed Friday. More than I should have, actually. Okay. Bye.
> Poppy Astalis: OH MY GOD. PLEASE IGNORE. MY SISTER SENT IT BECAUSE SHE SAID I NEEDED TO GROW SOME BALLS. PLEASE, PLEASE, PLEASE IGNORE.

I snorted. I made a mental note to let Poppy down as nicely as possible. She wasn't made of the same material as Arabella. She wasn't into dating me for the social status or sordid story. Whatever the fuck Poppy saw in me, she genuinely liked it. That made her endearing, even if I thought she was high on the insanity spectrum (and maybe high in general) for seeing me as anything other than a manipulative douche with a hara-kiri streak.

The third message was from Luna. I took a deep breath and told myself it was just my best friend—who I'd spent every single day of my life with, short of the last few months.

Luna: Whenever you're ready.

It was all the invitation I needed to jam my feet into leather Prada sneakers and head out.

The moon peeked through the clouds, shouldering past the last strains of sunset, and I thought, *fitting*.

"How do you like this baseball bat?"

Trent Rexroth opened the door, examining the club in his hand from all angles. Threatening me with heavy objects had been a running gag in our families ever since it became apparent I was smitten with Luna.

They used the word *smitten* because *batshit crazy* wasn't cute. But everyone knew I was *smitten* with chicken wings and vintage Tumblr porn, not with Luna. With Luna, I was in fucking *everything*. Love. Lust. Obsession. Take your pick.

Not that I ever told her that.

Not that I was even sure she knew.

I waltzed into the Rexroths' house, ignoring the baseball bat Trent swung playfully at random objects. He and I were cool. He and my father, Dean, were actually best friends. Trent had even coached my Little League team back in the day, and he'd introduced me to football. I stuffed my fists into the leather jacket over my hoodie (I didn't do varsity jackets; even as captain, they were fashionably insulting) and followed him inside.

"How's your middle finger?" Trent asked.

"Still working overtime, sir. Speaking of phallic gestures, Dad said to call him."

Was I making small talk? I was. But why the fuck? Apparently, I really was on edge.

"Your dad can pick up the damn phone, then," Trent retorted.

Edie, his wife, called from upstairs, "Language!"

I raised my eyebrows at Trent, and we both laughed as Racer, Luna's seven-year-old brother, darted from the family room to the landing, thrusting his toy car in my face.

"Knight! Look! Look what my sister got me from Boon! There's five of them, and it's not even my Christmas present."

"That's awesome, bud. Your sister is a pretty cool chick." I ruffled his curly hair, looking up at Trent in question.

There weren't many guys as big as I was, but Trent was one of them. He pointed upstairs.

"Good luck."

"Why would I need luck?"

"She's a girl in her late teens. Luck can't hurt, kid."

I shook my head, trying to downplay my nervousness. I was pissed. Pissed at the four months we'd spent playing virtual hide-and-seek. Pissed at the slap I still felt on my skin. Pissed at North Caro-fucking-lina. And pissed that I'd kissed Poppy Astalis for the entire world to see. If Luna found out, she would think I'd been dipping my dick in everything that moved.

That wasn't a true representation of how I'd spent the last four months, and I needed her to know that. Then again, I didn't want her to know that, because it was so fucking tragic, my goddamn soul wanted to wedgie me.

I climbed up the stairs to Luna's room and knocked on her door, pushing it open without waiting for an answer. She was sitting on her bed, her MacBook in her lap, and she looked up at me, exactly the same as I remembered her. With perfect gray eyes and that perfect tan skin and those perfect lips—and the slightly uneven teeth, the shit that took her from conventionally pretty to a breathtaking siren. My face broke into a smile, even though there was nothing remotely pleasing about the mess called our relationship.

"What if I wasn't decent?" she signed, grinning.

"I was counting on it." I ran my pierced tongue over my lower lip.

"Sorry to disappoint."

"It's never too late to rectify the situation."

"You're so bad." She chuckled, shaking her head.

"You're so good."

"What's wrong with being good?"

"Less easy to corrupt."

Silence.

"Ask me again," I said.

"What's wrong with being good?" She rolled her eyes.

"Nothing," I answered quietly. "Nothing is wrong with you, Moonshine."

Immediately, Luna's tight expression melted. She put her laptop on her bed and stood up, moving toward me.

I wrapped my arms around her and inhaled her shampoo, and skin, and entire being, squeezing my eyes shut and thinking, *home*. How could she feel like home? She went limp in my arms, and I felt her shaking. Sobbing. When she withdrew from me, her face was twisted in pain, but there were no tears. I frowned.

"What's eating you? Please let it be me."

She tried to laugh, but it died in her throat. "I need to tell you something."

"That makes two of us. Ladies first."

I wanted to tell her: You need to come back. Or maybe we can do the long-distance shit. I don't care. But you slapped me, and that meant something. It meant that you care.

I also wanted to say, I know you don't believe this could work, but not trying is no longer an option. For four months I've wanted to give you this ultimatum, but it felt weird to do it through Skype. But now you're here, and I'm not letting you go before we sort this shit out.

Then I wanted to add, I kissed another girl in front of everyone, and it felt like cheating.

And to promise her, It meant nothing. She meant nothing.

Moonshine tapped her index against the side of her thigh, considering her words, when Edie's voice pierced the silence between us from downstairs.

"Luna! Can you come down, please? Dad and Racer went to get Theo from camp, and I need you to help me choose Racer's mini-car for Christmas."

Theo was Edie's brother. He was autistic, high on the spectrum. He split his time between a developmental center in Orange County and the Rexroths'. Luna hung out with him like a boss, and he loved her so much, he barely tolerated my being close to her. Luna offered me an apologetic smile and ran downstairs, leaving me in her room.

I paced between the turquoise walls. There was a blackboard behind her bed, with a lot of shit she scribbled on it. A couple unfinished to-do lists. Some pictures of her with Racer, Theo, Edie, and Trent. And *me*. There were some pictures of me. Including one of me licking Luna's cheek with a mischievous smile while she was screaming her lungs out when we were on a roller coaster at Six Flags two years ago. Luna had been hell-bent on not buying the overpriced photo, but my indulgent ass had bought two copies and slipped one in with my Christmas card to her. Mainly, I remembered her voice when she'd screamed, how it had sounded in my ear.

Throaty and fun and sexy and...welp, shit. I had a hard-on now. *Think sad thoughts, Knight. Sad thoughts.*

How about the fact that it was one of the very rare times I'd heard Luna? How she only produced sounds when she was hurt or surprised or really scared. (Which wasn't very often, maybe once every few years. She was badass like that.) See? Now the hard-on was under control. Half-mast, at best. I rearranged myself and continued exploring her board.

There were tickets to charity events she'd gone to, letters from selective-mute pen pals all over the world, and pictures of rescue dogs she'd helped find homes for, with their new families.

I walked over to her queen bed and plopped down on it, noticing her phone flashing with incoming messages. I liked that she had friends at this new place, even though it drove me mad I wasn't a part of that section of her life. I wanted to be everywhere—to be unavoidable, as she was to me.

Ping.

Ping.

Ping.

Ping.

So apparently, her college friends were clingy as all fuck.

Then again, Luna would do that to you, with her huge heart and warm smile. I glanced at her phone, knowing I shouldn't but feeling my self-resolve tattering.

Moonshine didn't have any social media accounts. No Twitter, Instagram, Facebook, or Pinterest. She sent us weekly emails telling us how she was doing, sometimes adding pictures of her with her roommate, April. There'd been one picture of a dark horse. I remember being slightly jealous of Onyx and wondered whether that meant it was finally time to seek professional help for my obsession. But how much did I really know about her life? Only what she was willing to share.

Plus, it wasn't like I was going to *open* the goddamn messages. Just glimpse at her screen when the phone was still locked. All I'd have to do was tilt the phone. Fucking sue me for moving it an inch. As it happened, I didn't even have to do that. The screen flashed with another incoming message before I touched it, ridding me of (almost) all of my guilt.

Josh:	Is it crazy that I already miss you?
Josh:	I can't stop thinking about our night together.
Josh:	Thank you for giving me your most precious gift. It meant the world to me.
Josh:	On the plane heading south to see my parents. Send me pictures of your Thanksgiving table. I'll do the same. Thinking of you. x

I'd have fallen on my ass if I wasn't already seated.

I half expected the floor to open up and swallow me into a black hole as my eyes traced the text messages over and over again. My jaw was clenched so tight, I felt my teeth crumbling to dust.

Who the fuck was Josh? Where did he come from? I hadn't heard about any Josh. And I spoke with Edie and Trent almost every day. Luna gave him…what, exactly? Her virginity? Yeah, bro. No fucking way. That belonged to me.

Yet there it was. Plain and clear. He thanked her for their night together. For the *precious* gift she'd given him. I was going out on a limb here and guessing it wasn't a gift card from fucking Target.

Luna had slept with someone else. Someone else named Josh. He'd touched her and kissed her and spread her legs and put his fingers in her…

I needed to leave.

That much was clear. Not because I didn't want to demand the entire story behind Josh, but because I knew I was not in any condition to have a conversation with anyone other than a trained assassin, to get rid of Josh. *Josh.* With his fucking generic name. *Josh.*

Joshua.

Jesus.

Fuck.

Leave, Knight. Leave. Otherwise, I would lose my shit, and there was no way of knowing what I'd do. I would never hurt Luna physically. But I didn't trust myself not to say something that would bury her. I didn't trust myself not to tear her fucking house down, brick by brick, and ruin everything in her life like she'd ruined me. But I couldn't go downstairs and dash out the door like some damsel in distress. She didn't deserve to see the devastation on my face when I finally got the wake-up call.

Ring, ring!

"*Hello, who is it?*"

"Reality. Guess what, dumbass? Luna isn't different. She just didn't want your sorry ass that way."

Feeling pathetic, and subhuman, and half-functioning, I did what I'd done a thousand times before: I opened her window and slipped out.

The words chased me all the way up to my room.

Miss you.

Can't stop thinking about our night together.

Thank you for the most precious gift.

Slamming the door didn't help. The text messages seeped through the crack. I could still see and feel them on my eyeballs. My phone started buzzing.

Luna: Knight?

Luna: Where are you?

Luna: Did you go back home? Why?

I paced back and forth, running my fingers through my hair, tugging at it until I felt chunks of it ripping out. *Calm down, fucker. Calm down.* My body was sizzling with adrenaline, and I knew once I crashed, devastation would take its place. But first, I was going to explode. And I couldn't explode on her. No matter how much I hated her right now. How much I wanted to smash her fucking heart for doing that to mine.

A few minutes later, Luna put two and two together.

Luna: Oh God.

Luna: I'm so sorry.

Luna: I didn't want you to find out like this.

Luna: What business did you have looking at my phone?

Find out? Find out what? That she had a boyfriend? That she'd moved on? That she was in fucking *love?* That while I'd been waiting and pining and agonizing for eight years—since age ten when Lilith Blanco slipped me a note asking to be my girlfriend and I'd told her it would never be serious because all the parts of me she wanted already belonged to Luna Rexroth—*she* was fucking another dude in college? I turned off my phone, stuffed it into my duffel bag, and threw my door open.

"No visitors," I barked. "And no questions either."

Dad yelled at me not to yell. Mom coughed that I was her favorite psycho, and she was here if I needed to talk. Lev was in his room across the hall, probably with Bailey on the phone, listening to her bullshit ballerina stories.

She is friend-zoning you, bro. That's where your dick goes to die. Break the cycle before Bailey finds herself a Joe or Josh or FUCK.

The doorbell rang on cue, and I heard Dad telling Luna I was under the weather.

Damn straight I was under the weather. I was so far down under the weather, I was in goddamn hell. It was hard to make out Luna's reactions, because it was in sign language, but Dad kept telling her he was sure everything was okay, and I was a moody *sonovabitch*, and she should enjoy her time in Todos Santos and not worry about me.

Ten minutes later, I heard scratches outside my window. I was still standing with my back to it, staring at a wall, wondering if it was wood or concrete and calculating the odds of breaking all my fingers if I punched it.

The scratches turned into knocks.

"Go away." My voice was too husky, even to my own ears.

I didn't turn around, because I knew if I did, I'd see her face, and she'd disarm me from my anger. She turned me down three times, slapped me for messing around with other girls, then slept with some douchebag. I had every right to be furious, and I was done being the understanding, designated BFF.

Good thing she didn't get us friendship bracelets with hearts and unicorns. I'd probably wear that shit too, just to see a smile on her face.

Another knock on my window.

"Not fucking interested. You're mute, sweetheart. Not deaf. Even that isn't real, though, right?"

I began to stuff my gym clothes into the duffel bag just to do something with my hands. What the fuck was I saying? I couldn't even control the bullshit leaving my mouth. I already regretted it. It was a low blow, no matter what she'd done. As far as she could tell, I'd fucked the better half of the town, in several positions, so I got it—the hypocritical angle. Thing was, I didn't care.

I didn't want to be right.

I wanted to be mad.

Mad that Luna, the only girl I'd ever loved, had friend-zoned my ass, not because she had some mega-internal problem with getting it on with a dude, but because I'd gotten it all wrong and she didn't even like me that way.

Surprisingly, she still went at it on my window.

I wasn't completely in charge of my actions, or my thoughts, *or* my emotions, hence I did the dumbest thing in the world. I asked a question I wasn't prepared to hear the answer to.

"Tell you what—you want to be indulged? For one fucking time, we'll do it my way. If you didn't sleep with anyone else, knock twice, and I'll turn around and let you in. If you *did* sleep with Josh, knock three times, and do the honorable thing and let me have my fucking moment in private. Because I deserve it, Luna. I goddamn *earned* it."

My back was still to my window when Moonshine knocked the first time. My heart, all embers, flared in flames. I fisted the strap of my gym bag and squeezed. Then came the second knock. I took a breath and looked down, noticing that my clenched fist was trembling.

Don't knock again. Don't knock again. Don't, Luna. Don't.

The third knock had desperation in it. An apology. A silent prayer.

I dropped the gym bag, squeezing my eyes shut.

She slapped my window a few more times, and I heard a rare yelp. She was a frantic animal, begging for help. I heard another slap, then another, then another as she tried to break the glass. I picked up the bag, walked over to my door, and closed it behind me.

For the first time in almost eighteen years, I knew Luna and I faced something I couldn't fix. Something I didn't want to fix.

I was fucking done.

CHAPTER FIVE
LUNA

I examined my bloodshot eyes in the mirror of my bathroom, applying another layer of scarlet-hued gloss on my lips.

Guess that's what three days without sleep would do to you: red-rimmed eyes and a lip color to match. But I couldn't get through to Knight, no matter how hard I tried. I'd waited for him outside his door every morning. He'd breezed past me, usually with his phone glued to his ear, ignoring my existence all the way to his Aston Martin. I'd nearly fallen trying to climb up to his window again, only to find it secured and locked. I'd waited for him in his gym's reception area, pretending to be reading a brochure about hot yoga classes, only to have security personnel sent to tell me that a gentleman had requested I leave the premises so he could walk back to his car.

Knight treated me like a common stalker. And if I were being honest with myself, I wasn't exactly *not* one. I just needed him to hear me out.

Now, we were about to go to the Spencers' for our annual Thanksgiving dinner, and we were going to share a table, and a meal, and a *space*, whether he liked it or not. I was going to sit across from, or next to him, and I didn't know if I was elated to finally get to see his face or terrified of seeing what was on it.

I tapped the rich, crème ceramic of the sink, shifting from foot to foot on the checked black-and-white marble of our heated floors, ignoring the messages popping up on my phone, which was propped on the edge of the counter.

Josh: Everything okay?

Josh: You're probably busy. Just tell me you're good when you have time?

"Baby, we don't want to be late. Are you finishing up?" Dad called from downstairs.

Racer simultaneously knocked on the bathroom door, shouting, "Luna, Luna, Lunatic! Come on!"

"Don't call your sister that, you little rascal," Edie chided from downstairs.

She was so PC about my selective muteness, even though sometimes, when we were all alone, I'd actually answer her with words. Mainly *yes* and *no*. I didn't know why I felt so comfortable around Edie. A part of me thought she loved me extra hard because she knew my own mother didn't.

I tried wiping the redness from my eyes to no avail and opened the door, grabbing my baby brother by the collar and jerking him into a hug. I wore a lavender wrap dress with ruffled edges I'd borrowed from Edie. I hated dresses. There was nothing I liked more than blending in with the furniture and making myself invisible. But desperate times called for desperate measures, and I'd stooped so low as to wear a revealing, tight dress that might make Knight look at me with something that wasn't sheer hatred and revulsion.

Fine. I was a sellout.

A sellout who needed a way to reach her best friend.

"Wow, Lunatic. You're really pretty." Racer squeezed my waist, looking up to scrutinize my face with his big, cobalt eyes.

I took his hand, and we descended the stairs. When Dad and Edie saw me, their eyes flared, but they didn't comment about the makeup or the dress. They'd gotten tired of asking what was wrong with me and why I wasn't hanging out with Knight and Vaughn.

Shoot. *Vaughn.* I hadn't even considered him as a complication. Had Knight told him about Josh and me? My gut feeling said no, because Knight was overprotective of me. Then again, judging by his behavior the last few days, a reconciliation wasn't in our cards. One thing was for sure—if Vaughn knew, I would find out tonight. He wasn't known for his diplomatic skills.

"Beautiful." Dad kissed my temple, and I relished the tenderness in his voice.

When he let go of me, Edie was there to catch me in an extra-tight hug.

"I don't know what's going on, but I'm here." She clutched me to her chest, whispering in my ear, "I will always be here. I love you."

We got to the Spencers' carrying three different casserole dishes, five bottles of wine, and a dessert Dad had ordered especially from Los Angeles. Some fancy hot cakes with ice cream inside them that needed to be consumed at room temperature. Such were the Thanksgiving feasts my parents and their friends hosted—lavish, over-the-top, and picture-perfect.

I was the only imperfect thing about the picture, including the perfect house, perfect meal, and perfect people surrounding me.

Hugs and pleasant small talk ensued the moment we walked through the Spencer family's door.

Jaime and Melody Followhill were already there with their daughters, Bailey and Daria. Daria's fiancé, Penn, and his sister, Via, were also there. They were like foster children to the Followhills, which I guess made Daria and Penn's love affair a little forbidden, but I didn't judge them. I'd always thought my being with Knight would be weirder. Because we had actually grown up together. I'd seen him in diapers. He'd watched me studying the back of a tampon box for the instructions with horror in my eyes and had even tried to have a go at how to do it before we'd both toppled over, laughing.

Baron and Emilia Spencer looked Oscar ready with his second-skin-style suit and her pumpkin-hued dress—floor length and bare-shouldered. Vaughn, who took pleasure in looking like a hobo, awarded me with half a distant yet conspiring smile, which meant he definitely wasn't privy to whatever was going on between Knight and me.

A trickle of hope slithered its way to my gut. If Vaughn didn't know, that meant my relationship with Knight was salvageable, right? Knight hadn't said anything that'd make Vaughn see me in a negative light.

He still protected me.

I didn't even know what my goal was. Up until three days ago, I'd been keen to give this thing with Knight a chance. Then for twenty-four hours or so, I'd been planning a future with Josh—whose messages I'd been dodging the past three days, too hysterical to pay him attention. And all of a sudden my only wish was…what? To get Knight back? He was never mine to begin with. To beg for his forgiveness? *He* was the one who'd pointed out we were free to mess around with anyone we wanted. Yet I was expected to explain myself. I'd even felt guilty. But now, as I stood here, waiting for my verdict, I wasn't exactly sure why I had ever agreed to go to trial.

Knight slept with girls. All the time. He flirted and dated and locked them in Vaughn's media room and did unthinkable things to them behind the dark wooden doors. He crawled into my bed with their sweet, flowery, needy scents all over him.

Why was I being so apologetic and remorseful? Why would I mess this thing up with Josh to try to soothe Knight's wounded ego? Why had I let him hinder the entire progress I'd made these past four months just because he wasn't comfortable with my new life?

The only thing I was at fault for was slapping him, and that was months ago. But I shouldn't have done that, and he deserved an apology. But that was the extent of it.

Getting kicked out of gyms, nearly falling off window ledges—why was I indulging his vindictiveness?

Suddenly, my blood simmered with heat. All this time, I'd been trying to apologize for something Knight shoved in my face on a daily basis when we'd lived close to each other.

I excused myself from the adults' company, waltzing into the Spencers' kitchen and helping myself to a glass of spicy red port specially prepared by their Portuguese vintner, because of course, when you were a Spencer, having your own vintner was a *thing*.

I caught Daria—blond, tall, and too Gigi Hadid to look real— and Penn, who basically looked like Leonardo DiCaprio circa 1996, making out against the kitchen counter and pretended not to notice their picture-ready existence. The doorbell chimed behind us, and they disconnected on a grunt, panting hard and smiling at each other.

I wanted to throw up into my port. Not because I didn't like them—I did, I loved them, they were a part of my family—but because I knew what, and who, was coming through that door.

"It's Knight! I've been dying to catch up with him." Daria clapped excitedly, leaving Penn and me in the kitchen together without even sparing me a hello.

We nodded at each other. He leaned against the kitchen counter, jerking his chin my way.

"How's college?"

I smiled, pointing at him.

He shrugged. "I'm happy wherever she is." His eyes drifted to the space Daria had occupied a second ago.

That sounded like something Josh would say. Suddenly, I missed Josh. Josh, whose only sin was to be the cause of my rift with Knight.

I unlocked my phone and sent him a quick message in answer to the ones he'd been bombarding me with.

Luna: Everything is great. Sorry I've been silent—a lot has been going on, but it's okay now. We're just starting dinner. I miss you too, and I really can't wait to get back to Boon. x

When I looked up, the kitchen was suddenly full of people, including Knight, his mother (Rosie), his dad (Dean), and his little brother (Lev). Lev and Racer sneaked together to the great room with Bailey on their heels.

Rosie squeezed me into her wheezing chest and kissed the crown of my head. Dean narrowed his eyes at me playfully, ruffling the hair I'd tried to straighten for the past couple hours.

"Having fun at Boon, Lu?"

I circled my index and thumb in an OK.

"Good, good."

When it was Knight's turn to acknowledge me and all eyes were on us, he tilted his chin up in hello. He didn't take a second look at my dress or my made-up face or my dolled-up hair. Just gave me a nonchalant wink and moved to the port, helping himself to a generous glass. The blush on his cheeks indicated he'd already slipped in a shot or four before they'd arrived. He wore a white V-neck shirt, a navy-blue blazer, and camel-hued skinny jeans, his hair a delicious, unkempt mess. He was thumbing his phone, not really paying attention to anyone, uncharacteristically distant.

Vaughn, who now stood next to me, looked between us and cleared his throat, silently asking what the hell was going on. Knight scratched his eyebrow, tossing his phone in the air and catching it with precise speed and accuracy.

"Anything to share?" Vaughn grumbled.

Knight threw his entire drink down his throat when our parents weren't looking, clucking his tongue with a devilish smirk. "Sorry, not into sharing. You never know where shit's been, you know?"

Vaughn whistled low, looking between us. "And so, the little innocent creature has fangs. The plot thickens."

I swallowed.

Knight grinned. "Someone's thick here, all right, but it's got nothing to do with the plot."

"You're butthurt," Vaughn mused.

"Nah. The only butts in danger of hurting are the ones I'll be plowing into when we go to Arabella's party after this boring dinner." Knight spat out the word *boring* like I was the one who made it so.

I could feel my anger climbing up my toes, making every cell in my body burn. *Arabella? What about Poppy?* I wanted to yell my lungs out but settled for flashing the boys a dazzling, I-don't-give-a-damn smile, not wanting to cause a scene.

My fury reached another peak when we'd sat at the long dinner table, with brown, hand-decorated china, personal pumpkins painted by Lev and Bailey, yellow candles, and handmade napkins sewn with real threads of gold. Everybody was chatting, laughing, and drinking warm cider and wine, enjoying their butter-roasted turkey. Knight sat next to me, probably because he knew he'd be bombarded with concerned questions if he didn't, and continued texting under the table, taking no part in the conversation.

"Put the phone down, Son," Dean said at one point, and Knight didn't even look up from the screen.

Dean put his glass of water on the table—he never drank alcohol—and looked directly at Knight with the familiar intensity of a man who could set the sky ablaze.

"Honey," Rosie tried, dabbing at the sides of her mouth with a napkin.

This time, Knight did look up, tucking his phone in his front pocket. It was one of the things I loved about Knight the most. He was respectful and loving to his mother.

"Sorry, Ma."

"Sorry sounds right," Dean muttered into his forkful of white asparagus.

"I agree. Sounds are awesome. I love sounds." Knight threw his arms in the air, digging into his food all of a sudden like he'd been starving for days.

I shrank into my seat next to him, staring at my meal like it was going to help me if I begged it hard enough with my eyes. I had a lot to say to Knight, but I couldn't do it at the table.

"Do you have anything to say?" Edie, with her no-bullshit approach, speared Knight with a look, her utensils clattering to her plate.

"Plenty, Mrs. Rexroth. I have plenty of things to say," he chirped.

I knew, even though he could hide the signs from others, he was drunk. *Again*. Knight had always been careful with alcohol—at least up until Vaughn's party—so this was alarming.

Then again, I hadn't been here for a few months. Maybe this was his new normal?

"You're walking on thin ice," Dean warned in front of all of us, which I knew would only push Knight over the edge. He was a carbon copy of his father. When pushed, he pressed harder.

Knight smiled, tossing a piece of roasted yam into his mouth and chewing. "I've been good at breaking things lately. One more layer isn't going to make any difference."

"Okay, now." Emilia's voice rang out over what was beginning to sound a lot like a fight between Knight and everyone else at the table. "Change of subject. Are you guys going to do something interesting before Luna goes back to college?" She looked between me, Knight, and Vaughn.

I wanted to die right there and then. Emilia obviously hadn't paid attention to the general mood. Knight snorted out a laugh and shook his head. Frowning, I turned around to face him. I was reaching my tipping point, but I really, really, *really* didn't want to ruin it for everyone else.

He surprised me by looking directly at me for the first time in four days.

My eyes told him to shut up.

Honestly? My mouth almost did too.

"Oh, look. Luna's puppy eyes. My favorite guilt trip." He smirked, turning around and addressing the entire table. "To your question,

Aunt Emilia, I'm not sure if I'm going to do something nice before Luna's departure, but I sure as hell know Luna did something nice this past weekend. So nice, in fact, that her partner thanked her for the precious gift. She's always been charitable, this one."

I choked on my water, trying to cough out the liquid that slipped down the wrong pipe.

Now all the utensils at the table dropped in unison. Someone gasped. A chair scraped back, and I realized it was my father who'd stood up. Edie shot up right after him, clutching his shoulder in warning.

Baron Spencer leaned back in his seat at the head of the table. "*Boy.* Excuse yourself right now before your stupid jeans aren't the only thing that's distressed about you."

"Happily, Uncle *Vicious.*" Knight smiled, throwing his uncle's dodgy reputation back at him before standing up and strolling toward the stairs.

My father made a move to follow Knight at the same time Dean did, but my legs willed themselves to push me up and raise my open palm in warning. I needed to speak to him. *Alone.*

"I'm going to kill him," Dad hissed, his voice so full of power and disdain, I wondered what kind of man he'd been when he was Knight's age.

It hurt that I couldn't even look him in the eye when he said that because all I could think of was that he knew I'd had sex.

"Be my guest," I mouthed. "But first, let me deal with him."

I stalked up toward Knight, trying to digest what had happened at the table. He'd basically told our entire extended circle that I'd slept with someone. He'd ratted me out. I moved up the stairs and through the door of the media room, which he'd left open, knowing I was following him.

He laughed bitterly, walking over to the bar by the window and plucking a bottle of water from a mini-fridge. I caught him before he had the chance to unscrew the cap, spinning him in place by his shoulder so he faced me. I started signing to him with my hands, but he captured both my wrists, shocking me as he backed me against the wall until my spine hit it lightly, his eyes completely dead.

I was barely able to hold in my gasp. Knight had never touched me in a way that wasn't warm, fuzzy, and fully consensual. His smile told me he'd figured my mind couldn't wrap around this new way of touching and we were now playing by different rules. His eyes were as red as mine—he obviously hadn't gotten a lot of sleep either—but it was everything else about him I couldn't read. I realized it didn't matter if it was fair or not; Knight wasn't faking the pain. He was devastated, and I couldn't deny his feelings, no matter how hypocritical it was of him to act on them.

The heart doesn't ask for permission to feel things. It simply feels.

"Now, now, Moonshine. You're not like your little boyfriend, Josh Cooper. You have vocal cords, and if you're too pussy to use them, you obviously don't want to patch shit up badly enough."

Josh Cooper. He knew Josh's last name. How had he found out? It didn't matter. What mattered was that my hands were still clasped in his fists, and I was trying to wiggle them free, feeling my heart pounding so hard I thought it was going to escape my chest. He was taunting me. Challenging me. He never had before.

Tears made my eyes sting, but I didn't dare let them fall. I heard people arguing behind the closed doors of the room. Knight's fingers tightened around my flesh.

"Leave us the fuck alone," he yelled at the door, still staring at me.

I heard some more arguing, then Vaughn opened the door and peeked inside. He looked directly at me, with a nonchalance that implied he'd come to ask what would be our favorable dessert.

When he saw the scene playing before him, he grinned. "Finally, some tough love."

"Shut up," Knight snapped.

"Loon, they want to know you're okay," Vaughn said flatly.

I nodded. I didn't know why I nodded. I wasn't okay. Far from it. But I was going to see this thing through with Knight, no matter the outcome.

"Remember, Knight. She can talk. *Make* her."

Vaughn closed the door with a chuckle, and I looked back to Knight, hoping I didn't appear as frightened as I felt.

"He's right." Knight licked his lips, growling. "You can, and you will. If you want me in your life, that is."

I opened my mouth, but nothing came out. He smiled devilishly. I never knew he could be like this. So cold. So mean. Such a bully.

"Not up for it, Moonshine? Let's try another tactic. Was he good?" he sneered, his tone dark and low, his breath fanning my face gently. "Did you *come*?"

I was so blindly hurt by his behavior, I actually pretended to think about it. The answer, by the way, was no. It wasn't that Josh wasn't good or gentle—he was both those things. It just hurt too much. Physically. Mentally.

But watching Knight's face morph from cocky to unsure was worth it. For the first time since I'd known him, I took Knight's pain and drank from it like a well of strength.

He'd hurt me, so I hurt him back.

I felt the tears pushing their way down my cheeks but held my chin up, staring at him defiantly. He schooled his features, leaned toward me, and brushed his nose along my cheek.

"Did you think of me when he fucked you?" His lips curled into a smirk I could somehow feel deep in the pit of my stomach.

I shuddered, feeling my jaw clenching. My knee was close to his groin. I could kick him from this angle. I wanted to. His nose grazed my ear seductively, his tongue slipped out, the warm metal of his piercing flicking my earlobe.

"Tell me, did he fuck you hard or slow? Probably slow, huh? Josh Cooper seems like a nice chap. A good, solid…"

I went for it. I kneed his balls. Only I wasn't as fast as Knight, who was a spectacular athlete. He moved back just in time, grabbing the back of my knee, spinning me in place, and throwing me against the wall as he boxed me from behind.

Trapped. I was trapped. Between this giant guy's arms. A guy I no longer really knew or could even trust.

"It was a mistake!"

I slapped the wall I was pressed against, the words piercing my throat and burning it with their intensity and weight.

I swiveled around. He let me. His eyes widened for a moment. I'd given him what he wanted—my words. And now he didn't know what to do with them.

Frankly, neither did I.

Crap, I'd spoken aloud.

I'd spoken to Knight.

I'd said something.

Produced words from my mouth.

Jesus Christ. I'd done it. *I did it.*

And it hadn't been to tell him I loved him, that I wanted him, that I'd ached for him for years. We were fighting. Breaking. Putting an end to things that hadn't even begun.

I opened my mouth again, tracing the words, saying them quieter now.

"It. Was. A. Mistake. Not the part where I gave Josh a chance— but that I did it for the wrong reasons, while drinking."

I didn't mean to smile. The situation definitely didn't call for it. But I couldn't help myself. I'd tried to get to this breakthrough with dozens of therapists. And in true Luna Rexroth fashion, it had arrived at the worst possible time.

Knight took a step back, his face still grave but somehow entertained at the same time. He was a dash of the boy who'd give me the entire world thrown together with a giant, hard man who fought any positive feeling toward me.

"Were you conscious?" His voice was strained.

I didn't want to lie.

I nodded.

He pinched the bridge of his nose. "Then it really wasn't a mistake. Unless you slipped on his dick with your legs spread, I'm pretty sure it was intentional. There's a fucking limit to one's clumsiness. Even if that someone is *you*."

My smile collapsed; my eyebrows furrowed.

"Knight…" I said his name. Another different word. A word I'd practiced in secret for years.

He ran a hand through his hair, drawing a calming breath. The pain was smeared all over his face, like a sloppy painting. "Nah. It's cool. My fault. You need to be a special type of stupid to allow yourself to feel for your best friend what I felt for you."

Felt. Past tense.

But he'd felt something for me? I took a step toward him, cupping his cheeks, but he removed my hands from his face. My mouth quivered from the words it had produced earlier. Knight's eyes were shining—the first time I'd seen him anywhere close to tears.

"You're killing me, Luna Rexroth." He groaned, producing the sound I'd thought I'd pull out of him with a knee to the balls.

"I'm killing you, Knight? Have you ever stopped to wonder that maybe, just maybe, you killed me a long time ago?"

The words flooded from my mouth now. I felt alive. Raw. *Real.* I didn't even know I'd been feeling unreal up until now.

"Every day at school, your arm slung over a different girl's shoulders? Every time you smirked at your phone, texting someone else? Tenth grade, Jamie Percy yelled in the cafeteria that you took her virginity in the back of your car. Eleventh grade, your parents were called into school because there was a rumor going around that you'd initiated a threesome with two seniors. I died a thousand deaths before I inflicted the slightest of pain on your beautiful, tarnished heart."

Having a photographic memory sucked. I remembered every detail about our lives, and it poured out of my mouth without control. I couldn't stop myself now. Even if I wanted to. And I was beginning to want to. A lot.

"You slept with so many girls, Knight. Arabella. Shay. Belle. Dana. Fiona. Ren. Janet. Staci. Dozens of them. Or was it hundreds? Wait, there was also Hannah. Kristen. Sarah. Kayla—"

"Enough!" he roared.

Knight disappeared from my sight like a demon. I turned around to see him blazing toward the Xbox, tearing it from its hub and throwing it against the wall. I jumped back as he plucked the TV from the wall, smashing it against the couch before ripping the couch apart. He then turned around to me, stretching his arms wide, as if he were some sort of a game show host.

"Funny story time, Luna. You may want to sit down for this one. There were, as it happens, *no* other girls. None. I actually waited for you. I'm. A. Goddamn. Fucking. Virgin! Let that sink in for a second."

His voice boomed so loud, I was pretty sure everyone behind the door, and downstairs, heard too.

"Those stories you've heard? That was all they are. *Stories*. I saved myself for you like a goddamn Jonas brother. Forgive me for not wearing a purity ring and shitting all over my reputation just to appease your never-ending, silent demands that I need somehow, miraculously, to predict."

His fingers danced in the air, like my wants and needs were some kind of dark magic he wasn't capable of deciphering.

"The only reason I even associated myself with girls was so I wouldn't get shit from my friends and to take some of the pressure off of you—so you didn't think you were holding me back or something. Because, as a matter of fact, you were. I've been holding back for so long, you feel like a *chain*. A heavy, metal chain. I want to rip you apart, Luna Rexroth. I've been wanting to break away from you for a long fucking time, but you're stronger than me. Than this." He motioned between us, finally collapsing on the tattered couch, exhausted.

Speechless, a little hurt, and a lot proud, I felt my heart swelling in my chest to a point it took over my entire body.

It popped like a balloon the next minute when I realized his gesture was worthless now. He'd spoken about it in past tense. He'd *waited*. But no more. Now he wanted nothing to do with me. And why would he? I'd broken our silent pact. I was no longer a virgin.

"I appreciate that you saved yourself for me, but how was I supposed to know this? By the power of telepathy? The rumors were relentless, and you made out with Arabella in front of my face. Hell, you had Poppy's tongue shoved so far down your throat I was afraid she'd scoop out your tonsils in one picture. She posted it on Instagram. And what about all the girls I smelled on you when you came to sleep at my place? I had no reason to believe you were anything less than a walking, talking sexually transmitted disease."

"Arabella was a one-off. I was drunk and vindictive and frustrated. The scent of other girls? That was just me *hanging out* with them. Nothing more. You can ask Vaughn and Hunter. They'll vouch for me because they always laughed at me for it. Poppy…"

He stood up, taking a step toward me, bracketing my face with his big, warm palms. For some reason, I couldn't find the gesture reassuring. I was pretty sure he was going to crush me with his next words. He was going to show me exactly what happened when you made the legendary Knight Cole look like a fool or, worse, feel like one.

"Poppy and I did a charity thing for cystic fibrosis. For my mom. The parents at All Saints High were to donate a dollar for every Like she got on Instagram. We were chosen at random by the student body. I didn't even know her until two weeks ago, and I'm definitely, *definitely* not dating her."

I wanted to fall down to my knees and beg for his forgiveness, tell him Josh was great, but he wasn't him. That *he* was the one. That he'd brought his point home. And for the first time in seventeen years, I could tell him all those things. I could speak to Knight, even if to no one else. If I was being honest with myself, there was no one else I'd rather speak to than him. He was the center of my world.

"Do you love him?" Knight asked.

I shook my head. "No. I don't love Josh. He is sweet, but—"

"Save me the superlatives on Josh, Little Miss Clueless. Give me your phone." He reached his open palm to me.

"Why?" My voice was a little husky, a lot feminine.

I wondered what Knight thought about it. I looked down and saw the goose bumps on his arms when I talked, and it gave me a foolish hope that maybe things were still salvageable between us.

"I'm tired of feeling like the safe option you never want to take."

You were never the safe option. You are so risky, the idea of you makes my heart squeeze in my chest.

I started to give him my phone and stopped when I realized Josh must've answered the text message I'd sent him earlier, in the kitchen. And that Knight wasn't interested in my explanation at all, just in being proven right. The whole reason for this fight was because we weren't honest with each other, so him going through my phone would be more of the same bullshit. Him not trusting me. *No thank you.*

Knight's face morphed into the sad triumph of a man who'd predicted the apocalypse and now watched the fire of the sun blazing through forests and oceans and cities.

"No." My voice was barely a breath. "I'm so sorry, Knight. You either hear me out or you walk away empty-handed."

His lips curled with content disgust, something I never thought possible. "The first words she ever speaks to me in her life, and she decides to break my heart with them. For the longest time, I wished I could unthink you. Unlove you. Unbreathe you. I think I finally can."

He reached toward me, pressing his lips against my forehead. He didn't seem mad anymore, and that scared me. When he was breaking things around the room, at least I knew he was coping. Hurting. Working through whatever it was we were up against.

Now, with a clarity so piercing it burned my skin like a fresh cut, I realized the gravity of what had happened in the last few months. I'd lost my best friend and gained something worse than an enemy—an indifferent acquaintance.

We stared at each other with eyes full of tears. Only he was smiling, and I felt on the verge of dying.

"Please," I whispered. "Please, Knight."

"You have a beautiful voice." His hand slipped from my cheek to graze my jawline. He slanted my chin up so I could see the full tilt of his smile.

"*Please*," I repeated, begging. More wasted words. They felt like diamonds scattered on the floor after a burglary. With no one to claim them.

He pressed his lips to my hair. "Remember when I told you I always get even?"

I blinked. When had he said that? The tree house. *Yes.*

I nodded, defeated.

"Well, Moonshine, it's payback time."

CHAPTER SIX
LUNA

"Hurry up, we're going to be late!" April tugged at the sleeve of my peacoat as she pulled me out the door—just as I hung up on Knight's voicemail without leaving a message.

We were running through the crowded hallway, shouldering past students on our way to a Drum Kithead show.

Normally, I didn't do partying of any kind, but what were the odds of this band showing up at this shitty North Carolinian college again? Plus, it had been a miserable three weeks since I'd gotten back to Boon, and I'd spent the vast majority of them either texting, calling, or writing to Knight. Why I bothered was beyond me. He never answered, even the phone calls, passing on the chance to hear my voice.

Why had I been able to speak to Knight? I asked myself that question over and over again, and I always came to the same conclusion: it had felt like survival. A plea to my lifeline. And still, he'd walked away, just like Val. I was dying to reconnect with Knight… and also dying to know if I'd actually be able to speak to him again. Had it been a fluke?

Not talking felt like living inside a snow globe, with a thick layer of protection against the world. I knew I could, but at this point, it felt almost redundant to do so. No one expected me to talk. In a way, every day I didn't utter a word felt like an accomplishment. A competition between me and myself.

But with Knight, I broke all the rules. I wanted his attention, his forgiveness, his everything.

After the train wreck that was Thanksgiving dinner, Edie had pulled me outside when we got back home and offered me a glass of wine. I'd declined.

"Can I give you my two cents?" she'd asked.

I'd nodded. It wasn't like I'd had much choice, and besides, anything beat going into the house and facing my father's expression, probably a mixture of confusion and horror at the fact I had slept with some guy he didn't even know.

"The thing is…" Edie had taken a sip of her red wine, sprawling in her quilted hammock, stargazing. "You and Knight have known each other from the day you were born. You don't know anything else. You have no idea where the love starts or the familiarity begins. The lines have blurred so badly, you're both acting up and defying each other. Maybe it's best that you let it go, enjoy college, and revisit this thing with Knight on summer vacation. You have the right to be happy, Luna. And I've a feeling Knight is making you really unhappy right now."

"That's not true." I'd jumped to his defense in sign language. "Knight makes me very happy."

She'd slipped her tan leg past the hammock, her toes digging into the grass to stop its movement, then sat up and stared directly at me.

"I heard you talk to him. Out loud."

My eyes had widened.

She'd shaken her head. "Don't worry. No one else did. We gave you your privacy. Point is, you didn't sound happy. You sounded… hurt. That's not how I wanted to hear you when you finally spoke to someone who wasn't me."

But almost a month later, even though I knew Edie was right, I still couldn't shake off the need to stay in touch with Knight. I checked all of his friends' Instagram and Twitter accounts. Every day.

Even now, as we slipped into Josh's roommate Ryan's car, I knew I'd rather stay in my dorm, staring at the phone and waiting for Knight to get back to me, even though I had no evidence to support that he might.

I slid into Ryan's back seat before noticing that April had taken the passenger seat. When I swiveled my head, I realized why. Josh sat next to me in the back. He smiled, signing, "April called shotgun when she talked to Ryan on the phone."

The past three weeks had been what my childhood friend Daria would call *awkward central*. I'd taken a step back from Josh, telling him I still had feelings for Knight and couldn't be with anyone else. Meanwhile, April and Ryan had grown closer. Their blooming romance kind of forced Josh and me to hang out, even if we needed space from each other. But I couldn't fault my roommate for wanting to spend time with her new boyfriend.

April and Ryan shared a noisy kiss in the front.

Josh rolled his eyes and smiled. "How have you been?"

That was the worst part—seeing how kind and beautiful he was as a person, even when I'd brought my walls back up, even when I made him feel like a mistake.

"Fine." I used that damn word. "You?"

"Yeah. Good."

Thankfully, the ride was short.

When we arrived, it was the kind of gig where everybody was crammed like sardines into a darkened space no bigger than my parents' living room, the scent of warm beer and sweat wafting through the dense, smoky air—the kind of place even Vaughn and Knight couldn't usually drag me to. But after my disastrous Thanksgiving, I'd found that maybe Knight wasn't the only one with a shiny, red self-destruction button. I wanted to forget too. I wanted to drown in alcohol and sweaty bodies and loud noises no less than he did.

More than anything, I refused to stop. I was making huge progress—Malory said so herself. For the first time in months, I didn't dread the idea of her sending my parents updates about me, and I wanted to continue building friendships and getting out of my comfort zone.

There was a mosh pit and good vibes and—I had to agree with April—a really hot lead singer to drool over. I danced with Josh and lost myself in the music. By the second hour of bobbing my head and buying all of us rounds of drinks with my fake ID, I wondered if the recipe for giving up Knight was simply drowning in distractions.

I didn't have to wonder long. As soon as I felt my phone buzzing in my back pocket, I pulled it out and frowned. Knight's name flashed over a picture of him lifting up his shirt and winking at the camera, exposing his glorious six-pack.

He was calling me back.

Finally. After dozens of unanswered calls.

Expecting my words.

In front of my friends, who'd faint if they heard me speak.

Answering him would be dangerous, but I couldn't help myself, knowing he might change his mind if I waited to call him back. I excused myself and ran out into the alleyway sandwiched between the club and a coffee shop. I hit answer and jammed a finger into my ear so I could hear him better.

At first, I just listened to his soft breaths, feeling shudders of both pleasure and pain coursing through my body. His sheer existence excited me. Vaughn was wrong. Moving away from Knight didn't solve the problem. It amplified it.

"Hey," his gruff baritone said finally.

"Hi," I whispered, too afraid to be heard by anyone else. I hadn't spoken a word to anyone who wasn't him yet, but for some reason, when he was around I *needed* to speak—to claim his attention somehow. I still couldn't understand why I was able to speak to him, especially now. I was putting my new, meaningful friendships at risk for someone who'd made it clear he wanted to get even with me. Who sought revenge. Who craved my pain.

"How have you been?" I asked at the same time he said, "You need to stop calling me, Luna."

There was a beat of silence in which I digested what he'd said. He wasn't mean or menacing this time. There was no edge to his voice.

"What?" I gasped.

"I'm trying really hard not to hurt you, but I'm struggling. You need to take a step back before I do something I'll regret," he explained.

"Who said I can leave you alone?" I asked breathlessly, not really deciphering my own words. "You think I haven't tried?"

"Try harder, Luna. I know you can, because for about eight years, you *did*. Three unreciprocated kisses. You sleeping with someone else. You did a pretty darn good job, so just keep doing it, okay?"

I remembered what he'd said about my presence feeling like a metal chain. A heavy burden he wanted to shake off. Guess it had always been easy for me to choose Knight because I didn't have any options. Because Knight always chose *me*. But his choice came with a bigger sacrifice. He was the one getting me out of trouble, shooing off the bullies, making sure I had someone to sit with at recess. He was the one who constantly gave up the opportunity to actually date the hottest girls.

"Moonshine." He pushed through the fog in my head, pulling me back to reality. "Give it a rest. You're poking the bear."

"You didn't even say anything about my talking." I sulked, feeling the anger clogging my throat. I didn't know why it was so important to address it right this second. I could hear the smile in his voice.

"I always knew you'd talk, and not just to me. To everyone. I watched you crawl out of your shell, and it was slow, but by fucking God, it was beautiful. Have you spoken to anyone else?"

He sounded warm, conversational now—the Knight I was used to, who looked at me with admiration and delight.

I thought about my answer before giving it to him this time. "I'm working on it. It's strange to be without the gang, but I think I like it. I think I like being on my own. What about you? How's school? Football?"

This was what we'd come to. Two strangers making small talk.

I wanted to cry, and I had to bite my trembling lower lip to stop it from happening.

"We're winning, which is good. School is fine. Mom is…"

"What?" I panicked. "How is Rosie doing?"

"Fine." He amended his initial, worried tone. Still, that annoying word. "She's getting more intensive treatment, but she's doing well."

"Send her my love."

"Always."

Are you dating someone?

Who is she?

Is she pretty?

My thought process scared me. I'd never cared much for boys. Only that wasn't true. It just happened that the only boy I cared about was finally taking a step back, and now I knew how much he'd meant to me.

"Luna! Where the hell have you been? Josh is panicking that he lost you because he was the last person to see you." I heard April's drunken laugh just then and turned around, my mouth falling open.

I was caught red-handed, with my phone pressed against my ear. As soon as April saw it, she stumbled back.

"Whoa." She hiccupped, bracing herself against the redbrick wall.

I heard a dark chuckle coming from the other end of the line. "Have a good night, Moonshine." Knight's voice turned metallic before the line went dead.

Crap. Now Knight knew I was spending time with Josh, and he'd probably draw his own *wrong* conclusions. But he'd explicitly asked me not to contact him anymore, so I couldn't even explain myself. Not without ignoring the only thing he'd ever asked of me.

I stuffed my hands into my back pockets, smiling awkwardly as April paced toward me, her expression hooded. Now I had an entire new set of worries to obsess over. Had she heard me speaking? That could ruin everything.

"Naughty Knight?" She tapped her lips.

I nodded. She rolled her eyes as she approached me, looping her arm over my shoulders and walking me to the door. I let out a relived sigh. She hadn't heard.

"Why is the asshole calling you? Can't he take a goddamn hint? Jesus. What a douche canoe."

Of course, I did not correct her assumption because explaining to her how I was a selective mute would require me to also tell her what had happened. Tell her about Val. And that wasn't a story I was keen on telling. We went back into the club, and as soon as April spotted Ryan and Josh, she shoved me into the latter's arms, jumping on Ryan and wrapping her arms around his neck as she awarded him with a wet kiss. I fell into Josh's hands. As always, he caught me.

In the car, Josh glanced at me. His eyes told me April had given him the rundown. I liked April, but I hated the way she butted into my business.

"I know you said Knight is the one, and I respect that," he signed. "But would you ever give me a chance to try to be that other one? The second big love? The one you end up marrying? Because I'd like to apply."

I wondered how much of it was him wanting me and how much of it was him finally finding someone like him. The same age. Who liked the same bands and studied at the same school. Of the same heritage—more or less—who spoke sign language.

We had everything going for us, other than one thing: our hearts.

I squeezed his hand, biting my lip in answer.

He knew.

———

Three nights after the phone call with Knight, I was lying in bed, doing my usual Instagram routine to look for pictures of him. There were none. Maybe he didn't go to parties anymore? The prospect made me physically sick. For all my jealousy, I wanted him to have fun. I wanted him to be happy and meet girls and get over me. Because even if I didn't get over him, I desperately cared for his well-being.

When I came up empty-handed, I decided to look at Poppy's profile. I didn't expect to see much. I wanted to count the Likes on that kissing picture and cheer up when I thought about the amount of money they had collected for Rosie's cystic fibrosis foundation.

Poppy had posted four new pictures since the one that broke my heart. Three of them accordion related and of no importance to me. It was the last image that gave me pause. I clicked on it. She'd tagged a restaurant in La Jolla. It was of a giant milkshake with chocolate-covered pretzels, an entire donut, an enlarged Tim Tam to use as a straw, and three different ice cream scoops mounted on the glass. Next to the milkshake, was something that made my heart beat faster. Car keys.

Aston Martin car keys.

A distinctive Aston Martin car key, with a keychain that said *My Favorite People Call Me Daddy*, something Knight had found in Dean's drawer and thought it'd be funny to use.

Had Knight taken Poppy on a date? It was easier to tell myself they were hanging out with more people, but why wouldn't he go out with her? He'd said to leave him alone. That he wanted some space. This was perfect. *She* was perfect.

I knew it would drive me mad to think about it, so I chose not to. I threw off my covers and padded to my desk. Not, God forbid, to my typewriter, which was still untouched, but to my MacBook. Briefly, I wondered if something, or someone, would ever give me the courage to pick up a pen and write. I did write essays and short stories for school, but I never wrote anything I didn't absolutely need to.

I opened my search bar and Googled the one name that always sucked me into a black hole and made me forget. The perfect diversion from Knight.

Valenciana Vasquez.

I hit enter, sat back, watched the results roll in neatly, and started to dig.

CHAPTER SEVEN
KNIGHT

Footsteps thudded in the hall, and I stretched in the large bed, nudging the woman sleeping on my chest to wake up.

"Your husband's back. Pretty sure he won't be so happy to see a stud like me in his bed."

Mom looked up, blinking the sleep from her eyes. She swatted my chest, then coughed. "Hide. I wouldn't mess with him."

"I wouldn't mess with *me*."

I flexed my biceps behind her, and her coughs became loud barks that made me want to kill someone. Dad threw the door open, already untying his tie. He reached the bed, planted a kiss on Mom's nose, and flicked the back of my head.

"You're too old to cuddle with your mama."

"Don't say that!" Rosie shrieked.

"Seems like she's not really in agreement with you." I yawned.

Dad went into the bathroom and closed the door behind him. I squeezed Mom into my chest and kissed the crown of her head.

"He's probably crying while listening to Halsey on repeat like a little bitch." I yawned again.

"Language, boy."

"C'mon, we're not one of those fake families."

"What kind of family are we?" she asked.

"A real, kick-ass one."

Mom laughed so hard, I thought she was going to puke out a lung. When the laughter died and she looked up at me, she had that let's-get-real expression I perpetually hated.

"Have you spoken to Luna lately?"

"I have."

And had I fucking ever. She actually *spoke*. Which I didn't share with anyone, naturally. It was bad enough I'd ratted her out for sleeping with FUCKING JOSH (forever in capital letters, thank you very much) in front of everyone at a family dinner. There was no need to completely shit all over her trust.

Trent Rexroth had spent the day after Thanksgiving running after me across a park with that baseball bat. I had better stamina, but I'd let him catch me when I got to our deserted tree house, because let's admit it, I deserved a good beating.

When he'd finally pushed me against the old trunk, he just gave me a scary-ass look and promised, "If you disrespect my daughter again, in public or in private, I will spear your fucking head to my fence and feed the rest of you to the coyotes."

Plus, I kind of liked that Luna and I had our own secret, even though I was working through purging her out of my system. I'd lied. I didn't want to get even. I didn't want to hurt her. But I was done letting her hurt me, and that was something.

"And…?" Mom wiggled her eyebrows.

She was #*TeamLunight*. She'd even made herself a shirt with the hashtag for Christmas four years ago, when the concept had seemed real. My parents had loved each other in secret for over a decade. They still believed in star-crossed lovers and fairy tales coming true. Only they'd had a real obstacle stopping them from being together. And that obstacle wasn't some random dude's dick.

"She and Josh seem to be very happy from what I could tell."

Her face fell.

"Hey." I nudged her. "It's not like I give a crap."

"Of course you don't." She arched an eyebrow skeptically.

"Girls are lizards. They don't have souls."

"This is slander. Who says lizards don't have souls?" She pretended to gasp. "And how do you mean?"

"Cold blood. That's why you always shower with extra-hot water. Fact. Look it up on the internet." I pinched her nose just as Dad came out of the bathroom, freshly showered, wearing jeans and a Polo shirt.

"You're still here," he said, glancing at the door. "Can I bribe you with something to get some downtime with my wife? Another car? A nice vacation? Perhaps a kick in the butt?"

"Oh, you." Mom opened her arms.

Dad skulked into her embrace. A moth to a flame. Two unique pieces of an elaborate puzzle. The Coles were professional huggers. I swear Ma had a PhD in that shit.

"Lev! Levy boy," Dad roared. "Come here right now. Family cuddle."

"Can't," Lev barked from his room.

Dad rolled his eyes and grabbed his phone, turning off Lev's cell through an app.

"Hey!" Lev shouted. "I was talking to Bailey."

"Shocker," Dad and I drawled in unison.

Mom burst out laughing again. "I want every Cole man in this bed right now!" She patted the mattress.

Lev came running down the hallway, cannonballing onto the giant bed. We were all in now, laughing and talking. Mom ordered pizza, and we played twenty questions, with the loser having to get the pizza from the front door.

I didn't think about Luna. Or FUCKING JOSH. Or that first second every morning when I woke up and wanted to throw up because Luna had taken a dump all over what we'd had.

This was good.

This was for the best.

All I needed was my family—not another deserter who'd give me up.

———

After another grueling morning workout, I chugged down an entire bottle of BCAA water and slam-dunked it into the trash can on the way to my locker.

"Coming through. Beep, beep. Make way for the royal QB1, his highness Knight Cole."

The rest of my team pushed people down the hallway, half-joking but half dead-ass serious.

Some freshman turd mouthed something about my saliva and rummaged in the trash to retrieve my empty bottle. I couldn't give two fucks if he tried to replicate my DNA and make a ninja turtle out of it. It was becoming harder and harder to care about stupid things when your mother was one day closer to dying.

The football team dispersed, each player to his own locker. I reached mine, glancing over my shoulder. After making sure the coast was clear, I produced the letter I'd received this summer and opened it. It was wrinkled from being read five thousand times, but I read it again. It wasn't the first letter I'd received about this shitty matter, but it was the one I loved being tortured with the most because it offered action.

Meet me.

I dare you.

I didn't know why, but I especially liked reading it on days Mom felt like crap, one of which happened to be today.

Of course, drinking a bottle of whiskey before practice had helped too.

"Dafuq am I going to do with you?" I muttered at the letter, scanning the scandalous words. I shoved it back inside my locker, buried it in textbooks.

Slamming my locker, I saw Poppy's face. She stood right behind the door. Her sister, Lenny, was next to her.

"Hullo," she said in her Mary Poppins accent.

"Yo." I balanced my books under my armpit, ready to start for the lab.

There weren't many things I hated more than chemistry, but

seeing Vaughn's smug face across the hall morphing into something that strangely resembled intrigue was one of them. He slammed his locker and came to stand next to us.

What does the fucker want now?

Vaughn being Vaughn, he just stood there for the first few seconds, like a fucking creeper, staring at the three of us. No hi. No good morning. Nothing. Asshole had the social skills of a Post-it Note. It went to show that high school students were a special breed of idiots because dude was actually popular.

"Hey, Vaughn." Poppy smiled at him, mock-punching his arm.

Her sister rolled her eyes at the gesture. They were polar opposites, Poppy and Lenny. Poppy was more like a toned-down version of my friend Daria. She liked pretty dresses and putting highlights in her hair and knew how to distinguish one Kardashian from the others. Lenora was a different breed of chick entirely. Her wardrobe consisted of black shit only. She wore a lot of eyeliner and had a septum piercing. If you'd told me she'd lost her virginity in a satanic ritual on someone's grave, I wouldn't have bet against it. Seemed legit. What worked for Lenny was the fact that she was small and pretty, so she looked cute more than scary—like something Tim Burton would keep as a pet.

Lenny stared at my locker over my shoulder, not acknowledging my best friend.

"So, wasn't that milkshake fab? Thanks for taking us to La Jolla. We've never been before," Poppy chirped.

"It's La Jolla, not outer space. Proportions, Violet," Vaughn deadpanned.

"It's Poppy."

"Same shit."

"Not really. You could make an effort and remember," Poppy cried.

I saw her point, but trying to reason with Vaughn by being butthurt was like trying to worm your way into a serial killer's good graces by running naked in an empty field after handing him a machete.

"You're right." Vaughn yawned. "I'll remember next time."

"You will?"

"Yeah. Heroin is made out of poppies. Coincidently, you bore me to death."

Don't laugh, asshole. Don't you fucking dare.

"Someone's touchy. Is it shark week, Spencer?" Lenny asked Vaughn conversationally, examining her chipped, black-painted nails.

"Burn," I coughed into my fist, laughing.

"Nope, but if it's blood you're after, I'm your guy." Vaughn still didn't look at Lenny.

Lenny didn't look at him either. Was I witnessing a mating dance between two assholes?

Dear God,

If you are up there—which I'm not betting on, because why would you take my mom if you are?—please don't let these two reproduce.

The planet doesn't need a third world war.

Yours,

KJC

"Are you threatening me?" Lenora seemed about as outraged as a used napkin.

"Do you hear something, Knight?" Vaughn turned to me, frowning. "I hear buzzing. Like a fly or a cockroach."

"A cockroach doesn't buzz," Lenny noted. "Learn your insects, Spencer. You're about sixteen years behind on your material. Go on, Poppy. Get it over with so I can go back to my blissful existence sans this wanker."

I pieced together the picture, looking between them.

Vaughn was obsessed with all things British. *Spaced*, *Never Mind the Buzzcocks*, and *The Mighty Boosh*. He listened solely to British music: the Smiths, Kinky Machine, the Stone Roses. Sure, his heritage was English, but Vaughn cared about his heritage like I cared about the welfare of the Hawaiian blobfish. Plus, Lenny had an Instagram. It could have been her account he'd been checking that time. She was a prodigy artist, specializing in insane shit. And he was…well, an insane shit*head*. Oh, and an artist too.

Lenora was most famous in the hallways of All Saints High for getting on top of Christ the Redeemer to take a picture of the Rio view. Apparently, she'd also taken a thirty-year-old Brazilian model as a lover during her vacation this summer.

Vaughn and Lenora were a match made in hell, but they made sense.

"Just bloody do it." Lenny poked Poppy's ribs.

"Are you playing this Friday?" Poppy twiddled her thumbs, not even looking at me.

"Oh Christ." Lenny sighed, flinging her backpack on one of her shoulders and pinning me with a look.

"She wants to go out with you. *Alone*. On a real date. With flowers and a Kate Hudson film and possibly some heavy petting. Are you in or are you out?"

Good luck to Vaughn, because if there was one person to eat him alive, that would be this little ballbuster.

Last time Poppy asked me out, I'd dragged Hunter along, so she got the hint and brought Lenny too. Lenny had nearly stabbed Hunter with a fork, and then Vaughn had given me the stink eye when he heard about the outing. He'd asked why I hadn't asked him.

"When was the last time you went on a date?" I'd stared at him like he'd grown two spare heads and a pair of wings.

"Never."

"That's why."

"I'd do it for you," he'd deadpanned.

I'd called him on his bullshit then. Now I understood his sudden charitable offer.

"Yes," Vaughn answered for me. "He'll take her on a date. Now, can you remove yourself from our vicinity? I'm trying to eat here."

He produced a seven-year-old granola bar from his pocket, which I knew he had absolutely no intention of eating. Vaughn didn't eat. Publicly, I mean.

"Gladly," Lenora said.

"Do you do anything gladly? You look like the miserable spawn of Marilyn Manson and a blowup doll."

"Do you think blowup dolls can be impregnated, Vaughn? Shall I give you the talk about the birds and the bees?" Lenny squinted before her phone chimed. She laughed. She actually *laughed* as she shook her head. "Au revoir. And before you wonder, Vaughn—it doesn't mean a fancy pastry."

"My mom is French!" he yelled, finally snapping out of his usual ice-cold manner.

And just like that, Lenora and Vaughn disappeared in opposite directions, leaving me alone with Poppy.

"I do." I smiled.

Her eyelashes fluttered. "A bit early for that, but what the hell, if the ring is nice, I'm game."

I let out a laugh.

I'd cut off my balls and feed them to Luna's seahorses before I marry into your sister's family, dude.

"I do have a game on Friday," I clarified. "The championship game, actually. But we can hang out after. Just the two of us." I gave her a slow once-over, going for the kill with an I'll-chew-your-panties-off smirk. "Especially if heavy petting is involved."

"No promises."

"Well, prepare to watch a shitty cop movie, then."

She giggled. Her throat bobbed, and all I could think was *it's just a throat.* I didn't want to kiss it. I didn't want to trace it with my fingers. To strangle it. To cover every inch of it with my tongue and lips and teeth, like I'd imagined whenever I'd looked at Luna.

I reopened my locker and stared at the letter again, this time stuffing it into the back of my jeans. I needed something to hold on to.

A fresh hell to raise.

You want to be humored, Dixie? Joke's on fucking you.

CHAPTER EIGHT
LUNA

Winter break came blazing through my life, tearing hopes and plans in its wake.

Going back home felt like facing death row, with Knight representing a class of skilled snipers, all of them aiming their rifles at me.

I wanted to stay at Boon. I even went as far as considering going home with April, to Montana. Her offer seemed genuine, and she was trying to work out a scenario where Ryan, Josh, she, and I were going to hang out there before flying back to Boon. Alas, I didn't want to cower, and I didn't want to prevent myself from hanging out with Edie, Dad, Racer, and Theo just because of Knight.

Besides, home was so much more than just Knight. Edie had said Rosie wasn't doing well, and I wanted to check on her.

Racer had a toothless smile now. I needed to take pictures.

Daria was getting married. I wanted to be there for her.

I even missed Vaughn and his dark, angsty moods.

So I went.

Dad picked me up from the airport and carried my suitcase to Edie's Porsche. He asked about Josh, and even though I wanted to die from the prospect of telling him the truth, I couldn't lie either.

"We're just friends, Dad." I buckled my seat belt.

"Whatever you are, I support you, kiddo." There was a beat of silence after that. "I kicked Cole's ass."

My eyebrows shot to my forehead.

He shrugged. "More or less. He feels awful about it, if it makes any difference at all."

I looked out the window, watching San Diego zipping by on our way to Todos Santos. I hadn't spoken to Knight in weeks, but I knew our paths were bound to cross now that I was next door again.

Dad shifted in his seat, scratching at his stubble. "There's a pre-Christmas party at the Coles' tomorrow."

"I'll be there," I signed. I schooled my features, staring straight ahead. Every fiber in my body didn't want to go, but I'd be damned if I would disrupt everyone's lives just because of a heartbreak I'd seen coming years ago. If I didn't go, Edie and Theo wouldn't go either. Dad would have to save face and show up. He'd take Racer, who'd ask about Edie and me the entire evening.

"You don't have to." Dad frowned. His fingers drummed on the steering wheel. I knew he was uncomfortable.

"I'm more than happy to."

"Does that mean you and Knight talked it out?"

I'd done quite a bit of talking with Knight, actually. I felt guilty even thinking that. I'd given Knight something my father had begged me for, for years. My spoken words. Not that selective muteness was a choice. I'd tried speaking aloud to Dad plenty. It sucked that I couldn't give him the thing he wanted most.

"We're fine."

At least I hoped we were. I was counting on having no more embarrassing secrets Knight could reveal at the party, so really, how disastrous could it be?

I was a ball of nerves that whole first day back home, a knot of puke making it hard for me to breathe, smile, or shove food down my throat. I tried to write, but nothing came out. Tossing the MacBook to the wall in a fit, I grabbed my bike and decided to ride in the woods, where I knew I'd never bump into Knight. But I was too distracted and ended up falling flat on my butt twice. I couldn't remember the last time I'd fallen off my bike.

Actually, I could. The day Knight had saved me.

The world kept on moving, and I wasn't even trying to play catch-up with it. Edie and Racer made cookies and put on Christmas movies while I secretly Googled Val's name. One time, Dad caught me and asked what was going on.

"You look upset," he said.

I shook my head at that.

"What are you doing?" he persisted.

I shook my head harder, thinking, *Ruining my life*. That seems to be the theme lately.

Then the next day rolled around, and I realized I had to face Knight. I didn't want to go to the party. The only thing that made me drag myself out the door—every step feeling like I had a three-ton sandbag on my back—was that I knew he'd expect me to bail. He wanted confirmation of the fact that I was sad and lonely and in need of him.

Surprise, jerk.

Whether it was true or not, he was about to be served a big piece of humble pie. Hopefully he was hungry.

I showed up at the Coles' in my usual attire of boyfriend jeans, Vans, and a cropped yellow sleeveless shirt, ignoring the herd of women in gowns and men in double-breasted suits sipping expensive champagne. The party was in the backyard, which was as big as a wedding venue. Everything was red, green, or white, including the waiters' uniforms. They moved around, offering silver trays full of delicious finger foods and sparkling, golden liquid. I consciously worked on not scanning the place for Knight, and when Edie, Theo, and Racer disappeared into the kitchen to help Rosie and her staff, I found myself leaning against a round table next to Daria and Penn, just like at Thanksgiving.

Daria took a sip of her champagne and glanced around at the crowd, looking stunning in a red velvet dress.

"Vaughn is wearing a suit," she observed, and I nearly choked on my glass of water.

I followed her gaze. Sure enough, he was. He looked quite dashing too, with his black hair slicked back and his permanent frown smoothed into a blank expression. Vaughn always looked rich, even in tattered clothes. But now? Now he looked not only formidable, but…delicious. Daria turned to me, pressing the cold champagne to her cheek. Southern California was notorious for not getting the memo about it being Christmastime, and this year wasn't any different. The air was hot, dense with temperature and hormones.

"Who's the girl?" Daria pouted. "There must be one if he's making an effort."

"No idea," I signed.

"Of course you do. You're one of his best friends."

"Try Knight."

I hated that my mind went automatically to him.

Daria snorted out a laugh. "I would, but he's busy getting lucky by the pool. Which is, like, totes odd. I always thought you guys were going to end up together. Honestly, I'm glad you have a boyfriend at Boon. Knight is such a man whore. He'd be a terrible boyfriend to leave on the other side of the country."

He's a virgin, you fool! I wanted to scream. At myself, not at Daria.

Then I remembered that's what got me into this mess in the first place. The entire world and its sister thought Knight was dipping his sausage into every sauce on the counter.

How could I have known he'd been waiting for me?

Still, her words sank into me like deadly claws. My eyes darted to the pool, frantically looking for my best friend. I found him standing by the edge, clad in an eccentric navy-blue suit, a vest, and a pocket square in maroon red. His hair was tugged in every direction under the sun, and he looked outrageously sexy, talking to Poppy Astalis with his hand on the small of her back.

Poppy Astalis in the flesh, wearing an A-line, navy-blue dress and a maroon cardigan. They'd coordinated, I realized, and that made me want to throw up. My stomach churned, dipped, and shot an arrow of nausea to my throat. It didn't matter that Lenny, her sister, was standing right next to them, yawning provocatively in a simple black dress. Or that Hunter Fitzpatrick was standing next to Lenny, trying to strike up a conversation, his confident smirk collapsing with each passing second it became apparent she wasn't going to give him the time of day.

It was still obvious Knight and Poppy were together.

"I'm going to ask," Daria announced.

"Skull Eyes," Penn warned, his fingers curling around her elbow.

He'd nicknamed her Skull Eyes for reasons none of us could fathom. It was their secret, I supposed, and I loved that they had that—something that belonged just to them.

"What? I'm out of the loop. There's always drama in Todos Santos. I want to know. I *deserve* to know. It's my home field. Are you coming, Luna?"

I shook my head, but Daria being Daria, my consent was low on her care list. She grabbed me by the hand and dragged me through the Coles' garden, talking my ear off about honeymoon destinations.

She stopped abruptly, frowning. "Oh, one more thing. What'd you do to him?"

My eyes widened in question.

She rolled her eyes. "Don't play coy. He's obviously playing a game. What happened between you guys?"

I shook my head, shocked.

"Whatever. Don't say; that's fine. But don't you dare show Knight that you care about this bitch. That's exactly what he wants—a reaction out of you."

Was this him getting even? Did he still want to hurt me? I liked it better back when Knight would have chopped his own leg off before inflicting pain on me. I swallowed, willing her comment to roll off my back. By the time we got to them, a mist of cold sweat decorated my forehead.

"Howdy, guys. We've arrived. Hence, the party can start." Daria flipped her blond mane, smiling big at Knight and Poppy, waiting for introductions. Instead of meeting his gaze, I directed a salute to Poppy and Lenny, smiling. They were safer to look at. Knight made the introductions, and maybe he looked at me, but I was too proud to glance and check.

Hunter squeezed my shoulder and whistled low. "I have to say—every girl at this party is wearing a gown more expensive than the other, but you, Rexroth, look like an enchanting Lolita, even in your pajamas."

I wasn't wearing pajamas, but I wasn't going to correct him either. It wasn't worth taking my phone out and typing a comeback. I flipped him the finger instead.

"It's not pajamas, you wasted pile of scum. Don't you dare patronize her," Knight hissed through gritted teeth, heat radiating from his body.

Hunter's confidence melted. Daria's playful grin widened as Hunter threw Knight a dispassionate grin.

"Down, boy. You'll pop an artery and ruin your precious Burberry suit."

"I think my knuckles are the ones going to get messed up, and they've seen worse than your ugly face."

"Righto, time to calm down. Hunter was just taking the piss." Poppy rubbed Knight's back, slipping under his arm into an embrace.

Daria stared at them like they were a game she was still figuring out the rules to. Her smile screamed trouble.

"So, Poppy," Daria purred.

"Hmm?" Poppy batted her lashes.

They were two alpha females sharpening their claws in front of a thirsty audience. Poppy's message was clear: she was not intimidated. Daria's intentions were showcased perfectly too: she didn't like the British invasion.

"Knight here is like my baby brother, but he doesn't tell me anything. Are you guys an item?"

Poppy giggled in a way that made her so much less lovable to me than I'd remembered. My stomach clenched. Whatever Daria was getting at, I knew she was team Luna. I just wished she wouldn't probe. The sheer horror of being here next to them filled my annual quota for angst, and I didn't care for a second serving.

"I reckon we are." Poppy looked up to Knight, touching her unblemished cheek. "Are we not, darling?"

I looked away just as Vaughn appeared, saving—or ruining—the day. It really depended how you looked at it. I focused on breathing through my nose and staring at the back of a server's head. Vaughn gave me a peck on the cheek, throwing me off balance. He was not one for affection.

"Look what the pussy dragged in." Daria bowed down, tugging at the hem of her gown theatrically. "Question is: Which pussy was it that made you wear something you didn't steal from Salvation Army? Care to shed some light on the matter?"

"Daria, I see you are still putting that sharp mind of yours to good use," Vaughn drawled sarcastically. "If you must know, I lost a bet to my father."

"BS. You never lose, Vaughn." Daria knocked back her drink.

"I did this week," he clipped unflappably.

"Bummer. Thought you were finally trying to impress a girl."

"Girls are in the business of impressing me, not vice versa."

"Can't argue with that." She slammed her empty champagne glass on a tray, snatching a fresh one from a passing waiter.

Lenora made a show of gagging. Vaughn, who caught the gesture like an eagle waiting for its prey to show a sign of life, went for the kill.

"I see the mediocre artist does not approve. How is your dead kingdom doing, Miss Astalis?"

"Splendid. Watching your empire sinking slowly and having a jolly good time, Mr. Will-Never-Be-As-Good-As-His-Mummy."

"Jeez, your nerd-talk game is hot." Daria pretended to fan herself. "So, are you kids bumping uglies?" She pointed between Lenny and Hunter, obviously adding fuel to the fire.

"It's a work in progress," Knight said, slinging an arm over each of their shoulders and looking between them. I stole a glance at him, and our eyes met, then darted in opposite directions. Bile bubbled in my throat.

"I have a boyfriend," Lenny whispered hotly, her cheeks pinking.

"No one's buying that, Lenora. You need to be at least semi-tolerable for that to happen."

Vaughn was obviously turning on his charm this evening.

"We're going on a double date next week," Knight announced, and I couldn't help myself.

I let out a bitter chuckle. So he and Poppy were officially dating. Good for them.

"You seem hell-bent on making that happen." Daria eyed Knight curiously. "I wonder why."

"Just playing matchmaker, like my good friend Vaughn, who threw me into Poppy's arms so generously. Thanks, man."

"You needed a shove in the right direction," Vaughn said meaningfully, his eyes boring into Knight's.

Knight shrugged. "Anyway…three more couples to fix up, and I'll secure my place in heaven."

"Even if you find the cure for death, you won't be getting a free pass into heaven," I signed.

Vaughn and Daria, who understood what I'd said, burst out laughing. Knight ignored me, turning his head to Poppy, his eyes dropping to her lips.

"I can get a place in heaven, can't I, Sunshine?"

Sunshine.

I was Moonshine, and she was Sunshine.

If I'd had any doubt he was playing a game to get even, I'd just received my proof.

"Of course," she simpered. "I'll take you with me."

He leaned down, pressing his lips against hers. Kissing her. In front of me. Her mouth opened, and his tongue slid past her lips. I looked away, feeling something inside me collapsing. I felt the ground beneath me shaking. I needed to get out of there.

"Luna," Vaughn barked, staring daggers at Knight, who was still engrossed in the kiss. "Come with me."

"Where to?" I asked.

"The humble pie is getting cold. Better get Knight his fix."

My legs carried me after Vaughn as we moseyed through the lush grass toward the Coles' house. Even though I wasn't sure where we were really going, anything was better than standing there with a front-row seat to Knight trying to wrestle his tongue into Poppy's mouth, not stopping until he reached her liver.

I didn't know why Vaughn was saving me—if, indeed, he was doing that. He was the one who'd insisted I go away so Knight could get over me. Job done.

Inside, Vaughn started throwing doors open like he was looking for something specific. When he got to the laundry room, he motioned for me with his head to come inside with him. I did. I stood with my back against the wall. He kept the door ajar, crowding me with his back to it.

"You like Lenora," I signed.

I didn't want to talk about how much it hurt to see Knight with someone else. I didn't want to ask Vaughn how long Knight had had a girlfriend. I clutched the ragged ends of my pride with bleeding fingernails.

"I hate her." He let out a breath, and with it, his obvious frustration.

"Same difference."

"We're competing over the same spot at her dad's academy. She's her father's daughter. Connect the fucking dots, Lu."

"Is that what's bothering you?"

"What else could it be?" he scoffed.

"The fact that she might be more talented than you." I jutted my chin out.

He threw me a patronizing smile, stuffing his hands into his pockets and taking a step toward me. He seemed relaxed, like he was burning time until something important happened. Vaughn was a world-class planner. His life was a chess game, each step perfectly calculated and in complete harmony with his end game.

"You seem to be taking Knight's antics in stride. I'm proud of you. I thought you'd cower and break. You proved to be more resilient than I gave you credit for."

I tipped my head up, meeting his gaze. He was close to me now. Too close for comfort. Vaughn was beautiful, but not in a way I found attractive. Like a god-shaped sculpture. Gorgeous, lifeless, and so terribly cold. He captured my chin between his fingers, slanting his head sideways as his eyes traced the shape of my lips.

"Terrible, isn't it?"

My heart quickened. I wanted to step away. To turn my back on him and leave. To run back to my house. But running away from problems was getting old and had proved to be destructive.

My grays met his blues, defying him to finish his thought.

"The sacrifices we have to make to put things back in order," he explained.

"You wanted me gone," I reminded him.

"I wanted you *strong*," he amended. "You were no match for Knight, which was why you didn't have the balls to go after him."

"And now?"

My heart looped inside my chest. Why was I waiting for his confirmation? Who was he to decide anyway?

"Now the jury's out, and it's your job to prove it."

"You're mad at Knight for pushing Lenny into Hunter's arms." I grinned. I'd found Vaughn's vulnerability, dug it up with a little spoon.

"I'm never mad. Just fair." He shrugged. "Besides, this is about you, not me."

"Knight doesn't want me anymore," I signed.

I foolishly tried to goad him to tell me differently, but Vaughn was far too sophisticated to fall into this trap.

"You know, Luna, people dislike me because I fight mean. With no mercy. But what they don't get is that terror and arousal are very similar. Same adrenaline. Same incentive. Same reaction. What do you say, Rexroth? Are you ready to fight back?"

Before the meaning of his words could register, Vaughn leaned down and pressed his lips to mine ever so softly. We hovered between a kiss and breathing each other in, our eyes still open, but I didn't pull back. Didn't push him away.

Vaughn kissed the corner of my lips, murmuring, "You are delectable, Luna Rexroth. I could devour you and not even feel sorry for it."

He still wore a cunning grin when he was jerked back, and before I realized what was happening, Vaughn had been thrown on top of the washing machine and Knight's fist hovered in the air as he towered above him. Knight was bigger by far, and physically stronger. But that didn't stop Vaughn from smiling up at him, the flame of the devil's match twinkling in his pale eyes.

"If it isn't fucking Judas Iscariot himself." Knight narrowed his eyes, spitting on the floor.

"Careful, Cole. You're a taken man now. I wonder what your girlfriend is going to think about your little outburst. I was just kissing a perfectly single, shit-hot girl."

"Traitor!" Knight screamed in his face.

Vaughn straightened. "Traitor, as in I hooked up with the girl you love and now you're salty?" he asked conversationally.

Oh God.

Oh, Lenora.

"Yeah." Knight flashed a wolfish grin. "Exactly like that. You made Luna go to Boon." His entire body shook with rage, a stark contrast to his schooled features. "Poppy said she overheard you in the courtyard."

Vaughn shrugged, refusing to get pulled into the hysterical atmosphere in the room. "You babied her. You weren't equals and therefore couldn't be together. I sent her on her way, and look at her now. All grown up and ready to face you. Where's my thank-you?"

"I'm going to kill you," Knight whispered.

His expression scared me, but not enough to sit back and let him stake his claim. I didn't want to move on with Josh, but that didn't mean I didn't have the right to. Knight and I had never been together, and he was now seeing someone else. He had no right to be mad. I grabbed Knight's bicep, trying to pull him away from Vaughn.

He shook me off. "Stay out of this, Luna."

My eyes widened in disbelief. I was *part* of this. I slipped between them, blocking his access to Vaughn. Not that Vaughn needed my protection. He'd kill for a chance to brawl. I obviously hadn't thought the idea through, because now I was sandwiched between them, and Vaughn's groin was pressed against my butt, something Knight could see very well from his eagle-eye angle, being so much taller and bigger than Vaughn and me.

I opened my mouth, trying to yell at Knight, but of course, it failed me again, and nothing came out.

Knight took a step back immediately, giving me space. He worked his jaw back and forth. "Get the hell out. It's between me and Vaughn."

I shook my head, opening my mouth again. I knew I looked stupid. I felt it too.

Just say something.

"I'll throw you out," Knight said.

The hell he would. I gave him the finger and smiled. Here. One visual—a thousand words in it.

Knight advanced toward me, and I snapped.

"Stop being a hypocrite," I yelled in his face, unable to take it anymore. "You have a girlfriend now. You moved on. You don't have the right to get mad when I kiss other people. You don't own me."

As soon as I clamped my mouth shut, I remembered we weren't alone. I stumbled away from Vaughn, still at my back, until I hit the wall. When I turned, Vaughn stared at me in disbelief. The room spun like a ball gown before my eyes, the colors and shapes blurring together.

"Say something," Vaughn ordered, clamping a hand on my shoulder. "To me, Luna."

I opened my mouth. I didn't think I could do it, but a part of me desperately wanted to. I didn't want Knight to feel special. Like he had a hold on me. A power too great to be shared with others. I felt my throat clogging up with my words but pushed through anyway.

Do it. Do it. You can do it.

I tried, but I couldn't.

Opened my mouth. Closed it.

Then opened it again. After a few seconds, I closed my eyes and shook my head. I couldn't do it.

"Well, then. You keep saying you aren't mine, but all evidence points to the contrary." Knight's smirk implied he was slightly unhinged as he stared at me.

He was most likely drunk again. He was so good at disguising it at this point.

"As for you, Moonshine, I think it's time the tables turned. Unrequited love is a bitch. Time to taste your own medicine."

Then, Knight turned back to Vaughn and launched at him with so much force, I thought Vaughn's spine would snap like a twig. Knight grabbed him by the collar and threw him against the wall, then tried to punch him in the face, but Vaughn was quicker. He elbowed Knight's collarbone, knocking him down on his butt. The door flung open and Poppy, Daria, Lenora, Penn, and Hunter rushed in. It was a tiny room to begin with, so Hunter and Penn didn't have any trouble breaking up the fight by simply stepping between the two guys. Hunter pushed Vaughn, who didn't need much restraint because he was in full control, toward the door. Penn—who was a big football player—secured Knight's hands behind his back.

"You're a dead man walking," Knight spat at Vaughn.

Knight was red, his eyes glassy with anger. Vaughn sneered, once again looking bored out of his mind. Lenny and Daria pushed a crying Poppy out the door.

I realized it probably looked horrible from where she was standing. She didn't deserve to feel like the other woman. Things had gotten out of control. I squeezed Vaughn's arm.

"I'm off," I signed.

Rushing past the stairway, I saw Poppy sitting on the bottom stair, Lenny and Daria stroking her hair and comforting her.

"I love him!" Poppy cried.

My heart nearly spilled out of my chest, I hurt so much for her.

"I know, darling. But I wouldn't date a guy who's so hung up on someone else," Lenny admitted softly.

They all looked up at me when they heard my footsteps. I ducked my head.

"Saint Luna, what happened?" Daria asked.

She no longer looked smug and thoroughly entertained. I didn't answer.

I slipped back to my house, as I always did.

Running from conflict.

From the truth.

From my voice.

From my *silence*.

CHAPTER NINE
KNIGHT

"Nice shiner. Goes well with your shirt." Dad shifted his gaze from my black-purple eye to my indigo dress shirt.

He didn't ask how I got it. He knew he wouldn't get an answer. Months ago, I'd run in a circle that attended a betting ring/fight club called the Snake Pit. I sometimes used to fight there, especially to cover for Vaughn when the little asshole would disappear without notice—not often, but often enough that black eyes were the norm. Besides, it was pretty fucking obvious—with Luna making an early exit and Poppy clinging to the lapels of my blazer all night—that there were hormones and pussy involved.

Things with Dad had been different recently, though. He was snappier and less attentive. Couldn't blame him. He was busy trying to find a cure for Mom's illness. It just felt fake to let shit surface now. We were in a different place. We used to share di ganja in the backyard. Now, we were lucky to exchange two sentences without biting each other's heads off.

The party would have been a good time to break things off with Poppy, but I was so mad at Luna and Vaughn, I couldn't think straight. Winter break had just started, and if they were going to be making out all over town, they sure as hell were going to get a nice view of my junk grinding all over Poppy.

I knew I was being an ass. Poppy was a cool chick. Just not cool enough for me to curb my asshole ways, apparently. Anyway, she knew what was up, yet she still pursued me. The writing had been on the fucking wall since freshman year, when I'd followed Luna everywhere.

Poppy wasn't illiterate.

Even so, I'd literally spelled it out for her.

"I'm off." I threw a baseball cap on my head.

I didn't feel like sticking around, hearing my mom have a coughing fit. She'd been getting worse and worse lately, and sometimes— okay, oftentimes—I just wanted to run away from the sound of her body failing her. Failing all of us.

I wore black sweatpants and a rain jacket and jogged through the woods of El Dorado, heading to the tree house, the tree house I hadn't visited in four years—but hey, who was counting?

Me, actually.

I was fucking counting. Every single hour.

Day.

Month.

Remember when things were easy and simple?

Luna and I had decided we were too grown-up for the tree house when I was fourteen. Well, she'd decided, and I'd agreed. I'd agreed to a lot of stuff in the name of pleasing Luna, and I had to admit, it felt liberating to stop giving a crap. Even if I was just pretending.

When I got to the tree house and climbed up, I was surprised to see it in top condition. No dust on the mini-chairs, plastic table, and little makeshift kitchenette. The drawings we'd made were yellowed and curled around the edges on the wall, but still there. There were fresh flowers stuck in a tin can on the table. Sign language books stacked neatly on the DIY shelves. Someone had been cleaning the place, and I wondered if it was now occupied by new kids from the area.

I lay on the shabby carpet that smelled of dampness, old wood, and squirrel shit and closed my eyes.

"You had no right," I heard a voice from the entrance.

Rather than opening my eyes, I relished her voice, which I was still getting used to.

Soft.

Hoarse.

Sexy and gruff yet feminine, like Margot Robbie's.

Luna crawled into the tree house. It was snug for two grown-ass people. That meant she had to rest her thigh beside mine as she curled against the wall.

I opened my eyes, arching an eyebrow. "She talks again. Maybe all you really needed to start talking was for people to stop giving a crap about you."

Rewind. Stop. Apologize.

No matter how much I'd tried to get over FUCKING JOSH, I couldn't. The idea of him would haunt me to the grave. Perhaps even beyond. What if hell was watching Luna's sex tape with FUCKING JOSH on repeat?

Could you die twice? Thrice? My head was spinning. I needed to start looking into good lawyers. I was bound to kill the bastard.

"Don't change the subject." She looked around the room, hugging her knees to her chest. Watching Luna kiss Vaughn, or Vaughn kiss Luna if we're being technical here, was God's way of telling me he hated me on a personal, profound, go-fuck-yourself level. I shouldn't have cared. Vaughn being Vaughn, he'd done it to piss me off. He obviously had a boner for Lenny. It was all over his face—I'd check the crotch too, but gross.

Luna wasn't wrong. I had no right to get mad when minutes before I'd shoved my tongue down Poppy's throat. I'd been tortured by Luna for so long, tormenting her was now a knee-jerk reaction, though.

"You want to fuck around?" I sniffed. "Be my guest. But if you expect Vaughn to dick you, here's a friendly reminder: he only does blowjobs. But I can refer you to Hunter. He gives full service."

"Knight," Luna warned.

I still couldn't believe she was talking. It made me happier than a pig in shit and disturbed more than a pig on someone's plate, as bacon. Because she was becoming someone else, and that someone? I wasn't her best friend. Or her soul mate. I was barely her goddamn neighbor at this point.

"Fine. Sorry. Yes, I'll stop being a dick."

"Now."

"Old habits die hard, Moonshine."

"You were never a dick."

"Hmm, no. I was actually a seven-foot dick. Just not to you."

She gave me her pinkie silently. A peace offering, without saying so explicitly.

I curled mine over hers. "This place is neat as fuck." I scooted up to sitting, motioning toward the tree house with my finger.

"That's because I've been cleaning it on the reg. Or at least I was until I left for college." Luna bobbed her head.

I swiveled my upper body, staring at her.

"What?" Her nostrils flared.

"I don't know. I never thought you'd say something like 'on the reg,' is all. You sound completely…"

"Normal?"

"Yeah."

"Yeah." She nodded. "I used to talk to myself sometimes, when no one was listening. Like, to see if I had an accent or something."

That made me burst out laughing. Suddenly, the shitty holiday parties seemed centuries away. A spurt of optimism exploded in my chest. So what if Vaughn had kissed her? It wasn't like they were going to date. Plus, it meant she was no longer with FUCKING JOSH. So, really, today had been pretty pleasant. Even the shiner was badass.

"I have a question." I poked her ribs.

"Is it about Vaughn?"

"Yeah, but don't get cocky."

"Pretty sure you trademarked cocky, Knight. What is it?"

"Remember when you retrieved my bike from him?"

She nodded.

"What did you do to get it?"

"Told him if he didn't give it to me, I'd kick his ass." She puffed her chest, smiling.

I snorted, raising an eyebrow. "That did the trick?"

"Well, no. I kneed his balls when he refused. We were about the same height back then. I grabbed the bike and ran. *That* did the trick."

"You kneed Vaughn in the balls for me?"

"Honestly, I would knee Vaughn in the balls for sugar-free Froyo, and you know I think that's the work of the devil. But, yeah, you were upset. I stepped up. That's what we did for each other, you know?"

"Did?" I bit down on my tongue ring.

She looked down at her thighs. "*Do?*"

"Do," I said with conviction. "No matter how hard or stupid shit gets, Moonshine. Ride or die, remember?"

She nodded.

Fuck it. She deserved to know.

"Mom's not getting a lung transplant."

I didn't know what to expect. Probably a bullshit, long-ass speech about how it was going to be okay—even though it clearly wasn't—followed by an even more embarrassing attempt to find a silver lining.

Instead, Luna's face twisted with agony I knew took hold of every inch of her body. "Fuck."

She never cursed. Even in sign language. It felt good to hear her say that.

"Thanks" came my equally unlikely response.

"I'm looking for Val." She changed the subject.

"Fuck." It was my turn to curse. Honestly, though, I could count the number of times I hadn't said that word in a sentence on one finger. It'd be the middle one, by the way.

She nodded again.

"You feel guilty," I guessed.

"Don't I always?"

"You do." Unless there are other guys involved, of course.

Apparently, I wasn't done being Bitter Betty. Swear to God it felt like my balls had been surgically removed from the rest of my body.

There was silence, the type I'd grown accustomed to since I'd realized Luna Rexroth wasn't gross after all. I laced my fingers through hers. Closed my eyes.

"We can do this," she mumbled, trying to convince herself more than me. "We can be friends. We just need to remember we're not together, and therefore don't owe each other anything." She squeezed my hand, sticking to her eyes-on-the-ceiling strategy, speaking as if her words were written there. "Poppy is nice."

I didn't want to talk about Poppy. Or about how the one thing Luna had said about Val changed my mind about something—something I was going to do tomorrow, something I'd decided on a whim and wouldn't tell anyone about.

Right now I wanted to just be here in silence with my best friend. And somehow, I don't know how, Luna sensed it. So we sat there for what felt like two hours but was probably a lot less, until I opened my eyes again. Her eyes were closed too. I watched her for a while.

When she opened her eyes, it felt like she took something away from me.

"Let's jump," she said.

"I'm quite fond of my limbs, Moonshine."

"Stop being such a big baby."

"Big quarterback baby who just finished a football season in one piece and would like to keep all his body parts intact."

She crawled out of the tree house and settled on the branch. It was thick, but I doubted it could carry my muscular ass for more than a few seconds before snapping. I rolled my eyes and settled next to her. She slipped her hand in mine.

"Three, two, one."

It was a short, sweet way down.

———————

The next day, I sat on a bench, watching the sun slink into the ocean like a wounded animal disappearing into the woods to die alone.

I knew the woman sitting beside me had made one hell of a journey to come here, that she'd been waiting for days, weeks, months—who knew? who cared?—for me to pick up the phone and tell her to come here. Then she'd hopped on the first available flight to do just that.

And still. And still. *And still.* I was barely able to look at her face, gold-rimmed by the sun.

Pretty.

Young.

Lost.

Found. Maybe.

That was her version of the story anyway.

She smoothed her summer dress over her thighs in my periphery, sniffing the sea brine in the air. The action was compulsive. And annoying. And too close to the way I chewed on my tongue piercing whenever I was nervous.

"I was sixteen." She still spoke to the hands in her lap.

Sixteen when she gave up on me.

Sixteen when she handed me to my parents.

Sixteen when they asked her if she wanted them to send her updates and pictures.

Sixteen when she replied no.

She'd said so herself, in her letter to me, apologizing and assuring me she knew what I looked like now. I didn't ask how because I didn't care.

"Boo-fucking-hoo." I flicked my joint between my fingers, throwing it to the ocean and tucking my fists into my jacket.

"I didn't have a choice." She shook her head again, looking at her lap.

"Bullshit. Choices are all we have." I felt like our conversation had started from the middle. We'd hardly exchanged any pleasantries before we dove headfirst into the real mess.

"But, Knight…"

"Really? You drag your ass across the country, and all you have to say to me is a weak 'but, Knight'?"

She burst into tears. I turned my head to watch her, my face dripping nonchalance. She was tall, with blue eyes and blond hair. I wondered just how dark my dad had been to dilute the Reese Witherspoon genes she was sporting. We looked nothing alike, and that made me happy somehow. Proud.

"Don't send me any more letters."

"But…"

"Call me again, and I'll take it to the police. And never, fucking *ever*, bypass my parents when you want to get to me, eighteen or not."

"But…but…"

"Stop with the buts! I didn't want to open the case. You sure as fuck don't deserve to make that decision for me." I stood up, plucking a bunch of bills from my wallet and throwing them in my birth mother's general direction. "Cab fare back to the airport. Ciao, Dixie."

CHAPTER TEN
LUNA

I tried to ignore Knight's existence for the next few days.

I went surfing with Edie every morning, took Racer to the mall twice, and caught up on reading material for college. I rode my bike. A lot.

Even though I didn't actually see him, Knight was always there, hovering in the back of my mind. Everything I did was tainted with the vision of his face. To silence the demon with stabbing green eyes, I decided to dig deeper into Val.

Last night, I'd gone into my father's walk-in closet when he wasn't home, risen on my toes, and slid out the shoebox where he kept everything Val related. There were mainly legal documents, most of them about me—my birth, my heritage, and the documents proving he had full custody of me. I didn't know why he still kept them. I was nineteen and wasn't going anywhere.

Nowhere near Val, and nowhere at all.

The more I dug into my biological mother's case, the more I realized how much of a mystery she was to me—no address, no background, no relatives I knew of. She had a mother—wasn't my grandmother curious to meet me?—and not much else.

I decided to talk to Edie about it. Edie was a better bet than Dad because she didn't have an allergic reaction to the name Valenciana. I wasn't really sure why, because when I was four, she hadn't been immune to being screwed over by Val.

I found Edie in the kitchen, making sugar cookies with Racer. They turned around when I entered, both of them wearing matching *Why Are You All Up in My Grill?* aprons. Edie took one look at my face before she dropped a kiss on Racer's head.

"Go help your dad in the garage."

"Help him with what? He's watching a football game." Racer frowned.

"Well, he's old and nearsighted."

"No, he's not."

"He needs you to read the score for him. Go."

I plopped down on the barstool by the kitchen island, rubbing my face. Edie walked over to the fridge and took out two Bud Lights, popping them open and sliding one in my direction. I loved how she put the Mom cap on when I needed her to be the responsible adult and the Friend cap on when I didn't want to be lectured. She could always sense which version of her I needed and slipped into the role like a chameleon, changing her colors but still staying the same sweet Edie.

"What's the story, morning glory?" She tipped her beer bottle up, taking a sip.

"Val," I signed.

Edie gathered her long blond hair into a messy yet somehow perfect bun. "All right. I'm listening."

There was always a dash of guilt thrown in when I mentioned Val to Edie. After all, one of them was an MIA birth mom who wanted nothing to do with me, and the other was a girl who'd met me when she was a teenager herself—nineteen, as I was right now—and immediately took me under her wing, sacrificing her youth for Dad and me.

"Have you ever tried to find out where she was?"

Edie shook her head, peeling the label off her beer bottle. "Your dad doesn't like talking about her. I doubt she's in the country anymore. Last we saw her, when you were four, she was deeply troubled."

"I want to find out."

"Why, Luna?"

"Why?" I threw my hands in the air, wanting to punch someone. "Because I can't move forward! Because I have no roots, so how can I know where to grow, in which direction? Because she is my past!"

"Exactly. You can't do anything about your past. Focus on your present. On your future. Hell, on anything other than that woman."

I shook my head. I needed to know.

Edie looked around. Her shoulders sagged with a sigh. "If we open this can of worms without telling your dad, he'll be devastated when he finds out. And he *will* find out. I can't betray him, Lu. You realize that, right?"

I looked up at her. I didn't want to do it. Every fiber in my body didn't want to do it, but I dug out my manipulative streak, dumping it between us on the kitchen island, baiting her. Guilt-tripping her. For the first time in my life, I did something completely selfish.

"I don't have the money for this, Edie. Or the connections. I deserve to know."

Edie's teeth sank into her full lower lip. She examined her sugar-dusted fingers, her huge wedding ring catching the sunlight streaming from the large windows.

I thought about Knight. About how he refused to open his adoption case. Last time we'd spoken about it, he'd said, "I have two functioning parents with their shit together. Why would I let some random walk into my life and mess it up?"

He had a point. But Knight wasn't like me. He didn't need answers. He dripped validation. He was vastly loved and admired by everyone we knew.

Edie turned around, giving me her back. She braced herself on the kitchen counter, thinking. I hated myself so much for putting her in this situation.

"I'll hire a PI, but you have a week to tell your dad," she announced metallically. "I'm not lying to my husband, Luna."

As a gesture of good faith, I spoke the words to her, "Thank you."

She dipped her finger into cookie dough on the glossy marble of the counter, licking the pad of her finger thoughtfully. "Whatever it is you're looking for, I hope it's peace and not a relationship. She doesn't deserve you, Luna. She never did."

My perfect streak of avoiding Knight (and vice versa?) ended on a Wednesday afternoon the day before Christmas Eve. Clad in my checked Vans, mustard-hued beanie, boyfriend jeans, and a cropped sweater that showed a hint of abs from all the cycling I did, I was headed down to the dog shelter on Main Street for a pre-Christmas adoption day, one of the busiest days of the year. I hugged Eugene and Bethany, the elderly couple who ran the shelter. Eugene had white caterpillar eyebrows and wore a uniform of suspenders and hiking boots. Beth was a willowy thing who was always on the move. I'd come in before the other volunteers to help clean up, arrange the refreshments on tables, and print out leaflets for prospective adopters.

Since Eugene and Beth didn't speak sign language, I had to type on my phone to communicate with them. I'd been volunteering with them for many years, and communicating was never an issue, but today, they were squinting at my phone more than usual, rubbing their eyes when staring at the tiny text. I hadn't considered that they were getting older.

My heart was drenched with sorrow. I tried to open my mouth and speak. The wall had been pierced—why not try again? But nothing came out. I closed my mouth, snagged a blank page from the printer, and wrote with a thick Sharpie, *I'm so sorry. Maybe I should go?*

Beth ripped the page in half while it was still in my hand, snapped her fingers together, and smiled.

"Our grandson, Jefferson, studied sign language. He's going to become a speech therapist. Let me call him."

The last thing I wanted was someone else added to the mix. As it was, the place was going to be teeming with people, my least favorite creatures to hang out with. But I couldn't exactly shut down the idea either. So I watched as Beth coaxed her grandson (rather aggressively) to stop by the shelter on his way back from the gym.

Half an hour before we opened the doors to the general public, the volunteers started trickling in. They were mostly faces I recognized, but that did nothing to calm my social anxiety. Most people smiled tightly when they saw me and made themselves scarce to keep things a little less awkward—for them, not for me. Not that I cared either way, as long as I was back to being my blissfully invisible self.

I was arranging leaflets on red-clothed tables when Beth shrieked behind me and said, "Oh, lookie here! My favorite English rose."

My blood froze in my veins. I could practically feel whatever was left of my calm evaporating from my body, like mist, even before I heard Knight's voice muttering, "Shit."

Shit, indeed.

I resumed my leaflet arrangement, keeping my back to them, like nothing had happened.

So what if they were here? I'd been volunteering in the shelter for eight years, practically since I was a preteen. Today was going to be wonderful. Puppies and elderly dogs alike were going to find new, loving homes. I was going to make the most out of it. Besides, Knight and I had agreed on a truce.

"Knight Jameson Cole. How's your mama?" Bethany bellowed behind me.

"Well, ma'am. Thanks for asking. And yourself?"

"Been worse."

"But never looked better."

"You little charmer." She let out a hearty laugh. "Is that how he caught you, Miss Astalis? With his smooth tongue?"

"Ma'am, you haven't the slightest clue," Knight drawled.

I bit down on a grin and rolled my eyes. He'd gone there. In front of a senior citizen. The horndog.

"He makes me so happy," Poppy gushed, clapping her hands together.

I wanted to gag. The only thing stopping me, in fact, was Bethany calling for me to come say hello to my good, *good* friend.

We lived in a small town, where everyone knew Knight Cole and Luna Rexroth were a package deal. He'd come to the shelter with me so many times, his mere presence here with someone else felt like a slap in my face.

Truce, Luna. Truce. He's not yours, remember?

Drawing a calming breath, I turned around and plastered on a polite smile as I made my way to them. I waved hello to Poppy and Knight just as the door behind them opened and a person I assumed was Jefferson walked in.

Everyone went silent.

Jefferson was, for lack of other words, uncomfortably stunning, even in his gym clothes, sweat making his shirt stick to his six-pack. I'd always been drawn to people with distinctive faces—a scar, a crooked nose, chipped tooth. Anything imperfect went.

Knight's saving grace was his eyes. Everything about him was perfect to a T, an all-American superhero who could slide comfortably into Chris Evans's shoes and give him a run for his money. But his eyes were slightly different colors, one the shade of moss, the other more hazel. He was imperfect, but only if you looked really closely. Too closely for his comfort. Too close for him to ever allow. I could never fall in love with a hundred-percenter…but Knight was a solid 99.99 percent.

Jefferson, however, was three-figure perfect: thick, silken mane the color of sand and a jaw squarer than a Rubik's Cube, à la Scott

Eastwood. Since I was the reason he'd arrived, I was the first he reached out to for a handshake when Beth started with the introductions. I normally wasn't hot on physical contact with people I didn't know, but something about the situation pushed me into getting out of my comfort zone—or rather, someone. *Knight.*

Jefferson gave me a gentle squeeze, punctuating the gesture with a wide smile. He couldn't be much older than twenty-two. I didn't know why I was expecting someone older, considering his grams had mentioned he was still a student.

"Grandma Beth asked if I could save the day." He grinned, his teeth sparkling like in a cartoon.

Typically, I wouldn't answer him, in sign language or otherwise. But I could practically *feel* Knight's gaze putting more layers of clothes on me, one item at a time, to try to hide me away, as he tried to fence me back into being timid and shy. Not today, though.

"I appreciate it. You must be so busy," I signed.

"Never too busy to be a beautiful girl's knight in shining armor."

I smirked. Interesting choice of words. Karma was definitely working extra hours today.

"She's not a tortilla chip. No need to put so much cheese on it." Knight tousled his own hair, his eyes drenched with disdain as he threw Jefferson a scowl.

Jefferson was still staring at me and shaking my hand, his chiseled face smiling radiantly at me. "Actually, I'm vegan," he deadpanned.

"I'm vegetarian." My eyes bugged out.

Why was I surprised again? His grandparents ran a shelter. They were both vegetarian. Eugene and Beth looked between us, sharing a sly smile before they left to open the shelter doors to the general public.

"What are the odds?" Knight feigned interest. "I bet Harry Styles was both your favorite Fifth Harmony member."

"Harry Styles was in One Direction," Jefferson pointed out.

Knight spread his arms triumphantly. "Damn, son. You walked

right into the trap. Not the kind of information that should occupy your brain cells."

Again, Jefferson ignored him. Our palms were still clasped together, and I made no hurry to withdraw mine.

"I'm Poppy!" Knight's girlfriend offered in her dangerously smooth British accent, thrusting her hand in Jefferson's direction.

He turned from me, his face opening up when he saw her. "I adore your accent."

"I adore your grandparents! I've been volunteering here for three months. Mainly over the weekends. Shame we never bumped into each other."

She was overeager to sell him to me by pointing out how attractive he was.

"I usually volunteer on weekdays. I give the shelter dogs a live acoustic performance. It's less dumb than it sounds, I promise."

"Doubt it," Knight grunted.

Poppy elbowed his ribs. Michael Jackson's eating-popcorn GIF played in my head. I stifled a smile. This was surprisingly entertaining.

"It doesn't sound dumb at all. I wish you'd come on the weekends," Poppy purred, her gaze slicing to me.

"Maybe I will."

"I'm the boyfriend by the way." Knight cut through their flirtatious exchange, offering Jefferson his big hand.

Jefferson laughed and shook it. "No disrespect, man. I was actually baiting Luna." He turned back to me. "You come here on weekends?"

Knight's jaw ticked.

"Used to. I go to Boon in North Carolina now."

"Crying shame."

"I still have winter break."

Jefferson clutched his shirt where his heart was and threw his other fist in the air. "We must accept finite disappointment but never lose infinite hope."

"You sure know your Martin Luther King Junior, sir." I grinned.

Knight rolled his eyes. "Real subtle, bro."

Poppy poked her lower lip out, looking between us peculiarly. Of course she was happy if Jefferson and I rode off into the sunset together; then she could have Knight all to herself. Little did she know, I had no intention of spending time with her boyfriend this winter. Our last encounter in the tree house had been a bid to keep the boat from flipping over, but Knight and I were both smart enough to know we were still on troubled water.

Half an hour later, the place was jam-packed with families and couples crouching and cooing over crates. I had no time to think about Knight, Poppy, or even Val. Jefferson shadowed my every move, acting as my voice.

Three hours into the event, we had already managed to send twelve dogs home with their new families. I peeked at Beth and Eugene, who were laughing with their friends in the corner of the room. They looked relaxed and happy. Between Poppy and the other volunteers, we had it on lock.

Knight never left Poppy's side. He texted on his phone with a gloomy scowl. Every time he looked up and our eyes met, I turned around and struck up a conversation with Jefferson.

"So. You and Knight," Jefferson said when we were closing up.

He picked up Goldie, a golden retriever pup, letting her lick every inch of his face. I laughed at Goldie's eagerness.

"There's no me and Knight."

"You should tell that to his eyes. They've been putting extra time in on following you everywhere today."

"He has a girlfriend." I shrugged.

"Poppy deserves better."

I couldn't argue with that. I plucked Goldie from his embrace, rubbing my nose against her fur. Jefferson continued staring at me with an intensity I was too inexperienced to decode. He leaned forward so we were hunched together behind the register. He'd just opened his mouth when Knight appeared in front of us, rapping the counter with his knuckles.

"A word," he hissed my way.

I tore my gaze from Jefferson, playing dumb.

"I don't talk."

"To me you do."

"Think again."

"Don't make me embarrass you, Moonshine." He smiled impatiently. "Because I will. And make a damn good show of it."

"I hate you."

"Good. It will make our conversation much easier, and we'll be on the same page so you can return to Ken over here."

"You're a delight," Jefferson observed.

Knight shot him one of his football-hero smirks that seemed to dismantle ticking bombs. "And you're in my fucking way." His gaze shot back to me. "*Now.*"

I knew Knight would make the rest of the evening hell for Jefferson, Poppy, and me if I didn't oblige, and we still had to help clean up the place.

Reluctantly, I slid from behind the register and joined Knight outside on the sidewalk. Main Street was buzzing with shoppers, bright lights, and the dense scent of fresh winter air, cocoa, coffee, and baked goods. My mouth would've watered if I wasn't so furious.

"What the hell was that?" I signed, then jerked my thumb behind us as Knight slacked against the wall, squeezing his eyes shut.

He looked worn-out. Frustrated. Exhausted. If he was so distraught, why didn't he break up with Poppy? Why did he keep this charade going?

"I can't," he said simply. "I can't fucking look at you anymore. It's wrong. I know. It's hypocritical. Hell, I know that too. You owe me nothing, but you slept with someone else, and it's the only thing I can think about when I look at your face, no matter how much I want to see anything *but* that."

He turned his body fully toward me, opening his eyes. I watched as they hardened while he arranged his indecipherable mask. The one I couldn't get through even before Josh.

"Screwing FUCKING JOSH. Kissing Vaughn. Flirting with Ken. You've really become quite a hussy, haven't you, Luna?"

"Jealous?" I smiled sweetly, folding my arms over my chest.

Inside, I was fuming. How dare he? How dare he parade his gorgeous girlfriend around while giving me grief? How dare he belittle me? And how dare he slut-shame me when *he* was the very person who used to raise riots when people said words like *slut* and *hussy* around him?

"Jealous? Why would I be jealous? Guy's a vegan. He probably doesn't even have the energy to fuck you. Ken here is no competition for me, and we both know it."

"Tell that to your girlfriend," I murmured, and we twisted to watch Jefferson and Poppy through the display window of the shelter.

They were huddled in the corner of the room, Poppy showing him something on her phone. She laughed and swatted his chest. Once again, I realized I couldn't dislike her, even if I tried. Her only sin was being interested in the same guy I was in love with.

Knight looked back at me, jutting his chin out.

"Nice comeback. You open that mouth for FUCKING JOSH, too?"

His words burned hot with lust; they were sweet poison glossed over an apple I knew better than to bite.

He was picking a fight again. I locked my jaw and narrowed my eyes at him. He'd never been this cruel to me before. I got that he was hurt, but he had no right.

"Not to talk, of course. You're too precious for talking, aren't you, Luna? But maybe to suck his dick?" Knight cocked his head sideways, his eyes dead. "C'mon, Luna, is that what it is? You tasted dick and realized how good it is, and now you can't get enough?"

I turned around and started for my bike, dashing down the road.

He grabbed my arm and spun me around.

"Let go, or I'll slap you again."

"I'll take your wrath over your indifference," he deadpanned, unblinking.

"I'm not giving you a choice."

"Would people stop saying that? There's always a fucking choice." He threw his head back, laughing manically.

"Are you drunk?" I scrunched my nose.

"No," he shot back automatically.

"You seem drunk."

"What makes you say that?"

"When you're drunk, you're mean."

He was spiraling again. And I was talking to him. *Again.* Because I didn't know how to stop. I didn't know how to cut him out of my life, even when he cut *me* so deep.

"You can't half-ass a relationship, Knight. Either you're in or you're not. You're with Poppy now, but you treat her like crap. Every time I'm in the room, you put your relationship with her on the back burner. You don't let me move on without faulting me for talking or flirting or kissing other guys. Guess what? I *can*. More than that, I *will*. We had our chance, and we blew it. My fault. Your fault. Does it really matter now?" I spoke quickly, breathlessly, my chest rising and falling rapidly. "I will meet someone else. I will sleep with someone else. I will *love* someone el—"

He cut me off with a searing kiss, slamming my back against the wall in the process. Lacing his fingers through mine, he pinned my hands to the wall beside my waist, caging me in. I growled, knowing we were somewhere public, doing something wrong.

He has a girlfriend. Break the kiss, Luna. Now.

"That's where you're wrong." His tongue ring swirled across my lips teasingly, his kiss hot and incredibly deep as he thrust his tongue into my mouth again. "There will be no one else, Moonshine. I will never let you get over me."

He took my jaw between his fingers, and I had a moment of epiphany, very similar to the one I'd had when he'd saved me from the car crash.

Knight was not a good guy.

He wasn't even a decent one. But he'd been my protector. My savior. My guardian angel. Now that he'd quit that role, all bets were off. The precious prize became the prey. My halo was broken. My free passes—no longer free.

"I really do hate y—" I started.

"You already mentioned. Let me assure you: I don't give a fuck."

With that, he crashed his lips against mine again. This time, I wrapped my arms around his neck, exploring his delicious mouth, his furious lips, his tongue and the barbell in it—the way he whirled it inside my mouth, devouring me with an urgency I didn't know someone so cool was even capable of.

Trailing his tongue ring from my mouth to my neck, leaving tingly shivers of desire in his wake, he whispered, "I will make you so fucking wet for me, Luna. So fucking ready. And. I. Will. Never. Fuck. You. Never give you what you want."

My eyes bugged in shock at the same time I heard Poppy's voice piercing through the foggy cloud of lust surrounding us.

"Knight?" Her posh accent sounded frayed.

Like if you pulled more words out of her mouth, they'd come out in one thread. She stood there, the evening light twinkling behind her in a gorgeous backdrop, in her sensible navy dress and her Wizard of Oz shoes, unshed tears brimming in her eyes. She looked about as ready to work hard at the shelter as I looked ready to be a KKK poster child.

I cupped my mouth. I didn't trust myself not to apologize aloud.

You did this, Luna, I wanted to cry. *It is because of you she feels this way.*

Knight stared ahead, like she was a wall he had to bulldoze through. Jefferson came out of the shelter. He stuffed his hands into his jacket's pockets, looking between all of us. I was still caged between Knight's arms. Jefferson put his hand on Poppy's shoulder. I couldn't help but notice the disappointment in his eyes when he looked at me.

"How'd you get here?" he asked her.

Rather than answering and risking an outburst, Poppy tilted her chin in Knight's direction.

"Let me take you home."

Her gaze lingered on Knight one more moment before she shook her head. They turned around just in time for me to gather my wits, slip from between Knight's arms, and run to my bike. I didn't even care that I was running again. That he was chasing me. That Beth and Eugene still needed help. Anything to get away from my angel turned devil. I unchained my bike, flung a leg over it, and sped back to my house. I heard cars honking and Knight cursing behind me, but I did not dare look back. This time, neither of us was going to save the other.

This time, we were on our own.

CHAPTER ELEVEN
KNIGHT

"Are you going to let it ring for eternity?" Mom looked up from watching *Fried Green Tomatoes*.

The shit I endured in the name of my love for her was on another level. I was 99 percent sure if she hadn't been so sick, I'd have bathed in hot lava before I'd watch an angsty chick flick.

"That's the plan." I sent the phone call to voicemail for the fifth time.

Mom frowned. "Texas area code? Who do you know in Texas?"

"Probably a college thingy." I kissed her forehead, motioning to the screen. "Look, you're missing your favorite part, where he tells her he's not really there for the barbecue but because he thinks she's a shithead."

"You want to go to an out-of-state college?" she persisted, eyeing me carefully. "Because you know you can, right?"

"Mom, drop it."

"Knight," she warned.

I rolled my eyes and stood up, advancing to my room. She was in a probing mood, and I wasn't in the business of denying my mother anything, especially when she'd spent the past week throwing up mucus, retching all night. Dad had put pillows all around their bathroom floor, and they sat there all night, every night. I heard them talk and laugh and whisper. Whenever she felt good enough, anyway.

In the mornings, when her massage therapist arrived, Dad would disappear to one of the spare rooms downstairs, his eyes bloodshot. Earlier, I'd followed him into his study silently. I'd found him bracing his desk from the other side, his back quivering as sobs rippled through his body. My dad. The mighty Dean Cole. Crying.

Not that there was anything wrong with that, but it was another stepping stone in our demise as a family.

The Cole men didn't cry.

Not when they lost their mothers. Their wives. The quiet, gorgeous loves of their lives.

Things were changing, and I didn't know how to stop them. Luna was living elsewhere and no longer mine. She was speaking. She had friends. Boyfriends. Mom was dying. *Really* dying. Dad was consumed by it. He could barely look at Levy and me. Whether he felt guilty or just generally pissed was beside the issue.

"Don't run away from the conversation." Mom coughed.

The doorbell rang.

I gestured in its general direction. "That would be Poppy," I said. It was the first time I'd been glad she'd stopped by.

"You guys are going strong." Mom's face melted instantly.

She wanted me to be happy. To be in love. I was one of these things, for sure. But happiness wasn't a part of the package deal.

"Suppose."

"She seems very smitten with you."

That word again.

"Are you happy with her?" Mom's eyes clung to my face, begging for crumbs of truth.

"Sure."

"You've never had a girlfriend."

"I've had plenty of girlfriends."

"No one serious."

"I'm not a serious guy."

"You're the most serious guy I know, Knight Jameson Cole."

My phone rang again. Texas. *Motherfucker.* I killed the call, then sent Dixie a string of middle-finger emojis before tucking the device into my back pocket.

"Better answer the door before Poppy gives me the third degree." I smiled apologetically.

I took Poppy to the front porch. I wasn't in the mood for sitting in my room. Maybe I subconsciously wanted Luna to see us, but she had drawn her curtains and made sure I couldn't peek into her room. Not that I was looking.

Okay, I was looking. Sue me.

God, why her? Why couldn't I fall in love with the nice English chick who actually wore dresses and talked all the time?

Poppy and I sat on white rocking chairs overlooking the cul-de-sac, me drinking Gatorade to nurse hangover number five hundred for the week, her cradling a glass of orange juice.

"How's your mum feeling?" she asked, staring at the yellow liquid swimming in her glass.

She'd brought over homemade cookies, which my mother gushed over and took a bite of, even though her appetite was shitty nowadays. Poppy, for all intents and purposes, was perfect. Only problem was, she wasn't perfect for *me.*

I shrugged, still staring at the street.

The street where I'd played with Luna.

Where I'd kissed her on the steps of her house.

Where I'd tugged at her braids.

Thrown water bombs at her.

Run around laughing when she'd thrown water bombs at *me.*

Where we'd drawn with chalk on the cobblestones, bounced on hippity hops, and fell asleep on her front lawn, our heads touching, as we'd waited for the fireworks to explode every Fourth of July.

Then I thought about how I'd treated her. Taunted her. Kissed her. Belittled her.

I couldn't stop myself from doing any of those things, even when

I wanted to. Desperately. The more my mother weakened, the more I drank. The more I drank, the more mean Knight came out. It was a vicious cycle. I knew there was only so much Luna would suffer before she flipped on my ass. She was a proud girl.

"I don't want to talk about my mother," I said frankly.

"Obviously." Poppy slapped her forehead. "Sorry. Can we talk about what happened yesterday? About us?"

There is no us.

"Okay."

"That thing with Luna—"

"Luna and I are unfinished business." I bit on the tip of my tongue ring after slicing into her speech. "We'll always be unfinished business. Now. In five years. When we're eighty. That's the deal; it's always been the deal. You knew it. You saw us up until senior year. We were always together."

That was Poppy's in to break up with me. I'd handle it with grace. I'd still take her to prom. But there was no reason to keep up with this bullshit.

"I get that." She swallowed hard. "Let's try again. I'm willing to give you another chance. If you want it, that is."

I don't.

I spun toward her, studying her face: the soft planes of her cheeks, her carefully brushed hair, flawless little Neiman Marcus dress. She could be someone else's Luna, someone else's everything. A guy like Jefferson's, maybe.

"Look, Poppy, I know you said we'd give this a chance—"

"Please." She cleared her throat again, chuckling in embarrassment. "Please don't make me beg. I know you don't feel it yet, but I do. I can feel it. There's something here. And Luna is heading back to North Carolina in a bit. It's not like you can explore whatever it is between you two."

All valid points, but I didn't think it was right to string her along.

Thing was, Poppy was practically pleading to be strung along, and I had too much shit on my calamity plate to muster the self-control I needed to push her away. She begged to be here for me, and the orphan mutt that I was, I couldn't deprive her of the dubious pleasure. She was convenient as hell. Plus, I no longer had to pretend to be fucking anyone else. I had a steady ride now.

"I get what you're saying, but I'm a shitty boyfriend." I gave it one last run. "I cheated on you. In your face. I didn't mean to hurt you, but I did."

"No. I know. It's just that…" She looked around, shrugging. "I saw the look on both your faces. Luna is not going to let you kiss her again. She regrets this. I want this, and I'm willing to take the risk."

Was that what she'd seen? Luna regretting it? My blood sizzled in my veins.

"You're going to regret it," I said quietly.

She grinned, standing up and ambling my way. She parked her ass in my lap, knotting her arms around my shoulders.

"I'm not the queen, you know," she said huskily, her gaze dropping to my lips. "You can touch me whenever you want."

I took her mouth in mine and tried to drown myself in her beauty, giving her a sweet lie to hold on to.

"Yes, you are." I erased Luna's kiss from my lips, replacing it with Poppy's sweet, soft petals. "You're my queen."

When the next letter arrived on Christmas Eve, obviously violating my request, I burned it in my backyard and sent Dixie a video of the whole thing.

Knight: Is it a wonder that the no-show who knocked you up left your ass? You're clingy as all fuck. Get it into your head: I'm not interested.

This was my best Vaughn impression. Being an asshole was goddamn hard work.

"You smell like ashes," Dad pointed out as we slicked our hair back in front of his gold-leafed mirror.

Two peacocks in Kiton Ombre suits—it was one of the rare times this past year we'd actually done anything together, which didn't escape me. Before Mom's lung transplant debacle, we'd still had hope, so we'd still been close. We'd spent a lot of time together. Not anymore.

"Are you okay?" He ripped his gaze from his reflection, giving me a sideways glance.

I used two fingers to dab Clive Christian cologne on my neck. "Are you?" I asked casually.

"Don't dodge the question."

"Ditto."

"You're infuriating."

"I am yours," I said by way of explanation.

He grinned proudly. I liked that look on Dad, the one that made me feel like I belonged in this world. In this house. In this family.

"I'm working night and day looking into experimental treatments." He shook his head, referring to my mother. "She'll be fine."

"Do you actually believe that?"

"I have to, or I'll go mad."

"Don't go mad. You're already straddling the line of insanity."

"Straddling is quite the feminine word."

"Then you're punching sanity in the face sometimes. Hard."

"Much better." He let out a sad laugh. He caught my gaze in the mirror. "Break up with Poppy yet?"

I passed him the cologne, rearranging my moussed hair. "She's a little young for you, old man."

More laughing, without the sad aftertaste.

This felt good, like old times.

"So you haven't forgiven Luna for that guy yet."

"She hasn't asked for forgiveness," I admitted, taking a step back from the mirror, wondering if I should confide in him.

Mom wouldn't understand this part. I didn't think any woman would. Dad might, although we hadn't had talks like that in months. Still...

"I can't stop thinking about them." I dropped my hand from my hair. "I mean, about him..."

"Inside her," Dad finished for me, turning around and leaning against the sink, eyes blazing. "You keep rewinding it in your head. How he touched her. How she felt to him. How he felt to *her*."

"Stab me with your razor and get it over with."

"I would, but what about the new tiles?" he deadpanned.

I pretended to scratch my nose with my middle finger. We had the same twelve-year-old's sense of humor. He swatted the finger away, grinning with confidence.

"At the risk of sounding ancient..." he started.

"Here we go." I rolled my eyes.

"Know what the problem with your generation is? You refuse to understand that love has a price. That's what makes it significant, pungent, rich. It costs you anger, jealousy, heartbreak, time, money, health..." He stopped, snarling at his last word like a wounded beast.

I looked away. Watching my dad love my mom sometimes felt like watching a chest being shredded open, the heart still beating inside. It was too raw, too real.

"Food for thought—is she worth it? You have to pay your dues, you see."

I snorted, thinking about what he was going through with Mom. "No one is."

He clapped a hand on my shoulder. "When you refuse to pay your dues to love, sometimes the price goes up. There's an inflation, and you end up losing more than you'd bargained."

Don't I fucking know it, Dad. I shook my head, thinking about Dixie. *Don't I fucking know it.*

If you ever wondered how douchebags were born, this is the exact recipe: admiration that leads to false self-entitlement, multiplied by enough money to sink a battleship, divided by good genes and formidable height.

I was allowed to open my Christmas gift first, since I'd won the state championship earlier in the month, leading All Saints High as captain. It was on the night I took Poppy out for the first time. The night I'd had to finish an entire bottle of vodka to go through with fondling her. She'd tasted different than Luna, and smelled nothing like her. It was like making out with a bottle of Chanel No. 5—bitter and about as sexy as licking a fish.

As it happened, my gift was a blue-leather-strapped Ronde Solo De Cartier watch, with my varsity number—sixty-nine—(yes, they allowed it at All Saints High when your name was Knight Cole) in gold.

As I said, I wasn't born a douchebag. It took hard work.

"We're so proud of you."

Dad and his best friends and business partners, my extended family—Vicious, Jaime, Dean, and Trent—squeezed my shoulders. Even Penn gave my arm a friendly punch.

"Thanks." I secured the watch on my mammoth wrist.

"Man, you could go pro with your stats. Why the hell aren't you trying?" Penn whistled, slinging his arm over his fiancée's shoulder.

I threw a pointed glance at Mom, who was talking to her sister, Emilia.

"Yeah. Foot-in-mouth moment on my part. My apologies." Penn winced.

After consuming three Marines' body weights in food, hearing Daria and Penn going on about how fucking amazing they were (file under: jerks. The recipe for making them is different), Vaughn announcing that he wanted to study in Europe to a room full of people who let out a collective sigh of relief (file under: mega asshole. Don't ask me how to make a Vaughn; only his ruthless father is capable of that), and Luna working really hard on making herself extra-invisible (which only made my ogling more apparent), we all retired to the Rexroths' drawing room with alcohol and dessert.

My parents, of course, had no idea just how intimately I was acquainted with alcohol at this point. Mom was busy not-dying, and Dad was busy helping her not-die. Plus, I'd always been a resourceful son of a bitch. I'd been able to hide, disguise, and downplay how drunk I was, in and outside of the house. I was a high-functioning, shitfaced drunk at this point.

Luna, of course, was right. Even when I hid my alcohol breath, she could tell when I was intoxicated because when I was, I was mean to her. I didn't want to be. But staying sober, sharp, and present felt slightly worse than dealing with her disappointed gaze.

Luna tucked her legs underneath her butt and settled on the carpet by the fire. She nibbled on a cookie and cracked open a book called *The Dark Between Stars*. The doorbell rang.

"Who has the social audacity to drop in on Christmas Eve?" Uncle Vicious seethed in his usual diplomatic fashion as I stood up to get the door.

"Ask your son," I told him.

I knew it was a dick move to invite Poppy and Lenora, but in my defense, it really wasn't my idea nor my doing. Vaughn had practically requested I extend an invitation to the sisters. Since he and I were still beefing about the kiss with Luna—which had occurred because he'd thought he was teaching me some fucked-up lesson, and I thought he was being a little pussy about it—I figured, why the hell not?

He'd said he needed to talk to the younger Astalis about some internship she was about to steal from him. Didn't know. Didn't care. I just knew it was a good opportunity to cement the fact that I wasn't heartbroken.

Because I wasn't.

Fuck Luna.

Oh wait, someone else already had.

Awesome. The inflation on my love was clearly skyrocketing. But really, I cared more about the fact that I *didn't* care than anything else. Confused? So was I. All I knew was Luna, once again, had managed to friend-zone my ass in the tree house, and I'd taken it, *again*, because apparently, I had a side gig as her doormat. To make everything much, much worse, Luna was now flirting with people like Jefferson in front of me and kissing my best friend. And I shouldn't care, but I did.

The girls moseyed into the drawing room, carrying a homemade funnel cake and an awkward silence like a half-dead animal behind them. Luna refused to look up from her book, acting completely oblivious to the situation.

Daria pinned me with a death glare from the couch, curled around her fiancé. "Smooth, Cole."

"Also, thick, long, and hard. Your point?" I flashed her a smirk, whispering under my breath.

"Astalis." Vaughn stood up.

Didn't take a genius to know which sister he was referring to.

Lenora offered him a steadfast gaze. "Spencer."

"Did you make the funnel cake?"

"No, why?"

"I would very much like to see my family and friends avoid being poisoned this Christmas," he quipped.

"Lo and behold, he does have a heart. Would you believe I am literally surprised to hear that?"

"I might not know my insects, but you clearly have no clue what the word *literally* means. A quick word," he demanded.

"I know quite a few."

"I'm well aware."

"Why is Vaughn talking British now?" Daria mumbled, looking around dumbfounded.

Emilia and Baron stared at their son and the English girl, fascinated. It was like watching a car crash—or your pet Chihuahua standing up on two legs, reading Shakespearean poetry while sipping on black tea.

"Shall we…" she said at the same time he huffed, "Let's go upstairs to…"

I glanced at Luna. Her eyes were still stuck on a page, but she was grinning.

Lenny nodded. "After you."

They disappeared upstairs, leaving the rest of us in the drawing room.

I made quick introductions, noting the chilly smiles the Rexroths offered my girlfriend, before retiring to the backyard with Penn, Daria, Via (Penn's sister), and my new best friend of late, beer. Daria invited Luna. She politely declined.

An hour later, I went in for a quick bathroom break. It was locked. Instead of going to any of the others, I waited. Luna opened the door a minute later, her eyes red-rimmed.

"Yo," I said. Which sounded horribly stupid.

She bypassed me, but I snagged her wrist. Her shoulder pressed against my chest.

I grumbled into her ear, "I'm sorry."

She froze in her spot, staring at an invisible dot on the opposite wall.

"I am. I do. I…" I shook my head. "I didn't mean it, last time we saw each other."

"Which part?" She looked up at me, her eyes a shade darker.

"The words. Only the words. Not the kiss." I did mean the kiss.

"Why are you still with Poppy, then?"

If nothing else, her directness was admirable.

"Because forgiving you comes with a price I'm not willing to pay," I admitted.

"I never asked you to forgive me."

I smiled tiredly. "See?"

She shook her head, slipping from me. From us.

But I wasn't ready. I wanted her tortured, not gone.

"Ride or die, Luna Rexroth," I yelled to her back. "You're my ride or die."

CHAPTER TWELVE
LUNA

There was nothing I wanted more than to avoid the Cole residence until I flew back to Boon, but I couldn't deny Rosie.

In her defense, she had pointed out in a text message that Knight wasn't going to be home. I felt stupidly grateful. Rosie's only request had been that I bring a blank notebook and a pen.

I showed up at her doorstep at six in the evening, wondering if Knight was with Poppy, then reminding myself I wasn't supposed to care. Lev led me to Rosie's bedroom upstairs. The Coles' mansion was a nod to everything soft and southern. The furniture was classily upholstered or painted khaki and beige, with iron and crystal chandeliers everywhere, a vintage pottery collection, and ivy covering the courtyard walls.

As I moved down the vast hallway, a nurse brushed past me, making a quick dash downstairs while rummaging in her bag. My heart twisted in pain. I wondered what it felt like to be just a job for some people.

People who were in charge of your fragile life.

I pushed the bedroom door open. Rosie sat on the throne of her bed, looking like death.

I took a step back as I absorbed the image of her gaunt figure and braced against the wall. I'd seen her on both Christmas Eve and Christmas Day, but she'd been wrapped in luxurious gowns and well-tailored coats that had hidden how thin she was. Her cheeks were sunken, her eyes rimmed with dark shadows. She motioned to me with her clubbed finger, holding a piece of used tissue.

"My darling girl." She smiled through what I could see was great pain.

Gingerly, I stepped into her realm, forcing myself to return a beaming smile. I was so wrapped inside my own heartbreak, I hadn't fully considered what Knight had had to deal with in my absence.

His mother was dying. That was the blunt, awful truth.

Rosie patted the space at the foot of her bed, and I perched on it, my eyes never leaving hers. She had all kinds of machines hooked up on her nightstand and an emergency button installed on the wall.

You have a nurse, I wanted to scream, to sob and collapse into her arms. *You never had a nurse before.*

But I'd die before making it more difficult for her.

"How are you?" I signed instead.

"I'm going through menopause." She stared skyward. Tears began to pool in her eyes.

I didn't know what to do. What to say. I hadn't been expecting that to come out of her mouth. Foolish and self-centered as I was, I thought she wanted to talk to me about Knight, about our obviously strained relationship.

"I'm too young for menopause."

Rosie wasn't one to dwell in self-pity, and she'd never once complained about her illness, so I wondered why menopause was the tipping point.

I put my hand on hers. Squeezed. "It's okay." Was it, though? "Does Dean know?" I searched her soft eyes.

She shuddered in a breath, nodding and wiping her tears with the tattered tissue, leaving clouds of it on her damp face. "Yes, but I don't talk to him about it. I don't talk to any of them about those things. I'm strong for my boys. But sometimes…" She bit her lower lip, her teeth shaking against it to the rhythm of her sobs. "Sometimes I need to break too."

"You can always break with me." I held myself together with everything I had, willing myself not to cry. "Tell me how I can help."

I meant it with a ferocity I didn't know I could feel. I wanted Rosie to get better, even if it was obvious she couldn't. She'd always been there for me—taking Knight and me on playdates and getting me out of my out-of-his-wits, then-single father's hands. She'd gifted me special editions of her favorite books on my birthdays—the number of books equal to the age I was celebrating—because she knew I valued her literary opinion. Growing up, when I'd had no clue what to do with my hair, she and Emilia—Vaughn's mother—had learned how to braid it because they knew how much I hated going in for an appointment with a stranger.

When Edie had stepped into the picture and took over, Rosie still came to braid my hair every few weeks, just to keep seeing me. "Havana twist or cornrows?" she'd asked. I'd always signed *cornrows*. "Good girl. That's the only thing I know how to do."

"Luna…" Rosie held my hand now. She stared at our laced fingers like she was committing the image to memory before it was too late.

I tried stopping the shudders rippling through my body, the tears that demanded to come out. How come my parents hadn't told me it was this bad? But of course they hadn't. I'd been so busy on *me-me-me* island, I never bothered to sail to other territories and check in on her. Sure, I'd asked. But why hadn't I called? Why hadn't I done more?

"I'm not sure how long I have," she admitted, "and I need your help regarding a few crucial matters."

I already hated the sound of this, because I knew whatever she was going to ask me to do would break my heart—and that I was going to do it without fail. Because she wasn't being melodramatic. She *was* dying.

I nodded.

"I need you to be there for Knight, even when he pushes you away. And he will push you away. He will do anything he can to make sure you don't see him break. But he will break—in outstanding fashion, as he does everything else," she chuckled.

Yes. I rubbed my thumb along her hand, back and forth. This one was easy. "Even if he pushes me away. Even if he refuses it. I will always be here for him."

"When the time comes," she said, flipping my hand over and staring at my palm contemplatively, "I want you to give him and Lev something very important. Something I want us to make together. Paid work, of course. And we don't have much time. It will require some writing from you."

"Writing?"

"You are a writer, are you not?" She smirked.

I wanted to be. I didn't know if I had it in me. But what better excuse to try—and to fail—than honoring Rosie's request?

"Anything," I stressed. "I'll do anything for you."

"It will require some back-and-forth emails. We don't have much time. It will be intense. Will it interrupt your studies?" Her expression turned cloudy.

"Anything, anything, anything." I shook my head, almost violently, squeezing my eyes shut. The hell with my studying. "What more? Tell me. Please. I'll do it."

"My final request is somewhat controversial but important nonetheless. I want you to do something very special for me, Luna. Something I can't ask from my sons for obvious reasons, but it would break my heart to know this wish was not fulfilled."

My heart was about to explode. I held my breath.

"I want you to make sure Dean moves on. He is far too young not to experience love again. He is far too beautiful, inside and out, not to be admired. I know my husband. He wants to be a martyr. To show me that he cares, that I was—am, *am*—" She coughed again, her voice strained. "—the only person for him. But it's a title I never claimed. I know his love for me is the Big Bang. I don't mind him settling on another quiet planet afterward. He needs to move on, Luna."

Dumbfounded, I blinked. Up until now, I'd agreed to do things that were up to me. I could fulfill this mysterious writing project, even if I had to spend sleepless nights and drop out of school. I would be there for Knight, even if he kicked me out, demeaned me, and fought against my attempts to make amends. But how could I convince my godfather, my dad's best friend, to fall in love again after losing his wife?

Rosie saw the doubt on my face and brought my hand to her beating heart. It beat so slow, I could barely feel its faint pulse.

"It's very easy, really. I know the way. Grab your notebook. I'm going to give you the play-by-play of how this is going to happen."

I took out the notebook and my seahorse pen, and I started writing.

"You're coming with, Saint Luna, and I really don't care that you'd rather skin a live elephant. It's about making a statement." Daria flung her lush, blond hair back, applying another layer of shiny lip gloss in front of my mirror.

New Year's Eve was my idea of hell, especially if it was celebrated with a wild party.

I was still shocked that Daria was here to begin with. In my house. In *my* room. Daria and I had never been close. I was too shy to try; she was too exasperated with my general weirdness to understand. We'd reached some kind of understanding when she moved away, but I still treaded lightly around her like she was a magical unicorn: with equal measures of fear and respect.

"Team Daria, woot woot." April pumped her fist from the

screen of my MacBook, on Skype. It felt surreal, having two genuine girlfriends. Not that they replaced the hole Knight had left in his wake. It was a different kind of friendship—less intense but entertaining all the same.

"So what's the plan?" April leaned forward, her gaze following Daria around my room, starstruck.

I couldn't blame her. Some girls were born to rule the world. Daria was painfully clearly one of them.

Daria plopped on the chair in front of my MacBook. "We go to the party, Knight sees Luna looking like a million bucks, and he dumps the English tart."

"That's not nice," I pointed out, shifting inside the red skater dress Daria had handed to me and insisted I wear.

"Oh my Marx, who claimed to be nice?" Daria stared at me, horrified. "What a mediocre goal to have in life."

April gave us two thumbs-up, nodding. "Yeah, dude, this chick is your ex's current girlfriend. You're not supposed to protect her. Why did you two break up, anyway? You never even said."

"Break up?" Daria lifted a perfectly plucked eyebrow.

No. No, no, no. I'd totally forgotten I'd told April this little white lie to cover for the fact that I was an emotional mess when I arrived at Boon.

Daria swiveled her head to me, screwing her pouty lips into a scowl. I thought of signing to April that Daria didn't know. Daria would get the hint. She wouldn't rat me out. But it didn't feel okay to lie to April anymore. She was a friend now.

"I'm sorry," I signed, my shoulders sagging. I really was.

April shook her head. "It's okay. We'll talk about it when we get back to Boon. Break a leg, Lu."

"I'll try not to."

"Oh, and, Lu?" April smiled, just as I was about to close the MacBook. "You're not the girl I met the first day we arrived at Boon. You're much stronger. Make sure he knows that."

The beach house where Daria was throwing the party belonged to one of her rich friends and sat on Huntington Beach. The owners were two architects who lived in Europe half the year. It looked like an elaborate fishbowl. The floors and walls were all made of glass. You could see the blond sand and tranquil ocean under your feet. The living room, huge and mostly empty, spilled onto a large deck with crystal bannisters. The only proof people inhabited the carefully designed space was the second floor I'd caught a glimpse of when we parked. There was some light furniture scattered around there.

Who could live in such a place?

"Stephannie!" Daria squealed as she hugged a girl who looked like the dark-haired version of her. They held each other for what seemed to be a century before disconnecting. Daria introduced us and told Stephannie (who pointed out that her name was spelled with a double N—why couldn't rich people just let normal names be?) that I couldn't talk, but I could hear and text, waving it off like it was hardly an issue.

And so, Stephannie didn't treat it as one. It was definitely refreshing.

"Where is Penn?" I asked Daria as we wandered to the deck, where she began arranging drinks on a long table.

She tossed her glossy hair, her signature move. "Oh, trying on suits with his friends in New York. He's taking the wedding thing uber seriously." She rolled her eyes, laughing.

"Don't you?" I panicked. One thing we could credit our parents for—they sure gave us good examples of how successful, happy marriages should look.

Daria shrugged, pouring champagne into tall, thin glasses with an accuracy that would make an AA counselor flinch. "I take the marriage seriously. The wedding? Not so much."

My eyes raked over her face, searching for clues. Daria was

one of the most materialistic people I knew, so hearing her say that surprised me.

She put the empty bottle of champagne on the table, popping open a new one.

"Look…" She turned to me. "When you find the one, all the other details blur together. I don't know what I want to wear when I wed him. I don't know what my hair is going to look like or how many guests I want to invite, or if I want a beach wedding or one in a fancy hotel or to elope in Vegas. All I know is that I want to be with Penn. Every hour. Every day. Every year. And that's enough for me. It's more than enough. It's everything. Don't you feel like that about Knight?" She cocked her head.

I wasn't so sure anymore. Our relationship was such a mess. He was torn apart by his mother's situation and me sleeping with someone else, and I was scrambling to become normal, finally out of my parents' nest, with banged-up wings and frayed feathers. We both had so much going on. Communicating effectively was not our strong point these days.

An hour later, the place was jam-packed. Vaughn came with a bunch of his artsy friends, skulking in the corner of the room. They looked much older and terribly worldly. Knight walked in with Poppy on his arm. She wore a canary-yellow minidress and a sweet smile. They were talking and laughing.

They looked happy.

Genuinely happy. I didn't know what had happened between the day before Christmas, at the shelter, and now. But whatever it was, they seemed to have overcome it. Overcome *me*. Maybe I needn't fulfill Rosie's wish after all. Maybe Poppy would be there to pick up the pieces so I didn't have to.

So I didn't *get* to.

"Don't look at him, and definitely don't say hello," Daria warned fiercely when she saw me looking.

I cradled my glass of champagne and glared at the wall. This wasn't me. I wasn't one to play games. Then again, Daria was now blissfully engaged to a guy who'd once made a promise to ruin her life and hated her guts but now adored the ground her fancy heels walked upon. I was morbidly single. She obviously had game, and I could use a few pointers.

Hours dragged. Music played. People laughed. When it became apparent that Knight and Poppy weren't going to acknowledge us, too engrossed in their own little universe, Daria dragged me to the dance floor and convinced me to shake my butt. It was nearing midnight, and the acute sense of time running out slammed into me.

"The plan isn't working," I complained to Daria as she twerked against my thigh, throwing her head back and forth to "Lollipop" by Lil Wayne. I felt like a broken Cinderella. My carriage was going to turn into a pumpkin soon, only this was not a fairy tale—more like a Halloween nightmare. I hated that Knight could see what I said if he wanted to. Even from across the room.

"Honey, making a guy jealous is like getting a fine ass. You have to work hard for it." She waved me off, twirling in place and sipping on her champagne. "Act like you don't care."

"I do care."

"Ugh, I know. Which is so awful, isn't it? Guys are trash."

We danced until my feet screamed in agony, threatening to fall off. The entire party seemed to pour itself onto the deck for the ten-second countdown welcoming the next year. Everyone stared at the dusky sky, dotted with stars, while holding their drinks. I realized to my horror that, other than myself and Daria, everybody was hugging a significant other they could kiss. Jesus Christ. How had I not noticed it before? We were going to look so pathetic.

Well, maybe not Daria. Daria had a famous fiancé with NFL plans in his future and an engagement ring any girl would murder for. Yup. This sounded like a classic *me* problem.

I spotted Knight and Poppy standing in the far corner of the area, his head bent as she whispered into his ear. A shudder ran through my spine like an earthquake. The countdown started. I couldn't unglue my eyes from them even though I knew I should. That the entire point of being there was showing Knight I didn't care.

"Ten!"

"Look at me, Luna. Not at them." Daria snapped her fingers in front of my face.

"Nine!"

"Jesus, Saint Lu. He wants you to react this way!"

"Eight!"

"Luna."

"Seven!"

"Luuuuuuunaaaa!"

"Six!"

"Don't make me do something crazy."

"Five!"

"Bitch, you're more basic than an android."

"Four!"

"Last warning, Rexroth."

"Three!"

"You asked for it."

"Two!"

"Actually, I always wanted to know…"

"One!"

I didn't have time to catch Knight dipping his head farther down to kiss Poppy. Daria clasped my chin, tilted my head in her direction, and pressed her lips against mine as claps and shouts erupted around us, fireworks exploding in the air and in the pit of my stomach. Her soft, warm lips crashed into mine, the flavor of her watermelon lip gloss invading my mouth. I groaned, not used to the pliability of kissing a girl. Or kissing in general. The only boys I'd ever kissed were Knight and Josh. And Vaughn, I guess, if you could count it.

God, why wasn't I stopping this? I let Daria deepen our kiss, my eyelids dropping shut of their own accord. She felt surprisingly good, and not just physically, which I guess was expected. When her tongue slid past my lips, I knew the shouts and barks around us were *because* of us. We had an audience. Daria always had an audience. Only tonight, she'd decided to put me in the spotlight to make a point.

I reciprocated, tonguing her mouth, shuddering at how hot and sweet the kiss was. I realized I'd changed. I was no longer the girl who hid behind her parents, and Knight, and Vaughn. I had desires. I was real. I was whole.

With and without Knight, I was complete.

Daria had stolen the attention from Knight—*my* attention from Knight—and forced him to pay attention to me. A genius move, if I really thought about it. Maybe that's why I cupped one of her cheeks as our tongues danced together, my eyes still closed, and felt both of us smiling into that kiss. A smile that spoke a thousand words we never said to each other:

Thank you for having my back.

Thank you for tonight.

Thank you for being the wonderful, crazy, ruthless you.

"All right, show's fucking over," a gruff voice grumbled, and I felt the fabric of my dress pulled back.

I didn't have to turn around to know it was Knight. Daria grinned my way, arching an I-told-you eyebrow. Her lips were swollen, pink, and puffy. Her normally perfect hair a tangled, sexy mess. God. We'd full-blown made out. I could still feel my heavy-lidded eyes and my pulse dancing across my lips.

I waved Knight off, giving Daria a hug. She squeaked in my arms, and we both shared a giggle. This was about friendship, not some stupid attention-grabbing moment.

Knight tugged me away again, gatekeeper that he was.

"Luna," he seethed.

"Oh, for fuck's sake." Daria rolled her eyes. "Not everything's about you, Cole. Although, I guess she's Saint Luna no more, huh?" Daria winked, ignoring the death glare Poppy tried to spear her with.

It was like Daria had injected some of her personality into me with that kiss. Maybe it was the adrenaline. Maybe it was the alcohol, or perhaps the attention and the way I was really growing tired of Knight refusing to let me move on while parading his girlfriend in front of me. In all probability, it was all of the above that made me do what I did.

I rolled my eyes, opened my mouth, and spat out actual words in front of everyone.

"You're not the boss of me! Not even a colleague. Not even an employee. Barely an acquaintance." A ruthless smile blossomed on my lips.

Daria sucked in a shocked breath. Knight stumbled back, pain written all over his beautiful face. Most of the nearby partygoers didn't know I couldn't speak, didn't know the significance of what I'd just done, so they just stared on, ready for some blood to be shed.

"When did you become such a bitch?" Knight narrowed his eyes at me.

Finally. *Finally*, we were doing what we should have done years ago: deal with our emotions. Let the anger, frustration, and lust out. Stop tiptoeing around one another, pretending like nothing had happened when so much had.

We'd fallen in love.

We'd fallen in lust.

We'd broken each other's trust.

I smirked the patronizing smirk he'd taught me very well as I strutted my way to the door. I flipped him the finger without looking back to watch his reaction.

"Since you made me one, KJC."

CHAPTER THIRTEEN
LUNA

Why had I asked for this?

Why had I *begged* for this?

Why had I put myself in this situation in the first place?

I blinked back at Edie, who had her face buried in her hands, her shoulders quaking.

Normally, she was strong for both of us.

Normally, she knew what to do.

But nothing about our situation was normal.

It terrified me that so much had changed in such a short period of time. My life had derailed from the endless straight line I'd been sailing along to a roller coaster with no beginning, middle, or end.

I was living in another state.

Knight hated me.

I hated Knight.

Rosie was dying.

I'd kissed a girl. And pardon the poor cultural reference, but I'd liked it.

I'd really liked it. Not enough to change teams—well, maybe… though the only person I'd really ever wanted was my best friend— but enough not to regret it. That was a complication I couldn't even focus on right now.

I'd broken a heart. Well, might've. Josh had stopped texting me. His unanswered messages were piled up in a neat corner of my phone's memory like broken dreams, hung on a clothesline, damp from my tears of guilt.

And now this. The indigestible news I somehow still needed to swallow. The report sat between Edie and me, on the table, waiting to be acknowledged.

I stood up, slapped my open palm on the table, and yelled, "No!" Only I didn't do that.

I darted up and paced from side to side in our kitchen, throwing my head back and letting out a rabid laugh. "Good riddance!" Only I didn't do that either.

I broke down in tears. I ran to my room. I felt. I *felt*. Or I wished I had.

In reality, I just sat there, staring at my mom. My *real* mom. The one who'd been there for me from the moment she knew of my existence. The one who counted. Edie.

"Is that all he's given you?" I whispered.

I hoped my voice would shock her into pulling herself out of her meltdown. It worked. She peeked at me between her fingers, then straightened in her seat, wiping the tears from her face.

"The private investigator?" She cleared her throat, trying to be cool.

I knew she would be cool about it. Knew she wouldn't make a big deal of it, make a show, make me feel uncomfortable.

I nodded.

"He said she'd been living in Rio for the past eight years with her mother. Worked a job selling knockoff perfumes at a mall down her block. No partner, no kids, no family. Had a cat named Luar. She seemed to have gone through a really dark time. She died of an overdose eighteen months ago."

My biological mother was dead.

I should feel devastated. I should feel free. I should *feel*, period. I poked my lower lip, tugging at it, not sure how to react.

Val was still my biological mother.

Also, the woman who gave me up.

The woman who'd screwed me *over*.

The woman who'd wanted to use me as a pawn.

But also the woman who named her cat Luar—*moonlight* in Portuguese.

Val wore many hats in my life. All of them had painted her in an ugly way. People were wrong. I wasn't Saint Luna. I was capable of hating too. I just didn't know it until now. Somehow, I stood up. Edie rose to her feet after me.

"You have a mother," she stressed, slapping her palm over her chest. "You have me, Luna. You'll always have me."

"I know." I smiled.

"Speak more." Her expression softened.

"I try. I've been trying my whole life. It's just that…when the words come out, they do it of their own accord."

"Don't you get it?" She held my arms, giving them a gentle shake.

She had a goofy, lopsided grin—one I'd catch on Dad when he looked at her lovingly. She'd always had the courage to look at me and not through me.

"You're free now. Free to speak. Free to talk. Free to be someone else, not the person she made you when she walked away."

"I know," I whispered.

But did I? What if this didn't free me? What if I was destined to speak in random bursts?

We both shifted from foot to foot. There was a major elephant in the room, and we needed to address it.

"Your dad needs to—"

"I'll tell him," I cut her off.

Yes. I knew what I had to do, what I was capable of doing. Val was no longer here to remind me my words didn't matter, that my voice held no weight. Edie was right. It was time to shed the dead skin of the person I was and to become someone else.

The person Knight needed.
The person Dad, Edie, and Racer deserved.
I was going to talk to Dad.
With words.

"Come in."

Dad looked up from the paperwork on his office desk, still clad in his suit. He shuffled some papers around for the sake of doing something with his hands, flashing me a tired smile. There was something pathologically wary about his expression when he looked at me nowadays. Love dipped in misery, wrapped in a bitter crust of pity.

Not disappointment, though. Never disappointment.

I closed the door behind me, moseying to the camel-colored leather armchair in front of him. I sank into it, the weight of what I was about to do pulling me down. Without breaking eye contact, my nails dug into the tender flesh of my palms until they pierced through my skin. I breathed through the pain.

I could do it. I'd done it with Knight. With Edie. At a party full of complete strangers.

But somehow, this was different.

My father had been tricked by Val. She got pregnant on purpose. He hadn't wanted me. Yet he had been forced to raise me on his own for the first few years of my life. And it hadn't been easy, with my lack of communication. They'd called him the Mute because he didn't speak much, but his daughter truly crushed him with misery over her lack of words.

"Is everything okay?" He furrowed his brows, seeming to realize the atmosphere in the room had shifted. Maybe that I'd shifted too.

I used to be dependent. Small. Scared. The last few months had changed me. And I was still evolving, changing like clay—spinning through tiny changes that made small yet significant differences in my life. Each dent shaped me.

I opened my mouth.

He dropped his pen.

My lips moved.

His eyes widened.

I smiled.

He listened.

"Not everything," I whispered, aware of the way my lips molded around the words.

Sadness laced in my victory. The only reason I was able to speak was because my birth mother had died. There was no reconciliation possible. I'd lost something permanently—but gained something else.

I reached for his hand across the desk, clutching it with shaky fingers. Free at last. The pen he'd been holding a second ago bled ink onto his new leather planner. I only noticed because everything was illuminated, like I was on ecstasy or something.

"I have a confession, Dad."

I wasn't sure how I expected him to react. My father had tried everything to get me to talk. I had award-winning speech therapists knocking on my door, the best psychologists and experts in the world at my disposal. I'd seen his back shake from weeping dozens of times when he thought I wasn't looking, as he mourned the words that never left my mouth.

Then, I wasn't ready. Now, I was.

"Luna…" He put a shaky hand to his mouth.

I dragged my hand from his, fanned my fingers on his desk. "Val died," I said.

"How do you…"

"I asked Edie to hire someone to investigate. I'm so sorry, Dad. I didn't mean to hurt you. I needed to know."

He made a sudden move. The bleeding pen rolled across the

desk and dropped onto the carpet. He shook his head, paused for a second, then stood up, rounding his desk and yanking me to my feet. His eyes bore into mine, saying so many things he'd bottled over the years. I thought he was going to hug me, but to my astonishment, he got down on his knees, staring up at me, his eyes twinkling.

"You're talking." He looked puzzled.

I laughed. I actually laughed, which was horrible, seeing as my moment of greatness was tainted by the death of my biological mother. But then I started crying too. Tears ran down my cheeks, following one another along my neck, soaking my shirt. Talk about bittersweet moments.

"I mean…are you?" His throat worked. "Talking?"

"To some people." Guilt, guilt, guilt. Piles upon piles of messy, black, foggy guilt.

"Some?"

"You. Edie. Knight."

"Since when?"

"Since…a few weeks ago."

"Luna," he whispered.

"Dad."

"Say it again."

"Dad." I smiled. He closed his eyes. Took a deep breath.

"*Again?* Please."

"Dad."

His shoulders shook. Not with sobs. With happiness. Happiness I'd put inside him. I was drunk on my newfound power.

"Tell me again." His voice was soft.

The pen behind him spread blue ink all over the lush crème carpet.

"Dad. Trent. Mr. Rexroth. *Father*." I wiggled my brows, and he opened his eyes, laughing. The crow's feet fanning around his eyes squished up his entire face adorably.

"What about your brother?"

"What about him?"

He gave me a *really?* look, and I pulled him to standing. I buried my face in his chest, inhaling him. I hated that he looked like a man who'd just been released from prison. Happier. Lighter. I'd sentenced him to a reality he hadn't wanted, caged him into a situation he'd struggled with every day.

"I'll try. I…I don't control it, Dad. It's not like that. Yet. I'm sorry." I swallowed. "Aren't you…mad?"

"Which part should I be mad about? The fact that my daughter wanted to understand her past better and I obviously failed her if she felt she couldn't ask me about her birth mother, or the fact that you've just given me the only thing I've truly wanted since the day you stopped talking?"

"The first one. Definitely the first one." I laughed.

Melancholy dripped between us. This was the big moment. The top of the hill. Me, talking to my dad, telling him I knew my mother was dead. He didn't look surprised. Why didn't he look surprised?

Ever the mind reader, he cleared his throat and looked down.

"You knew about Val," I said. There was no accusation in my voice.

He nodded. "It seemed redundant to bring her up after all these years. Plus, she hurt you in such a vital way, I couldn't bring myself to think what would happen if—"

"It's okay," I cut him off. I got it. I did.

"God." He shook his head, pulling me into another hug. "Your voice. It's beautiful."

"I love you," I whispered into his suit. My words had life, and weight, and a pulse. I said them again. "I love you, Dad. I love you. I love you. I love you."

He lifted me up like I was a little girl, spinning me in place and burying his nose in my hair. Tears rolled down our faces. The pen bled the last of its ink, marking this page in our lives forever in my father's office. I knew, with certainty that made my heart swell, that he was not going to replace that carpet.

He was going to look at it every day, remember the day it had happened, and cherish it.

"I love you too, baby girl."

CHAPTER FOURTEEN
KNIGHT

"There's an Emergen-C pack and Advil on the kitchen counter. You know your way around, and if you need anything, ask Vaughn. Or call. You can call me too."

Emilia, Mom's older sister and Vaughn's mother, practically shoved me out the door, delving through paper bags for all the shit she'd brought Mom. She looked tired, worried, and secondhand sick. I spat phlegm into one of the plants by our door, ignoring the pulsating heat radiating from my body.

"Remind me why I'm getting kicked out of my own house again?"

"You spiked a fever last night. You're not well, Knight. You know you can't be here next to her."

"Fine. I'll take the guest room downstairs. I won't go anywhere near Mom."

"*I'll* be taking the guest room."

Emilia finally plucked a pack of chips from a bag. Salty snacks were good for Mom. She'd lost a lot of sodium. "I want to take care of my sister. Besides, even if you took the downstairs bedroom, you still have the flu. You're a germ-ball, excuse my bluntness."

I shrugged. "Been called worse."

"I promise I'll keep you updated. I made you some chicken noodle soup. It's in a container near the other provisions. I'll ask your uncle to report back if you haven't touched it, so no funny business. Don't worry, honey. She'll get well."

"She can't get well." I smiled bitterly, my eyes darkening. "We both know that, Aunt Em."

Emilia's throat bobbed with a swallow. She looked down. Why did people do that? Look down when things got too real? What was on the ground that was so fascinating, other than my mother's impending grave?

"But she can get worse," Aunt Em whispered.

She stepped into the house then, pushing the door closed in my face before pausing. "Oh, and I'm not sure what your current status is, but if you've decided to pull your head out of your butt and you're swinging by Luna's, please send her my condolences and let her know I'm here if she needs me."

I was midstride when I turned around sharply, pushing the door back open.

"Condolences?" I could feel my eyeballs dancing in their sockets.

Emilia dropped her paper bags, peaches and garlic rolling on the floor.

Our parents had refused to get the memo that Luna and I were no longer BFFs or whatever bullshit term they called us. But that didn't bother me as much as the notion that something bad had happened. Condolences meant one thing.

"What's going on?" I braced my arm against the door, making sure she knew she couldn't get rid of me before she explained herself.

I was burning like a thousand angry suns on their galactic period. The fever had come out of nowhere. Vaughn said it was probably because I'd nearly combusted watching Luna make out with Daria the other night.

When Aunt Emilia didn't answer immediately, I stepped back into the house, ignoring my general dizziness. Getting into her face, I bared my teeth.

"Speak."

I knew if Uncle Vicious ever found out I'd behaved even mildly aggressively with her, he'd castrate me and make dangling earrings out of my balls for his pretty wife.

Emilia's jaw tightened. "Step back, *boy*," she growled.

Maybe she didn't need Uncle Vicious to make the earrings for her.

I decided to step back because it was the quickest way to make her talk.

"Her birth mother, Val, died."

"Jesus." I covered my mouth, running my palm along my face. "How is she coping?"

Moonshine was entirely unpredictable when it came to Val, so I didn't know the level of devastation I was dealing with here. I just knew she'd been looking for Val, and now she'd found her—probably not in the state she needed her to be.

"I thought you could fill me in. Edie hired a private investigator, and that's what he came back with." Emilia frowned. "How do you not know this, Knight? You used to be like siblings."

Siblings, my ass. I needed to see Luna. Now.

Hold on a second—did I? Because last time we hung out, she'd yelled at my ass.

Yeah.

No.

I needed to.

Crisis trumped anything else. Even my mansion-sized ego.

Fuuuck.

She quickly amended. "Soul mates."

"Thanks for making it creepy."

"She needs you."

"Tough luck."

I could be a stubborn motherfucker. *So no, then? Not going to Luna?*

Shit. I needed a fortune cookie or something to make the decision for me.

"This can't be about a little college fling. What really happened, Knight?"

Everything. Everything happened.

Luna had moved on. I'd stayed behind. Mom got sicker. Dixie was healthy and pushy and depressingly alive. Apparently, God had a twisted sense of humor, and the joke was on me.

Emilia cupped my cheeks, pulling me closer. I was over a head and a half taller, but she still looked every inch the person in charge between us. It was in her eyes. They were like the ocean on a perfect summer day. Flat and blue and calmer than anything life could throw at them.

"You're so stubborn. So…tunnel-visioned. You're such a…"

"Cunt?" I offered indifferently.

"A *guy*." She bit her barely contained smile. "We always thought we were going to have girls, Rosie and me."

I couldn't help but smirk, mainly because all they had were boys. And we were about the most testosterone-filled creatures in the history of mankind. Sometimes I wondered if I had blood or jizz in my veins.

"Sorry to disappoint. Then again, I was adopted. Mom, at least, had a choice."

"There was never any doubt you were a Cole, Knight. You weren't a choice; you were destiny."

I waved her off. Mom and Emilia had the tendency to go full-blown *This Is Us* on my ass when I brought up the A-word (adoption). I never understood why they were so butthurt about it. It wasn't like *they'd* fucked some random and given me away.

"Speaking of adoption, are you sure your son is yours? Because you're like oil and water." I tried to disconnect from her embrace, but the Leblanc sisters, for all their tininess, cuddled like Olympic wrestlers.

"Yup. I have four stretch marks to prove it."

"I bet he carved his name on the walls of your uterus too, warning off any potential future siblings. The bastard."

Aunt Em laughed, her bright blue eyes shimmering with joy. She had Mom's laugh, and I could already see myself making her laugh when Mom wasn't around anymore, just to get a taste.

"What's so funny?" I frowned, finally managing to pull back.

"I bet you didn't mean to say the uterus thing out loud."

Shit. "Sorry. My filters are broken."

"Your manners too. You know I love you like a son, but you need to get your butt out of here." She smacked said butt lightly.

I did. I knew that. But I was feeling particularly loyal to Mom and particularly vindictive about the rest of the world.

"I only have one mother."

———————

Burning.

I was burning.

Like a nice, hot vacation in hell.

I woke up with my blanket sticking to my body, glued by cold sweat. Everything was so wet, for a second I thought I'd pissed the bed. I ran a hand over my head and found my hair soaking, like I'd just gotten out of the shower.

I slid out of the bed in the Spencers' guest room, still clad in my black Tom Ford sweatpants, and grabbed my joint and a lighter from the nightstand. I slipped my socked feet into a pair of slide sandals. I didn't bother putting on a shirt. I headed to the kitchen for a glass of water before going on the porch for a smoke, but once I was out of bed, I continued past the kitchen to the front door, tossing it open like a moonstruck monster.

Any more bad ideas, ass face?

Fresh blood pumped in my veins as I climbed up to Luna's window for the first time in months, a fucked-up Romeo in a story that was definitely a comedic tragedy. She'd made it clear she wanted nothing to do with me. And I'd made it clear I didn't care.

I wasn't done throwing Poppy in her face every chance I got. But it didn't matter. Emilia was right. Luna needed me. I refused to believe we were two strangers with a past, that our miles-long memories were nothing, that our first kisses were nothing, that the way we molded around each other was nothing, that our blood oath wasn't worth shit.

Her window was locked, as I expected it to be after everything that had gone down between us, and the curtains drawn together. I knocked once. Twice. When she didn't answer, I took a deep breath, looked away, and drove my fist into it. I knew the window was double glazed and I'd need more than a punch to break it, but the loud thud was enough to let her know I wasn't playing.

Luna rushed to the window, throwing the curtains open and frowning at me, heat dancing in her eyes.

"I just thought about *Romeo and Juliet*, and I remembered…" I swayed back and forth, losing my balance on her roof. *Shit.*

She probably thought I was drunk, not dying. I was the boy who'd cried wolf. Or, you know, tequila.

I braced on the edges of her window and continued. "And I remembered that Juliet told Romeo not to swear by the moon. Do you know why she did that, Luna? Do you know? Because I do."

We'd studied the play last year in English Lit. That Shakespeare dude was majorly depressing. I studied Moonshine's horrified face as it morphed from pity to anger in the span of a heartbeat.

"She told him not to swear by the moon because the moon changes, Luna!"

No answer.

"*You* changed on me, even though we were in this together. You never ever let me have a say. I stayed the same, and you just…you just changed!"

She stood there staring, like I was a fucking off-Broadway show. Mildly interested. Mostly terrified. Definitely waiting for the punch line.

"Let me in," I croaked, ignoring the shivers coursing through my body.

She shook her head at that. Sadistically, almost.

"No, huh?"

I made myself comfortable, parking my ass on her roof and fishing in my sweatpants pocket for my joint and a light. Might as well. She wasn't going to back down, and I sure as hell wasn't going back home before I knew she was okay.

"Give me one good reason." She crossed her arms over her chest. It was the first time I noticed what she was wearing. Or lack thereof. Holy fuck. A tiny, orange nightgown, the hem made of lace. An actual piece of lingerie. Who'd given it to her? Who did she wear it for?

None of your goddamn business.

"What's with the nightgown?" I asked around my joint, lighting it up. My tone was notably more cheerful. Flu and fever be damned, my cock already felt better. I would give up national security secrets for the opportunity to see the outline of Luna's nipple. Seeing her half-naked felt like all my birthdays crammed into one.

"Daria gave it to me for Christmas."

I made a mental note to make a voodoo doll of my blond neighbor and punch it in the tits. I puffed on my joint and stared at the sky, thinking about what to say next.

"Knight, what are you doing here?"

"I heard about Val." I exhaled in a thick cloud of smoke.

"I'm fine," she said.

I remembered how she felt about the damn word but couldn't help but agree with her—she didn't seem upset. But maybe Val was just an excuse. Maybe I just couldn't stay away.

I cocked my head. "Open the window."

"Does your girlfriend know you're paying me a late-night visit?"

"Does *yours?*" I blurted, exhibiting my fine, toddler-aged maturity.

I hadn't even seen Poppy since New Year's Eve. She was still sulking about the tantrum I'd pulled at the party because of Luna and Daria. When I'd told her I was sorry it couldn't work out between us, she'd said she just needed time to get over it. That *we* were not over. Chick was more persistent than an STD. Not that I was comparing. Some STDs were treatable. Point was, she had plenty of girlfriends and a sister who made Lucifer look like a Care Bear. Couldn't one of them convince her I was a bad idea? Even *I* knew my boyfriend game was trash.

"Wow. You're a piece of work."

"A piece of work who *worked* his entire life protecting your ass." I smirked around my joint. "Open up."

She closed the curtains. Apparently, tough love wasn't the way into New Luna's heart. You live, you learn.

"Moonshine." Just to be an ass, I tossed the joint toward the Spencers' artificial pond across the lot before banging my fist on the window again. "Please."

"Why?" came her muffled voice from behind the curtains.

"Because you need me right now."

She let out a yelp that was supposed to be a laugh.

"*Fine*. Because *I* need *you*."

She didn't say anything to that. *Interesting*. Was this the angle I'd been looking for? I elaborated quickly.

"I have the flu. And I *don't* have a shirt. And I'm living with the Spencers. Doctor's orders because of Mom…"

She pulled the curtains and cracked the window open, taking a sidestep to let me in. I slid into her room, inspecting it first, wary that it had changed somehow, just like she had. I let out a sigh of relief when I found everything in the same place. Even our pictures. That was the first thing I looked for.

"Jesus Christ, Knight, you're shaking. Why are you shirtless?" She snapped out of her anger and finally got the picture. Luna put her tiny, warm hand on my chest. I shivered against it. I looked down. My skin was full of goose bumps, and even I had to admit, I was on the corpse-looking side.

"Look at me," she gasped, taking my face in her hands. "Knight, you are completely blue. It's freezing outside."

I tried to laugh it off. "It's SoCal, Moonshine. I think I'm fine."

"I'm running you a hot bath."

"Your dad will know I'm here."

"Who cares!" she boomed. "Take off your watch."

I set my watch on the nightstand as Luna dashed out of her room, leaving me to stand there and process the fact that going outside shirtless in January, in the middle of the night, in the desert, with a serious case of the flu and a fever wasn't one of my finest life decisions. She came back ten minutes later, with a huge towel draped over her forearm, and dragged me down the hallway.

"I don't need you to take care of me," I whisper-shouted, digging my heels into the marble floor. I'd come here to take care of *her*, for Christ's sake.

"I'm not offering. I'm stating." She practically bared her teeth.

When we got into the bathroom, the bathtub was full of hot water, steam curling out of it like it was a cup of tea or something.

"Shouldn't people with fever get lukewarm baths?"

"It's not that hot."

I chanced another look at the tub. "I'm going to get third-degree burns from that shit." I pointed at it, shaking my head. "Nuh-uh. I'm going to look like Two-Face if I dip half my body in."

"You're getting in," she informed me.

"No, I'm n—"

She took off her nightgown. Just like that. The entire thing.

No bra. Just a pair of white cotton panties. Her nipples staring back at me. Dark and tiny and pebbled and *fuck*.

Dear Santa,

I always knew you were real. Thank you for giving me the gift I wanted, even if it's three years and one week late.

Yours,

KJC

She lifted one ridiculously toned leg over the ceramic of the bathtub and got in, but she was still standing. I took in everything, inking it to memory. Luna had actual abs from surfing and riding her bike. Her tits were small but full—they'd look perfect in my palms. Slender arms. Sleek all over. She looked like a fantasy. A sweet torture.

She reached her hand out to me. "Together," she whispered.

Cunning little thing, she knew I'd bathe in lava if it meant touching her. Growling, I yanked down my sweatpants, staying in my briefs. (I didn't want to scare her away. I wasn't being funny—my dick was so big, at this point I called it Knight Senior and myself Knight Junior.)

I stepped in with her. She put her hands on my shoulders and lowered me so we both sat down, facing each other. My theory proved to be correct. Girls were cold-blooded. The water was boiling. I shook inside it, thawing slowly. I looked down. I could see the veins under my normally tan skin, like thick ropes. Everything looked fragile, pale, unfinished. I was as sexy as a lizard.

(Yet she was still nearly naked.)

"Your lips are purple."

She took a loofa, dipped it in the water, and started rubbing my chest. It felt illegally soothing, and I couldn't help but moan.

(By the way, she was still nearly naked.)

I was proud of myself for not coming in my briefs. Knight Senior hadn't gotten the memo that the rest of me was dying and decided to sport a freaky hard-on that threatened to tear the fabric it was stretched against.

"Did you take anything for the cold?"

"Yeah. Two Advil."

She was *still* mostly naked. Did I mention that? Her tits. Her cute belly button. Her endless legs. All in my face. Incredible.

"I'll make you some tea," she said.

"I hate tea."

"You'll drink tea."

"Give me one good reason to."

"I'm asking you nicely."

I gave her a do-we-know-each-other? look.

She rolled her eyes. "I'll let you touch my boob."

"Nipple too. I don't want any side-boob action. That doesn't count."

"Fine!" She threw her arms in the air, exasperated but smiling.

"Sold." I smirked.

She leaned forward, advancing toward me.

I stopped breathing altogether. I wanted to ask what she was doing, but the smart part of my brain—a tiny, neglected corner I saved for family trivia nights—told me not to say anything in case she didn't notice she was doing it. She wrapped her arms around my neck, and our chests pressed together.

Her.

Bare.

Tits.

On.

My.

Chest.

My dick throbbed between us in the water, and all I needed to do—all I *wanted* to do—was remove the thin fabric of our underwear and drive home, screwing FUCKING JOSH out of her. She nestled her head in the crook of my neck and sighed.

"I've missed you," she whispered.

"I've missed us," I admitted brokenly, my heart crumbling inside my chest.

What the hell was wrong with me? Why couldn't I be an asshole, like Vaughn? Why did I have to crumble at the first sign of her vulnerability?

I chugged the stupid tea and passed out, Luna by my side. For the first time since we'd known each other, she was the one holding me, and not vice versa. We were both mostly naked, in only our underwear, her body pouring heat into mine.

I tossed, turned, and sweated out my fever the entire night, my eyes closed, the rest of me awake. Thinking, wishing, *willing* myself to sweat Luna out of my system the way I did the fever but knowing damn well that some syndromes were incurable, and she was one of them.

The next morning, I woke up groggy and disoriented. Luna brought me clear broth, tea, and two Advil. Then she sat at her desk and refused to look away until I'd consumed all of them. I still felt like shit, but better.

She stood up as soon as I was done with the tea, moving for the door. "I'm going to go grab a shirt for you from my dad's closet. I don't want you to walk around shirtless, even if it's just to Vaughn's house."

"Not so fast." I held up a hand.

She stopped at the threshold, turning around to me.

"Your tit"—I pointed at her nightgown-covered chest—"and I have a date. Now, I have no actual preference for which tit you're giving me, but I drank two teas and that broth that tasted like sewer water. I think that qualifies for something."

"For what?" She crossed her arms across her chest, raising an eyebrow.

"Sucking your nipple."

"Dream on."

"Dreams are just our reality on hold, Moonshine."

Hesitating, she peeked into the hallway, then closed the door behind her, locking it for good measure. I crooked a finger in her direction, coaxing her to come closer to the edge of the bed, where I sat. She took measured, careful steps, stopping about a foot from me. I could hear her heart beating. Or maybe it was mine.

Silently, she slipped off the straps of her nightgown, letting it slide down her thighs. Her body was glorious. Curvy everywhere, with a flat stomach and wide hips. I leaned forward and reached for her, hooking my arm around her lower back and jerking her to me. Her abs were in my face. I looked up at her. She was breathing fast and heavy.

"How far can I take this?" I murmured into her navel, my tongue playing peekaboo and darting into it for a delicious stroke. Her throat bobbed.

Beat.

Beat.

Beat.

"Well, you won," she finally groused.

Fuck yes I did.

Tentatively, I pressed my hot, pierced tongue over her hip bone, slowly dragging it up her stomach. She shivered and tried to pull back, but my hands slid from her lower back to her ass, cupping it to keep her pressed against my face.

When I reached her breasts, I traced the outline of her right tit with my tongue before pressing my piercing to her nipple and playing with it, sucking and tugging with my teeth.

"Ah," she shuddered against my face, and I hungrily swirled my tongue around her puckered nipple, again and again, until her thighs shook and clenched.

"Knight," my name fell off her lips like a broken prayer.

She yanked my hair. I was still sick, my head still pounding like a drum, but I could be in the middle of open-heart surgery and still suck her nipples like it was my job.

Her sweet cunt taunted me, and I moved to tease her other nipple, sucking on it hard and slow, building pressure, wondering if I could get away with more. She was moaning, raking her fingers over my hair and back, when I started rubbing her ass cheek with my thumb, back and forth, casually moving my hand to the front. It took me a few minutes to gather up the courage to dip my hand between her thighs and press it against her panty-covered pussy. Even though I still worked her nipples, I held my breath, knowing she was going to shoo me away in a second.

Only…she didn't.

Her thighs opened up for me in silent approval, and I fell backward to the bed, taking her with me. I kissed her everywhere but her mouth—not because I didn't want to devour her but because I was sick. I still had my hand between her legs possessively, even though I didn't exactly do anything about it yet. I just didn't want to retreat. It was a parking space in downtown LA—I'd worked hard for this spot.

Moonshine was on top of me, tilting her head to the side and letting me kiss her neck, shoulders, and tits, when I figured out the best way to get my fingers in her cunt would be to flip us over. So I did. Now I was on top. I shoved my big palm into her small panties, dipped one finger into her pussy, and it was so wet and warm, I wanted to die inside it.

"You're dripping," I breathed. It almost sounded like a cry.

She bucked her hips toward my hand, and I started fingering her, my dick pulsating against my briefs with every kiss and thrust.

I had Luna Rexroth in my bed. Well, technically, her bed. My fingers inside her pussy. Hot and sticky. Naked, save for the panties, which I nudged aside. The unlikely scene barely even registered, even before she did the unthinkable.

She put her hand on my dick through my briefs, curling her fingers around it.

"Please don't do that," I groaned into her neck, rubbing her clit with my thumb faster and faster. I was pretty darn proud of myself for finding the clit right from the get-go, seeing as how I'd never fingered a chick. I felt the little nub and went to town on it. All the shit I knew about sex, I'd learned from porn, so I knew the clit was the end game and that torturing her with fingering was stage one in chain-orgasms-landia. I did it all by the book. I was a good student, but I had no experience to think of, because I'd been waiting for her.

Only she hadn't waited for me.

Nope. Your brain's not gonna go there right now, asshole.

"Why not? Am I doing it wrong?" she half moaned, half pleaded.

A lot of football groupies begged for my cock, but it always sounded needy and annoying. It felt like a song coming from Luna's mouth. Not a shitty song. Not something by Katy Perry. A classic. Dare I say it? An Elvis Costello song.

"Everything you do is perfect, Moonshine, but I don't wanna come in my briefs."

"Why not? Is it bad?"

I shook my head, sucking on her nipple. We were so inexperienced. So clueless. *This.* This was what I wanted. To figure it all out together. And even though I had the notion that coming in my pants was not the studliest trick in the book, I couldn't hold back.

"Oh, fuck. Fuck." Without thinking, I took her hand and shoved it into my briefs. Her little fist wrapped around the silky, hot length of me immediately, and she gasped.

"That's what you do to me, Luna Rexroth."

"I love it."

I love you.

Of course, I wasn't dumb enough to say this. Not when we were in a compromising position and she wouldn't believe the words.

Her hips began to buck and grind against me, and her eyes popped open in shock. "I think I'm…"

Coming.

She was coming. I could see it on her face. The way her eyes rolled back and she let out little frantic, throaty moans that almost broke my dick in half from all the blood rushing through it.

Smugness spread across my chest like hot wax. It was so pathetic that this was the first orgasm I'd given someone other than myself. It was even more pathetic that by the astonished look on her face, I could see Josh hadn't been so successful in hitting the big O, and that made me stupidly, ridiculously, tragically happy.

She came all over my fingers at the same time I came all over her hand in my briefs. I'd never come so hard in my life. I was pretty sure I lost a pound or three in the process. I just came and came and came, the stream never-ending. And she was still holding my hard cock in her fist. I pulled my fingers out slowly, still staring her dead in the eyes. Her heavy-lidded eyes flared when I slurped every single drop of pussy juice from my hand.

"You're insane," she whispered contently.

"I'm going to eat your cunt until you go numb with orgasms," I quipped, serious as a heart attack.

It took us a few minutes to pull our shit together and get dressed. Luna combed her hair with her hands, cleared her throat, and dashed toward the door.

"Okay. Yeah. So. The tea and the broth. Oh, and the Advil. Coming right up."

"Moonshine?"

"Yeah?"

"You already did all those things." I motioned to the Advil pack and empty bowl and mug sitting on her desk. "You were going to get me a shirt."

"Of course," she mumbled. "I knew that, obviously."

Flustered, she made a beeline to the door, bumping into a wall on her way out. She took her phone with her before she left the room, throwing an accusing look my way. I stayed in her bed, sniffing the scent of her pussy on my fingers and replaying what had just happened on a loop. Her nipples against my tongue. Her clit swelling against the pads of my fingers. I stretched, patting the nightstand for the Cartier I'd removed before I got into her bath yesterday. My hand rested on something. An envelope? A letter?

I knew a repeat offense of getting into her shit was going to get me kicked out of her life for good, so I practiced self-control. I reached for my watch. There. Good boy. But as I did, I couldn't help but notice FUCKING JOSH's name on the sealed envelope.

She writes him letters now?

I flung up, ramrod straight, grabbing the letter. Self-control my ass. This wasn't a goddamn chocolate cake. The letter was already sealed, so I had to work with what I had. I angled the envelope toward the rays of sun drifting in the window, as far away from me as possible, reading the text through the somewhat transparent, thin paper. I couldn't make out much, but here's what I did read clearly:

"...and I want you to know that, of course, I love you."

Of course, she loved him.

Of course.

She loved him, and if I wasn't careful, I was going to *hate* her.

Something came to me then. A switch flipped in my brain. Luna and I were never going to be even as long as I was still holding my bullshit V-card for her. We weren't equal.

FUCKING JOSH was always hovering over our head, just like Poppy.

Only difference was, I knew I would drop everything and be with her. I couldn't say the same about Luna—especially with this fucking love letter to another guy in my hand...

Fury crackled in my veins so hot it burned past my skin. My jaw locked, and I felt my teeth grinding. She *loved* him. I'd drunk her pussy juice like it was the nectar of the gods, and she pined for him, still.

As a friend.

As a lover.

Who the fuck cared?

Were they going to bump uglies as soon as she returned to Boon? There's no way she would wait for me. She hadn't before...

I merely passed her time until she got on a flight back home.

She must feel high and mighty too, since she wasn't exclusive with FUCKING JOSH and wasn't technically cheating. I was. I was a goddamn cheater, something I hated with a passion.

No matter how pissed I was, this time I wasn't going to be a pussy about it. I didn't bail. I didn't throw a fit. I just placed the envelope right where it belonged, pulled my sweatpants on, and waited for the stupid-ass shirt.

When Luna came back, I thanked her for the tea, the shirt, the soup, and the Advil. I kissed her nose, smiled, and got the hell out.

I was going to kill Luna with kindness.

And dance all over the grave of our friendship.

CHAPTER FIFTEEN
LUNA

I spent the rest of my week either with Rosie or in the tree house, working on Rosie's project. Guilt gnawed at my gut for not telling Knight about what I was doing with his mom, about how she thought she wasn't going to survive much longer.

There were better, nicer places to be than in the tree house. But I went there because sometimes, in the afternoons, Knight would show up with a six-pack of Bud Light. Although I could talk now, he still hadn't asked for my words and was content with silence. I'd drink a beer. He'd drink five. He'd stare into the woods. I'd write and erase. Delete and rip papers from my notebook, working on his project unbeknownst to him.

He didn't ask me what I was doing.

I didn't ask him about Poppy.

I also didn't ask if we could do the things we'd done in my room again, even though it was pretty much all I could think of other than my Rosie project.

I could practically envision Daria hitting me with her straightener for spending time with him, for letting him into my panties while he had a girlfriend. Hell, I hadn't even let him kiss me when he *didn't* have one.

The one thing I did tell him, breaking the silence once, was that I was flying back to Boon at the end of the week.

"Bummer." He burped, throwing an empty beer bottle through the window and watching as it dunked right into the front basket of my bike. He'd smirked to himself. "Have fun there with FUCKING JOSH."

It was like we'd never shared that moment in my bed. That intimacy. I tried to remind myself what I'd been told about him by his own mother—what I knew about him firsthand: Knight didn't show vulnerability. He was so deeply wounded by being constantly on the verge of being an orphan that he stuck his chin out and hid the pain.

When he felt threatened, he pushed people away. But he needed me.

"How long are you going to punish me, Knight?" My eyes blurred with the fresh tears that clung to my lower lashes. "How much longer are we going to dance this twisted tango?"

He bent his head down, plucking a fresh beer from the pack. He'd been drinking so much lately, I could hardly tell when he was sober.

"I don't know, Moonshine." He'd cracked the beer open, downing it in one chilling gulp. "I hope we find out soon."

"Did Uncle Dean ever hurt you?" I asked Rosie the next day, furiously writing in my notebook.

She'd given me some great notes today, notes I was going to dig into later, notes that reminded me how deeply entwined my life was with Knight's.

Rosie looked like I'd just asked her if the sun was hot.

She burst out laughing, not even bothering to hide her delight. I felt my cheeks heat, watching as she began to cough, a barking sound that made me wince.

She was loud, but I didn't worry. Knight and Lev were never

here when I stopped by. She wanted the project to be a secret, and I understood why. No son wanted to know his parent had lost hope she'd make it to celebrate his next birthday. No son deserved to know his mother was contemplating the eternal, dreadful question: How do you tell your children goodbye?

"Can you elaborate?" I blinked.

She sat back, blowing a lock of hair from her eyes. "Where do I begin? Oh, yes. Dean dated my sister, for one thing. *And* took her virginity."

I gasped, which only made her laugh harder.

"Emilia's?" I signed.

She nodded. "Bet you didn't see that one coming, huh, kiddo?"

"But he loved you!" I frowned, my hands moving fast.

I was thoroughly outraged. I knew Uncle Dean and Aunt Emilia had been a thing for half a second in high school. I didn't know they'd been so serious, or how Rosie had gotten over it.

How would I react if Knight had slept with Daria? I'd kill them both, that's how, and Daria wasn't even my sister. Yet I'd kissed Vaughn. Hell, I'd kissed Daria too. I was no less responsible for the pain distribution in my relationship with Knight than he was. My sins were just more...*casual*. Spontaneous. I hadn't meant to hurt him, but that didn't mean I hadn't.

"Hmm...let's see. Then he spent the next decade or so—give or take—bedding anyone with a pulse, besides me, of course." Rosie tapped her smiling lips. "Threesomes. He was big on threesomes. We were neighbors for a while, and he always had a few girls go up to his apartment. I'd meet them in the elevator, warn them off about his mysterious STD that turned groins green. He wasn't impressed." She snorted.

"How could you forgive him?" I signed.

I was half-angry that she had at this point. Who was I kidding? Maybe even fully. Dean Cole had done a ton of threesomes. I don't know why it surprised me. He did have a wild streak about him. But he was so…so…in love with Rosie. From the moment he was born, it seemed.

"How could I not?" Now it was her turn to look angry. "You only get one life, Luna. One stab at this thing called happiness. Why deprive yourself of things you want just because they weren't given to you the way you hoped for them to come? Life is like a book, a long chain of scenes threaded together by circumstances and fate. You never know how thick or thin your book is, so you better make the most out of every scene, enjoy each chapter."

"But Uncle Dean—"

"Didn't pay?" She arched an eyebrow, grinning. "Did he not, though? Didn't he chase me around like a lovesick puppy? Get blackmailed by Uncle Vicious? Marry me knowing I might not have children? Commit to me knowing he would almost definitely outlive me? What about his sleepless nights for the past six years? The hospital visits? The emotional toll? The fact I am going to make our children orphans? Yeah." She patted my hand, like I was a precious, naïve thing. "If you think you've found something good without anything bad in it, it just means you haven't examined it close enough."

When we'd finished, I rode to our tree house with my head almost hitting the front basket. The weight of my decision slumped my posture. I wasn't going to tiptoe around Knight's intentions anymore. Rosie was right. Life was unbearably, excruciatingly short. I wanted to be with Knight. He needed to know that before I flew back to Boon. He needed to know that I loved him.

But also that I was done being the other woman.

I wanted to be the *only* woman.

Yes, I had slept with someone else while trying to move on with my life. But that had been *my* choice. Did I wish I had known the truth? Yes. Would knowing it have made me wait for Knight? Maybe. But I hadn't done anything wrong, and he couldn't keep holding a grudge like it was the end of a cliff he was dangling from. He had to let go. He had to. For our happiness.

I wanted to kiss him again. To open my legs for him—*again*. Let him lick and bite and taunt me. Let him punish me and cherish me. He was my everything. My only sin was fighting what we had because I'd thought I wasn't worthy.

When I arrived at the tree house, I dropped my backpack against the trunk and toed my Vans off. As I climbed up, I realized the light inside was on. Knight was here.

Chipped bark dug into my nails as I grasped the trunk hard, knocked back by the sight in front of me.

Knight.

Knight and Poppy.

He'd brought her here.

To our spot.

Not only had he brought her here, but they were both naked. *Completely* naked. He was lying on top of her, removing locks of hair from her neck, kissing it softly, his glorious, tan body enfolding hers. His triceps and broad back bulged with perfect muscles, and his tousled, brown hair fell across her face. She arched her back, her breasts full and lily white, meeting his pecs.

They looked like a beautiful dream and my own ugly nightmare. I couldn't move. I couldn't breathe. He was losing his virginity. To Poppy.

He was giving to her what he didn't want to give to me.

He wasn't done making me pay. At this moment, I wasn't sure he ever would be.

"You feel so good," Poppy moaned into Knight's mouth.

I shivered. I wanted to throw up. I *needed* to throw up. *God, make it stop.* They couldn't do this. It was wrong on so many levels. He didn't love her. He cheated on her. With me.

"I want you inside me." She rolled her hips toward him again, and I didn't dare look down and see him bare, aligning himself with her.

"Sunshine," he croaked.

Of course—the sun was stronger, bigger, and more important than the moon.

Knowing when to accept defeat, I'd learned, was an art. Giving up too fast was cowardly. But not giving up when all the signs pointed to long-lasting heartache was dangerous too.

I could no longer afford to put my heart on the line.

Once upon a time, Knight had been my protector.

But nowadays? Nowadays, he was the very thing I needed protection *from*.

And the person to shield me from him was myself.

Years of being noiseless had taught me how to slip into places without making a sound. I could be eerily quiet. The irony was, the same silence that had helped me go up undetected also helped me climb down from that tree without making a sound. When my feet hit the soft ground, I wobbled to the farthest corner I could find, deep in the woods, and threw up against a tree trunk, ripping chipped bark off of it with my fingers.

I didn't stop until my stomach was empty and my fingernails were gone.

Knight (Two days ago): When are you leaving 4 Boon?

Knight (Two days ago): Sup with you, L?

Knight (One day ago): Someone call ghostbusters, Moonshine just learned how to ghost.

Knight (One day ago): 👻 👻 👻 👻 👻

Knight (Three hours ago): Your dad just told me you flew to Boon yesterday. What the fuck? Are we playing this game again?

Knight (Three hours ago): Fuck you, Luna. Fuck you.

CHAPTER SIXTEEN
KNIGHT

I hadn't meant to pick up her call.

Unfortunately, life was hell-bent on fucking me in the ass, sans lube, the day I answered.

And in the great scheme of things, did it really matter?

Also, at least Dixie was alive. Val wasn't.

Also, I was in no position to make a decision about my next meal, let alone my long-lost biological mother.

Also, was this an earthquake, or had I really drunk enough to make the world spin like the teacups in Disneyland?

Mom had been taken to the hospital again, and after spending two nights in a row under harsh florescent lights watching her wasting away, I took the Aston Martin for a ride. So far, so normal—only I did it with a bottle of my old, destructive friend Jack Daniels.

The bottle was empty by the time I reached the beach.

It was cold, windy, and well past ten at night. I was pretty much alone, which was a relief and a lonesome curse. I threw the bottle into the ocean and screamed at the endless horizon until my lungs burned. How tauntingly beautiful and deceiving the world could be. With its palm trees and stupid oceans and Spanish villas and poisonous women who look like nymphs rising from the water.

Woman. Not plural. Just the one.

I told myself the drinking problem I was unabashedly flirting with had nothing to do with Luna and everything to do with Mom. But that was bullshit, even to my own ears. First of all, I wasn't flirting with the problem anymore. I'd moved in with the bitch and put a ring on it.

Second, it had everything to do with Luna. Everything.

Fucking Luna, who'd just bailed.

Fucking Luna, who always went hot and cold on my ass, and I kept on coming back for more. After screwing FUCKING JOSH. After kissing Vaughn. And Daria too. Shit, why was I so happy she'd let me finger her cunt? She'd probably seen more dicks than a public urinal.

Shut up, shut up, shut up.

Collapsing on the sand like a sack of bricks, I held my phone in front of my face, scrolling the contacts. I didn't want to talk to Vaughn, and Hunter was a shitbag. The rest of my friends were dumbasses with first-world problems and couldn't relate to me if they had a fucking brain transplant. Dad had enough on his shit plate, and anyway, we still weren't really talking. My aunts Emilia and Melody were at the hospital, fussing over Mom, and I wasn't sure how much Trent and Edie knew about what was going down with Luna and me, so it felt awkward to cry in their laps.

My screen flashed with an image of a bull's head and read *Deadbeat Dixie*. The bull's head was my own personal sick joke. Because it was the shape of a uterus, and that's what she was for me—a hub for nine months until she spat me out and gave me away.

There wasn't even an inch of me that wanted to answer her, but I still did because I was too alone not to accept the love of those I hated.

"Hello? Knight? You there?" she asked frantically, the desperation in her voice telling me I wasn't the only one surprised I'd picked up.

The wind beat against her receiver, and I could hear she was outdoors.

I grinned, even though I'd never been so sad in my entire miserable life.

"Knight? Are you okay?"

No answer.

"Baby, tell me where you are."

"What do you care?" I hiccupped. "You live in fucking Texas. Does it matter if I'm stuck in a sewer? You can't do shit about it," I taunted.

"Honey…"

"*Honey*," I mimicked, letting out a wretched laugh, rolling in the sand. I bet it wasn't a pretty sight. My grown-ass, six-foot-three quarterback figure drunkenly rolling on the beach like a whale trying to find its way home. For some reason, I still had the phone to my ear.

"Knight, listen…" She hesitated.

"Now's not the time for dramatic pauses. Kind of in the middle of being shitfaced here, and not really in the mood for coaxing your ass."

"I'm here." I heard her swallow.

"Yeah, yeah." I rolled my eyes. "Talking about my feelings is low on my to-do list, Dick—can I call you Dick? Seems fitting."

"No, Knight. I mean literally here."

Godfuckingdammit, is anyone ever going to use that word correctly?
"Huh?"

"I'm here. In California. In Todos Santos. Where are you?"

"Why?" My voice suddenly sounded sober, but that was about the extent of it.

It just surprised me was all. I hadn't known she was planning another visit so soon.

"The thing is…I kind of…well…" She sighed.

Please, God, I hoped she hadn't gotten knocked up again, by someone local this time. Life was too short to deal with random half siblings, and my life was doing a fine job being a train wreck without any added drama.

"I never left," she finished.

"You stayed here through Christmas and New Year's?"

I couldn't help it. I laughed. I didn't even know why I was laughing.

"Yes," Dixie said seriously. "You looked like you could use someone, so I wanted to make myself available to you. Where are you?"

"I…" I looked around me before remembering I didn't need a savior. Especially in the form of Dixie.

"Where?" she repeated.

"Nah. I think I'm good." My smirk was back.

"Knight," she warned.

"Aw. Look at you. Playing the doting parent and shit. Did you read a book about parenting? Bet you're an expert now, huh?"

"Tell me where you are right now."

"And if I don't?"

"I'll tell your parents you're an alcoholic."

That made me choke on my laughter. Hilarious. I stopped rolling and stood up, swaying back and forth. Everything spun. My throat closed in on my last meal.

"You go do that." I hung up.

She called again immediately. I picked up. I was looking for a fight. Hell, if Vaughn were here, I'd have punched him in the nuts just to start one.

"Miss me?" I asked.

"You've been drinking a lot recently."

"She's sharp too. Whaddaya think? Did I get my brains from you or daddy dearest? By the way, who is daddy dearest, exactly?"

"It's not a conversation for now."

"Guess it's a conversation for never."

She sounded like she was running. Where, I had no clue. I didn't care either. All I cared about was that I had a punching bag I could go to town on.

"Knight, stop moving. You're zigzagging," she snapped.

First of all, I didn't even realize I was moving. Second of all, and more importantly, how did she…?

I looked up and realized she was descending the stairs from the promenade to the beach. Hot damn. She'd found me. I had no clue how, but she had. I turned my back, walking away from her. But my intoxication slowed me, and she was fast because of her eagerness to help. She caught me in three strides and yanked me by the back of my Balenciaga jacket.

"Knight Jameson Cole, you do not get to drink your troubles away and talk to me like this. I'm worried, you understand?"

I turned around, chuckling in her face. The laughter made my stomach feel even emptier. "No. I don't. You're nothing to me. A simple no one who has yet to understand her role in my life. My mother—my *real* mother—is dying in the hospital, and the girl I love is on the other side of the continent, fucking some douchebag named FUCKING JOSH she thinks she fell in love with. And I'm putting up with this shit and keep chasing her ass because…because… because I can't *not* have her in my life. Don't *you* understand?"

I pushed her. Not aggressively but enough to make her stumble away from me. "You did this to me. Now I'm this broken puppy begging for love. I would take any crumb Luna throws my way. I'd self-destruct in order not to deal with what's waiting around the corner for Mom. You made unconditional love conditional for me. You fucked nature in the ass, Dixie. You don't do that. You don't mess with nature."

She stood there and took it as I pushed her again. She stumbled backward. The waves broke at our feet. I opened my mouth, and swear I got drunk again just smelling my own fucking breath.

"And all because of what? My biological father didn't want you? Did he dump you for someone hotter? Didn't want to put a ring on it?" I shook my head, chuckling. "Did you get pregnant to trap him? Did it not work? Did he bail because he was too young? Because he was too old? Because he was too *married*? Who's the sad fucker who created me? Who's the asshole I share DNA with, who was smart enough not to get trapped by your annoyi—"

She slapped me across the face. I tripped back, falling on my ass. She advanced toward me, and for a minute, I thought she was going to strike me again. Was I above hitting my biological mom? I was too drunk to remember. My gut feeling told me yes. I didn't flinch. I let her run to me in full force. She stopped a few inches away, collapsing on the sand beside me and bursting into sobs.

Jesus H.

"Uh…" I stared at her blankly, getting more and more sober by the nanosecond. The chilly air and the train wreck also known as Dixie was like a bucket of water. She was crying so hard I thought she was going to have a heart attack or something.

"I believe it is my turn to have a meltdown, ma'am," I pointed out dryly.

She wiped her tears away, her eyes meeting mine, zinging with fury. "You wanna know why I never mentioned your dad to you? Not because he dumped me. Or because he was married. Well, maybe. Maybe he was both those things. The truth is, I never told you about him because I don't know his name, okay? I didn't even know I was pregnant for the longest time."

I scratched at my imaginary stubble. How dumb was she, exactly? How had she not known she was knocked up, and for how long?

"Explain," I gritted out.

We were still on our knees, on the sand.

"I was a cheerleader in high school—"

"Big surprise."

"*Knight*," she warned.

I waved at her to continue.

"I was a cheerleader in high school. It was sophomore year. We got invited to a college party in Dallas through one of my friends' older brothers. Somethin' big. I was a good Christian girl, Knight. I didn't want to have sex before marriage. We were dancing…drinking but not too much. I remember feeling dizzy and sitting down. Then the next thing I remember was waking up in my own bed, feeling numb all over. My body was sore, but seeing as I'd danced all night, I didn't think much of it. There was some spotting in my underwear, but I figured I'd gotten my period. I'd only had a couple spiked punch cups, and I drank lots of water throughout the evening. I didn't want to start probing and asking questions, to be a problematic, hysterical chick. As far as I was concerned, everything was okay. My girlfriends had known I wasn't feeling well, so they'd taken me home."

Well, spank my ass and call me Sandra. I had a feeling I was about to hate myself a little more after hearing my how-did-I-get-here story. For the first time, I didn't throw shit at her and let her finish.

She took a deep breath. "Three months later, the symptoms started. They were creeping in on me slowly. You were so smart, Knight." She shook her head, tears brimming in her eyes. "Even in the womb. I was hungry all the time, and my breasts were tender. I didn't have any nausea or anything, so at first, I chalked it up to hormones. I remember polishing off two plates of chicken fried steak and my mama telling me I ate like a pregnant girl, and that's when I remembered I hadn't had my period in a while. The next day, I went to buy a pregnancy test. I told myself there wasn't a chance I was pregnant. I'd never had sex in my life, and when you're young, your period is not always regular. Imagine how shocked I was when all three tests were positive."

I hung my head, drawing in a breath. I had to admit, she was unlucky more than she was an asshole.

"I dug into my memory, trying to figure out what happened. Then I remembered the party. I went and confronted my friend's older brother, the one who threw the party, but he was cagey and insisted no one had touched me, said I was making it up because I wanted to pin the pregnancy on some frat boy with a rich daddy. The news about my pregnancy broke. My parents were crushed. They couldn't show their faces at church. Neither could I. I dropped out of cheer. My grandmamma stopped taking my calls, crossed the street when she saw me walking by. My friends took a step back. Nobody wanted my reputation to rub off on them. Two weeks after I became public enemy number one, I found a note in my locker. Anonymous."

She reached for her bag and hunted inside it, producing her purse. She sniffed as she explained as an afterthought, "I take it with me everywhere I go. Every time I think about you, Knight, and feel like I don't deserve to live in this world for giving you up, I read this. Horrible, I know. I'm not proud of it either, you understand? Just because something bad happened to me, I went and did something bad to my baby. Only I always knew I was protecting my boy. I was introduced to Rosie and Dean before I was sure I was giving you up. The adoption agency made the connection, and giving you up became bearable because I knew, without a shadow of a doubt, what kind of mother Rosie was going to be."

Dixie handed me a crumpled piece of paper. It was yellow, torn. Dissolving at my fingertips like fairy dust. I unfolded it with careful precision, knowing how much it meant to her.

Dix,

They would never tell you, so I guess I will.

You were roofied, girl. Dragged into one of the upstairs bedrooms when things at the party started getting out of hand. There were five guys. All of them from a Dallas college. Didn't give their names. They had just lost an important football game, they said, but who knew what division they were, who they played for? There was shouting and screaming inside the room you were in. Your friends...maybe like a couple of them, tried to open the door, but other guys kept pushing them away. No one saw because there was a fight going on downstairs. Your little friends were damn scared, girl. Too damn scared. By the time the three girls threatened to call the police, it was too late. They already did the deed, and everyone knew. But the girls didn't want to get in trouble with the boys, and telling you would mean facing what they did.

I know it's too little, too late, but it was not your fault, Dix.

It was not.

Remember, the only way you could have prevented it was not showing up to that party.

I hope your parents will find it in their hearts to understand what happened because it kills me to see you so sad.

Smile, Dix, maybe something good will grow out of this.

P.S. Please don't try to trace this letter back to anyone. You'll never find out who I am.

Sorry.

I handed it back to her, the air pregnant with whatever response I was going to give her. I was still undecided on what I wanted to say. Frankly, I didn't want to say *anything*, but I knew I had to at some point.

She stood and offered me her hand. I didn't take it but followed her to my feet. So. My dad was a rapist with rapist friends. She was undoubtedly a victim. She'd stayed here during the holidays because of my miserable ass. She'd given me up because she didn't know I existed until it was too late. She probably would have gotten rid of me with a hanger if she could have. Didn't matter. None of it mattered anymore.

I blew out air, fishing for the joint in my back pocket.

"I need to get back to the hospital." I started for the stairs leading to the promenade, shaking with rage and humiliation and all-consuming guilt for not responding to her story.

Dixie ran after me, her footfalls silent on the cool sand.

"In this state? No way I'm letting you."

"Refresh my memory. When exactly did I ask for permission?"

"Let me give you a ride."

"No thanks. Last time someone rode you, I was the result. Didn't work out too well for me." I wanted to throw up on myself. But I'd still said it.

"Why are you doing this?"

She was crying now. I'd made her cry. But I couldn't stop myself.

"Shit, where are my manners? I'm sure you've been screwed plenty since then. I'm good."

"Good? You're drunk!"

"So?" I turned toward her, amused. "I can count on one hand the times I'm *not* drunk these days."

She dug her fingernails into my forearm, spinning me in place. I jerked my arm away, baring my teeth like an injured animal.

"How dare you?" She slammed her little fists in my chest. "How dare you talk to me like this after I opened up to you? How dare you belittle my tragedy just because you're so consumed with yours?"

Stumbling backward, I took her in. For the first time since I'd met her, she stood up to me. I didn't know what to make of it. I just knew I'd undoubtedly screwed the whole thing up, and it was ten minutes in my life I couldn't take back, even though I knew they'd haunt me the rest of my days.

"Shit," I mumbled. "Sorry. You're right. Those last two comments were bullshit. I know you didn't ask for it. I'm just a little stunned, finding out about my father being…"

"How dare you treat life so fleetingly, knowing what Rosie is going through?" she continued, ignoring my apology and shoving me upstairs, toward the promenade. "Even if you have no regard for your own—what about others? What if you run over someone else's parent? Hurt a child? An elderly woman? *Anyone*, really. You get behind the wheel, you put everyone at risk, not just yourself."

"Dixie, I—"

"You are a disgrace to men, not only for talking so ill of a rape victim but for constantly getting behind the wheel when drunk."

Whoa. How did she know *that*?

"How do you—"

"You get your butt into my car right now, young man, and pick up your car tomorrow morning, after a hearty breakfast and a long shower. Am I understood?"

Speechless, I stared at her. She sounded so boring and moral and…right. I sidestepped, allowing her the space to slip past me.

Gingerly, she soldiered toward her rental car, glancing back every now and again to check I was still here. As I rounded her vehicle to the passenger seat, I caught a glimpse of a freshly glued quote, *Do you follow Jesus this closely?* and shook my head.

"Sorry," I said again when I buckled up. "About my dad. Not about being born."

"Zip it, Knight."

"Yes, ma'am."

Three things happened simultaneously after my soap opera encounter with Dixie:

One, I stopped answering her calls again. I still sent her text messages informing her I was okay, even though I was not, but I just couldn't face her.

Then, she'd been an annoying little background noise. Now she was a reminder of my dark, debauched existence.

Two, school started. After what had happened in the tree house, Poppy finally—*finally*—got the hint. She steered clear of my ass like I was radioactive. Which, to her, arguably, I was. Of course, that created a whole other set of problems. I passed her locker that first morning, noticing it was spray-painted in hot pink: *DUMPED BY KJC*. Someone had plastered a photoshopped

Instagram picture of her with a dumpster fire in the background. I ripped it off before she could see it, but rumor was she still spent the vast majority of the day locked in the bathroom, presumably not taking five hundred shits.

Three, Mom was discharged from the hospital.

I headed home straight after school. I discarded my backpack at the door, scrubbed my hands clean (germs and Mom weren't tight), and padded upstairs toward her room. Usually Hunter and I hit the gym straight after off-season. Not today. I wanted to see for myself that Mom was okay. Maybe it'd inspire me to go the entire day without drinking a bottle of who knew what.

Okay, who was I kidding? The entire morning.

Fine, an hour. Whatever.

I pushed Mom's door open, stepping into her bedroom and stopping on the threshold.

Dear God,

I'm a decent guy. I always buy the toffee-tastic cookies from Girl Scouts, knowing no one else in their right mind would buy the sandy motherfuckers. I explained masturbation to Lev so my dad wouldn't have to. And I didn't kill Vaughn, even though he touched Luna. Why do you hate me? What gives?

Not so faithfully,

KJC

"The fuck?" my dad grumbled, snapping his head in my direction. He was butt naked, and I do mean it literally—his ass staring back at my face—in bed, with Mom underneath him, his face strategically...*there.* I shook my head.

"Get out!" Dad grabbed something from the bed and hurled it toward me.

I squeezed my eyes shut.

Please, God, if you still have any remorse toward me, let that shit not be a dildo or a vibrator.

I heard something rubbery and hard falling to the floor.

Really, God? For real?

"Dean!" Mom chastised.

I slammed the door so hard its wooden frame cracked at the edges, and I dashed down the hall to my room. My lunch was shooting up my throat, and I was glad it was one of the rare times I didn't have a hangover or was simply plain drunk.

Fuuuuuuck.

I needed to tell someone. Who? Vaughn and Hunter would taunt me into my grave and beyond. All my other friends had the mental maturity of a LaCroix can. I texted Luna on a whim, conveniently ignoring the fact she hadn't answered my last trillion messages. I didn't know what had made her flip, but I'd been working extra hard on being a douche before sticking my mammoth fingers into her, then pretending nothing happened, so she had a variety of reasons to choose from.

Knight: I just saw something.

Knight: You cannot ignore this.

Knight: I caught my dad going down on my mom.

Knight: I can't unsee it, Moonshine. It's burned into my retinas. Forever.

Knight: Answer me for fuck's sake. Seriously? It was just a bit of fooling around. Nothing has changed. You're still my best friend.

And my only lover.

And the reason I woke up every day instead of giving up.

I had to keep her in my life, even at the price of making said life unbearable.

She could still have FUCKING JOSH.

Fuck him. Love him. Build a shrine to him.

And I'd still be here.

Waiting. Pining. Watching the time stretch between us like an endless ocean.

I tossed my phone onto my bed, letting it drown in heaps of black satin, then plopped down next to it. I rubbed my eyes like I could wipe off the memory of my dad doing what he'd done to Mom.

Uncle Vicious had once jokingly said life was not an easy phase in one's existence. I now understood what he meant. Life felt like a chain of calamities strung together. What helped me go through it was reminding myself of famous people who went through bad shit and were still alive. It was kind of creepy, but it helped. Like, Joaquin Phoenix had watched his brother die and had to call 911. Keanu Reeves had lost his baby and the love of his life eighteen months apart. Oprah Winfrey had been a fourteen-year-old runaway after being sexually abused. Charlize Theron watched her mother shoot her father to death in self-defense.

These people still lived. Laughed. Breathed. Got married. Had babies. Moved on.

Statistically, I could too.

Yet sometimes, I watched from the outside and wanted to fist-bump myself for still functioning. Staying in bed for eternity was goddamn tempting.

"Hi."

The small voice jerked me from my thoughts. I sat upright in my bed. *Mom.* She was clad in a green robe that hugged her thin waist. Her face looked flush and young. Almost healthy. Happy. Like Luna after I gave her an orgasm.

Note to self: Never put your mom and orgasm in the same sentence. Even in your head.

"Yo."

"You were early."

"And you were busy." I propped my chin on my knee, not giving a damn it was kind of feminine, looking up at the ceiling.

She let out a breathless laugh, pushing off the doorframe and taking a seat beside me. Her leg pressed against mine. She nudged me. It took everything in my two-hundred-pound body not to roll my eyes like a fucking Kardashian.

"How about we don't talk about it?" I wasn't above begging.

Was I really above anything at this point?

"Come on. I'm sure you know all about the birds and the bees."

"Right. So we *are* talking about it."

"Sex is natural."

"Not the type Adriana Chechik taught me."

"Adriana Chechik the porn star?" Mom's eyes twinkled with amusement.

"No, the astronomer. Don't play coy now."

She laughed, tousling my hair. "How are you feeling?"

"Shouldn't I be asking you that?" I arched an eyebrow.

"I'm feeling great, actually." She chuckled. "And you? How is my son?"

"Fine," I grumbled.

I've been drinking at least a bottle a day since Luna left, but fine.

"Great, great, great."

I can't fucking breathe without thinking about life without you.

But unloading on her would be a bitch move. Talking to Dad about it was out of the question. We both needed to cool down. He fucked my mom. With toys. *Not* cool.

She cupped my face and tilted my head up. Our gazes locked.

"Knight Jameson Cole, you build your walls high and thick, but I see through them. Tell me what's bothering you. It can't be my health, because I'm here and feeling better. Is it about a certain gray-eyed girl who flew across the country recently?"

She bunched the collar of my shirt in her fist, lowering me to her. She placed my head in her lap, threading her delicate, pale fingers through my hair, running them back and forth over my skull. Goose bumps rose all over my skin. She used to do this to me all the time when I had meltdowns as a kid. Calmed the hell out of me.

"Talk to your mama, boy," she whispered.

My words spilled like acid, a tsunami of confessions. I told her everything: About what had happened at the dog shelter. About kissing Poppy in front of Luna. About Luna kissing Daria in front of *me*. About the night I'd sneaked into Moonshine's room again (omitting the sexy parts—just because my dinner was ruined didn't mean Mom couldn't eat this decade too) and about how I tried forgetting about her. About how I'd invited Poppy to our tree house to settle the score with Luna.

"Maybe she saw you." Mom pursed her lips.

I frowned at the wall in front of me, painted black with the Raiders' logo on it. "Fat chance."

"Why's that?" Mom persisted.

"Because Luna would have flipped."

She'd almost killed me with her glare when I'd fondled Arabella, who was about as relevant to my life as a thoroughly used condom.

"Would she? Does that sound like Luna? Flipping out on you? Especially seeing as you did nothing wrong technically, simply spent time with your girlfriend?"

Inside my girlfriend. Or that's what it had looked like, anyway.

Mom had a point. Maybe Luna had seen. Maybe that was the deal breaker. I'd said I wouldn't rest until we were even, but now, when she thought we were, it didn't feel too good.

No. It didn't feel too fucking good at all.

"Do you love her?" Mom asked seriously.

"No," I shot out.

Yes.

Why was it so hard? Because it was pathetic? Because it was unrequited? Because I wasn't even sure who Luna was anymore? Talking and fucking and *living* without me, across the country, while I was losing my mother to cystic fibrosis.

"Well, then." Rosie threw her hands in the air on a breezy smile. "No harm done We don't need to talk about it anymore, do we?"

She was about to stand up. I straightened from her lap, sitting.

"Wait."

"Hmm?" Her lips pursed in a victorious smile.

"I do. I love her." I paused. "I love her, but I'm not sure I know her anymore."

"You love her, but maybe despite growing up together, you also grew apart?"

I shook my head. No. That wasn't it. "I can't outgrow Luna. It's like outgrowing your heart. Impossible. It grows with you. What do I do?" I ran my hand across my close-shaved jaw. "What the fuck do I do, Mom?"

"Well, that's an easy one." She smiled. "You go after her. You grovel. You win your girl back. Life's too short not to be with the person you love."

Going to Boon in the middle of the school year, with my mother sick, was insane. I knew that. But leaving things unfinished with Luna was, somehow, even crazier. How many hits could our friendship take before exploding like a piñata?

I was done hitting the piñata. I didn't want the candy inside it. I just wanted the fucking piñata. Was that too much to ask?

"I can't leave you." I took Mom's hand.

I was playing a dangerous game, cajoling her into giving me permission to do it. Truth was, I was demented enough to up and leave, taking my chances. I tried to reason with myself. Mom had just gotten discharged from the hospital. She could handle being without me for a long weekend. Or for a day. Jesus. It might just be one day. Maybe Luna didn't want to patch shit up. Maybe she had finally given up on my sorry ass.

"You must." Mom squeezed my hand.

"Why?"

I humored her. Rosie Leblanc wasn't big on having me away from school. As it was, I wasn't the most accurate dick in the urinal. I wasn't a *bad* student per se, but I'd be lying if I said Ivy League colleges were lining up at my doorstep.

"Do you want me to be honest?" She scrunched her nose.

"No. Please lie through your teeth." Another eye roll nearly commenced.

Mom looked down, flattening her palm over my linen and brushing it absentmindedly.

Bad idea. This shit is ninety-nine percent spunk, one percent fabric.

"I need you to do this for my peace of mind." Her gaze cut to mine, her blue eyes shining with emotion. "From a selfish point of view, I want you to win Luna back because knowing you two are together would make me so happy."

I tried to swallow but couldn't. I wanted to tell her to stop talking nonsense, but I couldn't do that either. Finally, I got up, tucked my chin, and regarded her with the same cool, lazy expression I'd learned from my father. From his friends.

Nothing gets in. Nothing comes out. If bottling feelings was a sport, I'd be representing my country in the Olympics.

She stood up and took my face in her hands, pressing her nose to my pecs. I froze before wrapping tentative arms around her. I kissed the crown of her head.

"Can I tell you a secret?" she whispered into my shirt, sending warm breath to my chest through the fabric.

I didn't say anything. Of course she could.

"I love your brother and your father more than I love myself. I would die for them. Fight for them until the bitter end. Go against the whole world for them. But you…" She dragged her face up to look at me. Her eyes were full of tears. "I've always loved you just a tiny bit more. My regal, rebel boy. My legendary hellraiser, my sad prince, my unlikely savior, my beautiful, broken Knight."

I gulped, looking down at her.

Don't say it. Don't say it. Don't say it.

But I couldn't *not* say it. The moment seemed too real and raw.

She brushed my cheek and gave me a smile so genuine and powerful, I thought it could outshine the sun.

"What if tomorrow never comes?" I whispered.

"Then, my darling boy, we'll make the best of today."

CHAPTER SEVENTEEN
KNIGHT/LUNA

KNIGHT

I spent the cab drive from Charlotte to Boon drinking mini-bottles of whatever the fuck alcohol I could find at the airport and popping a couple Xanax. The fake ID, paired with the fact I was running on zero sleep, made me look way older than eighteen. Unfortunately, I was past the stage where a few shots of Johnny made a difference. I was on edge. Agitated. Rubbing my knuckles back and forth against my jaw. I'd busted them open last night punching the tree house tree trunk. Just for old times' sake.

"You good?" The driver shifted in his seat, glancing at me in the rearview mirror.

"Fine," I clipped, tapping an unlit joint on my muscular thigh.

You know you have a problem when, before you meet the driver waiting for you at the airport, you meet a local drug dealer to get a fresh stash.

There was a brief silence as we zipped past green rolling hills, the backdrop of a cloudless blue sky and Charlotte's towers twinkling in the distance. So this was the place that stole Moonshine from me. Already I hated it.

When the driver pulled up at Boon, I slapped a few bills in his hand and wheeled my suitcase down the cobblestone path. A redbrick colonial building the size of a hotel stood before me, framed with lush, trimmed lawns on both sides. A herd of church-mice-looking girls in matching pastel cardigans and ironed hair poured from the double doors of the college. They stopped and eyed me curiously, exchanging looks and hugging their textbooks to their chests.

"Can I help you?" One of them cleared her throat, pushing her glasses up the bridge of her nose.

Was it that obvious I wasn't cut out for higher education? Maybe because I smelled like a liquor store and a dodgy one-night stand.

"Can you?" I flashed my lazy, lopsided smirk that put women in a spell even I couldn't fully understand.

Their frowns liquefied in an instant.

"I'm looking for the dorms."

"Men's or women's?"

I stared at her blandly. "They're not coed?"

"It's a Catholic college." The revelation was followed by a headshake.

"Women's," I clipped.

Shit just got a whole lot more complicated, as shit tended to where my life was concerned.

The girl pointed at a sign with white wooden arrows directing visitors to different sections of the campus. Her fingernails were colorless, thoroughly chewed. "You take a right and walk until you see the building with the pink flag."

"How misogynist." I bit down a smile, wondering how Luna had felt about that.

She hated wearing anything pink or girly, the exact opposite of Daria.

The girl flushed, drawing circles on the ground with her toes. "Thank you for saying that."

"Huh?"

"Thanks for knowing it's kind of offensive. Beautiful men...I mean, handsome men like yourself are..." she started, but her friends jerked her away, giggling and heading toward the cafeteria.

Are *what?*

Say, it sweetheart. I could use a little ego boost before I come face-to-face with Luna.

When I got to the lobby of the girls' dorm, there was a man about two thousand years old behind the front desk, with a Ron Weasley–orange toupee, flipping a local newspaper that lay flat in front of him. His brows were high as he read a fascinating article about the fish prices in Asheville.

"Wrong dorm," he said without looking up from his paper.

Instead of gracing him with a response, I dropped my designer backpack on his desk with a thud, fishing my wallet from my back pocket, plucking a few bills, and throwing them his way like confetti.

He didn't look up from the paper. "Do you understand English?" he grumbled.

"Only when it suits me. What's your price?"

"Why must there be a price tag on rules? Why can't we just follow them blindly?" He licked the tip of his index finger, flicking a page.

An impatient smirk tugged at my lips. He was still staring at his paper.

"Because humans are corrupt, and rules are boring."

"Speak for yourself, young man."

With an exasperated sigh, I took out a few more Benjamins, boomeranging them across his desk. There was maybe a couple grand in total covering the surface before he finally looked up.

"What's her name?"

"Rexroth. Luna Rexroth."

"And your intentions?"

Entirely sinister.

"She's my girlfriend," I lied, unblinking. "I came to visit her from California. I want to surprise her in her room."

I could see his gaze drifting to the row of spare keys under his counter. I didn't dare breathe.

Do it, old man.

He didn't budge. I took my wallet out and emptied it on his desk, the remainder of my cash raining in front of his eyes. I didn't break eye contact.

"How do I know you're telling the truth?" he asked.

"Do you know her?"

"Yes."

Casually, I unlocked my phone and threw it into his hands. My screensaver was a picture of me hugging her and kissing her cheek while she smiled into the camera. It was pretty obvious we knew each other and liked each other. He lifted his bushy, white eyebrows, examining the picture before handing my phone back to me.

Finally, he lowered himself to the wall of keys, searching for her name.

"I'll need you to leave your ID here."

I slid my driver's license over the counter.

"No spending the night on the premises. No loitering. Straight to room 601. And if I see you getting anywhere near girls who are not her, I'm calling the cops."

"I need one more favor," I said.

He looked up at me, Luna's room key dangling between his meaty fingers.

"Namely, one more set of keys…and a lemon."

LUNA

If you're ready to fall
Please do it with me
Ten o'clock. Water tower. Is where I will be.

Broken Knight

I'd found the note under my pillow—where I kept the book I was reading that week—like a tooth, forgotten by the tooth fairy. A wish. A promise. Knight knew I'd lift the pillow because he knew me. Knew us.

Knight was at Boon.

At my college.

In my dorm.

He wanted me to meet him at the water tower.

He was away from his mother.

His friends.

His school.

Away from his *Poppy*.

That alone should've made me run into his arms. I'd made a promise to Rosie. But only for after she wasn't here anymore. I didn't have to put my heart on the line just yet. I wanted my heart to be free a little longer.

Before I moved to Boon, I used to organize my time in accordance with Knight's life. When it was football season, I'd crammed activities into my schedule to make time move faster. I'd volunteered more, taken longer bike rides, and read entire fantasy series back to back. When he was free, I dropped said activities in favor of being with him—even when he'd flirted with other girls, when the rumors about his lothario ways had cut me open and made me bleed green with jealousy.

When I'd left for Boon, I'd needed to fill my life with distractions. I had done so by mimicking life as I saw it worn by other people. To my surprise, I was a pretty good actress—a miserable one without Knight but decent nonetheless.

I munched on the straw of my fruity cocktail, my legs folded as I sat in the nightclub next to April, Josh, and Ryan. I flipped my phone over to watch for the time.

Ten minutes to ten.

I couldn't make it in time even if I wanted to. *Good.*

The music pounded so loudly, it felt like it was coming from inside my head. I squeezed my eyes shut and tried to remove the vision of Knight waiting for me on the top of the water tower, in the cold.

It felt a little redundant not to use my voice with my friends, now that I had spoken aloud to Knight, Edie, and Dad, but I was still thankful to have people in my life who liked the old me. This was where I belonged. With my new, genuine friends I'd made on my own, not because our parents were best friends.

I checked my phone again.

Eight to ten.

It took about twenty minutes to get to the water tower by foot. Probably ten with my bike, which I didn't have with me. What was he doing here anyway? There was only one way to find out, and I wasn't dumb enough to risk crumbling in front of him and opening my legs again.

Josh and Ryan stood up to get us more drinks. April leaned forward and slapped my knee, scowling.

"That's it," she shouted over the music. "I'm staging a one-person intervention. You're the most awful datee ever."

"Datee?" I spelled out each letter. April was pretty good at making up words.

"Person you date." April rolled her eyes and exhaled, sending a lock of her colorful hair flying.

"It's not a date," I signed.

Josh and April had presented this outing as hanging out. Since there was nothing romantic about strangers grinding against each other on a dance floor, I'd believed them. Plus, I didn't want to stay in the dorm in case Knight showed up. I still hadn't told April he was here, but I figured tonight, I'd have to come clean about plenty of things to my roommate.

April was so understanding, she didn't even care that I'd lied to her about my relationship with Knight and told her he used to be my boyfriend.

"Come on, dude." April patted my thigh.

I was wearing ripped boyfriend jeans and a hoodie, a stark contrast to my friend's purple minidress.

"The guy is legit in love with you. If you're not going to let him screw your brains out again, at least have the decency to tell him now."

"I did," I signed. In the letter I gave Josh, I'd explained I just wanted to be friends.

"Well, then stop dangling yourself in front of him like a shiny prize. He had a taste once, and now I'm sure he wants a rerun." April barked out a good-natured laugh.

Suddenly, I remembered something very important—I'd never told April I slept with Josh. My jaw dropped.

"Had a taste?" I arched an eyebrow.

The only people who knew about Josh and me were my family, as Knight had so generously offered the information at Thanksgiving dinner, Josh, and me.

April waved her hand, laughing more awkwardly now. "It's not a big deal."

"Oh, it's not?"

"Guys talk."

"Last time I checked, you're not a guy."

"Well, Ryan is, and I'm his girlfriend, so he told me. It's not like the entire school knows. Or cares. Just a few of our friends. Jesus, Luna, you're not five. You think your alcoholic, scumbag crush who's screwing someone else to get back at you is better than Josh?"

"Don't you dare talk about him like that." I slammed my empty drink on the table.

I understood fully that April was on my side, but I hated that she spoke badly of Knight without really understanding where he came from or what he was going through.

"Why not? He wasn't even your boyfriend. You'd never protect Josh like this, and he's been nothing but nice to you."

"I don't want nice." I narrowed my eyes at her.

Really, what I'd meant to say was *I don't want anyone who isn't Knight*.

I flipped my phone over again mid-argument. Ten past ten. My heart hiccupped.

"Of course not." She gave me a sarcastic smile, leaning back in the leather booth. "He doesn't treat you like shit and, therefore, is an awful candidate as a boyfriend."

"Knight doesn't treat me like shit."

"You're right. That would imply that he is treating you at all, wouldn't it?"

Her words stung so much, I physically recoiled. "Why are you doing this?"

"Because." She took a deep breath. "You're hurting yourself, and you need to open your eyes and see the situation for what it is. You will always be poor Saint Luna because you insist on taking the mutt over and over again."

"He's no mutt. Stop saying that."

"He screwed another girl."

"He had every right."

He did. I realized it now.

April ran her gaze over me, her eyes sad and disappointed.

Twenty past ten.

April was trying to help me—but that didn't make her right. I'd portrayed Knight as the villain, when really he was a misunderstood prince. I hadn't agreed with all of his decisions, but he didn't want to hurt me. Not truly. He wanted to stop hurting, and he sometimes ran over people in the process.

I darted up, helplessly searching the bar. Josh and Ryan were leaning against it, laughing between themselves. Ryan said something that made Josh shake his head, pretending to finger-shoot his temple. I felt my fury rising from my toes to my head.

I looked back to April, smiling now, mustering every ounce of self-control I had in me.

"You know," I spoke, my voice dark and smoky, coming from the depths of my soul.

Her eyes widened in disbelief, her cocktail glass—blue liquid, like the tips of her hair—slipping from between her fingers and crashing on the floor.

"I take full responsibility for everything that happened this entire semester. The whole Knight debacle. The thing with Josh. I didn't handle it well, did I?"

I could see the confusion flashing in her face as it reddened, her pupils dilating like ink.

"But don't assume you know the entire story from where you're standing. I have so much to explain to you—if you're willing to listen—but know this, April: You've helped me. Helped me in ways I could never repay you for. Thank you."

"What the fuck, Luna?!" April's eyes glistened as she stood.

Wordlessly, she slapped me across the face. I felt the burn crawling from my cheek to my neck, spreading, pinking my ears with embarrassment she couldn't see because of the tan hue of my skin and the dim light of the club.

I lifted my head and stared at her. Every muscle in her face was shaking. Her expression told me I revolted her. In truth, I repulsed myself too. She thought I was a liar now, and she had every right to feel embarrassed and betrayed.

I should've told her the truth—all of it.

I should've stood up for myself long ago.

I should've been more stern with Josh when he ignored my rejections.

I shouldn't have accepted Knight's half-hearted fumbles while he was with another girl.

I was worth more. I deserved more.

"Good luck getting yourself out of this one." She looked hurt more than anything else, and I knew she had every right to be.

A firm tap on my shoulder made me turn around. I don't know

why I expected to see Knight. There was no reason for him to be here, other than the fact that, true to his name, he had the tendency to save my day.

It was Josh. His dark eyes were like two globes of misery, the weight of all the heartbreak in the world seemingly dimming his light. Seeing him hurt felt like a punch straight to the gut.

"I'm sorry," I whispered. "It's not that I spoke before this…" I licked my lips, looking around helplessly.

God, he didn't deserve it. Any of this. How difficult was it to not break a heart? I'd always been so mad at Knight for doing this to me. Maybe he hadn't meant to either. Maybe hearts were like carefully tended flowers. Sometimes they just wilted, no matter what you did.

Josh took a step back, shaking his head in disbelief. His hands trembled as he signed to me.

"You talk," he said.

I nodded. I felt ashamed talking to him. Not that it was bad. Not that my breakthrough didn't make me proud. But the fact that I'd hidden it from all of them for so long… I'd hidden a lot of things from my friends, and it was payback time.

"Since when?" he signed, too stunned to show any negative or positive emotion.

"Since…a few weeks ago."

He shook his head, without saying anything.

"How?" he finally asked.

I was about to lose the boy I loved, so I threw my fears and phobias off a cliff was what I would have said, but I knew my honesty would rip him to shreds.

"Family crisis," I answered.

The tears blinded me. Somehow, I could still see the melted figures of my friends through them, looking like clouds through a rain-stained window. April stood next to Ryan, and now they both faced me. Josh was starting to retreat, walking backward out of the club, out of my life.

Then he stopped. Smiled. It looked genuine. I could tell, even in the darkness of the club.

"Good for you."

I couldn't even form a response.

"I wish I'd known earlier."

I didn't know if he meant about loving Knight or about my talking.

"I lost the ability to speak freely when I was a baby," I tried to explain to them, even though they looked more hurt about my lashing out at April and hiding a secret from them than anything else. "It's not like I ever spoke in public or…"

I stopped, clamping my mouth shut on the lie. I'd spoken at the New Year's party Daria dragged me to. I was changing. I could no longer afford the comfort of being quiet and different. People were done cutting me slack.

I squeezed my eyes shut to rid myself of the tears so I could see Josh better. He signed again. "You should go back to Knight. To California."

He wasn't mean. He was truthful. He knew it was something in California that had caused my breakthrough. Or so he thought. But if I hadn't known them—April, Ryan, and Josh—I would never have stood up to Knight. Maybe I wouldn't have had my breakthrough. Who knows.

"I never meant to hurt you," I told him.

"I know."

"I don't want anything to change," I almost begged.

April was the one to answer. "Luna, we always wanted you to win. We just didn't know we weren't on your team."

Before I slipped out of the club, Ryan clutched my arm in a bruising grip.

"We thought you were different, not just another rich, spoiled, holier-than-thou Todos Santos bitch. Turns out, you're exactly like the stigma. Self-absorbed, beautiful, and a liar. It's over for you, Rexroth. Boon's over for you."

"Ryan!" April jerked him away, pushing him back.

"Ryan's wrong about you, but not about Boon. Go to Knight," Josh signed. "You're his. You belong there. With him."

He was right.

He was right, and Knight was here. At Boon.

I planted a soft kiss on Josh's cheek, then my legs carried me outside on autopilot. I tumbled over a stair, righted myself against the wall, and lurched forward like there was an invisible line, pulling me.

I didn't want to waste any time calling an Uber. I started for the water tower, tears stinging my eyes.

I was going to tell Knight I wanted everything.

Every single drop of him. No Poppy. No Arabella. No clingy girls he threw crumbs of attention to. I wanted to devour every single bite of the Knight Cole cake, and I wasn't going to settle for less.

The water tower was across Boon's football field. I jogged through the dewy grass, flinging myself over the tower's ladder, not even bothering to check the time. How late was I? An hour? Probably more. Maybe he wasn't even here anymore.

With every trembling move of my feet, my hands choking the cold, rusty metal bars, I became more aware of the abyss beneath me. The water tower was three stories tall. I could fall. But instead of fear, I was filled with determination.

No, this was like the tree house.

That's what we did.

We met high. In the sky.

Above everything.

And everyone.

I climbed up with careful precision and slid through the white metal bannisters surrounding the water tank. The surface beneath me was all rusty metal, cold and damp. I flung myself over the railing, out of breath. Panting. I closed my eyes, too chicken to see if he was still here. Silence cocooned me. I exhaled a shaky breath.

Please be here.

But then I felt our invisible rope, loose around my neck, and knew, without even opening my eyes—he was no longer tugging.

"Remember this game?" Knight's husky, gritty voice boomed in the air.

My eyes snapped open. The planes of his deity-like face registered, and like all the other times I'd seen him, my heart flipped in my chest, nosediving to my stomach like an Olympic diver.

He was sitting with his long legs crossed, a lemon cut in half between us. I looked down at it, realization sinking in. I smiled.

"Fair warning: I practiced all day." Knight grinned, his eyes raking up my body until they met mine.

I tried to swallow the ball of excitement in my throat. He was so beautiful. And so *here*. I wanted to ask him a thousand questions: Why *was* he here? When had he landed? When was he going back? What about Poppy?

But all I could do was shrug.

"I have a good track record of winning. What are we betting on?"

We used to play this all the time when we were kids. There was always a bet involved. He'd always let me win—a mischievous smile playing on his lips as I shoved the victory in his face. He was going to let me win this one too.

Knight stroked his chin thoughtfully.

"If you win, I promise to leave you alone," he said gravely, holding my gaze, letting his words sink in.

"And if I lose?" I croaked, ignoring the pain dull in my chest.

"If you lose…" A boyish, devastating grin found his pink, full lips, making my knees stutter, bones hitting bones. "I fuck you."

Lethal silence. I didn't know what to say. That's what he'd come here for? To screw me?

Distress, anger, and lust warred inside me. I opened my mouth, choosing my next words carefully, reminding myself this was Knight. That he had a special flair for self-destruction, and when he felt wounded, he fought back. I reminded myself that Knight always let me win this game, despite his poker face.

"Are you still with Poppy?" I asked.

"No." His eyes didn't waver from mine.

I let out a shaky breath. "No?"

He shook his head slowly.

I tested the waters. "She finally dumped you."

He gave me an exasperated look. "Sure. That's what happened."

"If we sleep together, will you tell people?"

His facial muscles didn't move an inch. "Not even gonna answer that question."

For all his foul play, Knight wasn't like Josh. He never kissed and told people about it. Never confirmed his Casanova status. And until mere weeks ago, he had remained a virgin. For me.

"I would like to negotiate the terms of my win." I cleared my throat.

"I'm listening."

"If I win..." I bit my lower lip. It was impossible to say this without sounding patronizing. "If I win, you stop drinking and start attending AA meetings."

He didn't even blink. "I agree to your terms."

"I'm not some prize," I added, scoffing as an afterthought.

"You are to me," he said frankly, his tone void of emotion.

"And I'm not a whore."

"I'm well aware. I'm not buying you, Luna. I'm merely making a point."

"What is the point?"

"That once you're with me, you won't be able to touch anyone else. Want anyone else. Feel for anyone else."

I already know that, you fool.

I took a deep breath, leaning forward and snatching one half of the lemon. It was cut precisely in the middle. He always played fair. Knight took his lemon. Our eyes met, and we shared an identical smile.

I couldn't believe I was doing this. A quiet, tiny part of me wanted to lose, but my competitive streak wouldn't let me. And Knight would protect me by losing anyway. Not to mention, he'd make love to me if I asked him to, bet lost or won.

"Whoever flinches first, loses. Ready?" He tapped my nose.

"Ready."

We bit into our lemons at the same time. The bitter, sour juices exploded in my mouth, making my eyes water, but I schooled my facial expression as best I could, my eyes roaming Knight's face as he nonchalantly took bite after bite of the lemon's flesh, his eyes dead on mine, as if he were eating an apple.

I took another tentative bite from the lemon, panic trickling into my gut along with the sour tang of the fruit. He should start making a face right about now. He always made a face. Then he'd secretly eat the entire thing, unflinching, after I did my victory dance.

Knight took another bite, his entire demeanor teetering on the verge of indifference.

What was he doing? Why wasn't he wincing? The rule was, if neither of us recoiled, whoever ate the lemon more quickly and thoroughly won. Knight had only won one time, when he'd wanted to take me to prom and I'd insisted I didn't want to go. He'd cared so much about giving me this high school experience that he hadn't allowed me to win. This, I was beginning to understand, was his second strike.

I was officially in trouble.

On my third bite, I began to gag. My tongue burned. I felt my brows furrowing.

I flinched.

Crap, I lost.

The lemon rolled from between my fingers, knocking Knight's knee. He picked it up and threw it over the side of the water tower gate, into the abyss, offering me his hand. I took it, realizing I was shaking. My whole body trembled with adrenaline, anticipation, and the winter chill. He yanked me to sit in his lap, cupping one of my cheeks and looking into my eyes. The tension between us made my insides liquefy. Drowning in his gorgeous eyes, I struggled to breathe.

"You didn't let me win," I whimpered, understanding for the first time the consequences and what was about to happen.

We never backed down from bets. We always followed through when the other person challenged us.

"Why didn't you let me win?"

"You're equal to me—not the same Moonshine who left Todos Santos." His warm, lemony breath tickled my cheek as he lowered his face to mine. "But whoever you are, I will crack you too."

His mouth slanted on mine, and our bodies molded into one. I deepened the kiss, sliding my tongue between his lips and letting our tongues play together, flicking his piercing and feeling his primal groan vibrate from his stomach and into mine. We kissed like starved, angry animals, with a passion that burned the sky above us.

His hand slid into my hoodie, cupped one of my breasts, and pinched my nipple. I moaned into his mouth. He did it again. The third time he did it, instead of releasing the pressure, he flipped my hoodie up and sucked my nipple into his mouth, keeping his eyes on mine as he grazed his straight teeth over it. I shuddered so violently, I thought I'd come from that simple touch alone.

It was freezing outside, but I was scorching hot, my blood rioting at an unnatural temperature. I let my head drop back, my entire body following suit, as I lay down, fumbling out of my jeans, kicking them off. Suddenly, I wanted nothing more than to have him inside me. He chuckled at my eagerness.

"A bet is a bet," I muttered.

Knight slid his index fingers to the sides of my underwear and took them off. I flushed even more, not knowing it to be possible.

"Why are you looking at me like that?" I panted.

"Because." He paused, swallowing. "I want to remember the moment you officially became mine."

I was so dazed, I hadn't even noticed he was naked at this point. Completely naked and fully sheathed. He must've put the condom on while kissing me into my mini-climax. I'd been rocking back and forth, chasing his touch.

His tan, strong body was like crushed silk wrapped over steel as we lay down on the rusty metal. Soft, light curls peppered his chest, and I ran my fingers through them, mesmerized. He took my wrist and lowered my hand to his penis, wrapping my fingers around the shaft.

"You're mine," he stated. "Always fucking have been, Luna. Say it."

"I've only ever been yours, Knight."

"The last year didn't happen." He choked on his words.

I nodded at first, accepting the denial. But then I stopped. I didn't want to acknowledge some parts of it either. But it had happened. It had happened, and yet we'd somehow still ended up here together.

"It did happen, though."

"I know."

With that, he eased into me slowly, kissing my nose, my cheeks, my lips, my forehead. Even though I was wet and ready for him, it still hurt a little at first, but then he stopped, letting me stretch around his girth, before he began to make sweet, agonizing love to me. He moved in and out of me like he was giving me something so much greater than an orgasm. Slid into me to mark me. Agonizing, liquid heat began to gather under my navel, and my thighs trembled around his waist.

"Oh, Knight." I ran my fingers through his hair. Why had I fought this all this time? Why had I rejected his advances when he was everything I ever wanted?

"I...I..."

I'm going to come so hard the entire state is going to know.

He shut me up with a dirty kiss full of tongue and stubble. He didn't, I realized, want this connection we had diluted by words. We'd never needed words. Our relationship thrived even when I'd given him no words at all.

This was really happening. I was having sex with Knight.

Knight Jameson Cole: Quarterback. Prom king. The best looking jackass in town.

But also, Knight Jameson Cole: Closeted alcoholic. Adopted son. Gentle soul. And the most pure-hearted man I'd ever known.

I started panting hard, burying my fingernails in the muscles of his shoulders. I knew I was going to scream, and there was no way to stop it. The orgasm was just too much. Too strong. Too full of emotions.

"Come for me, Moonshine. Come all over my cock."

I exploded, shattering between his arms, seeing stars in different colors and sizes and shapes, at the exact same time he jerked into me one last time, emptying inside me. My cry pierced the air surrounding the water tower.

After that, we just lay there, him still on top of me, slowly softening inside of me. We breathed each other, the scent of sex intoxicating both of us into heavy-lidded smirks.

"Thank you," he whispered, kissing the tip of my nose, looking skittish all of a sudden—almost endearing. "For a perfect first time."

I smiled sadly. "You don't have to pretend, Knight. I appreciate you sparing my feelings, but I saw you with Poppy. I understand."

"No, you don't," he said flatly.

My eyebrows shot up in surprise. "But I saw... I came to the tree house and..."

"Figured as much. I couldn't go through with it." He pulled out of me slowly, rolling away from me and gathering me in his arms. The chill began to pool around us, like a blanket, frosting our bodies. We shivered against one another. "I couldn't let both of us waste our first time."

"But how do you know mine was a waste?" I asked honestly.

Knight chewed on his tongue piercing, looking elsewhere. I realized it still hurt him. That it always would.

"The morning after I snuck into your room, I saw the letter you wrote to FUCKING JOSH. I didn't open it. Just held it toward the sun so I could read whatever I could get from it. You said you loved him. After I left, I spent all this time dissecting what you said, and I realized you never told him you're *in* love with him. You choose words so carefully and intelligently, Luna. I knew this wasn't a mistake. You understand the meaning of words. That's why you don't use them lightly. That meant I still had a chance. And I figured, I'm losing my mom. I'm not ready to lose my best friend too. I'm not going down without a fight, Luna. I'll take whatever you're willing to give me. If it's friendship—so be it."

"I don't want to be your friend anymore," I said, pulling away to catch his gaze.

His face hardened, his lips thinning in pain. Only this time, the invincible mask didn't harden around his face, like clay. I could see the full range of his emotions. Hurt. Terror. Anger. Annoyance.

My beautiful best friend. From whom I kept a secret. A secret about his mother.

You're going to hell for this, Luna.

"I see." He frowned, trying not to sulk. "That's cool."

But it wasn't cool. We were never just cool. When we were together, we were blazing hot.

"I want to be your *girlfriend*."

CHAPTER EIGHTEEN
LUNA

I'd never been a rebel.

Not much of a rule-breaker either. On my best days, probably a daredevil tomboy who abided by the rules but tiptoed around the red line of propriety.

But the combination of wanting to stick it to April, who was still in shock from the fact I could speak, and not wanting to part ways with Knight made me sneak him into my room, even though I knew it could land me in hot water. Maybe even get me kicked out of the dorm.

"Why not my hotel room?" Knight inquired on our way to my dorm.

"Because I'm done being a pushover."

And because my room was way closer.

"Who pushed you over? I'll maim them."

"My roommate, April. But that one's on me, Knight. I'm the one who's going to deal with this."

"Technically," Knight murmured, his erection pressed against my ass as he rained drugging kisses all over my neck and shoulders once we'd made our way to my hallway. "The old man in the lobby told me he'd call the police if I stayed the night. But also technically…" Knight slid his hand into the back of my panties and curled his hand around my ass, dipping a finger between my folds. "You're damn good jailbait."

Swallowing a fit of giggles, I unlocked the door and tiptoed inside the room. I was expecting—hoping, really—that April had opted to sleep at Ryan's, seeing as we'd fought without properly making up. It would be perfect if she walked in the next morning and found out all the space she took in our little closet—none of it for me, my clothes were still in suitcases—was now equally divided between us. And that Knight was sound asleep beside me, just like Ryan was beside her almost every night.

My hopes were crushed when I noticed her silhouette under her covers, her back to us, her even breath telling me she was asleep. Alone.

Thank God Ryan wasn't here. I wondered if they'd had a fight.

I motioned to Knight with my head to follow me in, closed the door, and flung myself on the lower bunk. Sliding in, I jutted my chin in invitation. He took off his shoes, neatly folded his coat and put it on the back of my chair, then slipped into bed with me. I fished out my phone to send him a text message. If we spoke, April would wake up. She was a light sleeper.

Luna: You'll need to sneak out before she wakes up. Which is usually around ten on weekends.
Knight: K.

He was staring at his phone but facing me. We were pressed close to each other in the snug bed, our faces glowing in our phones' lights in the otherwise darkened room. There was so much I wanted to ask him.

Luna: So...are we?
Knight: Together?
Luna: Yeah.

He looked up from his screen, the shades of green in his irises arresting my heart. How could I ever have let him slip from my fingers? How could I have given him up? Who even *cared*? Love is selfish. Love is raw. Love is unfair, and unpredictable, and unstoppable.

He looked back down to his phone.

Knight: Can I answer you in another form?
Luna: Like a dance?

His chest quivered next to mine as he tried to control his laughter. His smile was glorious. It was the one weapon he could unleash to completely defuse me.

Knight: Yes but better.

He tossed his phone between us, taking my face in his paws and drawing my lips to his. His mouth collided with mine, and he traced his tongue along the seam of my lips before plunging in and kissing me hard.

I groaned, against my better judgment.

"If I do this, we can't wake up your roommate," he whispered.

I nodded. He put his mouth in my ear and swept his tongue along the lobe before shoving it inside, making me swallow down both my giggles and shudders. I was horny. I was *never* horny.

Okay, not exactly true, but I'd never wanted to be filled the way I did right now. My breaths became harsh and short when his playful tongue found its way from my ear to my throat, tracing the delicate column at its center, his hands working my jeans, lowering them again. I'd expected him to give my breasts special attention, but instead, he slid down to the foot of the bed, his face level with my groin.

My heart began to beat faster. He looked up at me, silent. Dark. Contemplative.

I widened my eyes in question.

Sorry—his mouth curved around the word, but no voice came out. Then, in one harsh motion, he ripped my cotton panties from my body, throwing them on the floor. Before I could register what was happening, his face was between my legs, feasting on me. *Feasting*. His tongue thrashing against the walls of my sex.

"Jesus," I breathed. "Yes."

He put a finger inside me, filling me completely with his tongue and fingers. He drilled into me so deep I could feel him everywhere. He curled his finger when he reached the deepest part of me, hitting a spot that made hot honey pour from my chest to my groin. He took one of my butt cheeks in his big paw and hoisted me slightly up and to an angle that allowed him to shove his tongue deep inside me, and then he did something wonderful. He rolled the tip of his piercing inside, where his tongue couldn't reach, tickling that same sensitive spot over and over again.

Oh, God. Oh, God. Oh, God.

I felt liquid pouring out of me and into his mouth. It was probably a trickle. Still, I was ejaculating. Or something close to it. All over his face. I could feel my sheets dampening underneath me and my sex dripping through his fingers that held my ass. He made the groaning sounds of a lion gorging on a gazelle. I was coming so hard I couldn't stop it. Spasms ran through every inch of my body. I jerked and tossed, grabbing the side of my pillow and biting it hard as wave after wave of ecstasy coursed through me—atom-splitting, mind-blowing, nerve-tingling sensations I could never fully describe.

The climax was so intense, it felt like I was under a spell. Knight took his tongue out only when my ass hit the mattress with a soft thud. When I chanced opening my eyes and watching him, I caught him wiping his soaked chin with the back of his hand and licking the rest of my juices, still staring at my groin like it was some mystical creature he was trying to decode.

You know everything there is to know about it, I wanted to assure him, still lying half-naked in my hoodie, with my ruined panties somewhere on the floor of this room. He didn't even look at me as he used his thumbs to open me up again, staring at my inside carefully. It felt almost clinical. I fought the last trembles of my orgasms as he lowered himself and flicked his piercing against my clit.

Oh, no.

"I can't," I whisper-shouted.

I was going to break from another orgasm of this sort. Or worse. I had zero control over my muscles. I was actually afraid I'd pee on him or something. Knight seemed like a kinky dude, but I was sure he'd appreciate the heads-up.

"It's too much."

Flick. Flick. Flick. Suck. Knight may have been a virgin a few hours ago, but he'd probably made watching porn an art of sorts, because he was freakishly good at sex. And I mean, world-class good. Like everything else he did, he was confident in bed, and as he alternated between sucking my clit into his mouth and flicking it with his tongue, I found myself trying to fight off another orgasm that threatened to tear me in two. I scooted my butt up, trying to escape the tormenting pleasure that chased me, but he pinned me to the bed, flicking my clit faster, sucking on it harder.

This time, I cried into the pillow, tears of happiness sliding from my cheeks. I kept the pillow on my face, knowing there was a pool of my lust for him underneath us, and before I knew what was happening, he was on top of me again. But this time, it wasn't love we were making.

No.

He was fucking me.

Drilling. Slamming. Pushing. Punishing with his jerky, deep thrusts. I thought he was going to nail me into the mattress until I couldn't unglue myself from it, and knew for a fact it must feel like sitting on a roller coaster for April on the upper bunk. She was going to hate me.

"Knigh…Knight…go…s…s…slow…slower," I stammered as his sweat began to rain down my face. It was so hot, I was nearing my third orgasm. Fourth, if you counted the water tower.

His lips dragged along mine. He bit the tip of my lower lip and tugged it, like a lion warning his cub. "Fuck her, baby. Come for me again."

I'd always giggled when I read about women coming on demand. It seemed oddly unlikely. Like sneezing on demand. And I was seventy-five percent sure my coming had nothing to do with Knight's request. But I came nonetheless. He pulled out, ripped the condom from his penis, flipped my hoodie up and came all over my breasts, watching me as he did with a smirk on his face.

A minute later, he collapsed beside me. I stared at the wood of the upper bunk, to which I'd glued stickers of bands I liked and inspirational quotes that had helped me get through the period of time without him.

Knight flung his arm behind his head. I did the same. We both stilled as April shifted in her bunk, groaning something unintelligible. When she got back to softly snoring, we let out relieved breaths. I turned toward him, placing my hand on his chest, my other one plucking my phone from between the wall and the mattress, texting him.

Luna: Can I ask you something?
Knight: Anything.
Luna: Actually, two things.
Knight: …
Luna: How do I taste?

He didn't look up from his phone, which I appreciated.

Knight: Like cheap rubber.
Luna: ???

Knight: The condom from the water tower. But also sweet.
          And hot. And perfect.
Luna: That's better.
Knight: But also like the condom.

I swatted his chest. He grinned.

Knight: What's your second question?
Luna: You said what we did should answer my question. I
          don't think it did. What are we, Knight?

This time, he did look up, his gaze holding mine. He opened his mouth, not whispering the words, but uttering them loud and clear.

"We're everything."

CHAPTER NINETEEN
KNIGHT

I tossed all three mini bottles of mouthwash I'd consumed into the trash in my hotel room, washing them down with a bottle of water and mint gum. Luna and I were going to meet up at a diner three blocks from Boon, and I preferred not to smell like a piss-ridden alleyway. The alcohol on my breath was starting to stick, even when I wasn't drinking. It was in my sweat. In my odor. In my fucking veins.

This morning I'd snuck out of her room, but not before parting from her body in the most glorious way. She'd pressed her ass against my dick, wiggling it back and forth, begging for friction. I jerked off, came on her ass, then fingered her to an orgasm before leaving, because—why, yes, I *was* a perfect gentleman.

Before going to meet Luna, I called Mom. Her voice was strained, breathless, but she tried to hold back the coughs, asking me how I was doing in North Carolina.

"Good," I said. "Luna's my girlfriend now."

It felt stupid to say it in the same way it felt stupid to think it. We were so much more than steady. I was going to marry her. I'd known that with every fiber of my being before I was fully potty trained, for fuck's sake. I just hadn't known how to label it back then.

"Oh my goodness," Mom shrieked into my ear. She sounded relieved more than happy, and I tried not to let it dampen my mood. "I'm so happy to hear that."

"Happy or relieved?" I threw her tone back at her.

"Both," she admitted.

I had a flight booked for tonight. Missing school wasn't on my agenda—not because I gave a shit about it, but because I didn't want to add any more concern to my already troubled household. They were going to find out soon that the only reason I was still in school was because I had been the football captain and Coach would hunt me down and kick my ass if I dropped out. My grades were every teacher's nightmare. Based on them, you wouldn't guess I was literate, let alone smart.

I loved Luna, but nothing could keep me away from Mom for very long. This was the longest and farthest I'd ever been away from her.

There was silence on the other line.

"Mom?"

More silence.

"Rosie!" I barked impatiently, kicking the trash can in the hotel bathroom. The mouthwash bottles spilled over, rolling on the floor, knocking against the top of my boot. Without thinking, I reached for a fourth bottle and unscrewed it.

Damn it all to hell.

"Sorry," she choked on the word. "Drifted off for a second. I'm fine, baby. Totally fine. Just really tired."

"I love you," I growled, annoyed.

"Love you too."

I texted Dad asking about Mom, and he said everything was cool. I texted Lev and Aunt Em, cross-examining them, but they gave me the same laconic update.

Fine, fine, fine. I understood fully now why Luna loathed this word.

———

I sat across from my girlfriend in a dirty little diner that smelled like it had been deep-fried in its entirety. The walls, the red-vinyl booths, the tables—everything smelled of fried food, with the undertone of stale coffee.

Real talk? I wasn't Boon's biggest fan. If I had to give it a twin city, it'd be hell. Call me a shallow dipshit, but I liked my life in Todos Santos. With the perfect palm trees and mile-long white beaches and sparkling private pools and diners that were squeaky clean and brand-new. You could eat from the fucking floor at my local Denny's.

But Luna was here, wearing a tight green top that made her puckered nipples poke out, so naturally, Boon was my favorite place for this moment.

"How's Rosie?" She squeezed my hand from across the table. I wanted to sit on the same side as her but reined in my clingy-ass tendencies. I still hadn't told her the L-word. She had enough leverage on me as it was, so I held on to it like a nun holds her V-card.

"She's *fine*."

Then I remembered I couldn't bullshit Luna, and she didn't deserve to be bullshitted anyway.

"That's what they tell me. Wanna know what I think? I think it's nearing the end."

Luna bit her lip, looking down at her thighs. She was a terrible liar, so I deduced there was something she wasn't telling me.

"Do you know something I don't?" I dipped my chin, my throat working.

She shook her head, flipping the greasy, plastic menu a few times, pretending to read it. Upside-fucking-down. Nice.

Drop it, my mind told me. *Eighteen years later, you finally got the girl. Don't pick a fight and ruin this. Not now.*

What could Luna know about my mom that I didn't anyway? Nothing. I was on top of my shit in that department. I grilled Mom, Em, and Dad on a daily basis. Her doctors too. Short of gutting a random healthy person for their lungs and shoving them in my mom's chest, I did everything I could. Luna wasn't keeping anything from me.

"I'm hungry for something sweet. I think I'm going to go for the pancakes." Moonshine tucked a lock of hair behind her ear, her eyes roaming the menu. "What do you want to eat?"

"You," I deadpanned, flicking my menu across the table. She looked up. Giggled.

Her voice. Her fucking voice. I could drown in it.

"No, really?" She covered her giggling mouth and that chipped tooth she thought made her imperfect.

"*Really*," I maintained. "Put every dish on the menu in this place and your legs spread-eagle on this table and test me."

"Jesus, Knight." She laughed.

I sat back and smiled. It was easier to be my usual cocksure self when I was secretly drunk. And the good thing about mouthwash, I'd found out recently, was it didn't leave the stench of vodka or whiskey. Plus, because you weren't actually supposed to drink it, it packed one hell of a buzz.

"How'd your roommate react this morning?" I changed the subject from her pussy before my dick sprung out of my Armani slacks and ran to reunite.

Luna rolled her eyes, taking a sip of her giant glass of milk. "She yelled at me."

I winced. "What did you do?"

"Yelled back."

"Attagirl."

"Then she hugged me."

"Uh-huh."

"*Then* she apologized for slapping me."

"She slapped you?"

"Yup. I mean, I can't wholly blame her. She thought I was completely mute. I did a lot of apologizing of my own for keeping so many things a secret from her. Then I sent Josh a text message asking to meet him for coffee so I could apologize and explain. I feel like such a dick."

"Maybe because you were dicked all night."

Evidently, I wasn't going to be a supportive boyfriend. I just couldn't stomach FUCKING JOSH's name—even if I'd won the battle, the war, and conquered every inch of the land. I slid out of my seat and joined her, wrapping an arm around her shoulders and kissing her head.

"Just because you didn't tell them the whole truth doesn't mean you lied. You *didn't* speak at the time. It takes a lot of courage to do what you did, at age nineteen, and without the support of your idiot best friend. They'll get over the shock. Cut yourself some slack."

"What if I broke Josh's heart?" Luna's eyes filled with tears.

I took her hands and placed them on my chest. Her sweetness just about killed me. She wasn't sad for FUCKING JOSH specifically. She was sad because she'd made someone else feel shitty.

"You didn't do it on purpose. We break things all the time. It's called life. If you don't break, you don't live. You don't move. You don't try. You don't take chances. Breaking is a part of living. FUCKING JOSH will move on. He has to. You need to understand that sometimes, the consequences of your actions are destructive. You need to forgive yourself and make sure the other person knows you're sorry. You can't do more than that. You're not responsible for someone else's happiness."

She ate pancakes, and I had a BLT. I forced myself to finish the bitch so she wouldn't know how crazy lethargic I was from all the drinking. Since football season was over, I no longer gave a shit about my muscle tone. I wasn't even sure I'd go to college at this point. I might skip a year to stay with Mom. I knew I was definitely not moving out, and I wondered if that was going to be a problem for Luna, who seemed to want to stay here at Boon.

We strolled toward the water tower after that, hand in hand. I was boarding a plane later this evening. I didn't know the next time I could come visit. Technically, I could come next weekend if Mom was okay. But what if she wasn't? Leaving her side now felt like Russian roulette.

"So. This long-distance shit," I said, broaching the topic.

We both looked forward, at the water tower, not each other.

"We'll make it work," she said.

"We have to," I insisted. "And not just this year." I stopped. She stopped. The entire world stopped.

This was hard. And necessary. No man should have to choose between the love of his life and the woman who gave him life. But here I was, in front of some fucked-up Sophie's choice. The boy or the girl? The mother or the girlfriend?

"I'm not going anywhere, Luna. I'm staying in Todos Santos to be there with my mom. This year. Possibly next year. Definitely for the rest of her days. And if my mom…" I started, but she put her fingertips to my lips.

A tiny, barely visible shake of her head told me not to continue.

I cleared my throat. "Regardless of Mom, I will need to be there for Levy and Dad."

After.

"We'll make it work." She brushed her thumb across my cheek.

"I'll need you. All the freaking time."

"I'll try to transfer to UCLA. Might work. We'll see."

"Thank you." I was too desperate to do the chivalrous thing and tell her to stay here if she was happy.

How the fuck was I going to survive until then? If she was even going to get the transfer.

She rose on her toes, wrapping her arms around my neck. She touched her lips to mine. There was something about that kiss that promised more.

An *I love you.*

If she said it, I promised myself, I would stop drinking. I'd hold on to it in my darkest hours. I'd be good. Or at least better than I was right now. For her.

I love you, I told her in my head. *I love you, I love you, I love you.*

For some reason, it was important for me to hear her say it first. I was so obviously, blindly, pathetically in love with her, I needed her to show me this meant something for her too.

Her mouth opened. My goddamn heart was about to burst.

"Ride or die," she whispered.

I smiled, my disappointment leaking through the cracks of my soul.

"Ride or die, Moonshine."

CHAPTER TWENTY
KNIGHT

On my cab ride from the San Diego airport to Todos Santos, my fingers closed into a fist around three Xanax pills. I looked out the window, willing them to crush into powder so I could slide them easily into the mouthwash I had in a Starbucks cup. The high was faster when they were powdered.

The hospital.

I was going straight to the hospital.

The cherry on the shit cake, I thought as I tossed the pills into my mouth, was Dad refusing to tell me what was up. The worst possible scenarios rolled through my mind. Mom had sounded so weak on the phone.

She really is dying.

She's already dead.

She is brain dead.

Dead, dead, dead.

We were rich. We were healthy. We were strong. Invincible, really. So why couldn't we stop it from happening?

I resorted to texting Aunt Em.

Knight: Just tell me she's alive.

Emilia: She is.

Knight: Y is Dad being an asshole, then?

Emilia: Have you been taking care of yourself over there?

Uh-oh. She didn't even give me shit for my nonexistent grammar and for cussing Dad. Not a good sign.

Knight: Tell me what to prepare myself for.
Emilia: Reality.

I hated everyone. Other than Luna, maybe, but I couldn't talk to her before I had more information. It was the middle of the night in North Carolina now, and she had school tomorrow.

When the cab slid to the hospital curb, I stumbled out, the Xanax and alcohol already kicking it in my bloodstream. I decided it was probably a good idea to alternate between mouthwash and actual liquor when I almost threw up on the front desk while asking for Mom's room.

The overnight receptionist directed me to the end of the hall. As I zigzagged my way there, my phone began to buzz in my pocket. I took it out, hoping Luna had a sixth sense.

Alas, it was Dixie. I sent it straight to voicemail and texted, *All good, speak soon.*

My dad was standing in the hallway, looking like a piece of dried toast—crumbling at the edges, completely burned out. The minute he saw me, instead of hugging me, or telling me it was good to have me back, or asking me, oh, I don't know…how the fuck I was doing, he scowled and threw an accusing finger my way.

"You."

"Me." I pretended to yawn, getting near him.

Big mistake. Huge. Now he could smell the mouthwash. He wasn't stupid enough to think I'd gone all dental-hygiene crazy in the span of a weekend.

"Nice touch, son. Showing up here reeking of alcohol when your mother is hospitalized."

"Thanks, man. And I appreciate you keeping me in the loop as to what the *fuck* is going on with said mom." I collapsed onto a blue chair outside her room.

He was right, though. She didn't have to be healthy to know I looked like shit and smelled not much better.

"Where's Lev?" I asked.

"At the Rexroths'."

"Why not Aunt Em's?"

"She's on her way."

"Look, I'm not that drunk. Can I see Mom?" I rubbed my face tiredly, closing my eyes.

"No," he bit out, bracing his arm against the wall and looking down at his shoes.

She was asleep, then. I folded my arms, about to find a comfortable angle and call it a night. Mom could sleep for hours on end at the hospital. The shit they plugged into her, paired with the steroids, meant she went through spurts of random energy, followed by crashes and days of sleep.

I closed my eyes, mentally reminding myself to let Vaughn know I needed to bum a ride to school tomorrow morning, when Dad's loafer kicked my shin. Not gently either. My eyes cracked open.

"Wake up." He balled up the collar of my shirt, yanking me to my feet.

Suddenly we were nose to nose. I narrowed my eyes at him. He'd never been physical with me before. My heart started pounding.

"What the fuck is your problem?"

"You're my problem!" he seethed, baring his teeth. "Your attitude is my problem. Your selfishness, to just up and…and…leave for a *girl*," he spat the word out, his breath ragged as he flung his big arms in the air, pushing away from me. "You know what my problem is? My problem is your mom is not okay, and here you are, drinking and smoking yourself to death, thinking we don't know. Thinking we don't *care*. When, put simply, I'm trying to extinguish the fires in my life one at a time. My house is on fucking fire, Knight," Dad boomed, his voice ricocheting off the walls.

The entire hallway shook with his dark tenor. Nurses and patients peeked out of ajar doors, bug-eyed, and two male nurses straightened from their slumped positions against the reception booth and headed in our direction.

"Why don't you just go ahead and say it?" I smiled sardonically, opening my arms. "You wish you hadn't adopted me. One less bullshit problem to deal with, right? But you knew this was going to happen. She did too. You *knew* we'd be here someday, and you still had us."

Asshole drunk Knight had struck again. I really hated my intoxicated alter ego. He had no filters whatsoever.

What was I saying? Why was I saying this? Because there was a part of me that believed it to be true. My mother knew she was going to die young. She'd still adopted me. She'd still had Lev. His name meant *heart* in Hebrew, but it was lungs she needed. It was her lungs that failed her. And our hearts were broken.

"You set me up for this," I accused. "You gave me a family you knew was temporary."

"Newsflash, Knight. *Life* is temporary. Your mom could've been perfectly healthy and gotten run over by a truck ten years ago. Just because you take life for granted doesn't mean it is."

"Okay, Oprah. Spin this shit to suit yourself." I laughed bitterly, turning away and starting for the nearest door before we both exploded.

By the way my father's face had morphed from angry to shocked, I gathered my diplomatic skills were lacking while under the influence. The nurses clapped our shoulders, ushering us down the hallway.

"Emotions are running high, gentlemen. We understand this, but you need to take it outside. Get some fresh air. Calm down. We'll let you know if there's any change."

Any change? What did they mean, change? I let my legs carry me to the balcony off the first floor of the hospital. Dad and I stood outdoors, ignoring the drizzle. He shook his head, staring up at the black sky, letting the rain pour down on his face. He closed his eyes, looking half-dead. He raked his fingers through his hair and a chunk of it was left between his fingers. *Jesus.*

"You're an asshole for reducing Luna to being just a girl," I muttered, fishing for my phone in my pocket.

Dixie again. I killed the call.

Why can't you die, Dix? Why does it have to be Rosie?

"You're an asshole for judging your mom for having you and Lev," Dad retorted, pacing.

I wondered what the fuck was going on but didn't want to ask, because I knew he wouldn't give me a straight answer.

"I'm going to see her." I tested the water, pretending to make my way to the door.

Dad curled his fingers around my bicep, pulling me back. "Don't," he warned.

"Why?"

"Because."

"Because?" I gauged, assessing him coldly.

I was getting tired of being strong. Being indifferent. Being someone I wasn't.

He took a deep breath, his eyes fluttering shut. "Because she's in a coma."

Know how sometimes people say their entire world crumbled? I never quite understood what they meant until this moment. The moment where everything in my life shattered, collapsing one brick at a time. I toppled backward, my back hitting the wall, then slid down until my ass hit the damp ground. Dad stood in front of me, his head hung between his shoulders—a lowered, defeated flag. I immediately knew this wasn't about my drinking or the drugs. Neither Dad nor Mom knew the extent of the trouble I'd gotten myself into this year.

This is about Mom.

"How?" I heard myself asking.

"They put her in a chemically induced coma for her end-stage cystic fibrosis."

"When?"

"Earlier today."

"Why didn't you tell me?" My voice escalated into a scream.

"So, what? You'd fly back home thinking about it the entire time? Her hooked up to a ventilator, dying?"

"Dying?" I realized I sounded like a dumbass but couldn't help it.

What was I expecting to happen? For her to walk swiftly out of this place? Maybe do cartwheels all the way to the parking lot? It was too late for a lung transplant, too late for experimental treatments, too late, period.

Dad shook his head. It occurred to me that I needed to be there for him like he was there for me. I just couldn't. I couldn't think straight. I couldn't even breathe. I shook my head, stood up, and stalked back into the ICU, slapping the glass door, flinging it open. I could hear Dad's footsteps following me.

I took out my phone, ignoring the five missed calls from Dixie, and texted Luna.

Knight: My mom is in a coma.

Her answer came not even a minute later.

Luna: On my way.

———————

A bottle of whiskey.

Two more Xanax.

One Adderall because I needed to concentrate on shit in class. (See? Responsible adult.)

That was basically my menu for Monday, as Dad hurled me into Vaughn's car and insisted I go to school. I fought him on it. Of course I did. What kid goes to school when his mom is in a coma?

"This one does." Dad slammed the passenger door in my face, ignoring Vaughn, and Hunter in the back seat. "It's chemically induced. We have the situation under control. Show up to class, do your best, come back here, and we'll see her together."

I opened my mouth to argue again but clamped it shut when Hunter, behind me, said, "We'll take good care of him, sir."

"Hunter…" Dad dug his fingers into his eye sockets. "No offense, but I wouldn't trust you with an ant. Unfortunately, I have my plate full right now. Just go."

The entire way to school, Vaughn stole glances at me with his slanted, icy eyes. I realized things were dire when even he was on his best behavior. Dude didn't do pity and didn't cut corners. He had a mean streak a mile long and never missed an opportunity to kick you while you were down.

"Not sure drinking yourself into liver failure is the best course of action right now." He moved his gum from side to side in his mouth.

"Not sure I asked for your fucking medical opinion," I snapped, leaning my head against the window and closing my eyes.

Hunter sucked in a charged breath behind us. Someone pounded their fists from the inside of my head to my eyes.

I was pretty sure it was Dixie.

Hunter pulled my head off of a toilet in the school's bathroom. My face was wet. My hair dripped down my Armani shirt. I knew it was Hunter because I heard his voice growling, but I couldn't for the life of me open my eyes.

"This is even more pathetic than dying *on* the toilet seat. Fuckboy literally almost drowned *inside* a toilet."

Vaughn's voice came next. "I need to give Mr. Astalis my application. You have to deal with this mess."

"You asshole. What am I supposed to do with him?"

"Just put him in my car."

"You're seriously going to have him wait like this?" Hunter shrieked.

"He did that to himself." I could hear the shrug in Vaughn's voice. "Call it a hard-earned lesson."

"Can I just call *you* a cunt?" I wanted to say, but I couldn't. I couldn't move my lips at all.

I heard Vaughn tossing Hunter his car keys, and Hunter catching them and hauling me up. I was dragged, pushed, tucked inside a car, and buckled.

And by the time I knew what was happening, I'd passed out again.

––––––––––

"You smell like shit, and you're making my car smell like it too."

I didn't answer Vaughn.

"Passing out inside a public toilet bowl. Real classy, Knight. Hit rock bottom yet?"

"Not yet," I groaned, gaining consciousness. Everything hurt. Most of all? Living through this nightmare.

"I'm telling your parents."

"They know." I grinned, closing my eyes. "And they don't have time for this crap. But go ahead. Make things more difficult for them. Oh, wait, my dad is flailing to keep himself going, and my mom is in a fucking coma. Good luck getting a response from either."

Vaughn shook his head.

I laughed, even though nothing was funny anymore.

If I'd thought getting into Mom's room and seeing her hooked up to chirping machines that sounded like freight trains and were programmed to help her breathe would soothe my aching ass, I was gravely mistaken. Dad held my hand on one side, Lev's on the other. The three of us stood there, staring. Staring. Staring.

The notion that it was the end was so strong you could feel it in the air.

Not just the end for her but for all of us.

I used to get this idea that the end of the world was happening right in front of me, since I'd learned about Mom's disease at a young age. Sometimes I'd climb up the forest's mountain, look at the nothingness surrounding me, and think, *This is it. The end of the world. Right here.* Or it was when thunder cracked, and fog descended over the roads, misting the car windows. Or when I concentrated on that thin line between the skyline and the ocean, imagining myself sliding into it and letting it suck me into another dimension.

That was how it felt right now: Like there was nothing to come after this.

No graduation.

No football.

No more kisses from Luna under her covers.

This was where I ended, and nothing else began.

This was when I lost the person who'd built my life—the person who'd claimed me when the woman who gave birth to me couldn't.

Who was going to claim me now?

Where did I belong?

"Can I touch her?" Levy's voice was hoarse.

He wasn't so short anymore. He was fourteen now. I imagined it was even more difficult for him, to lose her when he was still so young.

Who'd tell him it was okay to screw up his first kiss when she was gone?

That there was such a thing as too much saliva?

Who'd give him female advice?

Take him suit shopping for prom?

Wipe his tears when Bailey broke his heart—and she was going to, I had no doubt. They were too tight not to hurt each other.

Me. That's who. That's what I decided anyway. I was going to up my big-brother game. I had to.

"Gently," Dad said, his tone like a whiplash, making my baby brother wince.

Lev disconnected from Dad. He took restrained steps toward Mom—like if he walked too fast, he'd shatter her. Her eyes were closed, her skin pale. Purple veins ran through her eyelids like spiderwebs. She looked peaceful, the blanket pulled all the way up to her neck. I thought Lev was going to touch her cheek, her face. Maybe her hair. To my surprise, his fingers curled around the edge of the blanket, pulling it slowly, moving it down to her waist.

"She hates to sleep with the blanket all the way up," he choked out, looking away, at the wall. A sob ripped from his mouth, coming out harsh, like thunder.

Dad stood like a statue, refusing to cope with the shit life had thrown at us, and stared at both of them—mainly at Mom.

I snapped out of it, shook off the headache and nausea, and gripped Lev's shoulder from behind.

"You're right, Levy-boy. She really does."

CHAPTER TWENTY-ONE
LUNA

I wished I could rewrite our last moment, the way I could in my little notebook.

The last, first moment I saw him again, after Boon.

The boy I fell in love with, the guy I fell in lust with, the man who'd be my downfall.

When I finally got to the hospital, my first vision of Knight was him gliding through the corridor with a death glare, rubbing a crying Lev's back, walking away from his father, who was shouting at both of them to come back.

Knight stopped when we came face-to-face, his expression unmoved. I didn't expect a kiss or a grand declaration of love, considering the circumstances, but when I opened my arms to hug them, he ignored the gesture, opting to jerk Levy closer to his side, like he was protecting him from the entire world, me included.

"Take us home?" he almost pleaded. "I want to drop Levy at your parents' and take a shower. It's been a long day."

I nodded. I'd figured he'd need some chauffeuring, so I'd made a quick stop at my house to pick up Dad's car before coming here. I normally shied away from driving, but I was beginning to understand that Knight's situation required a lot of adjusting. I was desperate to fit into his new, broken world and help any way I could.

I was already missing classes, skipping school, and falling behind by being here for God knows how long. But I would be.

Indeed, the price of Knight's love was expensive, but I had no trouble paying my dues.

As we drove silently, Lev sat in the back, sucking his breath in to hold back his sobs. His face was a wreck, his eyes red, his hands shaking in his lap. I didn't know what to say, but I knew I needed to say *something*. Anything. I cleared my throat, straightening in my seat.

"I'm going to pack you a bag, Lev, give you some pizza money, and drop you at Jaime and Mel's. I already spoke with them. You can sleep over at their place."

I watched through the rearview mirror as Lev's dimmed eyes lit up. I knew he loved Bailey dearly. She was his rock, as I was Knight's. Everyone in this family needed someone strong to lean on. I just wondered who was going to be there for Dean.

"You talk?" Lev was too exhausted to be surprised.

A sad smile played on my lips. "Yes."

"Since when?"

Since I decided to pull my head out of my butt.

"Since…it became apparent that I need to. A few weeks. Not more. How can I make this easier for you, Levy?" I asked.

It occurred to me that when someone is dealing with something so profound as losing a loved one, perhaps instead of telling them everything will be okay—while knowing that for the foreseeable future it won't—it would be better to ask for guidance on how to please them.

"Doesn't Racer have the new Zelda?" Lev asked.

"He does."

"We've been wanting to check it out."

"I'll drop it at Bailey's," I assured him.

After leaving Lev at the Followhills', I let Knight nap on the couch while I ran him a bath. He smelled like hell, a piece of information I refrained from sharing with him. I had just thrown a unicorn bath bomb into the water, watching the fizz and foam dance in pink and purple on the surface, when I felt his arms tightening around my midriff, his nose nuzzling my shoulder.

"Shower," he growled into my ear, turning off the running water. I closed my eyes, shuddering against his erection, which pressed against my butt.

"What's wrong with a bath?" I licked my lower lip.

"Can't fuck your brains out the way I want to in a bath." His teeth scraped along my skin, leaving goose bumps in their wake.

His large, ripped body moved toward the tub, unplugging it before flicking on the shower. The three showerheads came to life, and as steam gathered between the glass walls of the crème-and-black checked marble tiles, he turned to me, stripping.

I did the same. We took our clothes off silently. There was something clinical about it. Bitterly erotic. We were getting prepared to do something dirty in a place so clean, without any sweet words and reassuring promises.

"Are you sure you're in the right headspace?"

"I will always be in the right headspace to be inside you. You're my home."

He was totally naked now, his penis hard, long, and thick, pointing at me. He offered me his hand. I took it. He took my lips with his and kissed me so hard, I began to feel dizzy in his arms, swaying back and forth. He tasted like alcohol, but I didn't think confronting him about it would do me any good.

After, I promised myself. When we were both content and spent and napping in each other's arms, post-orgasm, I'd go harsh on him for the drinking.

He'd been too good at keeping his addiction under wraps.

I could no longer turn a blind eye or hope it was a phase.

It was here to stay, and by God, I wasn't going to let it.

Knight opened the shower door, helping me in and boxing

me against the wall in his arms, still kissing me deep and rough. I quivered against his bulging body. Everything about him was hard and strong.

You can afford to be a little soft from the inside from time to time, my beautiful, broken Knight.

"Condom," I murmured into his lips as he hoisted me up.

I had to wrap my legs around his narrow waist for balance. I wasn't on the pill, and even though I'd booked an appointment back at Boon, I wasn't taking *any* chances.

"I'll finish out." He spoke against my skin, already lined up to push into me.

I moaned. "Too dangerous."

"So why is your grip on me tightening? C'mon, Moonshine. What's the worst that could happen? A little baby Lunight? She'll be cute. Plus, cosmic interference and all. I'm losing a mother, gaining a kid. Sounds about right."

I was so shocked by his words, I found myself gaping at him as he pushed into me bareback, fucking me against the tiles. A few thrusts in, I forgot what had come out of his mouth. I forgot my own name. He pumped fast and hard, his soft, wet hair between my fingers as I cried out his name.

Knight could fill me to the brim even when he wasn't technically inside me. Just feeling his hot body pressing against mine was enough to set me off. I felt the climax from my curled toes, like an earthquake rising up to the rest of my body, an electric shock zinging through me.

"Knight, Knight, Knight."

I came so hard, I couldn't hold myself wrapped around him, and he had to catch me, groping my ass with a bruising grip. His harsh fingers against my delicate skin only made the orgasm more intense. It ripped me apart in the best possible way.

He pulled out of me at the same time I dropped to my knees. I didn't even know what I was doing. Worshipping him? Couldn't have been much else. I didn't know how to do the thing I wanted to do to him. I didn't have the first clue how to do it.

Still, I stared at his big hand, pumping his dick, so raw and large and close to me, and I wanted to.

I swallowed, licking my lips and staring at his manhood.

"Can I unload down your throat?"

He'd read my mind, his voice so raspy and hoarse, it felt like fingernails dragging along my skin. He looked drunk on what we were doing, and that made me feel powerful.

"I…I don't know how."

"Do you know how to swallow?"

"Ah…yes."

"Perfect. You passed the test."

I licked my lips again. I wanted this dick in my mouth.

The thought surprised me but also delighted me. I never thought I'd be into something like that.

Before I could articulate my next thought, not to mention form it, his penis was inside my mouth. It was bigger than I'd anticipated it to be somehow. I gagged as I felt the tip in the back of my throat, my eyes filling with tears. I could taste myself on his skin, and it embarrassed me as he thrust hard and grasped the back of my head, forcing me to gag instead of pull back, as was my instinct.

Instead of biting down on his cock—which a part of me wanted to do—I clamped my lips over his length, a knee-jerk reaction that matched the hot heat swirling in my stomach. He groaned, and I felt warm, thick liquid rushing down my throat. I kept swallowing and swallowing it, even though it tasted salty, earthy, and strong.

Honestly, a lot like low-carb noodles.

After, I closed my eyes, hugging my knees to my chest. I didn't know why I was so ashamed. I wasn't uncomfortable about what we'd done, but I was hurt by the way Knight had used my mouth to get off. So I just let the water rain down on my face and body. I heard him shuffling inside the shower unevenly, probably a little drunk still, and the scent of coconut and citrus filled the air—soaps and creams and salts everywhere.

"Hey."

I heard his voice. Soft. So soft all of a sudden. But I couldn't shake what he had said about having a kid, about not wearing a condom—or how he'd just shoved his dick into my mouth without warning and basically fucked my head.

"Moonshine." His hand clasped my shoulder.

I held back from wailing. This was not the right time to cry, not when he was drowning in troubles. Then again—was I really that girl? The one who let something like that slide?

"What's up?" He lowered himself to me, and I opened my eyes. He looked like a wreck. On the plus side, he also looked completely sober.

"I didn't like it," I whispered.

He took my hand and began to lather my arm in soap, up and down. He moved on to my other arm, his lips pursed.

"I thought you had an orgasm. I thought it was good for you," he said boyishly, his ears pinking to a deep shade of rose. "Well, fuck. I'm sorry."

"I did like it. But I didn't like the *way* we did it. You were angry. You didn't listen to me when I asked you to put on a condom. And that thing in the end…"

He stopped touching me and looked up. The water was pounding on us, like that time when he'd saved me on my bike. The memory soothed my aching heart. Then I remembered the Knight I was talking to wasn't the same boy who'd risked his life for me. That boy wasn't an addict.

"I'm sorry about the condom. That was… God, it was such a dick move. Shit."

He squeezed his eyes shut, shaking his head. He sat down in front of me, burying his face in his hands, his elbows on his knees. There was something so vulnerable about seeing him—big and athletic and formidable—naked. I shamefully loved and rightfully hated this view of Knight—fragile and imperious at the same time.

"I get like that when I'm drunk. Really mean. I'm so sorry… so sorry…"

I crawled into his embrace, prying his hands from his face. He wasn't crying, but his eyes were red.

"I'll never do it again. It was a fucked-up thing to do and a screwed-up thing to say. I didn't mean anything by it. I know we can't have a baby now. And trust me, I'm totally on board with that. We'll have lots of babies. When we're old and shit."

My heart stirred wildly behind my ribs. I tried to ignore it.

"About that other thing…" I cleared my throat.

"What other thing?"

"When you put your dick in my mouth, Knight."

"You asked me." He frowned, confused. "You said you wanted it there."

"What?"

"You *signed* it to me, Luna. You signed *I want this dick in my mouth*. I just assumed you meant literally because you dropped to your knees, looked at it, and licked your lips."

Oh my God.

I'd signed it. I had. Jesus Christ. Tears began to pool in my eyes. Relieved tears, with a dash of horror for believing, even for one moment, that Knight could ever do something so cruel to me. I knew his normal self never would. Hell, I'd let him sleep in the same bed as me since we were kids. But this was different. He was different now. But nonetheless, he'd done it because he thought I was into it and ready for it.

Now it was my time to lather his gorgeous, Greek god body with soap. I kept my eyes on every organ I cleaned.

"Knight."

"Yes?"

"Do you care for me?"

I hated to play that card when his mother was dying, but I had to. I'd made a promise to her, and I was going to fulfill the hell out of it.

He stared at me seriously, his thick brows furrowed. "More than anyone in the world save for one person. You two are a tie," he said.

My pulse began to thump in the back of my throat. "In that case, I need you to do something for me."

"*A-ny-thing,*" he enunciated, in the same way I'd told Rosie I would do anything for her.

"You need to stop drinking. Stop with the pills. I saw you taking them at the diner when I went to the bathroom and you thought I wasn't looking. And I know that wasn't a one-off. I mean it, Knight. I can handle anything life throws at us. But not this. You need to stay the same Knight I…" *I fell in love with.* "…I know and care for."

I couldn't bring myself to tell him I loved him, and not because of my ego or because I didn't believe it. But because he was drunk. He was always drunk when we were together, and I wanted to say it for the first time when he was sober.

If he was ever going to be sober. I was seriously starting to doubt that.

He pulled away, staring at me blankly. He looked so tired, so miserable, I wanted to swallow the words back and just let him be.

"Vaughn talked to you?" He squinted.

"No." Did Vaughn know we were together?

He got up, thoroughly soaped. "I don't know what to say. I drink occasionally. Who doesn't?"

"Many people." I stood up too. "Me, for instance."

"As far as I recall, you lost your virginity to someone while completely smashed. I kept mine. For *you.* So maybe *you* really shouldn't be drinking. Me, I'm no lightweight. I can handle my shit pretty good."

It was like a slap in the face, and he knew it. I took a step back, turning off the water and wrapping myself in a towel. I wasn't that

girl—the chick who was going to stick around in an abusive relationship, even if the guy was the love of my life. I'd seen firsthand what
bad relationships could do to you. Valenciana, aka mommy dearest,
had bounced from one millionaire to the other. They'd all abused
her—excluding my dad, of course.

"Moonshine." His voice softened again. He touched my shoulder.

I shook him off. He was mean and hateful, and he was going to
stay that way—periodically, of course—until he was sober.

"Get dressed. I'm taking you back to the hospital." My voice had
hardened.

"Baby."

"Don't *baby* me. I'm not your home. People don't ruin their
homes; they build them. They cherish them."

The ride back to the hospital reminded me of how I used to be
before Boon.

Completely silent.

CHAPTER TWENTY-TWO
KNIGHT

Lev was still at the Followhills' when Luna dropped me off in front of Mom's hospital room. She'd rushed to the cafeteria to get Dad a coffee and pick up a bag of clothes Vicious had left for my father. I was all alone now, pushing the ajar door all the way open.

What I saw inside stopped me in my tracks.

Dad, on his knees in front of my unconscious mother, holding her hand between his rough palms. It was the first time I'd seen my dad kneel, and I knew, without a shadow of a doubt, it'd be the last too. He took Mom's hand and kissed the back of it. His entire back was quivering.

"I'm trying, Baby Leblanc. I really am, but I don't know if I can do it without you. The scariest part is, I don't know if I want to. It's a terrible thing to say. I know. Trust me, I know that. But what is life without you? Please wake up, baby. Please. There's an experimental thing they want to try… They told me it could give you five more years. Five more years, sweetheart. Lev will be in college. Knight will probably have a kid or two of his own with Luna. I can't imagine us not babysitting the little monsters together."

I wanted to launch at him and hug the shit out of him, but I also didn't want to kill this moment. It was theirs. Moving was too dangerous. He needed to finish what he had to say.

Dad drew a breath. "Just try for me, okay? Try to get better? I'll fight the doctors. I promise. I'll fight everyone. I just need the smallest signal from you. Anything. Move your eyelid. Twitch your nose. Breathe on your own. Fart, for all I care! Anything, Rosie. Please. Please. Please."

I wanted it to be like in the movies. When his pleas for a miracle actually materialized, and she woke up, and everything was okay. Hell, I half expected it to be the case. That's the trouble with being a Generation X kid. They teach you dreams really do come true. Cruel assholes.

Dad stared at her for long minutes, not giving up, before his shoulders sagged and his head dropped to the mattress by her waist.

He looked up again, changing his tone from pleading to stern.

"Rose Leblanc, you can't die on me now. We still have a lot of work to do. Knight is out of control. Lev is too sensitive and emotional to grow up without a mother. And what about Emilia? What about our friends? Vicious, Trent, and Jaime will try to drag me out of the house to meet people—maybe fix me up with someone. I'll start drinking, I swear. I'll ruin all the progress we've made together."

Pause.

My heart broke for him. It didn't matter that I was still furious with him for how he'd treated Lev. Or me. Or the entire universe, for that matter.

Another growl left his mouth. "Take me with you." He whispered this time, broken and sad and resolute. "I don't want to be here without you, Rose Leblanc."

I swallowed, looking down at my feet. He wanted to die. I got it. If Luna's life were in danger, I'd want to go through whatever she was going through too.

"Ride or die," I heard him say, and my eyes darted up in shock.

What the fuck? It was the same as Luna and me. What were the odds?

"Remember? We carved it on the tree in the forest before the kids butted into our shit and asked us to make a tree house out of it?

I never forgot, Baby Leblanc. Ride or die. There will be no one like you. Nothing like you. You're a once-in-a-lifetime experience, baby, and I'm the lucky bastard who got you."

A sound between a groan and a yelp escaped me, and Dad's head snapped to the door, meeting my gaze. I closed my eyes. I was too self-conscious of getting caught seeing them like this. I'd rather catch them porking every day of the week for the rest of my life than witness this. It had gutted me like a fish.

"Knight."

I didn't know how much time passed before I realized he was hugging me. Or how much time passed before I hugged him back on the threshold of that room, between life and death, hanging by the thread, not here nor there.

I buried my face in his shoulder and tried hard not to cry. I still couldn't cry.

"This is the end, isn't it? You need to tell me," I said.

I felt him nodding, but he didn't say anything. I didn't want him to. It was too hard on all of us as it was.

"How much time?"

"A week, if we're lucky."

"Oh God. And the experimental thing?"

I wasn't even pretending I hadn't eavesdropped on his intimate breakdown. Tragedy and loss strip you off all those things—shame, humiliation, humanity. At some point, you just stop caring.

He shook his head, tightening his arms around me. I wanted to tell him so many things: That he needed to give Lev more attention. That we needed to prepare my baby brother for this. But for the first time in a long time, I just stole a moment alone with my father and pretended my mom wasn't dying, that I wasn't an addict, that my girlfriend wasn't unhappy with me, that I had my shit together.

I breathed in the traces of Dad's cologne, closing my eyes.

He'd carved the words *ride or die* on the back of the tree? How had I not noticed them carved on our tree house?

It was only when Luna wrote them to me in blood that they'd registered.

She was all I saw. Always.

Since telling Luna about Mom was easier than telling Lev, I decided to start with that.

I went to school the next morning right from the hospital. People were still so busy talking shit about Poppy, they hadn't noticed the changes in me, and they knew nothing about Mom. I knew Vaughn and Hunter would stop the gossip mill if people found out just how bad things had gotten with her.

There was something embarrassing and humiliating about death I had yet to uncover. It was a weakness everyone had—yet still, being affected by it felt shameful.

Luna picked me up from school ("You're fucking a freshman in college! Good for you," Hunter called when he saw me kiss her lips.), and we drove to the beach. I hadn't had a drop of alcohol the entire day, and I was snappy, on edge. I decided to make every effort not to piss my girlfriend off. I had a very strong feeling I was already walking a tightrope after our encounter yesterday, when I'd basically thrown her encounter with FUCKING JOSH in her face yet again.

The drive, like many hours of my life recently, passed in silence. Then Luna got us blue slushies and we settled on the sand, letting the freezing waves break on our toes.

"My mother has one week to live, give or take," I told her, looking at that magical sliver where the sky kisses the ocean—where little kids could get swallowed into another portal, apparently.

I wanted it to suck me in. Take me and Dad and Mom and Lev and Luna somewhere we could live without bone-crushing problems.

"Knight," she whispered, cupping my bent knee and giving it a squeeze. "I'm so sorry. I'm here for you. Whatever you need, baby. I took the rest of the week off from school, and my mom and Aunt Emilia said they'll be moving into your house until…"

I turned my head toward her, my face probably carrying a puzzled expression. How did she know all this, and why in the fresh hell wasn't she more surprised by this whole ordeal? It had certainly caught me off guard.

"I just heard them speak on the phone," she clarified, rubbing the back of her neck. Bullshit. Luna couldn't lie to save her life.

"Luna," I warned.

I didn't want to do this. I didn't. But Luna wasn't the only one with a great memory. I remembered the last time she'd acted weird when the subject of my mom's health came up. Like she'd known something I hadn't.

"I really don't—"

"But you do," I cut her off. "You do, so tell me."

Her face fell, her features tightening. She looked wary. I couldn't bear it. She was wary of me. I scrubbed my face, willing myself not to snap at her. I'd do whatever it took to keep myself together.

"Please don't lie to me," I pleaded softly, not looking at her.

"I knew," she whispered.

My heart broke all over again. Because I *hadn't* known. I was the idiot who still prayed while everyone around me was making plans, putting shit in motion. Everyone was preparing for grief, while I was still deep in denial. I exhaled sharply, my face still buried in my hands.

"She asked me to do something for you and Lev. We worked on it over winter break. It was a secret. I promised her I'd always take care of you, Knight, and I meant it."

"You knew it was coming," I repeated. "You knew she was dying. You knew, and you still let me come to you, to Boon, knowing I might not have a mother when I came back. And as it happens, I don't. She's in a coma. I'll never speak to her again."

I didn't know if the betrayal was really that big, or if the tragedy itself enhanced it. Either way, I knew one thing for sure: between finding out I'd be an orphan in the next few days, and that my girlfriend had known about it and hadn't told me, I was angry, in self-destructive mode, and not in the right headspace to be lovey-dovey.

Only this time, I bottled it in.

I couldn't call her ass out and lose her. She'd made a bullshit move—no doubt in my mind. She couldn't fuck someone else *and* keep something like this from me in the same year. Only, apparently, she could. I wasn't going to fight with her because I knew I'd lose control.

I couldn't do that anymore. Not after our little dub-con in the shower. No way, José.

I stood up, smiling tightly.

"Knight?"

"Sorry, baby. Nerves."

"You're scaring me."

Wait till you read my mind. That'll send you running to the hills in a heartbeat.

Actually, drunk Knight wasn't the only asshole inside of me. These days sober Knight was a miserable piece of work too.

"Don't be scared, Moonshine. I'm just trying to cope as best I can. Drop me at home?"

She frowned at me, still hugging her knees to her chest. "What? Why?"

"Homework."

"You expect me to believe that?" She raised an eyebrow.

Sometimes I still couldn't believe she was talking—and at times like this, wished she weren't.

"You can sit and watch if you'd like," I said, trying to give my lie wings.

"Sure." She followed through, standing up.

Wrong answer, bae. I needed to be alone, and I needed to be alone right now.

"Although…" I laced my arm through hers as we walked up the stairs back to the promenade, knowing how wrong everything about the situation was. "I'd only get distracted and try to put my dick in you."

It all sounded off. The proposition. My excuse. My smiles. Every single thing about it. But I could see she knew I was trying really hard not to be a dick. And being a dick was a knee-jerk reaction.

"It's okay," she finally relented, looking around, like there was some hidden camera she wasn't aware of capturing this debacle. "I was going to drive Lev to the hospital so he and Dean could have…a talk."

I practically sighed in relief. I needed a binge like Tom Brady needed a personality transplant. Urgently.

"Right." *Because you knew about this talk before I did* is what I left out.

"Are you sure everything is okay?" Luna stopped in front of her car.

This was my chance to come clean. To tell her I was mad at her for not telling me this. To blow shit up. But wearing my heart on my sleeve never did me any good. Last time I tried it, I'd pushed her away.

So I just offered her another one of the many smiles that never reached my heart and kept her close.

"Never been so sure in my life, baby."

CHAPTER TWENTY-THREE
LUNA

Texas area code?

I let the call go to voicemail, shifting in my chair in the endless, depressing hospital corridor. In front of me, Lev, long-limbed and lanky-framed, had curled into his father's arms, moans tearing through his body like a demon trying to claw its way out of him. Bailey was by their side, rocking back and forth as reality hit them in the face with full force. Much too young. Much too soon.

Edie, Dad, and Racer sat next to me, and we touched each other absentmindedly, grateful we still could. Dad's arm was thrown over Edie's shoulders. Edie held Racer close to her chest, and he clutched my hand in a death grip.

The entire cul-de-sac was in attendance. The Spencers. The Followhills. The Rexroths. Everyone had crammed into the waiting room of the hospital, supporting the Coles.

Everyone but Knight.

My guess as to his whereabouts was as good as anyone else's here. When I confessed to him that I'd known about Rosie's situation, I'd expected him to raise hell. Rightly so. I'd kept something fundamental from him. It was true that Rosie had sworn me to secrecy, but I could still understand his sense of betrayal.

I twisted in my seat as I remembered how his eyes had glossed over at my admission, his irises becoming two dark pools of blood.

Yet, instead of confronting me, yelling at me, breaking stuff, busting knuckles—the things Knight did to cope—he'd mustered a smile. An eerily disturbing smile that had made my heart beat like a wild beast's for all the wrong reasons. And while I wanted to respect his wishes to be alone, I also feared I'd completely blown it by letting him be by himself when he was hurting so much.

My phone buzzed in my hand. Another call from Texas. *What in the hell?*

I was waiting for Knight to show a sign of life. I'd left him dozens of messages. But answering phone calls was never on my agenda, let alone unidentified ones. People knew not to call me because I don't— didn't—speak aloud. In my mind, my talking was still enabled by random spurts of confidence, rather than being a regular occurrence. Many people in this room still hadn't heard my voice.

It seemed surreal to consider casually taking a call and starting to talk as if the last eighteen years hadn't happened.

When the third call from Texas lit up my screen, I excused myself and walked over to the outside area, sliding the door shut behind me.

I pressed the phone to my ear but didn't say anything.

"Hello?" I heard a desperate, female voice.

It sounded like she was running. Her panting blasted in my ear, and there was background noise of wheels squeaking, an elevator pinging, and cell phones ringing.

"Hello? Is there anybody there? Moonshine?"

Moonshine? Why would she call me…?

Knight.

"Who is this?" I retorted.

My whole body broke out in hives at the thought he was in trouble. A bad feeling settled in my stomach like a brick. I paced from side to side in the little garden.

"His mother."

I stopped pacing. Stared at the glass door. My fingers were going numb.

"His birth mother, I mean." She sounded far away now. Her running came to a stop.

"Where is he?" I demanded.

I didn't have time to be shocked. Knight's mother knew him? Was in touch with him? Everything about this screamed surreal and bizarre. My head spun. I stumbled down, forcing myself to sit on a wooden bench behind me. I was shaking like a leaf, unsure if it was from the cold, the adrenaline, or both.

"He's in the ICU."

"Visiting his real mom?" I struggled to breathe.

I heard her gasp on the other end and realized how insensitive that had come out.

"Sorry—I mean…"

"No, it's okay. I don't have time to get offended." She sniffed. "He is hospitalized. He overdosed."

"On *what*?" I screamed into the phone, shooting to my feet, slapping the door open and galloping back in, even though I had no idea where he was or how to find him.

"On everything. Alcohol. Cocaine. Xanax. They're pumping his stomach right now." I could hear in her voice that she was trying hard not to break.

"Is he okay?"

"He threw up most of what he'd taken, I think. But there's no way of knowing how much of it got into his bloodstream."

"Where are you?" I ran past our families to the other side of the floor, zipping by without acknowledging their existence. Luckily, everyone was too cocooned in their own misery to notice.

"I'm outside his room. They wouldn't let me in because I'm not…" She paused for a second, taking a ragged, shaky breath, before finishing: "Because I'm not family."

"Tell me where he is!"

She gave me the directions, and I practically flew there.

Dean couldn't know this. Neither could Lev. I knew it was a

horrible thought when my boyfriend was possibly fighting for his life in the same hospital as his ailing mother, but I loved the entire Cole clan, not just him.

When I got to the room number she had given me, I found her in the hallway. Petite. Blond. Velvet blue eyes and an ankle-length, unstylish dress I knew she'd get slaughtered for at the haughty Todos Santos Country Club. She was pretty but looked nothing like Knight. Maybe he looked like his biological father. To be perfectly honest, he very much looked like Dean, even though they weren't blood related.

"Hi."

"Hi." Her posture was bowed, defeated. Like a wilted flower.

"I'm the girlfriend," I said breathlessly, sticking my hand in her direction.

"I'm…" she started, biting down on her full lip.

Lips. That's what Knight had inherited from her. Her luscious, round Cupid lips.

"I don't know what I am to him." She put her fist to her mouth, trying to swallow back a sob.

Without meaning to—and perhaps without *wanting* to either—I wrapped my arms around her. Having the person who'd brought Knight into this world at my fingertips overwhelmed me with gratitude. As far as I was concerned, she was an ally, even if Knight didn't see her as one. She'd brought him here, hadn't she? That was enough for me to give her a chance.

"Dixie." She sniffed, trying to gather herself together. "I'm Dixie."

"Where did you find him? Did he call you?"

It made sense. He wouldn't have wanted to call anyone else with what we were going through with his mom, but Dixie wasn't wrapped up in that sorrow.

I put my hand on her shoulder and ushered her to the folding chairs lined up against the wall. We both took a seat. Silent tears slid over her cheeks.

"No."

"No?" I slid my hand from her shoulder to her back, rubbing it. By the way she collapsed against my hand—sobbing harder yet somehow more quietly—I gathered she hadn't been touched by another human in a long time. A very long time.

"You can tell me," I whispered.

"This is going to sound crazy to you, probably, but I followed him."

She pressed a tattered piece of tissue to her nose. Parts of it snowed down to her lap.

"I've been following him around for a while—only when he's alone. Never when he's with you or with his family and friends. I'm so sorry. I know it's wrong. But I'm worried. *So* worried. I can't sleep. I can't eat. I left my job—I'm a secretary in my father's company—and I've been living in a hotel off the promenade for months now. Knight's been drinking and popping pills every day. He is not okay. He needs help."

I closed my eyes, taking a deep breath. I knew Knight had been drinking heavily, but judging by what it had come to, I'd mistaken the severity of the issue. I'd chalked it up to stress from Rosie's situation escalating. He'd always been eccentric and moody. He was a goddamn teenager, for fuck's sake. Knight was also good at hiding his vulnerability behind his nonchalant smirk and herculean frame.

"So after you dropped him off at his house—God, I sound pathetic," Dixie said.

"Please continue."

To me, it didn't sound crazy at all. He'd rejected her, but she couldn't let go. I knew what that felt like, because the same thing had happened to me with Val but in reverse. If I could've followed Val around the world like a lovesick puppy, I would have. If I could have prevented her death, her addiction, nothing would have stopped me.

"Well, after you left, a Mercedes pulled up at the Coles'. Two big guys with gold chains came out. Knight met them at the door. They talked for a minute, then they handed him a small paper bag. When the guys left, I waited for Knight to come out, but he never did. I started calling him. He didn't answer, which wasn't out of character for my so...for Knight," she amended, shaking her head. "But I had a really bad feeling. Call it a mother's intuition, although if he ever heard me say that, he'd laugh in my face."

She threw her head back, staring at the ceiling. "The door was unlocked," she explained. "And I...and I..."

She'd walked in.

This was El Dorado, on a cul-de-sac where everybody knew everybody. Of course the door wasn't locked. Our parents only locked the doors at nighttime.

"It's a gated community. How'd you get in?" I scrunched my nose.

"Someone put me on the list."

"*Who?*" I pressed.

She looked away, shaking her head.

"I found him lying in a pool of his own vomit in the living room, unconscious. I called nine-one-one, flipped him over, and followed the ambulance with my car. It's been forty minutes since he got to this room, and they're not telling me anything. I'm scared for my baby."

She clutched the tissue in her fist, pressing it to her heart. "I don't know what I'm going to do if something happens to him."

"You did the right thing." I squeezed her thigh, trying to swallow and push the ball of emotion down my throat.

"Thank you, Moonshine. You've got such a pretty name. Very unique."

Blinking at her for a beat, I proceeded to burst out laughing. In the hospital. In the middle of a double Cole tragedy. Guess it's true that human nature is programmed to fight. And laughter is the best medicine for almost every problem.

"Luna," I corrected. "My name is Luna. Knight's the only one who calls me Moonshine."

She gave me a tired smile. "Despite everything, it's nice to meet you, Luna."

———————

Two hours later, I sat in front of Knight, who lay in a hospital bed just a few hundred feet away from his dying mother.

I had spent those two hours making plans—plans I should have made a long time ago. Plans that ripped me open. Plans that had meant unplanning big portions of my life. For him.

Plans, I knew, that might leave me bitter with him in five, or ten, or twenty years.

Plans to cancel myself so I could help him.

When Knight opened his eyes, he closed them again as soon as I came into view. He put his big paws on his face, half laughing and half wincing.

"Shit."

"Indeed."

"I've really screwed it up this time, haven't I?"

"Seems that way."

"How's Mom?"

I loved that he cared more about Rosie than himself. At his core, Knight was inherently unselfish.

"Same," I said softly. "I just came back from checking on her. Everyone's there."

"Do they know about this?" He opened his eyes again, motioning with his finger to his hospital bed.

I shook my head, running my hand over his high cheekbone.

He took a deep, relieved breath and nodded. "What time is it?"

To grow up, Knight. To collect the pieces of your broken spirit and patch them up for your family. For yourself. For me.

"Ten at night. How are you feeling?"

"Never been better."

I chucked his nose, leaning back.

He gave me a lazy, dark smirk, reaching for the collar of my shirt and yanking me so we were face-to-face. Half-dead and hospitalized or not, Knight Jameson Cole looked like every girl's wet dream and her daddy's nightmare.

"I'm hard."

"Stop it." I pulled away, standing up. "Stop pretending everything is okay when it is so unbelievably not."

As much as I wanted to, I couldn't touch him. Hug him. Break down because he was alive and *lucky*. So very lucky.

I needed to make a point, and it was high time I did before he joined his mother in an early grave. It was going to be the hardest, most selfless thing I'd ever had to do, but it was far more important than entertaining my romantic dreams.

Every day of my life, since the moment I'd laid eyes on this broken, beautiful boy, I had dreamed of him being mine. And now that he was, I had to let him go.

"I'm leaving you."

He rolled his head on the pillow to catch my gaze. He answered by ignoring me, yanking the IV from his vein and tossing it on the floor indifferently. I winced.

Dixie was outside, making calls to her family in Dallas, giving them updates about her son they didn't know but apparently deeply cared for—the same son who wanted nothing to do with her.

Knight next ripped his hospital gown from his broad pecs, getting ready to stand up.

"What are you doing?" I whispered.

"Chasing you," he said tiredly, swinging his legs to the side of the bed, his feet hitting the floor. He looked like death—exhausted and pale, a far cry from his usual self. "That's what you want, isn't it, Luna? I always have to fight for you."

"No." I shook my head. "I don't want that now. You don't understand, Knight. It's over."

Now he looked at me with different eyes. Darker. The air shifted, moved differently in the room. It bunched around my neck. I couldn't breathe.

"For real?" His voice leaked pain and apathy.

That's when I knew this was the right decision. He was close to giving up. I couldn't let him.

"For real."

"You can't do this to me," he said emotionlessly, stating a fact. "My mother is dying."

"I'm not bailing on our friendship; I'm breaking up with you. I will still be here for you every day. I dropped out of my semester to stay here as long as you need me."

I looked away so he couldn't see how sad that made me. Because it did. Boon had changed me, and I was walking away from my growth, from my own accomplishments.

But wasn't that exactly what he'd done for me all these years?

Missing football practices when I needed someone to hold my hand.

Sitting with me in the cafeteria, snubbing the rest of his friends, even though he knew he'd get shit for it.

Staying a virgin, and inexperienced, waiting for me to open my eyes, my heart, and—finally—my legs for him.

He'd given so much to me over the years. The least I could do was repay him with the same token. But not at the cost of watching him waste away. Not that.

"I told you I will not tolerate this behavior, Knight, and I won't. I made a promise to your mother to take care of you. This is my way of taking care of you. This is your wake-up call."

"You're the only thing I have left."

"You have your family."

He looked away, his silence speaking for him.

"You have us, your friends. Vaughn. Hunter. You have Dixie," I pressed.

His head snapped up, his thick eyebrows furrowing over his thunderous eyes. "I don't need—"

"Yes, you do," I cut him off sharply. "You do need her. She saved you. *Twice.*"

Dixie had told me about his meltdown at the beach the other day. Knight was obviously spiraling, and it was hard to watch. He needed some tough love, even amidst all the pain and anguish. He had to understand he couldn't get away with self-destructing.

"So you're team Dixie." He smiled acidly.

"I'm team *Knight*, and Dixie is on the same team, so I play nice." I slapped the wall, losing patience.

If someone had told me last year that I'd be the one to save Knight Cole and not the other way around, I'd have laughed in their face. He was so formidable. Untouchable. Powerful. Yet here he was, small and lost and in real danger.

"I don't want her on my team," he seethed.

"You're not the coach. You don't get to make that decision." I shook my head.

"Who is? Who is the coach?"

I knew the answer to that question, but it wasn't my answer to give.

I took a step forward and scooped his hand in mine. It was heavy and big. I couldn't believe these hands weren't going to touch and caress and pleasure me anytime soon. Maybe not ever. I hoped to hell the plan was going to work because there was a lot at stake.

Two hearts, two lives, and too many missed opportunities.

"I can't live without you," he croaked, flipping my palm so it faced him and putting it to his lips, tracing every line inside it with his hot mouth.

"So don't."

"But I also can't contain all this pain, Moonshine." He let out a desperate breath.

I stared at him boldly, perhaps more courageously than I ever had before. I could feel the strength oozing from me.

"Then let me carry some of it too."

CHAPTER TWENTY-FOUR
KNIGHT/ROSIE

KNIGHT

It was just a simple white gown.

"A long, satin chemise," Aunt Emilia had called it.

Like I had any goddamn clue what the fuck that was supposed to mean.

I stared at it, hung alone in an entirely empty section of the massive walk-in closet my father had built for my mother with his own hands, even though she was never big on clothes.

"Get her the white gown. It's her favorite. She picked it exactly for this occasion," Aunt Em had said to me.

Like the occasion was a wedding or someone's bar mitzvah. The detail to which my mother had gone to plan her own death made me sick to my stomach.

Frazzled, I reached for the hanger. My fingers were shaky. Withdrawal was a bitch even though they'd kept me in the hospital a few days and given me a ton of shit to help wean me off all the crap in my system.

I'd had every single goddamn symptom in the book—shaky hands, fever, sleepless nights, and blood pressure so low, it'd make a thrice-dead corpse proud. I was still taking medication that was supposed to help, and Dad had slapped me with a twice-a-week therapist for coping, maintenance, and all the other bullshit.

I'd hated every single part of my existence during those days in the hospital—especially because it kept me away from Mom. But I also finally knew I had no choice. There were so many things on the line. My family. Luna. My friends. Oh, also, my fucking existence.

So I hadn't sipped a drop of alcohol in six days—this was my seventh. Pills were out of the question too. Only reason I hadn't had a seizure and died from the abrupt cut off was, I suspected, that I wasn't asshole enough to steal Mom's thunder.

After I was discharged from the hospital, Luna and Vaughn had walked into my house, emptied the alcohol shelves and medicine cabinets, and then proceeded to empty all the mouthwash bottles and throw them in the trash. They'd concluded by double-locking the wine cellar downstairs. Vaughn had installed the second lock and did a jacked-up job too. My dad was going to kill him for chipping both the door and the frame when he was finally in a mood to pay attention to anything that wasn't Mom.

Which, let's be honest, wasn't going to be anytime soon.

On the third try, I managed to snag the dress from the hanger. Instead of bringing it straight to Dad, who was to help her into it, I just clutched it between my fingers, staring.

I needed a few more moments in this room, knowing what was about to happen next was going to put everything in motion and change my life forever.

My mother was downstairs, getting ready for her bath. She was back home. She was awake. After a week of back and forth, Dad had made the decision to take her out of her chemically induced coma so she could say goodbye. He'd made it clear—after fighting with the entire hospital staff and having Vicious, Trent, and Jaime walking the corridor with a harem of lawyers—that my mother was going to go peacefully, as she wished.

At home.

In her favorite white gown.

Surrounded by her loved ones.

And only after saying goodbye to each of us personally.

I knew why Dad had given me the task of bringing the gown. He could have asked anyone. Like Emilia, who was so good at being practical and moving things around. Or Luna, who'd stepped up and was resilient, quiet, and determined to help. He could have asked Edie, or Melody, or any of his friends. But he'd asked me.

He wanted me to be a part of this.

The second man of the house.

I brought the gown to my nose, closed my eyes, and inhaled deeply. It smelled like Mom—freshly baked goods, vanilla, citrus shampoo, and her sweet, natural scent.

Shuddering, I stepped back, opened the door, and stepped out of the walk-in closet, fingering the wood of the doorframe. I paused when I felt the uneven surface under my fingertips and looked sideways, frowning.

Carved on the dark wood, sloppily, like it was done with car keys, were the words that had kept me from drinking myself to death for the past six days. The words I couldn't bear not hearing Luna say again.

Ride or die.

ROSIE

I'd once asked my sister, Emilia, what it felt like.

To be normal. To be healthy. To be genetically privileged.

She'd said, "Days tick by, as you expect them to. Like fanning pages in a calendar. You make plans. Sometimes you forget them. Sometimes you keep them. Sometimes cancel them. But you never doubt you can make them. You let things—mundane things, like bad traffic or getting caught in the pouring rain or rude, inconsiderate people—ruin your day, not realizing how precious said day is. How unique. How this day will never come again. No day will look quite like it. And that's how you look back, years after, wondering where all the time went."

When she saw what was on my face, though, she'd added quickly, "But I learned a long time ago that maybe a reminder of the fact that we aren't here forever is exactly what we need to make the most out of life. And I learned that because of you."

This was why I'd decided to adopt my beautiful son.

To bring my younger son into the world.

To get married. To start a family. To love hard. Fiercely. With abandon.

This is why I never denied myself anything I wanted. Not only was life too short, but I wanted my beautiful family to remember that too.

Plenty of times I'd wondered if I was selfish to have a family.

But was breaking Dean's heart and walking away from him the selfless thing to do? I didn't think so. I knew in my heart that Dean would be miserable as long as I was alive and away from him. Just like he had been until we got together.

Was not adopting Knight going to help him? What if he'd ended up handed over from family to family in the foster care system? What if he'd been given to a family that didn't give him all he deserved? I *knew* I would be the best mother for him. And what if Dixie had been forced to keep him somehow, when she wasn't equipped nor in the right emotional place to care for her child?

As for Levy, he was a pleasant surprise. I hadn't been expecting him, didn't think I could ever get pregnant. But once I'd found out I was, I couldn't imagine my life without him. He was the most precious gift and loved beyond words and actions.

I've lived a full life.

A beautiful life.

I wouldn't take anything back. If I could do one more thing before I left this earth, it would be to *give*—give my loved ones a piece of advice, my love, and my approval.

Now I was living the picture as I'd imagined it in my mind, every day since I was a little girl and found out I wouldn't live to ripe old age, that I would probably never see myself with completely gray hair, deep-set wrinkles, and surrounded by beautiful grandchildren. The gown was beautiful, comfortable, and angelic. I lay on top of my bed, dizzy but smiling nonetheless, as I hugged my sister Emilia.

She stood up from my bed, wiping her eyes. "Who do you want to see first?"

"Levy."

When my young son entered my room, the first thing I noticed was how not completely young he was anymore. Of course, I'd seen him every day, save for the week I'd been in a coma. But he seemed to have gotten tall almost overnight. He was lanky now, his jaw squarer, his eyes less wide and exploring, more suspicious and slanted. He was going to be a gorgeous man one day, and I absolutely refused to be upset over the fact that I wasn't going to know what he would look like. Or over the nagging, eternal question of whether he was going to be with Bailey or not. I couldn't allow my thoughts to roam this way. I had to keep them on what was important. I patted the space next to me with a smile.

"H-how are you feeling, Mom?" He glanced at me from under his lashes.

He had great lashes. Like mine. I smiled at the fact I was going to stay on this earth forever. Through him. Through Knight. Through my husband.

"Good. You?"

"Yeah. Good."

"Liar."

He looked down, shooting a small smile.

"Break for me, Levy. I want to hug away your pain."

That's what we did for the next half hour. I just held him while he sobbed. I asked him to understand that even after I was gone, I still loved him, fiercely. Begged him not to feel the betrayal that can accompany the loss of a parent, to know that no part of me wanted to leave him and his brother and father behind. That I'd lived, breathed, and thrived because they were with me. That I'd fought for every day, until I couldn't anymore, because they were worth the struggle.

When Lev ran out of tears, and I ran out of strength, I let him nap on my chest peacefully, ignoring the dull pain and how badly it hurt when I was hooked up to so many machines, my lungs collapsing by the nanosecond.

When he stirred sometime later, looked up, and saw that I'd been watching him the whole time, he smiled. It was as though he needed this reassurance that I truly loved him. That I genuinely cared.

"Who do you want to see next?"

"Your brother, please." I smiled.

Lev nodded.

When Knight entered the room and closed the door behind him, I motioned to him with my finger.

"Your breath. Let me smell it."

"Mom." He rolled his eyes.

He was so tall. So gorgeous. Such a heartbreaker. Yet his heart was so loyal. The rest of him too. I was in awe of how good he was. How pure. The only thing I worried about was how he dealt with pain. I didn't want him to run to alcohol and drugs. I saw what it had done to Dean when we were younger. Knight's soul was much too precious, his heart too tender to deal with heartbreak. Just like his dad.

"Come on. You know as well as I do you will never deprive your dying mother of anything."

With a harsh exhale, he walked over to me, put his mouth to my nose. He smelled of mint gum and, underneath it, iced coffee. I immediately knew he was sober.

"Thank you." I grinned.

Instead of pulling away, he put his lips to the tip of my nose, awarding me a kiss. "How are you, Mom?"

"Better than I look."

"You look perfect."

"You're just being nice."

He pulled back, giving me a *really?* look. "Being nice is not even in my dictionary."

"Probably because you used the page to roll yourself a joint. How's your girlfriend?" I tried to elbow him good-naturedly in the ribs as he sat down beside me.

By the dark cloud passing over his expression, I could see something was going on.

"She dumped me."

"She did?" I asked cheerfully, not missing a beat.

Luna, Luna. Thank you, Luna.

He nodded, giving me a quizzical look before shaking his head. "It's stupid. This is not what we should be talking about right now."

"What should we be talking about right now?" I arched a playful eyebrow. I didn't want this to be heavy and sad.

He looked out the window, shaking his head. "I don't know. About you?"

"We know everything there is to know about me. I'm the least interesting subject in this household, and the most depressing one too."

"How can you be so calm about this?" He scratched at his jaw, the fine whiskers growing over it light brown dustings.

"First of all, this is not without hard work, trust me." I winked. "And second of all, I have faith in my plans for the three of you. I just need you to promise me one little thing."

"Okay." He sat up straight, eyeing me curiously.

I put my hand on his. "You stopped drinking."

"I did."

"You stopped with the pills too."

"That's right."

"And you're going to the counselor Dad found for you?"

"Like clockwork," he gritted out.

"She will never be yours if you go back to the way it was."

"I know." His voice broke. "I know that, Mom. I know."

"Promise me, then."

"I promise. No more bingeing. No more benders. No more alcohol and pills. I won't even take a Tylenol next time I'm sick."

Silence. I had to tread carefully around this one. I didn't want him suspecting anything, didn't want this part of the conversation to tarnish everything else we'd said. I knew he'd forgive me in time, down the line. But not now. And I couldn't burden him with more anger and disappointment for a second, as long as I had my breath in me.

"Can I give you one other piece of advice?"

"Of course, Mom."

"The grudges you hold against people? Drop them. They're not worth your anger. They keep you anchored to a place you shouldn't be."

"Can you be more specific?"

"No, I can't. But I can tell you one last thing."

"Okay."

I took his hand. Put the back of it against my lips. Smiled through my tears. "Parents are not supposed to have favorites," I started.

I knew my confession wasn't going to leave the walls of this room. Knight loved Lev with everything he had in him. He was a wonderful brother who'd volunteered to teach Levy's entire football team. He'd covered for Lev dozens of times when he'd sneaked into Bailey's house, and vice versa.

"But I do, Knight. I have a favorite. I love you so brutally, sometimes I'd lie awake at night wondering if you were the thing that kept me going when I couldn't do it anymore. When the pain was too much. I don't want you to ever feel you were less."

"I never felt that way." He smiled calmly, cupping my cheeks and staring deep into my eyes. "I never felt like I didn't belong. Not even for a hot second. I always knew you were my home. I'm just worried about what being home*less* will do to me."

"You will never be homeless, my darling boy. You will always have a home. I will be with you, even after I draw my last breath. Remember, my love. The sun will rise tomorrow. It always does. And don't you dare live one day of your life without basking in its glory. If you truly love me, you will respect my legacy. You will wake up tomorrow morning. You will grieve the loss of me. But with time, you will smile. You will laugh. You will *live*. You will push through and conquer your desires. You'll get your girl back, because she loves you, and you love her, and I've seen you from childhood—you were born for each other. You will give me beautiful grandchildren, whom I will watch over from heaven. And every summer rain, you will know it's me, saying I love you."

"Mom. Mom. Mom." He buried his head in my chest, wrapping his huge arms around me. "I'm not ready to let go."

"Go and save your princess, my love." I kissed his forehead. "She is waiting. Besides, that's what knights do."

It was when my husband entered our room that I finally broke down.

I was exhausted from being strong. Strong for Emilia. For Lev. For Knight. I knew Dean was in a state no less upset than they were, but with one distinguished difference: he had always been my protector. He'd always had my back. It was inspiring to watch as he'd fought with doctors, sought out specialists from all over the world, and turned over every rock, checked every corner, until we'd exhausted our options for how to fight my disease.

Now, I was the one in *his* arms. Lying against *his* chest. I sobbed into my husband's black polo shirt, clutching its collar, letting the moans roll out of my throat. The truth was, I was frightened and confused. One moment, I had managed to be calm and reasonable—logical, even. I wasn't going to feel anything. I was simply going to cease to exist. Just like any other human in the history of this planet.

Dead, alive, or destined to live. Simple as that. Other moments, I was panicking, struggling to breathe. The whole room felt like it was closing in on me. I was trapped inside my body, wanting to leap out with my breath still in me and run from it. From cystic fibrosis.

"I'm scared," I cried into Dean's chest. Because I was. God, I was frightened.

He stroked my hair and kissed the crown of my head. "Don't be scared, my love. I promise I will watch over you, even when you're there and I'm here. I promise this is not the end. I promise to come look for you in heaven. And if I'm destined to go the other way, I assure you, I'll find someone to bribe so we can be roommates in hell."

I broke out in relieved laughter, shaking against his body.

He pulled away, showing me his brave, glorious smile—all straight, white teeth. Then he pulled me into a bone-crushing hug again.

"Not only will you not get rid of me, Mrs. Leblanc-Cole, but I also promise I will make sure our sons grow up to be decent men, with big families. They will be happy and healthy. Even if it's the last thing I ever do, I'll make sure of it. I also promise to come to you every single month, twelve months a year, and show you pictures, give you letters, and keep you updated."

"Once a year will do." I grinned. "But if you slack, I will haunt you from there, wherever it is."

"Once a month." He shook his head, correcting. "We need a monthly date, to keep the flame alive and all." He winked.

This reminded me of something I absolutely had to tell him, something I knew he didn't want to hear, especially right now.

I put my hand on his chest. "My love?"

"Yes, Baby Leblanc?"

"Can you promise me something?"

"Anything."

"I know I'm the love of your life. I feel very secure in this position. No one will ever take it away from me. I gave you two beautiful sons.

I gave you a life worth living. I helped you overcome your addiction. No one will ever be able to replace me—"

"So don't ask to be replaced," my husband cut me off, a jolt of chill twinging his otherwise soft voice.

I felt his chest flexing and stiffening under my fingers.

"And *yet…*" I raised my voice an octave. "I forbid you to spend the rest of your life miserable and alone. I refuse to shoulder this responsibility. You're young, gorgeous, and amazing. You will need some help with the boys. You will find someone else. Promise me that."

"No."

"Dean."

"I'm sorry. I can't promise you I'll let anyone else in. I'm all out of heart space. It's you and the kids. Just because you're about to leave doesn't mean you'll leave here." He pounded his fist to his chest. "You think I didn't know this was a possibility?" He motioned between us, his voice steady. "I knew. I knew this could happen. And I still fought to be with you. I'm at peace with that, Baby Leblanc."

"I have a plan," I whispered, but he kissed me halfway through my sentence, brushing a lock of hair from my eye. Our faces were so close, it was easy to memorize every curve of his beautiful face. For a moment, we just breathed each other in, as we'd done the first time we met, inking one another into memory.

"Will you do me one honor?" I asked.

"*Anything*," he said again, which I now knew wasn't necessarily true.

"Would you please let me die in your arms, alone, just the two of us?"

He crawled into bed with me and settled behind me, sprawling me out against him as he wrapped his arms around me possessively. We stared at the door. Breathing. Waiting. Digesting.

He kissed my ear, trailing the kisses down my neck.

"Ride or die," he whispered.

"Ride." I closed my eyes, smiling. "Always ride."

CHAPTER TWENTY-FIVE
DEAN

"Talk about fucking awkward." I unbuttoned my Armani suit jacket, flapping it back to take a seat on the first pew overlooking my wife's open casket.

For the first second, I waited for her to scold me for dropping the F-bomb and then reality came crashing in.

Knight scooted away from Lev to make room for me between them. He glared forward, not taking the bait.

"We're wearing the same outfit," I explained, resisting the urge to put the final nail in my nonchalance coffin and nudge his shoulder.

Said outfit was black cigar pants, black loafers, and a black button-down shirt, complete with the black blazer Rosie was fond of. Normal attire for a funeral, especially your own wife's, but I needed to break the ice with my son.

I'd thrown every single negative thought that had crossed my mind about him at his feet. I'd been wrapped up in Rosie's coma, mentally climbing the walls of my sanity. And when I finally did talk to him, it was to force him to go to a counselor for his addiction. He needed more than to be bossed around. He needed a father.

Knight stared ahead at the elaborate stainless steel casket, his expression as flat and dead as Vaughn's. This wasn't my son. My son was an expressive, lively motherfucker with a sense of humor and natural charm. He was nothing like his sulky-ass best friend.

"Devastated," he finally drawled when he realized I wasn't going to look away until he gave me an answer.

"As you should be," I murmured.

"As I fucking am."

"Language," I sparred.

"Please, Dean. You use the F-word more than any other word in the dictionary."

Dean.

He'd called me Dean.

"I can't believe you're talking about suits right now," Lev gritted out, wringing his hands together, almost as if trying to rid himself of his own flesh.

He wouldn't look at the coffin. Only his hands. I couldn't blame him.

"We're not talking about suits," Knight and I said in unison, which made us glance at each other.

The only time we'd caught each other's eyes since he'd walked in on me going down on Rosie all those weeks ago.

The realization nearly skinned me alive.

I hadn't talked to my elder son in *months*.

I'd been too busy grieving a wife who hadn't even been dead, mourning her loss instead of enjoying her presence, enjoying our family while I still could.

Rosie. Rosie. Rosie.

I looked around at the two front pews of the church, which were filled with our friends and family. My wife had taken her last breath in my arms three days after she woke up from her chemically induced coma. My brave Rosie had hung on to her life longer than the doctors predicted, because she wanted to say goodbye to all of us. I'd been selfishly hoping she'd go in her sleep, that her heavy breaths would turn into shallow ones, then to no breaths at all. But she'd been awake, still squeezing my hand with whatever strength she had left. Her last words would forever remain carved on my heart.

"The sun will shine tomorrow, my love. I know."

"Because it must?" I'd asked her.

"Because it was the first thing Luna ever signed to me. When I did her braids sixteen years ago, I asked her if she was sad about her mother. She signed that it didn't matter. That the sun would always see her to another day. And you know what? It did. Smart girl."

"She is," I'd said.

"Thank you." My wife had smiled up at me. "For this life."

"Thank *you*," I'd answered. "For making me worthy of giving it to you."

I'd promised her I'd be strong, and I was going to be.

For her.

For me.

For them.

No more bullshit, half-assed dad. I'd been stuck in my own little Rosie-colored universe for far too long.

"Let me smell your breath." I clapped a hand on Knight's shoulder.

He turned and gave me a death glare, arsenic dripping from his pupils.

"Playing dad for the duration of the funeral?" He smiled tightly.

"I *am* your dad."

"Whatever you say, big guy."

He was bigger than me, and he knew it. Little fucker.

"Open your mouth."

"Sell it to me, Dean."

"Are you serious?" I felt a tick in my eyelid. "Do it, mister. Now."

"Or what?" he pressed.

"Or I'll open it for you, and that'll be the only damn thing people remember about your mother's funeral."

When he made no move, I stood up. I really didn't give a fuck about making a spectacle, and I think he knew it, because we were the exact same person. He was my mini-me, much more than sensitive, kindhearted Lev was.

Knight tugged me down by the hem of my blazer.

"Christ," he mumbled. He opened his mouth, still staring at me hard and defiantly.

I had a sniff. Sober as a nun. I leaned back, keeping my face hard and grim.

"Have you been eating tuna?"

Lev snickered from my other side. I took that as a little win, although it wasn't Levy I was trying to make amends with.

"Vaughn, Hunter, and Luna are taking turns watching me." Knight clapped his mouth shut, rubbing his jaw.

"I know." I sat back.

Vaughn accompanied him to the restrooms at school, even though Vaughn, apparently, was above taking a piss there. Luna shadowed his every move from the moment he left school, and I checked in on him every single hour. Hunter came at nighttime. Mainly, I suspected, to take refuge from the harem of girls he'd been bedding and dumping. I couldn't care less, as long as he took care of my kid.

"I'm not three," Knight said.

"Debatable," I answered flatly.

"Why am I being treated like a toddler?"

"Because you're just about as reliable—at least until you go an entire month sober."

"You suck."

He nearly goddamn sulked, and although he was giving me shit, I also acknowledged that he'd at least talked to me, which was something. Which was *everything* right now.

"Thank you," I said quietly.

He looked at me like I was crazy. Guess I needed to elaborate.

"I needed to suck and do my job as a parent months ago. From now on, I am going to suck like a whore in a brothel, kiddo."

"I can do whatever I want. I'm already eighteen," Knight said at the same time Lev coughed all over my inappropriate little speech.

"You are," I whispered, leaning closer to Knight. "But you want to get better. I know you do. And I also know why."

The service opened with a prayer by Father Malcolm, the same man who'd baptized Knight and Lev when they were born. Personally, I wasn't big on religion, but Rosie had wanted the kids to be baptized, and what Rosie wanted, she always got. Next, Emilia went up to talk about my wife. Then it was my turn.

I kept it light. I didn't believe in the afterlife, but if there was a slight chance Rosie was watching from above and she saw me shed a tear, I knew she'd haunt my ass to the grave, Casper the *Un*friendly Ghost style. Besides, I'd run out of tears over these past two weeks. The ruthless motherfucker I was prior to losing my wife had been shed and dumped behind.

I cried every night.

Sometimes all night.

Many times with the door open, when Emilia, Knight, Lev, and my parents could hear and see me. Pride was a luxury I could no longer afford.

When I made my way from the podium back to the pew, I expected Father Malcolm to wrap the ceremony up so we could get to the real nasty stuff. The part where I had to bury the love of my life. The part where I'd undoubtedly break.

To my astonishment, the next person to walk to the raised podium in front of Rosie's casket was my son's sometimes-girlfriend, Luna Rexroth. Her steps were brisk yet somehow full of trepidation. What in the ever-loving fuck was happening?

Luna Rexroth didn't talk. Was she going to communicate her grief about my wife's untimely death via telepathy?

I felt Knight shifting beside me, tugging at his collar and wiping his mouth. He couldn't look at her without getting flustered. Plus, he knew she hated crowds and people. Everyone goddamn knew that. Which begged the question—what was she doing up there?

I threw him a glance, asking just that with my eyes. He ignored me, his eyes still glued on her frame, wrapped in a long, black dress.

Luna cleared her throat and smoothed over an object she was holding—some kind of a notebook. She tapped it with her finger, nodding silently, as if having some sort of a conversation with it.

People began to look around, whispering. As far as the town of Todos Santos was aware, Luna Rexroth was a mute. Some knew it was selective muteness. Most simply didn't care.

"Save your girl," I ordered Knight without moving my lips an inch, still staring at her as she shifted from foot to foot, busily flipping the pages of her notebook.

Transfixed, Knight answered me, his eyes still on her. "No."

"No?"

"No. She needs to see this one through." He drew in a breath.

I was about to stand up and save my best friend's daughter from a debacle when she hurried to the edge of the stage, produced a small remote, and darted back to the center. She swiveled on her heels, giving the audience her back, punched the remote keys a few times, and a portable projector behind Rosie's casket came to life.

A picture appeared on the screen: Rosie and Emilia when they were no older than four and three, butt naked, their messy, curly hair the same shade of brown-blond, sitting in two buckets full of water, grinning at each other.

Luna looked back to the audience, took a shuddering breath, and opened her mouth.

"Here's the thing about love—it's an uncomfortable feeling. It pushes your boundaries. If any of you would have told me I'd be standing here talking to you a year ago, I'd have laughed in your faces. Silently, of course."

"Oh, my goodness."

"She speaks."

"Are you recording this?"

I heard all those whispers behind me and knew Luna was in great discomfort, but I couldn't help chancing a look at Trent, her father, who sat at the aisle behind me. He was smiling at the stage, his eyes shimmering. Pride radiated from every pore of his face.

The entire room was so quiet with scandalized shock, you could've dropped a pin on the floor and it'd make a colossal sound.

I returned my gaze to my son. He was smiling.

For the first time in months, he looked pleased.

Maybe not content.

And definitely not happy.

But there was something promising behind his jade eyes.

I looked back to Luna just as she clicked the remote.

"The truth is…" She sighed. "I didn't want to talk here. It was part of my promise to Rosie. She asked me to make this for Knight, Lev, and Dean so they'd remember her the way she wanted them to. Not in her last month, struggling, unhealthy, and fighting for each minute that passed. She wanted you to remember she'd had a good life and that she expects nothing less from you. This picture was taken over forty years ago, in Rosie's backyard in Virginia. Her first-ever memory. She told me it meant the world to her because she'd thought a bucket full of water was the most joyous thing someone could have before she moved to glitzy Todos Santos, with all the Olympic-size and kidney-shaped pools and the glorious ocean. She said Lev and Knight always asked her why she put them in buckets of water every summer when they were little. It was so they could remember that the small things in life count the most."

Luna smiled at Knight, giving him a wink.

Next was a picture of Rosie, Emilia, and me from high school. Em and I were seniors; she was a junior. I had my arm thrown over Emilia's shoulder, but it was Rosie I looked down at with a smile. Rosie stared at the camera, horrified, and although I'd lived many happy years with my beautiful wife, it still pained me to know I'd caused her a heart-break, no matter how minor, no matter how long ago.

"Knight, Lev, Rosie asked me to tell you about this moment. Said it was the moment she realized she was in love with your father.

But she chose not to do anything about it because she loved her sister just as much. This is a message from post-life Rosie to you, in her own words: 'Don't be a Rosie. Be a Dean. If you want something, no matter what it is, go for it. Falling in love is rare.'"

Luna's eyes were now on Knight, only Knight, and something in the room shifted. She wasn't merely speaking the words; she was *becoming* them.

"'Don't give up this precious gift. Chase it. Catch it. Hold it close. Don't let it go. And if it leaves anyway…'"

Her eyes clung to Knight, and for the first time—for the very first time since I'd known my own son—there were tears in his eyes. It gut-punched me to the other side of the room.

"*Fight* for it," Luna finished.

There were more pictures. More stories. One of us on our wedding day that captured me picking her up, crossing-the-threshold style, and walking away in the middle of a soul-crushingly boring mingling session with a few of my colleagues. I'd carried her to our vintage rental car, straight to the airport, and to our honeymoon in Bali, Indonesia.

Knight in our arms when he was one day old.

Lev's angry-red face right after birth.

Rosie's first lengthy hospitalization, where the entire family had sat on her bed. We'd played cards, eaten cinnamon mini-pretzels, and made up elaborate life stories for all of the staff who'd tended to her.

Each story lifted me up and brought me back to life. The audience laughed, cried, clapped, and gasped at the stories Rosie had left for us. And by the time Luna was done, no one remembered how weird it was that she'd spoken. Everyone was laser focused on the fact that Rosie had left us with such happy memories.

It was when we stood up, and people trickled up to her casket, that I understood why my wife had enlisted Luna Rexroth to do this for her. The finality of the situation hit me as if it were the first time I'd learned my wife had died. I clutched the back of the pew, righting myself.

Levy scurried to Bailey, who threw her arms around him, letting his pain soak into her like Rosie had for me countless times.

I closed my eyes and breathed through my nose, expecting Knight and Luna to have a similar reunion, especially after the exhibit of loyalty and trust Luna had put on. To my surprise, I felt a hand on my shoulder. When I opened my eyes, I vaguely recognized the woman in front of me. She looked like a distant memory. A yellowed, old picture, curling at the ends.

"I'm so sorry for your loss."

She sounded genuine. I nodded. I wondered at which point, if ever, it was acceptable to ask her who the fuck she was. Instead of putting both of us in an awkward position—truth was, I didn't *care* who she was—I smiled politely and moved toward the neat line of people who'd paid their respects to my wife and wished to say goodbye.

"Wait," I heard the woman yelping behind me. "We need to talk. I need to... I need... I need you."

I stopped. Turned around. She looked meek. Timid. Almost scared. Did she realize this was not the best pickup place in the world for newly singled millionaires?

I frowned, losing patience. "Yes?"

"Your wife asked me to come here."

"She did?" I smiled skeptically.

I didn't buy it for one second. Chances were, my wife wasn't keen on throwing younger blonds on my ass before I'd even buried her.

The little blond nodded furiously, swallowing hard.

"And you are?"

"Dixie Jones."

"Dixie Jones," I repeated the name, tasting it in my mouth before the penny dropped.

Motherfucker.

My eyes narrowed, and I immediately twisted my head to look for Knight. Suddenly I was rabid. I wanted to protect my kid like he was a baby and she was about to kidnap him. As it was, Knight weighed probably more than both of us. He could wear his birth mother as a scarf and forget to take her off when he walked indoors. He didn't need my protection, but it didn't make me want to give it to him any less.

"He knows I'm here." Dixie read my mind, taking a step back.

I obviously looked as distraught as I felt. I needed space. From her. What the hell was she doing here?

"What the hell are you doing here?" I echoed my thought.

She looked ready to explain, but the last thing I wanted was baby mama drama at my wife's funeral.

I held up a hand, shaking my head. Already people's gazes were beginning to turn our way. I was supposed to be with my friends and family, not talking to this young stranger. Dixie Jones was, I decided, not the sharpest pencil in the box, despite my wife's strange fondness for her.

Late. Late wife. I was never going to get used to it. Yet Rosie had wanted her here. I couldn't disrespect her wish.

"Know what? My son is eighteen. He is of legal age. If you want to talk to him, do. If he wants you in his life, I will give him my blessing."

She nodded.

I should have stopped, but I couldn't.

"If he doesn't…" I said slowly, fixing my gaze on her. "I will unleash hell on you if you come any closer to him. I'll bury you so deep in legal shit, by the time you come up for air, it will be your turn in a casket. He's been through enough. Now, excuse me, Dixie. I need to go say my farewell to the love of my life."

With that, I turned around and walked toward the woman I'd joined with between these pews two decades ago. Only then, she'd worn a wedding gown and a mischievous smile.

Only then, she'd promised me forever.

Only then, I'd taken it, knowing damn well forever wasn't going to be the longest time.

As I peeked into her casket, at her tranquil smile, her gorgeous, porcelain face, that white chiffon gown she loved so much, I knew forever wasn't long enough.

Not for a love like ours.

A little while later, I watched Levy hugging Bailey over my wife's fresh grave. I wanted to die.

I watched Luna engulf Knight in her slim arms. I wanted to dig a hole next to my wife's grave and settle there.

Everyone was in pairs. Such is nature—a special type of asshole.

Vicious and Emilia. Jaime and Melody. Trent and Edie. My parents. Rosie's parents. Even Daria, Jaime's kid, and her fiancé, Penn.

The soil above my wife's casket was fresh. Dark. Damp. It was not too late to pull it out. Not that I would. That would be crazy.

You've done crazier shit for this woman.

Staying calm was not an option, so I was trying to keep sane. Baby steps and all that bullshit. I blinked, looking away from the assaulting image of the ground swallowing my wife's casket. There were dozens of people around me, but somehow, the only person I could spot in the distance was Dixie Jones. She stood back, away from everyone else, chewing on her lower lip the same way Knight chewed on his stupid tongue piercing every time he was contemplating something or just being his usual, ill-behaved self.

A cheek pressed against my shoulder. I looked down. It was Emilia.

"She'd have been proud of you," she whispered.

"I know." *Not if she could read my mind.* Not if she knew all the dark shit that blazed through it like a storm.

Vicious, behind her, clapped my back. "I'm sorry."

"Me too, bro." Trent clapped my shoulder from the other side.

"We're here for you. We're always here for you," Jaime butted in.

Mel and Edie clung to me. Then the kids trailed over, embracing me from the back. The front. Everywhere. I was the center of a mass-hug in a matter of seconds. Everywhere I looked there were faces I knew and loved.

And it wasn't pity I saw in them. That was the part that kept me from breaking, from really digging a hole next to Rosie and lying there. There was admiration and determination instead. But still, I couldn't find solace in that. Not completely. Not until I felt Knight's hand on the back of my neck and saw my son staring right at me. He leaned in to hug me, so close his lips were on my ear.

"You told Dixie to fuck off?" he rasped.

Goddammit. I didn't want to lie to him. But I didn't want another explosive argument on my hands either.

"Knight," I said.

"Thank you." He drew me into a hug.

We crushed each other's bones, and the beef between us.

"I love you, Dad."

"I love you," I choked back. "I love you, I love you, I love you."

CHAPTER TWENTY-SIX
KNIGHT

I wasn't supposed to show up at school this week, for obvious goddamn reasons. I still did. Not to study, God forbid, but to catch Poppy alone, after her accordion class. Yes, she took an accordion class. Who was I to judge? I was a recovering alcoholic before it was even legal for me to drink.

I waited outside her class, loitering about, kicking invisible air to pass the time.

Apologizing to her was a knee-jerk reaction more than anything else, though I could see it was needed after taking a step back from the alcohol and pills and assessing the clusterfuck that was our brief time together. Specifically, the high note with which it had ended, when I was halfway through putting my junk in her trunk, before confessing that I just couldn't do it.

I couldn't do it with someone who wasn't Luna.

Not then. Maybe not ever.

That was the straw that broke Poppy's back. I'd watched her descend the tree trunk from our tree house, fall on her ass, and run in the opposite direction of my neighborhood, where she'd parked her car. Then, I'd had to go down and direct her the right way, which, of course, was more awkward than bumping into your one-night stand in an STD clinic.

Vaughn and Hunter had tried to tell me I shouldn't feel so bad, that Poppy had pretty much single-handedly managed our relationship for us, even when I'd tried to break up with her several times. But that was a cop-out, and I was having none of that bullshit.

I'd hurt her.

I'd wronged her.

I needed to apologize.

End of.

I caught Poppy timidly making her way out of class, staring down at the floor, wearing a huge-ass jacket and one of those big hats you only see in catalogs or on beaches.

"Are you a spy now?" I pushed off the doorframe and fell into step with her, shoving my hands into my front pockets. She was practically making a run toward the exit. Toward her car.

"Worse. I'm a hermit."

"How so?"

"Everyone's laughing at me. I'm a bloody joke, Knight. Because of you," she whispered hotly under her breath, tilting her hat down.

"I'm here to make amends."

"Pretty sure you're here to make my life a living hell."

"I deserve that." I sighed, still following her as we burst through the double doors and descended the stairs toward the parking lot.

Poppy stopped on the last step, turning toward me sharply. "Look. This is my first day here in a while. Please don't ruin it for me."

"It's mine too," I confessed.

"You've been sick?"

I shook my head. I didn't want to say it out loud. First, because I didn't think I could. And besides, I didn't want her to think it was some kind of bullshit way to milk forgiveness out of her.

By the way Poppy's face contorted and her lips clamped, trying to bite down the tears and emotions, I gathered I didn't need to spell it out for her. I was just relieved to know people weren't talking about what had happened in my family too much. Then again, people had to be a special brand of stupid to say anything about me—positive, negative, or otherwise—with Vaughn and Hunter around.

"Oh, Knight." She tore the hat from her head, dumping it on the ground. "I'm so, so sorry. That is horrible. How are you holding up? Are you okay?"

Was I okay?

No, I wasn't.

Not even close.

And in this moment, it felt like I might never be again.

I shook my head, swallowing down all the anger and sadness and bullshit.

"I will be," I lied. "Seeing how you grew up to be wonderful and kind and understanding without a mom, I know I have a chance of being semi-tolerable as a person. Maybe. But that's not why I'm here. It's not, Poppy. I'm here because I screwed up, and I want to apologize. I understand how shitty it must be to walk these hallways and have people talk behind your back. I'm sorry I was the cause of that."

More people began to pour out of different afterschool classes. A stupidly genius idea formed in my mind.

Full disclosure: It was mostly stupid, but I knew Poppy cared about saving face, and I didn't give a shit what people thought about me. I knew Luna didn't give a damn either.

"It's quite all right," I heard Poppy say as I noticed more and more people looking at us curiously as they went down the stairs to their cars. "I knew you were the king of All Saints High. I still chose to pursue you. It is my fault as well as yours." She sniffed.

"Please." I shook her shoulders, crying out all of a sudden. Her eyes bulged in surprise. They asked, *what the fuck?*

Mine answered, *just go with it.*

"Poppy, I know you dumped me, but I need a redo. I will do anything for a redo, babe."

So many emotions passed over her face, I thought she was going to faint.

She probably wondered why I was doing this. I wondered the same thing. Maybe I'd realized during Mom's funeral how loved she was, and I didn't want to leave this world unexpectedly one day, knowing so many people thought I was a world-class cunt. And to some, maybe I had been—certainly not on purpose, but it wasn't like that mattered to them.

"No!" Poppy cried overdramatically, and I wished I could tell her to take it down a notch or two. She flung her arms in the air. "I will not! I will never give you another chance, Knight Cole. I'm in love with another."

In love with another? Who the fuck was she, Billy Shakespeare? Who talked like that? Oh, that's right. Poppy. Poppy talked like that. She knew how to play the accordion, for fuck's sake. She probably knew Latin and how to tie a corset properly too. I almost smiled at that. Almost. Instead, I shook my head.

"Who's the douchebag?"

"I shan't say!"

Shan't? Shan't? I was vaguely aware of the fact that people were beginning to swarm around us, taking their phones out to record. I didn't mind an audience. I lived for it from Friday to Friday during football season. I just hoped to shit I could explain it to Luna if it ever leaked.

But deep down, I knew I wouldn't need to do any explaining. It was obvious she had whatever was left of my heart. I could never be anyone else's.

"Dude, I think she's, like, expecting you to challenge him to a duel or something. Bitch is cray," someone called out from a top stair.

I twisted my head and flashed him a murderous stare.

"Mind your business."

"Sorry."

I turned back to Poppy.

"I'm going to try to move on, but, Pops, dude, I swear on everything holy, it's gonna be hard." I then looked around and threw my arms in the air. "Anyone need a fucking bucket of popcorn? Get the hell outta here!"

The speed with which people scurried to their cars and back into classrooms actually would have made me laugh if it wasn't for the fact that I was newly orphaned.

Three minutes after, Poppy and I were alone in the parking lot.

I opened the door of her Mini Cooper for her. She smiled through her tears. I hated seeing people crying for me. Glass half-full: she was no longer crying *because* of me. So there was that.

"You're going to make Luna really, really happy," she said.

"Yeah?" I had the audacity to ask her, mainly because I felt guilty about talking about Luna with anyone else.

Poppy nodded. "You truly are a knight."

"That's punny."

"It's true too."

"Thank you, Sunshine." I kissed the top of her head. "P.S. Soccer is soccer and football is football. Not the same shit. Okay. Bye."

———————

One by one, I crossed shit off my mental to-do list to accommodate the new situation in which Mom wasn't alive.

Movie nights on Friday.

Family sushi each Saturday.

Our weekly what's-going-on-with-your-college-application argument.

Hushed gossip about Lev and Bailey.

I'd been working hard at it, perfecting the art of letting go. But I still fucked up sometimes. And those times…they hurt like a bitch. Like the time I'd casually strolled into Mom's room, expecting to find her in her throne of pillows and duvets, looking for some feminine advice.

I'd found her bed empty—*don't look so surprised, idiot*—and even though it was hardly news that she was no longer with us, I still allowed myself a nice forty-minute breakdown, consisting of punching everything in sight, ripping one section of the wallpaper, floor-to-ceiling, then proceeding to crack the TV from its base, seeing as I wasn't going to watch any more movies in this room.

But I didn't drink. I didn't drink a drop.

Even when my bullshit, Prius-driving, preppy-looking counselor, Chris, tried to "dig deep" and help me "find my way to mindfulness"—practically throwing me back at the hard stuff—I stayed true to my promise to Mom. To Luna. Most of all, to myself.

What now? I'd finished things with Poppy—finally—but I needed a plan.

There was no way I was going to approach Luna before I knew exactly what to say to her, and in order to know what that was, I required a woman's perspective—preferably a sane, knowledgeable one. Problem was, Daria was a mini-Lucifer, and I trusted her slightly little less than I trusted a bag of fucking rocks. Let me rephrase: at least I could use a bag of rocks as a trustworthy weapon. Daria was uselessly evil and at the bottom of the talk-to list.

Same went for all the girls I knew from school. They had hidden agendas. Either they hated me for my lack of interest in them or liked me enough to try to sabotage my efforts to get back with Luna.

I could talk to Edie, Mel, or Aunt Emilia, but the truth was, I'd been meaning to give Dixie the time of day to thank her for, oh, I don't know, saving my life, and so I'd agreed to meet her one more time on that bench in front of the ocean where I'd originally told her to piss off.

Only now, I was privy to some information I hadn't been aware of when I'd suggested she find her way back to Texas:

1. Dixie cared enough about me to stay here even when I hadn't wanted her to. She'd saved my life when everyone else was too busy hating me or being disgusted with my sorry alcoholic

ass. She never judged, even though I'd made no efforts not to judge her.

2. I needed a female perspective to help me with Luna, and Dixie was, indeed, a woman. An intelligent one, I was beginning to find out.

3. Dixie had told me she had a one-way ticket back to Dallas, and it somehow felt like losing two moms in the span of a week. I cut myself some slack for feeling that way, since my head was all over the place, but it didn't make the loss of her any less real.

Dixie was already waiting for me on the bench, hands in her lap, a timid smile on her face. I was fifteen minutes early, yet somehow it didn't surprise me that she'd been waiting here. Dixie was always three steps ahead and forever at my disposal since she came to Todos Santos.

Maybe that's why hating her was so pointless. It got old fast. Mom was gone now, and my entire range of emotions was directed toward either mourning her loss or putting a plan together to get Luna back. Dixie was no longer a threat because I wasn't worried Mom would somehow find out about her and feel replaced.

Dixie handed me a purple-and-blue slushie. Berries and grapes. My favorite, though we'd never discussed slushies, so my guess was it was one of the many things she'd found out by stalking my ass.

"Thanks." I took a big slurp, squinting at the sunset. She curled a strand of my tousled hair behind my ear in response.

"How are you holding up?"

Great. Small talk. Exactly what I needed. That and a hot bleach treatment for my anus.

"Fine." Everyone's favorite word.

"No, you're not. I'm relieved to see you hurting. Numbing the pain with substances would have made things much worse."

I wanted to shatter her hope to miniscule pieces. To tell her that, although I had been sober—as promised to *Luna*, not her—I hadn't been eating or sleeping. Every time I closed my eyes, I saw Mom. And every time I opened them, I saw a ghostlike vision of Moonshine walking away from me, getting farther and farther with each blink. I was shit-scared that, as time went on, Luna's sense of responsibility toward me would lessen. She'd go back to Boon. To April. To FUCKING JOSH.

I wanted to tell Dixie I was haunted by two women, that I had no room for her in my heart, in my brain, or in the space in between them.

Yet for the first time since we'd met, I didn't say any of that mean shit.

"When're you leaving?" I changed the subject.

Even talking about Mom with Dixie felt like a betrayal. I'd told Dad I was glad he gave Dix the third degree for attending Mom's funeral, but the truth was, I mostly pitied her while she was there. Yeah, she was alive and Rosie wasn't, but Mom had been loved. Adored. Cherished by an entire community and put on a pedestal by the men in her life.

I'd never love Dixie the same way. Hell, I'd have given my own life for Mom without even pausing to think about it.

"Knight…"

"It's a simple question, Dixie," I snapped.

Silently, she handed me an envelope. It was already torn open and wrinkled to death. I rubbed the back of my neck.

"Couldn't afford the glue?" I crooked an eyebrow.

"Read it." She ignored my bullshit, nudging me. "Please."

"And then you'll tell me when you're leaving?" I flashed a taunting smirk, trying to make her feel unwelcome, but no longer invested in making her feel unhappy.

"Then you will tell me if you still want me to leave." She jutted her chin up.

That piqued my interest. I took out the letter, and the first thing I noticed was the handwriting. It was like a bucket of ice water in my face. Because I would recognize it anytime, anywhere, even in my sleep. Neat and bold, all long strokes.

My throat went dry, my eyes drinking in every word as if they were water.

Dear Dixie,

I know I should stop writing to you. Maybe it's compulsive at this point. Thing is, I don't have much time left, and I cannot afford to leave this earth knowing I haven't done everything I possibly could to connect you two.

I understand why you're not replying to my letters when I send you pictures of him. It is frighteningly easy to get attached to our Knight. And by "our," I mean mine, Dean's, and yours.

Yours, Dixie. Yours.

He is gorgeous, isn't he? The most beautiful boy I've ever seen. But it's not just his good looks and athletic nature that make him so popular. I don't want you to think he's just another pretty face.

Did you know he is best friends with our neighbor's kid, who is a selective mute? She doesn't speak at all. He carried her backpack all through elementary and middle school, every single day, even when he was sick. Up until last year, when she graduated from high school, he had spent every recess and lunch break with her just so she'd have someone to sit with. He once punched a boy in the face for insulting her and got suspended. His heart is big and open and spongy. It's soaked in goodness. I swear.

He's funny too. I hope this doesn't come off as gloating, but he really is wonderful. Do you remember his father? Did he have a good sense of humor? Knight can bring me to happy tears when he puts his mind to it. And he does often. Especially when I don't feel well. He stands in front of my bed, like it's a stage, and tells me jokes.

This is not me trying to convince you to love him. I know you already do. This is me basking in the joy we should share, for our son is kind, and handsome, and healthy, and strong. My only regret is the circumstances in which I want you to reconnect with him.

Knight deserves a mother. Someone who will take care of him.

Lev deserves a mother too, although I would never ask you to take that role.

My husband, Dean, needs a companion.

I know you are single. I know you live alone. I know you never bounced back from giving Knight away.

Please, Dixie, don't take this the wrong way. I understand I sound judgmental and patronizing. Why should I assume you would want what's mine? Why would I think my life is so glamorously desirable that I'd invite you to slip into my shoes?

But know this: I'm not sending you this plane ticket to San Diego and reservations for a Todos Santos hotel because I pity you. I am doing this because I know, deep in my heart, that you can do all those things for them. If anyone should be given pity here, it is me.

So please give it to me.

I am willing to take it. I have no pride to spare.

Please come to Todos Santos.

Please meet Knight, our son.

Please try to reconnect with him.

Please keep this a secret.

And when my time comes, please be there for Lev and Dean. I loved every moment of raising Knight. Although unconventional and perhaps downright irrational, I would be honored if you could return the favor by being there for my family when they need a woman to lean on.

> *Sincerely,*
> *Faithfully,*
> *Lovingly and desperately,*
> *Rose Leblanc-Cole*

My hands shook so hard, I had to drop the letter because the words became fuzzy.

Mom did this. She'd invited Dixie. She'd thrust her into my life.

This wasn't betrayal. My seeing Dixie was fulfilling Mom's wish. She'd wanted me to bond with this chick. This chick, who didn't want anything to do with me but somehow found the strength to do something good for a woman she didn't know. Pay back a favor. I guessed I should be angry—angry that Dixie didn't want to see pictures of me, didn't want to make an effort or stake her claim on my ass.

But I wasn't.

Honestly, I thought she was a badass for doing something this selfless for Rosie, even though she didn't want to. She did this for my mom, whom I loved dearly. Besides, it didn't matter what had brought Dixie here. She hadn't quit at the first sign of me giving her shit. No. She'd *stayed*.

Stayed while I was an insufferable dick to her.

Stayed through my addiction. Ghosted phone calls. The breakdowns. The tears. The death.

She stayed even after Dad had told her to fuck off, and I'd cemented the sentiment by coming here and seeing her ass out myself.

Whoever this woman who gave birth to me was, she wasn't the selfish witch I'd believed her to be.

I picked up the letter from the ground and handed it back to her, searching for the right words yet somehow knowing they didn't exist.

"Okay," I said finally. Yup. Pretty far from being the right word, dipshit.

"Okay?" She tucked her chin to her chest, examining my face in my periphery.

"You really wanna stay?" I shrugged, aiming for nonchalance.

My heart beat wildly in my chest. *Goddammit, Mom. Looking out for us, even from the grave.* I somehow knew she would, knew there were a lot more surprises with her in them waiting for me down the line. That it was never really going to be over between us.

Guess Mom was like Luna in a lot of ways. We would always be unfinished business. She'd made sure of it.

"Yes," Dixie croaked. "I have a good job back home. My family has money. But I want to stay here, with you. I want to get to know you. Rosie wasn't exaggerating. You're amazing, and you're mine. I want to know the entire Cole clan."

I side-eyed her, hard. She shook her head, sniffing and wiping her tears with her thumbs.

"Not like that. Oh, God. Never. I haven't even…I've never…"

Her blush could start a fire. Was she a virgin? I mean, obviously not, she'd had me, but had there been anyone else since the night I was conceived?

"I've never had a partner." She answered my unvoiced question. "I'm not planning on having one either. I just want to return a favor to Rosie. She trusted me so much, she paid for my accommodation here. She even gave me access to your gated community. But more selfishly, I want to gain a son. If you'll have me, of course."

If I would have her.

Should I have her?

That was the million-dollar question. Because if I was going to let her up and leave everything she knew and move here, I needed to be damn sure I wasn't going to bail on her ass when things got tough.

"I have a test for you." I stood up, folding my arms over my chest.

She followed suit, darting to her feet. I tossed the empty slushie cup into a trash can a few feet away without even looking, my eyes still on hers.

Her throat bobbed. "I'm listening."

"It's about Luna."

"Your girlfriend?" she interjected.

She was already doing a great job being a nosy mother. I started strolling along the promenade, and she matched my step, hurrying beside me.

"No, she is not my girlfriend anymore. She broke up with me."

"Why?" Dixie asked breathlessly.

"Because I was an abusive, drunk idiot. Actually, I was being a real jerk to a lot of people. I hurt another girl trying to get back at Luna."

"What do you mean, hurt?" Her voice caught in her throat.

I immediately knew what she was worried about. I stopped, putting a hand on her shoulder. Surprisingly, she melted under my touch, the worry evaporating from the creases on her face.

"No, Dixie. Nothing like that. I kind of toyed with Poppy's feelings, but she pushed hard to stay with me. I didn't even want to sleep with her, though she wanted us to. So yeah, I hurt her, but not physically."

"Okay." She nodded. "Continue."

"Anyway, so Luna dumped my ass. She told me she'd revisit the subject of us after I've been sober for a while. But what's long enough? I just lost my mom. I can't lose her too. She is the only thing that matters to me anymore, other than Dad and Lev."

The charged pause in the air suggested I should add her name. I was nowhere near ready to even consider such an idea, though. Dixie had just passed the threshold between enemy and acquaintance. She had a long way to friend territory, and mountains and rivers to cross before she was family.

"So what's the question?"

I stopped walking. So did she.

I turned to face her. "How do I get her back?"

"You want my help?" Her eyes twinkled.

Did I? Hell yeah, I did. Luna had promised to be there for me, and she was but only as a friend. She knew I was sober, and she still wouldn't let me touch her. Kiss her. Feel her.

I got it. I'd screwed up. And she needed to give me an incentive to keep away from the alcohol and everything else. Especially now, when Mom was gone. But hadn't she heard her own words at the funeral? If you love someone, don't set them free. Smother the fuck out of them until they realize they have no chance of escaping. Yup. That was the sentiment I was down with, a method I was willing to try.

"Yeah." I stuck my fingers in my hair. "Yeah, I want your help, Dixie. That's the test," I added. "If you help me, you're in."

"And if Luna doesn't respond to your advances?"

I knew she'd asked mainly to know where she stood, that it had nothing to do with Luna and me, but the idea of failing made me want to throw up.

"We'll discuss it further if that happens."

"No," she said. "I don't agree to this. I'm about to hand in my resignation. So whatever happens, I want you to promise me I can see you twice a week. *Consensually*," she added, which made me want to laugh.

No more of her stalking ways.

"If you wanna meet up, I get to choose where we meet," I clarified.

"That's fine with me." She nodded.

"And I get to tell you when and for how long. We'll need to do things my way." I stubbed a finger to my chest. "Because your way proved to suck, Dix. No offense."

"None taken."

"So what's your Luna plan?" I asked, getting back to business.

With all due respect to my gaining a mother, I needed not to lose Luna first.

"Give me a little time to form the perfect plan. Meet you at my hotel at eight? We can order Chinese."

"I hate Chinese," I deadpanned.

"Sushi?"

"Sushi is Mom's and my tradition. So, no."

"Sorry." Her face twisted in apology, like she was the one responsible for Mom not being here. "How about donuts?"

"Donuts?"

"Donuts will be our thing. You love donuts."

I said nothing.

"Aren't you going to ask me how I know?" She grinned.

"Hmm, no. I'm alive, therefore I love donuts. Not exactly rocket science, dude. Carbs and sugar equal oral orgasms."

"Right. Let me be more specific, then. Your favorite donut is pistachio and vanilla, and you're partial to plain donuts too."

I hadn't had any donuts in the last few months, so it couldn't have been something she'd unraveled in one of her stalking sessions. "Now you're being specific. And accurate. *And* creepy. How do you know that?"

Although I enjoyed donuts, I also enjoyed having a fucking six-pack, and those two didn't go together. True, I was too young and too active to get pudgy, but Dad and his friends said it's about forming good habits, so you never find yourself looking sixty when you're forty.

Anyway, this conversation didn't majorly suck, so that was an improvement.

"Because when you were in my tummy, you were crazy for pistachio donuts." She blushed.

I just stared and continued staring at her, waiting for more.

"And milk. Oh, how you loved milk with your donuts."

"I drink a gallon a day," I confessed.

Fuck the haters. I had good, strong bones because of that shit. Also, Dixie was way more bearable than I gave her credit for.

"I indulged you, of course. I got us one every single day. First, I bought a whole thing of donuts in every flavor and took a bite of each. You kicked the holy Jesus out of me when I took a bite of the pistachio. So that's what you and I had every afternoon. Pistachio donuts with a big glass of milk."

"That's...cool."

"So, donuts and a plan?" She smiled.

"Donuts and a plan." I nodded.

CHAPTER TWENTY-SEVEN
LUNA

"There she is."

I heard a whisper behind my back as I flipped through clothing items absentmindedly. The voice was female. High-pitched.

"Word around town is she broke up with Knight the week his mom died. Heartless, right? That's after he'd taken care of her for years. He literally had no life other than her."

"Insane," another girl gasped.

Sometimes—more often than I cared to think about actually—people assumed that if I couldn't talk, I couldn't hear either. Or maybe I could hear, but it didn't matter. I wasn't going to confront them. I never had. Never would, they assumed. Only today, as I hung out with Daria; her mother, Melody; Emilia; and Edie, finding Daria the perfect engagement party dress, these girls were in for a rude awakening.

"Luna," Edie called from the crème love seat in front of the dressing rooms, cradling a glass of champagne next to the rest of the women. Daria was inside, trying on her fifth dress in the boutique. All of us tried our hardest to focus on the garments and not on the fact that we were faking the entire thing, ignoring the Rosie-colored elephant in the room, but I had to take a step back and pretend to look for something for myself so they wouldn't see me cry. I missed Rosie terribly. More so every day.

"…and now she's hanging out with Daria Followhill? How

fitting. All she needed to do was become a bitch like her to get in the cool kids' club."

The chatter behind me intensified.

"I hope Knight goes back to Poppy. At least she didn't play stupid third-grade games."

"Luna, baby, come. I think this one's the one," Edie said.

She must've seen the girls behind me, deduced that they were talking about me by the way they looked at me, and wanted to spare me the heartache.

Edie, Emilia, Melody, and Daria had gotten used to my speaking, just like everyone else around me, but they were still overprotective. They still worried I couldn't take care of my own business.

"Just one minute, Mom!" I yelled to Edie, loud and clear.

The chatter behind me stopped. So did their shuffling of clothes. I turned around, a serene smile on my face. It was high time I did this—stood up to the bullies myself instead of hiding behind Knight's broad, formidable back.

Set the record straight about what I was to him. What he was to me.

Shut them up by showing them quiet didn't mean weak. That being gentle and meek didn't mean there wasn't a storm brewing inside me. Still water runs deep. The people who were the noisiest and most popular in my school often had the most to hide. I walked over to the girls, the sound of my squeaking Vans the only thing audible in the store. I stopped a few inches from them, my smile widening.

I recognized them. Two senior cheerleaders: Arabella and Alice. I'd seen them both at Vaughn's party last year. Arabella had been all over Knight, teasing me about sleeping with him. Now I knew it wasn't true. It had never been true. Knight had only slept with me. I could rub it in her face, I realized. But I wasn't going to.

I was too old and too smart for her game.

"For your information," I said pleasantly, watching in amusement as Arabella clutched a feather-trimmed, sequin and tulle baby-pink dress to her chest, as if using it for protection from me. "I did not break up with Knight. We took a break while he attended to something much bigger and more serious than our relationship. He is mine. He was always mine. Not Poppy's. Not yours, Arabella. Not anyone's. And if I didn't make it clear before, I think I should now: I will destroy everything in my way, including your catty ass, if you ever say a negative word about him or me. Don't mistake my politeness for weakness. I merely let you keep him occupied while I sorted out my own issues. But now I'm here. I will stay here. I will always be here for him."

I took a deep breath, undeterred by the way they stared at me, wide-eyed and slack-mouthed, still in shock over the fact that I was speaking—and not just that but having fun handing them their asses on a platter.

"I love him. So very much. And anything you say about our relationship is not going to change that. So I strongly suggest you move on to your next gossip victim, or better, stick your noses where they belong. In your own business. And by the way, this"—I plucked the dress from Arabella's round-tipped, nude-colored fingernails, throwing the gown over my shoulder—"will look gorgeous on Daria at her engagement party. From one bitch to another, thanks."

With that, I turned around and marched triumphantly to Edie, Emilia, Melody, and Daria, who was now standing outside the dressing room in a green number, staring at me with an entertained smirk, her arms crossed over her chest.

I tossed the gown to her, and she caught it in the air.

"Proud of you, Saint Luna," she said.

"For standing up to those idiots?" I asked. "I should have done that long ago."

Daria shook her head, her grin widening. "No, for having perfect timing. I think your love declaration is appreciated, considering the circumstances."

"Circumstances?" I blinked. "How do you mean?"

Daria's gaze traveled to the glass door of the boutique. Through the windows, I saw something that made my heart blossom and almost burst out of my chest.

Knight, Vaughn, Dad, Dean, Jaime, Lev, Racer, Penn, Hunter, and the entire football team of All Saints High were standing there, each guy holding a sign written in Knight's awful handwriting.

Vaughn's read: *Luna*

Dad's: *Would*

Dean's: *You*

Jaime's: *Do*

Lev's: *Me*

Racer's: *The*

Penn's: *Honor*

Hunter's: *And*

Footballer: *Be*

Another baller's: *My*

Another baller's: *Wife*

Another baller's: *???*

Another baller's: *Chill.*

Another baller's: *Just*

Another baller's: *Kidding*

Another baller's: ...

Another baller's: (*Mostly*)

Another baller's: *Actually*

Another baller's: *I'm*

Another baller's: *Fucking*

Another baller's: *Serious*

Finally, Knight's sign was the biggest and held more than one word. It read:

Ride or die, Moonshine?

I opened my mouth, knowing how much was on the line. Knowing Knight, once again, had done everything backward. First the engagement, and then, right after, the declaration of love, which had yet to come. The patching-up part. The getting-back-together portion of the Knight show. But this was Knight for you.

He didn't do things by the book.

But he was sober.

And hurting.

And mine.

It was the easiest decision to make. The easiest by far. And the Rosie-colored elephant in the room was knocking over racks of clothes left and right because I knew she was somewhere up there watching this whole thing. In fact, I could practically hear her telling me not to settle for this before I heard the words I'd been dying to hear since the day he'd saved my life in the rain on my bike. Since the day I'd known I didn't love him as a brother. Not at all. He was the love of my life.

"Knight Jameson Cole," I said, loud and clear, not caring that we had an audience, that the saleswomen took out their phones to record this. That Edie, Mel, and Emilia had tears in their eyes. That Daria muttered, only half jokingly, that I was stealing all her thunder.

"You come here right now and tell me the L-word if you want to be my awful-wedded husband."

The entire football team erupted in laughter, and Knight's nervous smile broke into the cockiest, most arrogant, most adorable grin I'd ever seen on a human face. He made me weak in the knees. And I knew, impossibly, that this was the way it was going to be until my last day. My heart would always miss a beat the first time he entered the room—no matter how many times I'd seen him.

Tossing his sign behind his shoulder, he threw the glass door open and strolled inside, ignoring Arabella and Alice to his right. When he reached me, he got down on one knee, but instead of looking up at me, he bowed his head, like a warrior kneeling in front of his queen, his sword piercing the ground. Producing something from his pocket, he held a ring up in the air, no box. I recognized it immediately. It had belonged to Rosie.

Story was, Dean had given it to her on their second wedding anniversary. It was a round-cut, yellowish-green diamond, surrounded by much smaller diamonds. For every year of Dean's sobriety, he'd added one more mini-stone to surround the bigger one. At some point, he'd begun to decorate the band itself with precious diamonds too.

Knight's message was loud and clear. He sn't ignoring the issue. He was tackling it headfirst. He was promising me not only his heart and loyalty—but his sobriety too.

"I know I have been a terrible boyfriend. I know we're not together anymore. I know you deserve much, much better than what I've given you so far as a lover, not as a friend—other than the sex part. The sex part was…" He looked up, his eyes laughing as mine widened in horror and embarrassment. "I mean, let's admit it, Moonshine. We're the shit in bed, okay? No point denying it."

Dad cupped his mouth with both hands. "On with your speech."

Everyone laughed. I think it was the first time since Rosie was in a coma that our families were truly happy, and I understood why Knight needed this. This big, festive, out-of-this-world thing. We all needed it.

Knight shook his head like he was trying to rid himself from some naughty thoughts. "Anyway, to your request—your quite reasonable request, milady—I assure you, I love you. I'm in love with you. I'm crazy about you. Have been since age four. It was always you. Never someone else. Not even for a fleeting moment. Not even when I dreamed of moving on from you. Even when I hated you—or when I thought I did—I knew we'd be together. I knew. Our love always had a pulse. Sometimes it was faint. Sometimes it was beating so hard I couldn't hear anything else. But it would never die. It can't. I won't let it."

I took a shuddering breath, placing my hands on his shoulders, signaling him to get up. But he stayed put, still on one knee.

"I spent the night at Dixie's, trying to come up with a way for you to know I will never repeat my mistakes. I will never give in to alcohol and drugs again. Never self-destruct that way. But the only thing I could come up with was for you to give me a chance not to fuck up. Because if we're apart, how would you be able to know? I decided I'm coming to North Carolina, babe. You gave up so much for me, and I am happy to do the same for you."

I shook my head frantically. Violently, almost. Now Knight's smile was completely gone. His face a little paler.

"No," I said, letting the tears on my cheeks run freely.

"No?" He was still on one knee and not in a hurry to stand up.

I loved it. I loved that he was still in a vulnerable position. For me.

"No, we won't be going back to Boon. Boon changed me in so many ways, and I will forever be grateful for the journey, but my home is here. You're here. Our families are here. Some people can go to an out-of-state college and do their own thing. Not us. We'd be leaving too much behind. No, babe. We're staying. We'll study here. We'll overcome your addiction, and my inhibitions, here. We'll stay close to the street we grew up on. Where we fell in love. Where we fell apart. Where we broke and pieced ourselves back together."

There was a beat of silence after which Knight cleared his throat.

"So…is that a yes or a no? Because Dixie's been filming this whole thing outside, and I don't know how much memory her phone has."

A burst of laughter rang in the air. I was pleasantly surprised that some of it was mine.

"Yes!" I shouted. "Yes, I'd love to be Luna Cole!"

He scooped me up and kissed me for the entire world to see. My arms linked behind his back, my lips fused to his. It was the perfect princess moment I never thought I could have, with a prince I'd thought was everyone else's rake.

And when he finally put me down and stared at me, I knew what he was going to say before he opened his mouth. We knew each other so well. Too well.

"Always. Whenever. Forever," he mouthed, his lips still on mine.

I decided to complete his sentence, the way I'd imagined it in my head so many years ago.

"I choose you."

EPILOGUE
KNIGHT/LUNA

KNIGHT, ONE YEAR LATER

"Oh my God. Oh, Knight. Oh, Knight. Oh, Knight. Oh…"

"*Knight*. Yup. I know." I rotate between fingering Luna and pushing my tongue into her pussy. She is crazy horny these days, which makes *me* a horndog of massive proportions.

Yeah. Okay. I'm always a horndog.

Real talk, though—is there anything hotter than licking the cum from my fiancée's pussy and smearing it on her clit, playing with it as I fuck her until next Wednesday?

Yeah, I don't think so either.

I eat her out until she clutches my hair and yanks my head up from her groin, her eyes a gray storm. I can feel the diamonds of her engagement ring digging into my skull, and it makes my dick twitch in excitement. Who knew that Luna Rexroth, the tomboy, the mute, the kid no one noticed, was a bit of a freak in bed?

Not me, that's for sure. Life's full of surprises like that.

"I want you inside me." She sounds more angry than turned on now.

I can't help it. I nearly topple over, laughing. But she doesn't give me a chance to do that either. She pulls my big-ass frame atop her, traps my waist with her slender legs, and waits for me to plunge in.

I do. I fill her to the brim until her moans of pleasure have a dash of sweet ache in them. I move in and out of her slowly, bareback, making love to her, kissing her mouth.

Mine.

The center of her chin.

Mine.

Her nose.

Mine, mine, mine.

"Moonshine," I croak, her nickname like a cliff I'm about to jump from.

I can see the beautiful horizon splashing in front of me in all its glory. It is full of memories we're going to make, places we're going to see, moments that will define us forever.

Memories with Levy, who I talk to every day on the phone, sticking to my promise to be there for him.

With Dad, who is slowly crawling back into life.

With Dixie, who is trying her very best not to piss me off, and so far, I have to admit, succeeding.

And with the girl who was born to pull me through an inevitable tragedy.

The moon peeks at us from the curtain of our beach house, smiling.

You made it, it says.

We did.

We have awesome windows where you can't see anything from the outside, but we can see everything from inside of the house. We moved here six months ago, on the same day Vaughn packed his shit and moved to England.

People *were* surprised to find out we'd moved out of Todos Santos, but to me, it was the most natural thing in the world. I needed some time just with Luna before I tackled the real world—somewhere our parents and friends couldn't drop by and interrupt us. We're still only a short drive from Todos Santos—less than an hour when the traffic isn't shitty.

"Knight," Luna whimpers in my arms. "Faster."

"But what if…"

"Faster!"

Her nails sink into my lower back and *O-fucking-kay*….

It's settled, then. Pregnant ladies are batshit crazy. I thought Dixie was exaggerating. She's been coming here every weekend. We have dinners and trivia nights and the entire *Brady Bunch* bullshit together. She was the one who warned me that Luna was going to go over a lot of hormonal hurdles.

I thought she mostly meant the spurts of crying every time she sees a dirty puppy or a lone mitten on the street. But no. Luna is also hornier than a moose.

Not that I'm complaining.

"I don't wanna hurt the baby," I moan, trying to keep it PG-13 somehow.

I can eat my fiancée until my mouth goes numb, but I'm worried I'll hurt the baby with my massive cock. I'm not being arrogant or anything—it's a genuine concern. I don't want Knight Senior to poke its head or anything.

"Mommy, how come I only have one eye?"

"Well, son, Daddy poked it out while dicking me when I was pregnant with you."

Can't blame me for not taking any chances—especially as Vaughn has been having a fucking field day since the news broke. He called my fiancée a "teen mom" in the making when we Skyped with him (false, she is twenty), and when Luna admitted to craving ramen noodles, he replied that judging by the rush with which she got knocked up, he thought she had a particular taste for my dick.

And I couldn't maim him.

I couldn't even punch his face, seeing as he's so far away.

"Well, I'm about to hurt *you* if you don't speed things up. I've been on the edge of an orgasm for ten minutes now," Luna growls, pulling me back to reality.

"What if I hurt her?"

"You're not going to hurt her."

"How do you know?"

"You're not that big!" she exclaims, exasperated.

I pause, mid-thrust, staring at her with horror.

I know I am. I have statistics to prove it. We even used a ruler in the locker room back when I was a junior in high school. What kind of bullshit is this? Knight Senior doesn't need this negativity from the love of its life.

"Take that back right now," I warn, plunging into her so hard and so deep, I'm probably tickling her throat right now.

She is laughing. And coming. On my cock. And laughing some more. I really am the best partner in the world, if I may say so myself. Which I may. I mean, I just literally did.

Finally, the word literally said in an appropriate context. And I didn't even say it—I thought it.

"Isn't the second trimester supposed to be the most dangerous of all?" I ask as I continue to chase my own climax, thrusting in and out of her.

Luna seems pretty adamant that we're not hurting the baby, and she knows stuff about stuff. Also, she is a health freak and already loves this baby more than I love life itself, which means the nugget is in good hands. And belly, for that matter.

"This is not how pregnancy works, Knight. We can have sex. The baby is secure. You, on the other hand? Jury's still out on that, depending on how much you're going to play me like this in bed."

By the time I'm done with her ass, she can barely wobble toward the bathroom. I stay sprawled in bed, watching her naked figure moving around in the lit bathroom. Three months ago, when we found out she was pregnant, we were elated. Despite what a lot of people thought, the pregnancy was one hundred percent planned.

Yeah, yeah, I know. We both attend UCLA. We're both students. I have a job coaching a kids' football team, which pays shit and I do it mostly as chicken soup for the soul, but Luna just finished a project that actually made some decent money. We broke the news by accident a month ago, at Daria and Penn's much-belated wedding in Palm Springs. Luna wasn't drinking. Neither was Daria. Didn't take long to put two and two together.

"Our babies are having babies!" Melody Followhill proclaimed.

For some reason, it sounded accurately gross coming out of her mouth.

Our decision to have a kid wasn't made lightly. It was just that even as we ticked all the boxes a happy couple our age should aim for—engagement, a house, a big, black Lab called Johnny, and an ugly, rat-looking white Husky called Rotten—something was amiss. That something was Mom, of course, and not just the lack of her presence, but lack of the notion that there was someone to take care of. To fight for. To be there with.

The thing about Luna and me is we're caregivers by nature. I'm so used to taking care of her and Mom, and she's so used to trying to save the rest of the world, me included, that we needed someone to give all our extra love to.

Dad almost killed me when he found out I'd impregnated my fiancée on purpose at age nineteen. Luckily, Dixie calmed him down.

Luna is humming a song now. "Enjoy the Silence" by Depeche Mode. There's a little smile on her face. I wonder if the nugget is a girl or a boy. We keep referring to it as a she, because a part of us knows this baby signifies Mom somehow.

I wonder if the baby is going to have my green eyes or her gray ones.

If it will have her dark, smooth skin and my narrow, full lips.

I hope the baby will know we wanted a child before we even knew he or she was in existence. And that unlike our biological mothers, we would never let him or her go. And I don't mean after birth. I mean possibly ever. Maybe not even for college. Straight up, we'll be locking them in their room forever.

Okay, that's not good parenting. Never mind.

"I thought you hated that song," I call out to Luna, patting the bed to inform her that her five minutes out of it are officially over and it's time for round two.

"I do," she chirps, coming back from the bathroom and diving into bed gracefully.

Our place on Venice Beach is pretty neat. You can actually hear the waves crashing on the shore at nighttime, usually as a backdrop to the sound of tourists laughing and screaming, young people getting shitfaced, and the terrible music street artists play across from our balcony. I love the hustle and bustle outside, though. It reminds me how lucky I am and that I chose well—staying with the quietest person I know.

"Then why are you singing it?" I pull her close, nuzzling my nose to her neck.

Our hot chests bump into one another. Mine, hard and muscular. Hers, soft and round.

"Because." She smiles. "Edie loves it, and I love Edie."

"By the same token, you love anal," I muse.

"I do?" She cuts a no-bullshit glance my way.

"Yeah. Because I love anal, and you love me."

"Only on your birthday." She raises her finger in warning. "Apparently, I only love you then."

"And on national holidays," I negotiate.

"You've got yourself a deal."

"Canada's too. It's high time we show them some solidarity."

She laughs. So do I. I can't wait for the baby to start kicking and join the party.

That kid doesn't know how long we've been waiting.

How I always wanted them around.

How that day, shortly before Mom died, when I apologized to Luna for going bareback, it was a ninety-nine percent apology. Because I wanted us to have a child.

I wanted us to atone for what our mothers did.

Only Dixie is not the same woman I resented. Maybe she never was. Maybe sometimes we make people monsters in our heads because we can't understand them.

Maybe we don't understand them because we don't try to.

And maybe we don't try to because we're scared.

Either way, I've stopped being scared. Of love. Of feelings. Of forgiving.

Luna and I have carved each other's personalities since the very beginning. Needs. Wants. Morals.

And most of all, our love.

LUNA

I'm wearing a black dress that cannot hide the small bump in my lower stomach. I don't want to hide it. I'm proud of that bump something fierce. I feel whole while pregnant. I think I'm going to be one of those women who has a lot of children, biological and not biological, but I don't want to scare Knight by telling him this. He's not officially twenty yet.

Also, we promised each other to take it one step at a time, and we still need to get married before I pop this nugget into the world or before our parents have heart attacks because our child will be born out of wedlock—whatever comes first.

I'm pacing back and forth behind the stage's heavy, black curtains, knowing they're about to call my name. That I will get on this stage, and they will ask me questions. And I will answer them. At length. More importantly—with words.

That was part of the contract I signed when I wrote a book about my seventeen years of silence. *Silent No More* was dedicated to Rosie and to Val, two women who played very different roles in my life. One killed my voice. The other brought it back.

The book published last week and hit *USA Today's* bestsellers list. I am on the verge of signing my second contract with the same publishing house. I have no idea how I'm going to juggle school, a baby, a book, a husband, a life, *and* a trip to London to see Vaughn's exhibition next year. But I'm about to find out.

"Moonshine." My fiancé saunters backstage with a cup of tea and a small white box. He hands the tea to me. "How are we doing?" He drops a kiss to my forehead.

"Fine," I say.

We look at each other and laugh because we know what this word means. *Nothing.* It means nothing.

I take a sip of my tea. "Seriously, though? I'm excited more than scared."

"Good. Have a donut." He pops the box open, and I eye the carb-loaded treat inside.

"It has a green thing on it." I scrunch my nose.

"Yup. Pistachio."

"I hate pistachios."

"Nugget might like it, though." Knight rubs his cheek. "Worth a try."

"Why would Nugget like pistachios? That's random."

"Because I did."

I humor him for sharing this intimate piece of information with me, taking a tentative bite. Despite my disliking pistachio, I feel my stomach flutter immediately. It's like a little goldfish is swimming in my lower belly. My eyes widen on his.

"What? What?" Knight's grin might split his face in two.

I'm about to answer him when the event coordinator takes my hand in hers and pulls me toward the stage.

"They're calling your name. Good luck, Ms. Rexroth!" she says, just as I hear the claps and shouts.

I can also hear some whistling as I stumble to the stage and immediately detect their source. Hunter and Vaughn are sitting in the front row, slung low on their seats with Hunter pumping his fist in the air. Next to them, April, Ryan, and Josh are sitting and staring at me with smiles so big, I know my apology all those months ago was truly accepted.

I flew back to Boon to say goodbye, because I couldn't fathom the idea of not explaining myself to the people who had changed me so profoundly. Even though April and I had our disagreements, and even though we both did less-than-perfect things, we bridged it out.

And Josh? He's been dating one of the stable girls for a while now, and it's getting serious between them.

My counselor Malory is here too. I kept in contact with her after dropping out. Or more accurately, she kept in contact with me. She didn't want to see me crawl back to my old habits and has been delighted to hear I've been doing better than ever.

The event coordinator leads me to a stool in the middle of the stage as the host explains my book. For a minute, I am completely numb. I scan the room, drinking everyone in.

Emilia is smiling at me, a copy of my book in her hand.

Next to her, Uncle Vicious salutes me with a cunning smile.

Dad's eyes are shining with tears.

Edie is flat-out crying.

Racer, Lev, and Bailey exchange appalled glances. This public display of emotion is not exactly up their alley.

My eyes halt on Dean and Dixie. They sit next to each other, and both look at me intently, ignoring one another. But there's something there I can't seem to take my eyes off of: the fact that his pinky finger is almost entwined with hers on the armrest between their seats.

I know Dixie is still wounded and hurt from Knight's father, although the details of whatever happened have yet to be disclosed.

I know Dean is nowhere near close to moving on from Rosie.

But I also know there's hope for the both of them, and somehow, that makes me happier for them than I am for me about this book deal.

On her deathbed, Rosie asked me to bring them together, and for the past year, I've honored her request: hosting dinner parties, inviting them to restaurants, and making sure they're around each other, even as the excuses for them to meet up have dwindled and become more and more forced.

Last week, Edie told me she saw them having an ice cream together. A quiet outing. They didn't speak to each other. They did not hold hands. They simply marveled in the slow, creeping thing called love.

I caress my stomach, put the microphone to my lips, and open my mouth. Feeling the room take a collective breath, I try to hide my mouth with the mic, then start my story from the only beginning that truly mattered. Our beginning.

"It started with an abandoned toddler in a soiled diaper, but the plot twist was a boy with busted knuckles and a heart of gold…"

BONUS EPILOGUE
KNIGHT

DARIA AND LUNA KISS AT THE NYE PARTY, FROM KNIGHT'S POV

I walk into the New Year's Eve party with Poppy on my arm.

And I mean that literally. She is clinging to my arm like the rest of her body is dangling from a cliff, her coffin-shaped nails creating crescent-shaped imprints on my skin. She is draped in a canary-yellow dress with generous cleavage and needle-thin stilettos. She is trying too hard, which is a dick-shriveling trait. Of course, I can't tell her that. I can't blame her either. I would try hard too, if I had to compete with the love of my girlfriend's life.

"I'm so happy we decided to give this another go." Poppy turns to me, her smile somehow hopeful and miserable at the same time. She rises on her toes to kiss the corner of my mouth. "You won't regret it, luv."

I'm already regretting it as my eyes zero in on Luna Rexroth from across the room. She's my moon, my sun, and my royal pain in the ass. And she is wearing what must be a fucking bar napkin, sipping champagne with Daria Followhill.

Now, I have nothing against Daria. I grew up with the girl. But I trust her a little less than I trust a bagful of venomous snakes. This chick hasn't met a drama she didn't like. Shit-stirring isn't just her passion; it's her love language.

Poppy is clutching to me harder, pressing her tits against my chest. "Do you want to go and say hi?" she murmurs in my ear. "It's all right if you do."

Daria says something to Luna. Luna rips her gaze from me, suddenly taking acute interest in the bubbles in her champagne. I sling my arm over Poppy's shoulder, butthurt. I don't know what it is about my former best friend that makes me act like a toddler who's just been sent to the naughty spot, but every time she's around, I'm on the verge of bursting into a shit-eating grin and starting a brawl. Simultaneously. Guess it's true what Mom says: Pain is the price we pay for love. Dumbassery is the currency.

"Nah. I'm good." I curl my arm around Poppy's neck, pressing a kiss to the crown of her head. But then a few hours pass, and I'm not good. Poppy can sense it too. How I'm mentally checked out.

"This place is a drag. Wanna skinny-dip and get drunk?" I ask her before she can complain.

"It's almost midnight."

"So? I'm sexy when naked all hours of the day."

"Knight, it's New Year's Eve."

As if on cue, everyone in the place starts counting down the seconds. *"Ten!"*

I don't want to kiss Poppy, especially not in front of Luna, *especially* after what happened at the shelter, but what choice do I have?

"Nine."

It takes everything in me not to look at Moonshine. And still, my everything isn't enough. I sneak a peek.

"Eight."

Fuck, she's looking back.

"Seven."

I can feel Poppy's face inching toward mine. Poppy, my girlfriend. My *nice* girlfriend. My understanding, pretty, every-superlative-on-planet-earth-applies girlfriend. The one who didn't fuck a rando as soon as she landed in college. Yup. Her.

"*Six.*"

Luna is staring back at me, wide-eyed, like there's a freight train heading straight toward us.

"*Five.*"

Shit. Fuck. What do I do?

"*Four.*"

"*Three.*"

"*Two.*"

"*One.*"

Poppy's lips lock over mine, my eyes still open, glaring at Luna. Then Daria leans in and presses her lips against Moonshine's.

I repeat: Daria. Is. Kissing. *My.* Fucking. Moonshine.

This is where I lose it. I rip my mouth from Poppy's so fast she stumbles forward, almost falling flat on her face. I right my girlfriend and lean her against the wall like she's an inanimate object—the gentleman that I am—and pounce on Daria and Luna, separating the two like a chaperone at a prom who just spotted a couple slow-dancing without leaving room for Jesus.

"All right, show's fucking over." I serve as a barrier between them. I'm such a hypocrite. Watching women kiss each other is one of my favorite hobbies. I would make it my fucking profession if there were money to be made there.

Moonshine's lips are sleek with Daria's pink gloss, and smell of bubblegum. Extra-pouty after being ravished by the blond bombshell. She waves me off with an eye roll.

When she turns around and walks away, I tug her back to me. "Luna!"

"Oh, for fuck's sake." Daria bares her teeth, stepping between us, pushing at my chest. "Not everything's about you, Cole. Although, I guess she's Saint Luna no more, huh?"

Daria is lucky her fiancé is the size of a two-bedroom apartment in Manhattan.

Luna gives me a snort that tells me exactly what she thinks of me. And none of it is good.

What in the ever-loving fuck happened to my best friend? She used to be so sweet, so pliant, so agreeable.

So boring, a voice in my head snorts out. *Which was why you felt so easy and self-assured not to make a move on her. There was no urgency. No other potential boyfriends waiting in the wings, vying for her heart.*

Still, I'm pissed. *I* was the one who protected her for almost two decades. Who took care of her. Now she's going around fucking randoms and kissing people and…and…

Living life without asking for your permission? her sweet voice asks sassily in my head.

"When did you become such a bitch?" The words are out of my mouth before I can smash them between my teeth, break them into harmless alphabet letters.

But Luna doesn't seem offended. She just smiles serenely. "Since you made me one, KJC."

She waltzes off toward the door. I could run after her, or I could go back to Poppy.

I should do the right thing and go back to Poppy.

I do the *wrong* thing and chase Luna. Daria's laughter rings in my ears, piercing through "Heartbeat" by Childish Gambino. "The way you're showing your feelings passes as indecent exposure, Knighty Knight."

Seriously, how is Scully with this chick? Is he building tolerance so he can face, like, super-evil world tyrants?

Luna descends the stairway of the beach house, and I follow. I'm shackled with an invisible cord, one with a pulse and a life on its own, and I can't seem to shake it off, to disconnect from her.

"Are you gonna run away forever?" I bite out. "Is that your new theme?"

She doesn't turn around to face me, her feet slipping in and out of the golden sand as she rounds the house. "Ever considered a career in cinematography, Knight? 'Cause you're really good at projecting."

"Fuck me, Luna—"

"No thank you."

"I wasn't finished!" I'm losing my shit and eager to hurt her back. "I can't believe you waited all those years to talk only to spew so much bullshit."

"Why don't you spare yourself from my bull, then, and take a hike?"

"You looked like a whore back there." What the *fuck* am I saying? Since when am I shaming women—least of all the girl I love—for consensual sexual acts? Someone hijacked my mouth, and that someone is an eighteenth-century pig.

Luna laughs. Doesn't answer.

"I meant because Daria is engaged," I hear myself say.

"*Sure, Jan,*" Luna peeps. Which is when I officially lose all decorum (let's pretend for the sake of argument that I had one in the first place) and catch her wrist, yanking her to me and plastering her back against the house. The part we're pressed against is made out of glass and overlooks the master bedroom. There's a couple there, making out on the bed.

"Suddenly you care about fidelity?" Luna growls into my face. My whole body comes alive with our proximity. With her gaze. I can't keep doing this to myself. Gathering broken fractures of attention from her, using them as oxygen to pull through the next day. It's like collecting drops of water on a dry tongue.

"I always care about fidelity," I bite out back at her.

Luna arches an eyebrow. Her hand snakes between us, and she cups my junk, which is hard because: 1. I'm standing next to her. 2. I'm eighteen and alive.

"Tell me to stop." Her voice drops low, sultry now—I still haven't gotten used to it all the way—as she starts stroking me through my jeans.

Hot. Fucking. Damn.

I see what she's doing here. Exposing me as a douchebag, as a liar, as a hypocrite. My throat bobs with a swallow. I want to tell her to stop, but I don't *want* her to stop, and she knows it.

"Stop doing this to Poppy." Luna's voice breaks. "Just stop. She deserves so much more. She's nice. Sweet. Even to me."

She is about to withdraw her hand from my junk, but I grab it, pressing it harder. Her fingers curl around my shaft through the fabric, and I just might fucking come. We both shudder in the dark. It's the most erotic thing that's ever happened to me.

"Don't stop," I beg, croaking.

"One of us has to." She pulls away, wiping at her face. Her eyes are shining with unshed tears. "You mean the world to me, Knight Cole."

"But?" I ask brokenly. There's always a but.

"But sometimes the world is just not enough."

SERIES INSPIRATION

Struggling to picture the characters? Here are the physical inspirations for each character:

Daria Followhill—Nicola Peltz

Bailey Followhill—Chloë Grace Moretz

Penn Scully—Austin Butler

Knight Cole—Matthew Noszka

Luna Rexroth—Zendaya

Lev Cole—Patrick Schwarzenegger

Vaughn Spencer—Felix Mallard

Lenora Astalis—Jenna Ortega

Sylvia Scully—Lily Rose Depp

Hunter Fitzpatrick—Chase Mattson

Racer Rexroth—Andrew Davila

ACKNOWLEDGMENTS

I have so many people to thank for making *Broken Knight* happen. It was definitely one of the most challenging books for me to write, and at a point, I was beginning to wonder if I could write it at all. I had to take long breaks, in which some of my closest friends held my hand and made sure that I saw it through. Here they are.

First of all, I'd like to thank my beta readers—Tijuana Turner, Sarah Grim Sentz, Amy Halter, Lana Kart, Helena Hunting, and Ava Harrison—for their insane attention to detail. Lord, did you make this book so much better than it initially was. I owe you so much.

A huge thank-you goes to my editors. Firstly, Angela Marshall Smith (you know what you did, LOL), Jessica Royer Ocken (#OCD4Life), and Paige Maroney Smith. Thank you for constantly pushing me forward and helping me improve my craft.

Thank you, Letitia Hasser, for the amazing cover (in our opinion, anyway, right?) and Stacey Blake Ryan for the gorgeous formatting. Huge, huge thank-you to Social Butterfly PR, and especially Jenn, Sarah, and Brooke for their love and attention. It's so much fun working with you, and I love you so dearly.

To Kimberly Brower, my rock star agent, who is always one step ahead of the game. Thank you for your immense support in my career. It means the world to me.

There are some people who enter your life and change it for the best. Here are some of those people for me: Charleigh Rose and Vanessa Villegas, who loved Knight before she even knew him, and Marta Bor, Betty Lankovits, Lin Tahel Cohen, Avivit Egev, Keri Roth, Ratula Roy, Sher Mason, Lisa Morgan, Kristina Lindsey, Chele Walker, Nina Delfs, Yamina Kirky, Nadine, Amanda Soderlund, Ariadna Bastulo, Brittany Danielle Christina, Vanessa Serrano, Vickie Leaf, Sheena Taylor, Sophie Broughton, Leeann Van Rensburg, Tanaka Kagara, Hayfaah Sumtally, Isa Lopez, Jodie Wilkins, Aurora Hale, Erica Panfile, Stacey Edmonds, Lulu Dumonceaux, Julia Lis, and Sarah Kellog Plotcher.

Special thanks to the Sassy Sparrows group for their support and their love for this series, and to the bloggers who signed up for this book and decided to push it. Last but not least, I would like to thank you, the readers, for the amazing journey. For reading, and talking about my books, and making my dream come true.

It would be an honor for me if you could take a few seconds to leave a brief review of this book if you have the time.

Thank you x million,
L.J. Shen xoxo

ABOUT THE AUTHOR

L.J. Shen is a *USA Today*, *WSJ*, *Washington Post*, and #1 Amazon Kindle Store bestselling author of contemporary romance books. She writes angsty books, unredeemable antiheroes who are in Elon Musk's tax bracket, and sassy heroines who bring them to their knees (for more reasons than one). HEAs and groveling are guaranteed. She lives in Florida with her husband, three sons, and a disturbingly active imagination.

Website: authorljshen.com
Facebook: authorljshen
Instagram: @authorljshen
Twitter: @lj_shen
TikTok: @authorljshen
Pinterest: @authorljshen